SMASH
THE
WORLD'S
SHELL

DANIEL FLIEDERBAUM

To anyone who's ever felt scared and alone —
this story is for you.

ACKNOWLEDGEMENTS

FIRSTLY, I'D LIKE TO THANK fiction itself for inspiring me with its many-splendored, always-splintered words and worlds. I'd like to thank the 1997 Rodgers and Hammerstein *Cinderella* movie, which revealed unto my two-year-old self the phrase "impossible things are happening every day" and all the secret narrative magic that burbles inside and branches out from just those simple words.

I'd like to thank my mother and my father for indelibly molding my existence as a human being with their wisdom, support and saintlike willingness to listen to me enthusiastically and endlessly ramble about *Pokémon* for years and years. At the end of the day, isn't *that* the truest form love can take?

I'd also like to thank my brother, who taught me the value of sharing the TV remote control, even when it meant missing *SpongeBob SquarePants* reruns, because wow, elementary school me would have lost out on some amazing cartoons if I hadn't compromised. I'd like to thank my best friend, who shall remain nameless in the interest of privacy, for simply being in my life. I couldn't have done it without you, my dude.

I'd like to thank my adorably selfish cats, who are the real heroes here as far as they can tell. I'd technically like to thank toxic masculinity and stupid gender roles for giving me all sorts of juicy writing material, but toxic masculinity and stupid gender roles also gave me frustration and self-image issues, so I won't thank them and say I didn't.

I'd like to thank the simply splendiferous team at Water Dragon Publishing. Without their support, expertise and willingness to believe in me, this book would never have made its way from my hard drive into your hands and/or eBook reading device and/or smartphone.

I'd like to thank Twitter user @SeaSaltShrimp for her vibrantly fantastical, dreamily draconic cover art, and for being so wonderfully charming and polite as we hammered out the finer details of what it should look like. Dear reader, go browse on over to her Twitter page and give her a follow! She deserves it.

Finally, and perhaps most self-indulgently, I'd like to thank myself. I'd say I use L'Oréal — because I'm worth it — but after so many years of doubting myself to the benefit of literally no one, I've realized I'm worth far more than L'Oréal. I am a living, loving, breathing human being with endless stories waiting to burst out from inside. And my stories, whether they have dragons in them or not, are always worth telling.

SMASH
THE
WORLD'S
SHELL

PART ONE

SHARD AND ELLEN

I

ELLEN DELACROIX lay curled up in bed one evening, her nose buried in her phone. "Top Guild Operative Loses Limb to Vicious Dragon; Finds Motherlode of Orichalcum," declared the *Safe Zone Gazette's* digital headline in bold black letters. Pausing on a picture of the man, who had a stub where his arm had once been, she made sure to say a prayer to the Goddess — words of gratitude for his sacrifice, and a plea that her father wouldn't see this headline and double down on his refusal to let her join the Guild.

The room that had been hers ever since she was a small child surrounded her, familiar and cozy. Far beyond the open window, a shimmering silver dome stretched for miles and miles, lending the world a metallic tint. In the daytime, you could see the stygian monoliths that projected the dome looming in the distance, but most people didn't want to think about the dome or its Generators any more than they had to. Those were what kept the dragons out.

Ellen was not most people. She twisted restlessly beneath her sheets, eyes wide open. When her dad's snoring at last started to rumble from the next room over, she flung off her covers.

"C'mon, Delacroix, you can do this," she muttered. A deep breath in. A deep breath out. She lowered herself into a horse stance, arms in at her sides like she'd seen on the dataweb. Then, she struck out with her fist. A weak wisp of wind fluttered through the empty air and dissipated against the wall with a *puff* — her aeromancy. Her air magic.

Again, she punched the air, over and over, never making wind more powerful than a tickle. She grunted, barely resisting the urge to stamp her feet. No dragon would be fazed by spells so feeble — and tonight had been a good night. Tonight, her magic had worked.

What if I never get this right? whispered a traitorous part of her mind. *What if I'm always useless?* Ellen shook her head. Tomorrow would be better.

Hours later, her eyes snapped open in the darkness. The dregs of a strange dream flittered behind her lids, but already, it was slipping from memory. Rubbing sleep from her eyes, something caught her attention. There, on her shelf. A ring, glinting silver.

Ellen frowned. She didn't own a ring. Even though school was in just a few hours, she climbed out of bed. There was a note next to the ring — and that alone was an oddity, even ignoring how it got there. In this day and age, everything was digital. She picked it up and unfolded it, the paper crinkling loudly in the silence of night. *Use when alone,* it read. *May you bring peace and love to this world that needs it so.*

Weird, Ellen thought. On a whim, she slipped the ring onto her finger — it was a perfect fit. Mulling over what this could all mean, if it meant anything at all, she fiddled with the ring absentmindedly, twisting it once, then twice, then three times ...

And then her room was gone. In its place, trees upon trees stretched on forever; tall, leafy, ominous, their dim outlines lit by infinite specks from above: stars. The sky above her twinkled with starlight as far as the eye could see.

Ellen's stomach lurched — this shouldn't be possible. The Safe Zone dome blotted out the night sky. If she could see it like this, then she wasn't in the Safe Zone anymore. She was in the Wildlands, beyond the safety of the dome. Every moment she spent here was another moment closer to being scorched to death by dragonfire.

2

THE GRADUAL CRESCENDO of wingbeats meant that Keeper was back from his hunting trip — and that Shard's quiet time was over. The dragonling sighed, but extinguished the torch on the wall, trying to make it seem as if he'd been asleep. In the dark, he put away his easel and paints, hiding them in the usual spot — a hole in the ground. He took one last, lingering look at his creation, a picture of two dragons laughing together, before sealing the hole with a spell.

He braced himself.

The entrance, a slat in the roof enchanted to slide open on command, rumbled as it granted Keeper passage. "This is so awesome," Shard heard his clutch-twin announce. "I got three deer in one flame breath. That's gotta be a personal record." Keeper landed, his beating dragon wings blowing cool air over Shard. With a quick flame breath, Keeper ignited the torch again. "Anyway, I'm back. You cleaned my hunting trophies, right?"

Shoot, Shard thought. He had been so wrapped up in his painting that he'd forgotten. He ambled over to the entrance and kissed the ground at his brother's claws. "I'm very sorry," he said as he looked up, still pressed against the ground. "It must have slipped my mind."

Keeper shook his head, clicking his tongue. "Wow, seriously?" And though Shard knew it was coming, the swift kick to his jaw didn't hurt any less. He yelped, clutching his snout with his paws.

Keeper flew past his brother to the center of the shelter, red and scarlet scales glistening in the firelight. He dumped the meat from his cloth hunting sack onto the ground, and the delicious scent of fresh-killed deer filled the shelter within seconds. Shard kept his head down, but he could just imagine the amused, self-satisfied look on Keeper's stupid face.

A hot surge flushed Shard's cheeks, but he tamped down on it. Keeper was big and strong, tight muscles rippling up and down his body. With just a little more effort, he could do so much more damage.

When the sounds of eating had died down, Keeper spoke again. "Ugh, what am I going to do with you? I asked you to clean my trophies, and that would have taken like, no time at all? But you couldn't do something as simple as that! I mean, it's not like you even do that much. You get to just sit and meditate all day, then come here and do Agito knows what."

Ah yes, meditating, Shard silently quipped, *by which I'm sure you mean tending to the fields with my magic. Totally the same thing.*

Keeper's eyes narrowed as if realization had struck. "Were you painting again?"

"N-no, I was just … I was just relaxing." Shard tried his best to sound casual. His legs were starting to ache from crouching so much. Against his better judgment, he chanced standing.

"Bow," Keeper snarled venomously, and Shard immediately prostrated himself again, his heart pounding — he had to avoid another beating. If only there was someone who would take this seriously, someone who would listen to him …

"Listen," Keeper continued, his iciness gone. "I get that you're different, but you're never gonna get a girlfriend if you keep holing up in the shelter all afternoon."

Hot anger surged in Shard again, tense and dark. *Calm down,* he ordered himself. *Focus on getting through the night.*

Keeper took a deep breath and sighed. "You wanna eat?" Shard's growling stomach answered for him. Keeper laughed. "C'mon, you can stand."

Despite himself, Shard rose to his paws. He had always hated eating meat, but he loved the way it tasted. Yet, as his belly trembled in anticipation, a scene popped into his mind unbidden, the same one that always did when he was encouraged to indulge his carnivorous side: the deer, minding its own business in a lush meadow, when out of nowhere, a stream of fire scorched it to death.

"I think I'm good," Shard mumbled. "I um, I'm not actually all that hungry ... I mean, my stomach hurts, and uh, I'm trying to be less of a glutton anyway, so ..."

He began to back up, not once looking away from his brother.

Keeper sighed. "Sweet Agito, you're always such a bleeding-heart." Shard said nothing. He just had to keep quiet and he'd be free. Then Keeper would forget about him, and he could slip back in later. "What did Mom even do to you to make you so weak?"

Shard froze. "What did you just say?"

"I said you're weak." Keeper shrugged. "I mean, it's true. Mom ruined you. It's like ... we're drakes, not dragonesses. We're not supposed to be so *delicate.*"

"I see you've been spending time with Chieftain Inferno," Shard said through gritted teeth.

"Yeah? He's our uncle." Exasperation dripped from Keeper's forked tongue. "Of course I spend time with him. He could probably help you, you know. Fix your nonsense about Mom."

"Our mother is *dead,* Keeper." Shard stomped closer, flaring out his wings aggressively.

"Don't you dare." Keeper growled, deep and throaty, all pretenses of amicability dropped.

"Stop talking about Mom like that!"

"Don't tell me what to do, little brother." Keeper spat the last two words out as if they were obscene. "I could break you if I wanted."

An alarm blared in Shard's mind. Keeper was right — Shard didn't stand a chance. Not unless he used his magic. But to do so would be to betray everything that his mother taught him — use magic to protect, never to destroy. So instead, he bared his fangs and snarled.

Keeper's eyes blazed. In a red blur, the larger dragon twisted around and lashed his tail into Shard's chest. Shard wheezed sharply, landing on his back, pain exploding behind his eyes. Keeper tail-whipped him again. Shard's vision went fuzzy, and through the throbs, he heard Keeper cluck disapprovingly.

Shard stayed sprawled out on his back after that. How long exactly, he was unsure. The whole time, he forced himself to stay quiet, refusing to think about the hate boiling inside him.

Once Keeper started to snore, Shard finally allowed himself to crawl back onto his paws, rolling his shoulders to loosen them up. Painful jolts shot up and down his spine and he winced. Still, he forced his aching wings to carry him upwards, and he emerged into the night.

Outside, he could see more shelters dotting the area, constructions of red dried mud, standing tall against the forest and the moonlight. The dragons of his village slumbered inside each and every one, waiting for the new day.

Shard wound his way through the community. His deep marine-blue and brilliant turquoise scales sparkled ever so slightly as they drew upon the power of the starry heavens above. If he'd wanted, he could have used that cosmic energy to heal his wounds, but what if the glow woke someone up? Besides, storing some more energy never hurt.

When he was younger, he would seek out his mother's embrace after a night this upsetting. His heart ached at the thought of her — her soft, gentle voice, her kind words, her loving smile — but he shook his head. She was gone, and there was nothing anyone could do about it.

He thought of his paintings, of dipping a stone into his paint jar and running it across his canvas, leaving behind color, creating the image of a dragon he hadn't met yet — his first friend. What would they be like, he wondered? Would they enjoy his art? Would they be more of a storyteller, perhaps? Maybe they'd be fit and athletic in all the ways he wasn't, and could stand up to Keeper. The possibilities were endless.

After about twenty minutes, the river came into view. Plants sprouted along the banks: vibrant pastel-hued flowers, weeds, grassy green reeds and more. Gingerly, he lowered his front legs into the water and finally allowed himself to truly glow, heaving a relieved sigh as magic from the moon and stars flowed into his wounds, his cut lip sewing itself shut, pain draining from his throbbing sides.

In the river, he could see his reflection staring back at him. Shard was a mere six years old, an adolescent by dragon standards, but he did not have the sheer presence of the other drakes his age. Even now, he could see how scrawny he was. Where Keeper's body had chiseled muscles, Shard's was smooth and undefined. He didn't have horns yet, either, and he was on the late side for those as it was. Two wings, leathery like a bat's, were folded in at his sides, and his tail, curled in around his body, was rounded at the tip instead of ending in a sharp, threatening point like some of the other dragons in his tribe.

As he looked into the still surface of the water, his eyes stared back at him, one blue and one green. And though he didn't want to admit it, in them, he saw something like fraying threads.

Crack!

Shard snapped to attention at the sound, looking around for its source. And there it was: a human, stepping on a branch. She — he thought it was a she, at least; she was so slender — she froze in place, her blonde hair fluttering to a rest on her shoulders, her green eyes wide.

Shard and the human stared at each other. Neither made a sound. Concern for the tiny creature lurched inside him. She was so small and had no wings or scales to protect her pale skin, exposed on her hands and face where her garments did not cover. How did she go about her day without getting scratched or cut? She seemed so fragile.

But then, he knew his village would expect him to kill her. In the words of his uncle, humans were "thieving little apes." For whatever reason, they wanted a kind of metal called orichalcum. Dragons used orichalcum during funeral rites — at least, Shard's tribe did — but their deposit was so far away that it had been many, many moons since humans had raided the village for it. And what if humans used orichalcum for their funerals, as well? Shouldn't they be allowed to have some?

If he snuffed her out, he would be a hero. The other dragons would all pay attention to him, maybe even more than they did to Keeper. They'd praise him for exterminating one of the pests that invaded their lands and stole their sacred metal. And if he killed her, she would be dead.

Shard sighed. His shining scales probably terrified the creature. *I'd better dim them,* he thought. But before he could, the girl swung her arm forward, her hand closed in a fist. Shard tensed — this was how humans cast spells. He wracked his mind, trying to think of a way to counter it without hurting her.

Nothing happened.

Shard tilted his head. "The hell is she doing?"

The human gasped. "Y-you can *talk!?*"

"Um, yes? Can ... can *you?*" Shard blinked. A talking human? Was that possible? He stood, intending to fly to the other side of the river for closer look, sore body or no.

"S-stop! Don't come any closer!" The girl swung her arm again. This time a gentle breeze floated through the air towards Shard, tickling his snout. He blinked but forced himself to focus, finally letting his scales dim, fear replacing wonder. "P-please. I don't want to fight you."

The human loosened her stance just a little. "You can talk. You can really, actually talk ... And you really don't want to tear me limb from limb?"

Shard shook his head emphatically. He would not be like Keeper and the others. Not now, not ever. "I'm not a killer."

"Oh. Well. Okay, good." Silence. "I'd rip you to shreds if we fought," she said at last, puffing her chest out and broadening her shoulders. After that paltry display of magic, she was clearly posturing. Shard couldn't help but snort.

"Hey, I'm serious! There's nothing wrong with my magic!" she retorted. Loudly.

Shard's amusement vanished. "Quiet, please! You don't want to wake the other dragons up! I might be able to understand you, but they might not! Do you really wanna take that chance?"

In some less fear-addled part of his mind, he was a little taken aback — she sounded angry, not just afraid. And when had he said anything about her magic?

"Right, well. I'm gonna go now. Don't try anything funny when I turn around."

"Wouldn't dream of it."

"Good."

And with that, the girl retreated a few more paces, her arms still in front of her, ready to strike should Shard attack. Soon, though, she turned around and walked off.

"You uh, probably don't want to go that way," Shard called out. "You're walking right towards more dragons." It was true; if the human kept in that direction, she'd find herself smack-dab in the middle of the neighboring tribe's territory.

She grunted but turned back around. "I'll ask you, then. Which way is the Safe Zone?"

"The what now?"

"Big, silvery dome, all the humans live underneath it? Dragons can't get in because it's magic? You know, that Safe Zone?"

"Oh!" He hadn't known the human name for it. "Yeah, you're nowhere near that. You've gotta be like two days away, and that's if you're flying."

"... And if you're walking?"

"Um ... A really long time?"

She smacked her palm to her forehead, muttering an expletive under her breath.

"Are you okay?" The only response Shard got was the girl cursing again. She kicked a pebble into the river. It landed with a *plop.*

"Okay, gonna take that as a 'no.' How did you get out here anyway? Don't humans usually come in groups with those weird metal thingies with wheels?"

"They're called cars," she said, "and I ..." She trailed off, looking like she was contemplating something. "Are you offering to help me get home?"

Shard considered. Was he? At last, he admitted, "I guess? I can't exactly fly you back, but I'll do what I can."

A complicated expression colored her face as she stood there wordlessly. Just when Shard was about to speak again, she slipped something off from around her finger. It looked like a small band of metal. "It's a ring," the girl explained. "We wear them to make ourselves look better. I found it in my room with a note and well ... I think this is what brought me here."

"A note?"

"Something we write — er, leave symbols on to tell each other stuff, even when we aren't together."

Shard nodded. His mother had told him something about humans having symbols that made words before she died. He had never asked her where she had learned that.

"So, yeah. I put the ring on, and boom, I'm here. I have no idea where it came from."

"You had no clue where it came from, and you put it on?"

"Hey! I had no idea it would fling me Goddess-knows-how-many miles away."

9

A witty retort formed on the tips of his forked tongue. But wait. Human magic was different from dragon sorcery. "I'm guessing you had no reason to think it had been enchanted, then ... Did you do anything after putting it on?"

"I mean, I twisted it a few times?"

"Try twisting it again, maybe?"

She nodded and began to slide the ring around her finger, but stopped, her hand hovering midair. "Can I really trust you? You're a dragon."

Shard's frustration finally boiled over. "Sweet freaking Agito! What, do you I think snuck under the dome? That I left you a ring and a ... What did you call it? 'A note?' Dragons can't make those! I just ... just let me do something nice and help you, okay?"

Shard's eyes widened, an icy hand of fear clutching his chest. He had to apologize, had to fix this, had to do it now, now, before she got angry and violent ... She didn't. She simply stood there, unmoving and unreadable.

"... I-I'm sorry. That was uncalled for. A-are you okay?" he dared to ask. His panic seemed to release him bit by bit as he spoke.

The human took a seat on the dirt, and let out a long, tired breath, cradling her temple in her palm. "No, no, I'm the one who should be sorry. I'm being a real jerk. I'm just scared, you know? I've never been outside the Safe Zone before, and suddenly I have to rely on a dragon to get home. It's ... it's a little terrifying."

"Yeah ... Yeah, I get it," he said, truthfully. "Shard."

"I'm sorry, what about shards?"

"No, no," he clarified, feeling very stupid. "My *name* is Shard."

"Oh," the girl said, then paused, eyes glancing downwards. "I'm — I'm Ellen. I uh, wanna say nice to meet you, but I guess that's not exactly appropriate, what with the whole 'attacking you' thing. Sorry about that."

Shard snorted, but not without humor. "It's okay. Nice to meet you, too, Ellen."

"Uh, yeah. Now, let's see if this works ..."

She reached towards her ring again. Time seemed to slow down as Shard's mind raced. This girl — Ellen — she clearly had no training in magic, but she also definitely had the capacity for it. At the same time, she seemed proud of her powers, or at least like

10

she wanted to be proud of them and couldn't be. Maybe she didn't have anyone to teach her?

Oh, sweet freaking Agito. He couldn't imagine what it would be like to have his gift and to never have had the chance to develop it. Magic was the only thing he was good at. He liked painting, but he was absolutely horrendous at it. *And,* he thought, a beautiful, terrible idea sparking in his head, *she did try to apologize for attacking me ... Maybe ... just maybe ... we could get along?*

"Do you want me to teach you magic?"

Shard's breath caught in his throat — what was he thinking? Not killing the girl was one thing, but if he tutored her, she would have to come back. If she came back, then someone might see her. Someone might see him teaching her. Teaching a human. He'd be sentenced to death. Or banishment. Or worse. He had to retract his offer, had to play it off as a joke, had to say *something* to get out of this, because Agito knew —

"Are you pulling my leg?" Ellen wrinkled her nose. "Why would you teach me magic? I'm a human. We're *enemies.*"

A million responses tumbled around inside Shard, a million ways to back out. He used none of them. "You haven't done anything to me," he declared. "We're not enemies." Strangely, he meant it.

But Ellen didn't seem so convinced. "What's in it for you?"

"I just ... I just want a frie —" Shard started to say, but then he saw something in her emerald-colored eyes, something deep-rooted — she didn't trust him. But what would a human have that Shard wanted?

"I ... I'll think of something later, okay? And it'll be something really valuable, too, so make sure you can get it, whatever I decide I want!"

"Well ..."

"One lesson," Shard urged, despite his better judgment. "Just ... let's have one lesson, and you can decide if you want to learn from me after that."

Ellen pursed her lips and gazed far off into the distance, unmoving and inscrutable. Then she let out a breath. "All right. One lesson. If the ring works, should I be here at the same time tomorrow?"

"Same time tomorrow," Shard repeated, adding, "if the ring works." He really hoped it did. For her sake.

11

She gave the ring a determined look, grasped it, and took in a deep breath. She twisted the ring once. Twice. Three times. And then she vanished, replaced by a gentle breeze murmuring through the trees.

A rush of tense air tumbled from Shard's lungs. *What just happened?* he thought, blind to how his destiny had just been irrevocably altered. *How did she understand what I was saying? How did I understand her? Why did I offer to teach her magic?* If anyone ever found out, he could be exiled, or even killed. It was the stupidest choice he had ever made.

But was it so foolish? a voice in the back of his mind asked, a little whisper that pierced his cloud of worry. *You knew that Ellen, human or no, didn't hurt you or belittle you. That's more than you can say for most dragons.*

Shard gazed up at the starry sky longingly. The moon, perfectly round and dazzlingly white, hung above him. "I really hope this isn't a bad idea, Mom ..."

An owl hooted in the distance. For a moment, Shard could have sworn he felt his mother's presence.

3

I N A FLASH, Ellen's room reappeared, her wood floor hard against her legs — the ring had worked. Her room was still dark, save for the dim glow of the star stickers she had pasted on her ceiling as a kid. The grassy, earthen aroma of the wildlands still lingered on her pajamas.

The Wildlands. A giddy smile broke out on her face, and she slowly rose to her feet, her knees wobbling beneath her. "I was in the Wildlands," she mouthed, bringing her palm to her forehead. "Holy Goddess above, I was in the Wildlands."

Ellen was an elemental, someone who could awaken to and harness the magic of the four elements of air, fire, earth, and water, though she had only ever awakened air. Most elementals did one of two things with their lives: played blastball, a sport that used magic, or joined the Guild, the organization that tirelessly combed the Wildlands for orichalcum, the magic metal that powered the Generators. But with magic as weak as hers, Ellen could do neither.

Until now. Now, she had a tutor, someone who might help her strengthen her magic. Granted, her tutor was a dragon, but Ellen would do anything to grow her powers, no matter who she had to learn from.

Besides, Shard had had every opportunity to attack her and hadn't taken a single one. And they had communicated, exchanged actual words. Ellen could not think of how for the life of her, but she almost didn't even care that this was all so very, very impossible.

Almost. The image of the Guild member who had lost his arm flashed through her head. Was this really not a trap of some sort? She flopped backwards onto her bed with an irritated groan. She needed to learn what dragon sorcery could do, and anyone could post anything on the dataweb. The Echo Woods Compendium — a building home to a collection of books perusable by patrons — was her best bet.

Most compendiums had been closed a little more than fourteen years ago, their books' contents uploaded to the dataweb and the books themselves recycled for material. Unfortunately, information on sorcery was very limited, even online. Maybe, just maybe, there was something available in print.

And though her chances were slim, dreams of the Wildlands filled her sleep that night.

A few hours later, her alarm blared, announcing the start of a new day. Her eyes slowly opened, the remnants of sleep weighing on them like anchors. A floral breeze floated in through her window, the light of day tinted silver by the ever-present Safe Zone dome.

Groaning sleepily, she reached for her phone. With a swipe of her finger, she turned off the alarm, and hoisted herself out of bed.

In the shower, as the air steamed and the bathroom mirror fogged, she remembered what happened last night. Strawberry-scented shampoo foaming in her hair, she marveled at the complete incredibility of it. A ring from nowhere that took her to a talking dragon that hadn't killed her and wanted to teach her magic? It all was just too unbelievable. But when she went to change into her school uniform, there the ring was, right on her bookshelf where she had left it, tangible proof of the impossible.

Out in the kitchen, she grabbed a bowl of cereal and a banana, eating in the empty apartment. Her dad worked early on Tuesdays. Most mornings, she would wish he were there to eat alongside her, but today, it was a relief.

Goddess knows how Dad would react if he knew I talked to a dragon last night — much less agreed to meet him again. Not that she could blame her dad. Everyone knew exactly what dragons could do if they wanted. Him more than her.

The school day passed in a blur. By the time the bell rang at 3:00, the teacher's dull droning was already a mere memory. She gathered her phone and laptop, shoved them in her backpack, and made her way through the chaotic mass of milling students.

Presently, she passed by the school cafeteria, its large double doors wide open. Inside, kids chattered happily as they gathered over their phones, sharing videos and dataweb posts. Even over the din of dismissal, their laughter struck a chord. She found herself hovering in the doorway, watching everyone.

One of the other kids looked up from his phone and waved at her, smiling brightly. "Hey, Delacroix! We're playing checkers; you wanna join in next match?"

Ellen shook her head politely. "Oh, um, that's fine. Thank you, though."

The cafeteria was barely behind her when a second boy scoffed. "C'mon, have you ever seen Delacroix hang out with anyone? She's like, the dictionary definition of lone wolf." The first boy murmured something that sounded like agreement.

Ellen broke her pace for only a millisecond. It was a fair observation. But she didn't want any friends. Not now. Not ever. No matter how much she might think she wanted to be sitting there, laughing with them.

People always left in the end, and it always, always hurt.

Once out in the cool April afternoon, Ellen walked a mile through the streets of Echo Woods, the familiar, translucent dome hanging above her, birds chirping in the trees. She passed by the train station, an express bound for Haven City blaring its horn as it pulled away from the platform. Another few blocks later, Ellen spotted the food bank where her dad worked — the place where everyone in Echo Woods got their food. It had a blue truck parked in front of it, making a delivery. Roadways were ubiquitous in the Safe Zone, but cars were reserved for ferrying supplies and emergency and government travel. Once upon a time, Ellen remembered from history class, everyone had had cars. These days, trains were *the* way to cover long distances.

Next to the food bank was a community garden, where the voices of gossiping adults tending to their vegetables mixed with the laughter of children, who were young enough to find the whole thing a grand adventure.

Finally, she came upon the Shady Orchard Group Home, a small, yellow-white two-story building nestled midway between Ellen's home and the compendium. There was an old but sturdy wooden swing set on the lushly green front lawn, and from inside the house came more childish laughter. A tattered, raggedy doll peeked out a windowsill on the second floor, as if resting beneath pitch-black solar panels blanketing the roof — all sights Ellen had grown to love over the last two years.

She knocked on the front door. Footsteps *thumped* inside, and it swung open a second later. And then, lightning struck — standing in the threshold was perhaps the prettiest girl in the whole Safe Zone. A little shorter than Ellen, with brown skin, luscious, long, dark hair and a pair of round glasses, the girl had chocolate eyes both rich and splendorous. She was thin too, slender even. For the briefest of moments, Ellen's gaze couldn't help but trace the contours of her body.

"Hey there!" The stranger smiled wide and bright, extending a hand; her voice was infectiously cheery. "You must be Ellen. I'm Lana Pai, a new volunteer here."

Ellen cleared her throat. "Right, hi." Her cheeks flushed hot red, but she didn't need to remind herself not to say too much, not to put herself in harm's way for a pretty face. *Everyone leaves,* Ellen reminded herself. Ellen took Lana's hand, giving her a single, limp handshake. "I'm just here to read to the kids."

Lana smiled even more brightly than before. "Awesome! I'm helping the cooking staff, so I'll see you if you stay to help with dinner. Robert! Ellen's here!" She retreated back inside as a portly man hurried over, one of the fulltime workers.

"Ellen, glad you're here. I was just getting all the kids sat down for you. Be careful though. They're a little rowdy today."

Ellen nodded, undeterred. They stood in an entry hall painted in pastel pinks, purples and yellows. From farther in, the savory fragrance of tomato soup and grilled cheese wafted up Ellen's nose — signs of an early dinner. Her eyes lingered in the direction of the kitchen — the direction Lana had gone in. Then she frowned and forced herself to focus.

In the living room, about ten children, most of them younger than six, were waiting for Ellen on the carpeted floor, legs crossed, tittering excitedly.

"All right kids, Miss Ellen's here to read today!" said Robert. "What do you say to Miss Ellen?"

"Hi, Miss Ellen!" the kids chorused in that singsong way. Some of them swayed back and forth as they sat, angling to get a better view of her.

"Hello, everyone!" Ellen put on her brightest, most saccharine voice. It wasn't something she liked doing, but a syrupy disposition always made the kids so happy. Who was she to begrudge them that? "It's so good to see all of you; have you been good? Today, we're going to be reading a favorite of mine from when I was your age! Isn't that exciting?"

"Yes, Miss Ellen!"

She took her seat in a wooden chair in front of a white pulldown sheet. With a few taps on her phone, she pulled up a storybook app, and with a few more, a vibrant pastel picture appeared on the pulldown sheet, showing a log cottage on a scenic, green hill. "Once upon a time ..."

Everything went well until the end of the story. A shrill cry pierced the room, followed by a fluttering *swoosh* of air. The curtains ruffled, swaying. Ellen's head shot up from the storybook app, and she saw two kids tangled in a knot, their fingernails digging into each other — Tia and Luke.

Ellen sprang from her chair. In an instant, she had weaved between all the kids on the floor, who were looking on intently, and closed the gap between her, Luke, and Tia. With a gentle but firm yank, she pulled them apart. Technically, Ellen was supposed to get one of the actual workers if the kids started fighting — but she knew they trusted her here.

"Stop it, you two!" she scolded, keeping her hands loosely closed around their wrists. "That is not okay! When we're angry, we use our words — and don't think I didn't see that airblast. Magic is only for blastball games and dragons. You do not use it to hurt other people. Which one of you cast a spell?"

"Tia did!" Luke called out.

"Is that true, Tia?"

Tia's lips wobbled a single time. Then she wailed, tears streaming down her face. "This isn't fair! Luke was being *mean!* He said my mommy hated me!" Just like that, she leaped up and dashed out of the living room, the light *thump, thump, thump* of her footsteps heavy in Ellen's ears.

Ellen narrowed her eyes. "I'll talk to you later, Luke. Everyone! Story time is on hold for just a few minutes. I'm going to get Mr. Rob to watch you, so be good for him."

Peeking into the hallway, Ellen gestured over the portly man and explained the situation, then jogged upstairs. Floorboards creaked beneath her with each stair she climbed, until finally, she reached a long hallway lined with doors. Tia's room was all the way at the end.

Ellen rubbed her fingers together, a nervous tic she'd never quite been able to shed, then knocked. "Tia? Can I come in?" she called out. For a minute, all Ellen heard was Tia sniffling on the other side of the door. Then, just as she was about to enter anyway, the door inched open, revealing a chubby, tearstained face.

"… Am I in trouble?" Tia's voice was small.

"That's not up to me. But if you want to talk about your feelings, I'm here for you."

Tia nodded, but did not open the door any further. "Luke said Mommy's not coming back for me because she hates me. But he's lying! She's going to get better soon! She's not going to leave me!" Her lips were set defiantly thin, but her eyes told the real truth.

Ellen sighed, kneeling to be at face level with Tia. She, Ellen, of all people, knew the pain of losing a parent. "That must have really hurt your feelings. When you don't think your mommy or daddy loves you, it feels like your whole world is ending, doesn't it?"

Tia nodded again, and Ellen's heart ached. No one else should have to know what that felt like. "I'm so sorry. What Luke said was mean and cruel. But you can't use that as a reason to hurt other people, especially not with magic. Using magic like that is really illegal — do you know what that means? Adults can get in really big trouble for it. Promise me you'll use your words next time, okay?"

Clutching her arms around herself, Tia relented. "Okay … I promise."

"I'm glad to hear it. And I really hope your mommy gets better soon, too."

"Yeah … Are you magic, Miss Ellen?"

Ellen blinked. She had to spend a moment deciding how to answer. "… No. I'm not," she said at last. It was half-true, at least.

There was a reason her power was so weak — she was magically impaired. But she didn't need to share that.

Soon, Ellen's volunteer shift was over. She bid everyone as cheerful a goodbye as she could muster, and then emerged into the dusk. Once, she'd heard that in the Wildlands the sky turned brilliant shades of purple and orange at sunset, but here in the Safe Zone, it just got darker and darker, never anything but silver until it was pitch-black. Ellen had never known anything else.

As she walked, she realized she was shivering, hugging herself tighter and tighter. Before she knew it, her head was swimming in a fog of memories, her feet guided homewards by habit while her mind replayed the past, a movie she'd seen time and time and again ...

When she was diagnosed with magical impairment, she had been only five. Everyone at the lower school had been called to an assembly. The microphone screeched as the principal explained to wide-eyed children that today, they were all to be tested for magic. The children were herded into lines, some of them barely standing still, vibrating with excitement. Others had been less enthused; the high-pitched whine of someone begging to go to lunch had stayed in Ellen's memory all these years.

Ellen had been one of the excited ones. An animated, tooth-filled smile, the kind that can sparkle only on the face of an eager five-year-old, tugged at her mouth as she hopped from foot to foot on the gymnasium floor. She knew she had magic. She had no proof, save for the fact that whenever she closed her eyes, she could feel the flickering warmth of limitless energy within her. It was just a matter of learning to use it, she had been sure ...

The line flowed into a makeshift booth, thrown together from velvet-red curtains. In front of it, there was a computer set up, but Ellen had been too short to see the display. A teacher ushered her inside the booth. Ellen obliged happily, rushing through the drapes. Inside was a machine with what looked like a small waterwheel on it, suspended at about chest level with Ellen by a rod going through it. The teacher told her to try and throw a windblast at it.

Ellen remembered closing her eyes. She remembered picturing the magic inside her, shimmering like silver. She remembered her excitement all but boiling over as she punched the air.

A wisp of wind, barely a breeze, tickled the wheel, but it didn't even budge. The teacher typed something into a tablet, the keys clicking loudly. Ellen frowned. That had to have been a fluke. She punched one last time, funneling fiery determination into the movement. But the wheel merely shifted half an inch back and half an inch forth. Then it came to a rest.

And that's when Ellen was hurried out of the booth. The teacher smiled as he fed her honeyed, hollow assurances. "It's all right. My sister's wife is magically impaired; you can still live a happy life," he had said, uttering for the first time the two words that would haunt Ellen for years to come.

There had been a doctor's visit that afternoon in a sterile, blindingly white office. They had drawn blood, the sharp jab of the needle a vivid punctuation mark, a comma joining and dividing two eras of her young life.

The results confirmed it — Ellen's magic was feeble. Present, but so infinitesimally fractional compared to what a normal elemental could do that she likely would not even be able to awaken to the other elements. Her father and mother had sat her down afterwards and talked to her about it, offering only the same sweet nothings as the teacher at school. Ellen hadn't realized it at the time, but her mother's face had been so very pale, like she was hit harder by this than Ellen was ...

Ellen gritted her teeth. She *had* to learn magic. Even if Shard was a dragon, he could teach her — she would one day join the Guild with his help. She would protect the children at the home, first by volunteering, and then by keeping the dome running. Not just them, but all of humanity — it was her purpose. She wasn't good for anything else. And if she wasn't good for even that ... then what was the point of her?

The sun had long since set by the time Ellen entered her apartment building. Upon reaching apartment 317 on the third floor, she twisted the key in the lock, and was greeted by her dad snoring loudly on the sofa, his feet dangling off its edge. His balding head still had most of its once-luscious red hair. What struck Ellen the most about her father, however, was his face, creased with worry even in slumber.

Ellen shook her head. Just how hard was the food bank working him that he fell asleep when he got off early? Smiling with a hint of melancholy, she made a point of bringing her father his blanket and draping it over him as he slept. Lingering, Ellen saw exactly what she had hoped to: the furrows vanishing from his brow as he snuggled deep into the quilt.

Soon enough, the clock struck ten. Ellen stood in her room, the lights out, darkness bathing her. Letting out a breath she didn't know she had been holding, she grasped the silver ring. The metal was cool beneath her fingertips.

Here we go. She twisted the ring three times ...

Her room vanished, replaced once more by the starlit night. The delightful gushing of a river filled her ears. Vibrant foliage sprouted up alongside the running water: bushes, grass, reeds. By the riverbank sat Shard, his legs underneath him and tail curled around his body like a cat. "Hey. I was wondering when you'd turn up."

Ellen's throat closed. This apex predator towering above her had to be at least six feet tall, and that was sitting down on all fours. How tall would he be if he reared up?

"You in there?" Shard asked without the barest trace of aggression. Concern danced across his blue-and-green eyes.

Ellen forced out a cough and shook her head. "Sorry, sorry. I'm ready to start when you are!" She supposed she should talk to him a bit before jumping into things, but she didn't trust that the ring wasn't his just yet. Letting him know how little she knew was out of the question.

Slipping out of her shoes and socks, she took a seat and dipped her feet into the water. "Oh, that's cold!"

"You don't like it?"

Ellen shook her head again, a smile fighting to spread from one ear to the other. "It's amazing." Now that she was out in the Wildlands on purpose, the urge to shout for joy jousted with her fear. Home had never felt so distant — had never *been* so distant. But somewhere out there, nearby or far, far away, there was orichalcum to be found, the very stuff that made human society possible. The very reason people ventured out into the Wildlands and risked their lives.

Shard merely tilted his head. "I guess? It's just water. Don't you have rivers underneath the dome?"

"That's not what I mean. I'm just so far away from everyone I know ..." She trailed off.

"Huh. I can definitely understand not wanting to be around anyone else, that's for sure. Anyway, you wanna get started, or are we just gonna get our claws wet and chat?"

At that, Ellen had to chuckle a little. "Yeah, let's," she said, pulling her feet from the river.

"Keep your feet in the water. Being physically connected to one of the elements will help."

"I can't use water magic, Shard. Besides, I'm touching the air."

"It'll still help. Now, close your eyes."

"Uh, okay? I've never heard of anyone learning magic with their eyes closed." But Ellen did exactly as she was told. Shard just seemed so authoritative all of a sudden; talking about magic had undammed a reservoir of confidence.

"Seriously? This is like, the basics of the basics for increasing baseline magical strength." There was genuine bewilderment in his tone.

Ellen opened her mouth, a snarky comment dancing on the tip of her tongue, but she thought better of it. "All right. What do I do now?"

"First, put your hands together. Breathe out, and reach out with your magic. Breathe in, and pull it back. Then, when you breathe out again, try and push out farther than you could before."

"Okay." Ellen inhaled, the cool night air tickling the inside of her nostrils, and pressed her palms together as if in prayer. Then, she dug deep inside herself, to the innermost portion of her being and tugged at what little magic was there.

With an exhale, she forced it outwards.

And then she felt something — only faintly, but it was there nonetheless: the movement of the air itself, tingling against her skin. And yet, it wasn't her skin. Her senses, her very mind, had expanded beyond the confines of her body. But a moment later, she felt a burning ache — not in her muscles? Outside her body? She sucked her power back into herself and opened her eyes, panting.

"Holy ..." she gasped between breaths. "That ... that was amazing! How did I even do that?"

"Anyone with magic can. It's a great exercise for building magical strength." Shard paused. "Wait, what did you think we were gonna be doing?"

"I ... I ..." Ellen puffed. Remembering her workouts at the gym, she tried to steady her breathing as if after a run on the treadmill. "I thought ... I thought we were gonna be casting spells. Like ... like, you know, doing reps of shooting windblasts or something."

"Why would —" Shard stopped himself, considering. "I mean, we could do that. But you'd probably end up exhausting yourself physically before you got anywhere with your magic."

Ellen nodded; she supposed that explained why she hadn't been getting anywhere. But something wasn't quite right. "Wait. Can't I just do this on my own?"

"Sweet Agito, no! If you overexert yourself, you could seriously get hurt. You need a spotter for this exercise, at least at first. You'll develop a sense for it eventually, but by that point we'll have moved on to other stuff, anyway."

Was that true? Did he really need to be there, or did he have an ulterior motive? *Better safe than sorry,* Ellen decided. "Okay. That's good to know."

"One more time?"

Ellen nodded and closed her eyes a second time. When her breath started to come in ragged, Ellen heard Shard say, "Okay, that's enough. Stop."

Ellen's magic snapped back to her like a rubber band, a short sharp shock, and she was no longer able to feel things beyond herself. She yanked her feet from the river and sprawled out onto her back, eyes shut as she rested. "Okay ... I'll ... I'll take a ... a break and then get back —"

"Uh-uh, no way. This exercise is necessary, but you've got to take it slowly."

Too winded to argue, Ellen simply opened her eyes and glared at Shard defiantly. Whatever she was doing, it was amazing, and she never wanted to stop. But, if this was just the beginning ..." "Fiiiiiine."

Shard looked at her funny for a second. Suddenly, he made a strange sound, a staccato somewhere between a trumpet and a bird's call. It didn't register immediately, but she quickly realized: he was laughing.

"Wh-what's so funny?" she demanded, her cheeks tinting red. In the back of her mind, she thought how strange it was to hear a dragon laugh. She had never considered it possible before.

"Er, sorry!" Shard's eyes shot wide open, all traces of mirth gone. He was breathing heavily now, shrinking into himself as if waiting to be struck. "I shouldn't have —"

"No, no, it's fine." Ellen sat back up and raised an eyebrow — he had swung from a confident teacher back to a quivering mess in the blink of an eye. Such a change! "You didn't do anything wrong."

No answer. Then, warily, slowly, he spoke. "R-right ..."

"You gonna tell me what you were laughing about?"

"Uh, well. It's just ... that face you made was hysterical."

"It was?"

He winced again. "S-sorry! You were scrunching up your nose while twisting your lips, is all, and it was funny!"

Ellen thrust her hands up like stop signs. "Dude, relax! I'm not mad."

And with that, it was as if someone had released a valve on Shard; Ellen could see the anxiety rushing out as his posture loosened. What, she wondered, had happened to make a dragon of all things so scared? Well, maybe she could ease his mood with a little ribbing ...

"But hey," she volleyed, making sure to wear her slyest, wryest grin, "don't get so smug just because I can make a funny face. Your face is funny by default."

"You uh ..." Shard took a steadying breath. "You mean my natural good looks and charm? D-don't hate me because you ain't me."

"Sure, 'natural good looks.' Let's go with that."

"Ooh, going for the low blow, I see."

The two bantered, laughter seeping in where fear had reigned. But eventually, their repartee died down, and Shard began looking serious. Sad, even. "Hey, thanks for not being angry," he said. "I needed that."

"Uh, no problem, I guess." But Ellen found herself thinking that she needed this too, whatever it was. Not that she was going to say that out loud. "When should I come back?"

"So you *do* want to learn magic from me!" Shard pressed excitedly.

A taut silence passed. Ellen knew she should say no. Despite her grand aspirations for the Guild, she knew how dangerous it was to meet with a dragon, how impossible and suspicious this whole situation should be. And yet, when was the last time she'd had fun like this? She nodded but didn't speak, not trusting her own voice.

"Awesome. There's so much I can't wait to teach you, so you better be ready to learn!"

Ellen finally found her voice. "Trust me, that won't be a problem. And you never told me what you wanted for payment."

"Oh, uh ... I'm still thinking! But I'll have something for you soon, don't you worry!"

24

"I wouldn't dream of it."

Then, she twisted the ring three times, and everything fell still. She was back in her room. The sudden sounds of her dad snoring in the next room over sputtered like a lawnmower, cutting through the silence. It seemed to Ellen that the air was different in here. Dirtier, more suffocating. Duller. Outside, the silver dome glowed in the distance. She wondered how many elementals were risking their lives for it right now.

4

S HARD ROSE WITH THE SUN. The moon and stars had vanished to make way for the morning, so while the energy he'd stored the previous night still buzzed beneath his scales, he was just a little emptier than when he had shut his eyes.

He sighed. If only he could spend the day painting. But then, his work in the fields would go undone and he'd have to deal with the chieftain's anger. Not to mention the beating he'd get should Keeper catch him, or that he wasn't supposed to paint at all.

Finally peeling his eyes open, he saw light from the open roof streaming in. Keeper had already left. Perhaps he had gone for a midnight rendezvous with his girlfriend, a black-scaled dragoness named Firebug. She was Inferno's adopted daughter — Shard didn't quite know the full story, but her blood father had been killed by humans when Shard was barely a year old. He didn't remember the attack for having been so young, nor did he know Firebug all that well, but even with as few words as they'd shared, he couldn't imagine what she saw in Keeper. He knew they had been friends since they were very young dragonlings, but even then, the fact that anybody liked Keeper baffled him.

As he took to the skies, the cool spring air rushed beneath his wings. Below him lay a sea of trees that gave way to verdant pastures where their cattle grazed, and beyond that the golden expanse of the fields. In the far, far distance he could see mountains, snow-capped giants blotting out what lay beyond. As he flew, Shard thought back to the previous night, his meeting with Ellen still fresh in his mind.

He still couldn't shake his dread. Their lesson last night had gone well, but could this truly last? Lonely or no, with this, he was betraying not just his tribe, but every dragon who had ever suffered at the hands of an orichalcum-seeking human. The more he thought about it, the more his stomach clenched.

Presently, he came upon the Clearing, an area that had been deforested, leaving only a large circle of yellow-brown dirt. Everyone gathered here for a community meal in the mornings. Even so close to the end of breakfast, dragons were still there, some chatting with their friends before work, others peddling goods laid out on cloth blankets, ranging from food to stone tools to medicinal herbs. Shard sometimes traded small spells for berries he could crush into paint: enchanting wood to burn just a little slower, chisels that were just a bit sharper, anything that wasn't too magic-intensive. He always had to pretend to eat the berries, though.

At the far end of the clearing sat Chieftain Inferno — Shard's uncle. Magical energy radiated from his red and scarlet scales in waves, noticeable even from a distance. Sometimes, Inferno's horns would glow when he cast, and his eyes had turned golden with arcane might, something that only happened to the most fiercely magical dragons. Shard shivered at the thought.

Currently, Inferno perched on a stone platform, one he'd erected with his powers. The podium made sure that he, already one of the tallest dragons in the tribe, could look down on each and every one of the dragons he governed from on high. No one else was permitted on it unless he allowed them. Not his advisors, nor his Bonded mate, the green-scaled Emerald, nor even his son, Shard's cousin Spearhead.

The chieftain's eyes landed on Shard and his expression lit right up. He spread his wings and took flight, gliding above everyone else towards Shard.

Countless scenarios raced through Shard's mind. Had Keeper somehow found his stash of paintings and reported it? Had someone heard him with the human last night? Shard glanced over at his brother, hoping that he could glean some sort of insight, only to see his clutch-twin making lovey-dovey faces with Firebug. She was draped around his neck like a cloth sack, giggling and batting her eyelids coquettishly.

Just act as plain as you can; don't let them suspect a thing. It'll be okay, Shard ordered himself, forcing down a swell of nerves. He didn't believe himself for a moment.

Chieftain Inferno landed on the ground in front of Shard with a *bump.* Shard's heart beat wildly, a percussive *thud, thud, thud* that seemed to only get louder. He looked away, focusing on the ground.

Finally, the chieftain boomed jovially. "Shard, my little soldier! So good to see you!" He patted Shard on the head with a forepaw.

"It's good to see you, too, Uncle," Shard said mildly, but the word *uncle* tasted rotten in his mouth. *You know,* he wanted to say, *that nickname is a bit aggressive for me* — but the one time Shard had stammered that he did not want to be called a "little soldier," Inferno had laughed it off, deep belly laughter, but with an edge of steel in his narrowed eyes. Shard had never asked again.

Inferno glanced from side to side — as if every dragon in the Clearing didn't have their attention on them after that boisterous greeting — and leaned in. He whispered, "Now, I'm going to need to talk to you tonight! Don't worry, you're not in trouble, but it is important. Meet me here at sundown, and we'll talk, yes?"

Shard's blood ran cold. "Of course, Uncle," he croaked through a dry throat. *C'mon, c'mon! Get it together!* He could worry about his uncle later — the best thing to do now was keep his head down and not cause a scene. A frisson tingled his spine anyway.

Inferno nodded, satisfied, and returned to his podium.

"All right, everyone! It's time to get to work!" he declared. The sun was now truly beginning to peek out from over the horizon, its rays illuminating the Clearing in the colors of the sunrise.

As everyone began to file out of the Clearing, Shard spread his wings and took to the sky, traversing a meadow where dragons herded fuzzy white sheep along the banks of the deepest-blue rivers, until finally he reached a field of vibrant gold — the grain field. Landing in a small, cleared-away circle, his claws gave a light *thud* as he hit the ground. Curling his tail around him, he sat on his haunches and closed his eyes, drawing upon the well of magic deep within himself.

If a dragon flew high enough, they'd be able to see another nine dragons spread out, and then another ten elsewhere, and another ten further on. If they traced a line from dragon to dragon in each group, they'd see a pentagram with one dragon at each of the star's five points, and then five more at each of the vertices. All ten dragons were sorcerers, all of them sun sorcerers save Shard. They supplied the grains with nourishment by channeling their own magical energy into the plants, using the natural magical properties of the pentagram shape to boost their efforts. Several back-up sorcerers stood at their own spots in the field, ready to switch in if someone used too much magic and needed to rest.

If there were more night sorcerers, they might be doing this at night, but as it was, Shard had to use most of his magic on farming and then recharge at night. Of all his frustrations, this had to be the one he could least blame the other dragons for. Being a sun sorcerer — deriving your power from the daytime — was far more common.

Before the pentagram method had been discovered, the tribe had been dependent on the weather for their plants' wellbeing, but with this, they could farm worrying about one less factor. The sorcerers had to focus slavishly for hours on end, but that was a small price to pay for warding off starvation.

But as Shard worked today, it was all he could do to keep the energy flowing, much less provide his own magic for the plants. All he could think of was his meeting with Ellen last night, the follow-up tonight, and his meeting with Inferno before that.

Well, he reflected, scrunching up his snout in thoughtful determination, *I already offered to teach her, already gave her a first lesson. I'm not going back on my word. But if Inferno finds out …*

He remembered the last time he had gone against Inferno. After his mother's death, Shard had taken up painting as a way to cope, as an outlet for his anger. He hadn't hidden it, not at first. In the beginning, he'd painted out in the open, in the Clearing even. The other dragons had given him looks, but he didn't care.

He'd painted his mother, alive and well. He'd painted his family, together and whole and void of aggression. He'd painted her funeral, over and over, almost as a way to remind himself that he'd never see her again. The paintings had felt more real than the funeral itself had, in a way.

And then even that crumbled to dust around him.

He'd been painting outside his shelter one autumn night. It had been cloudy and cold, a nippiness in the air that promised snow in a scant few weeks. He had his easel and paints out and smoothed-out tree bark flattened on the easel, for this was before he'd learned to magic up canvases. He smiled as his rock glided across the bark. Peace still eluded him, but he felt numb now, and that was better than before.

Suddenly, there was the sound of pawsteps, and Shard looked up to see his uncle approaching him. All the other dragons were either at the Clearing or asleep in their shelters. Shard and his uncle were alone.

Inferno sighed, shaking his head mournfully. "I owe you an apology. I've let this go on too long. I know it hurts, but painting is a *dragoness's* pastime. You're a drake, Shard. The god Agito made us such for a purpose, and we would be fools to reject his design. There's a reason, you know, why we have two colors in our scales, whereas dragonesses have but one."

Shard bowed his head, looking down at the ground even though he wished he could just cover his ears and bolt off. He'd heard this all before, and he didn't care. He opened his mouth, but Inferno cleared his throat — a demand for silence.

The chieftain opened his mouth and spit — not saliva, but a jet of blue fire. Shard's eyes bugged wide open, but before he could do anything, his easel and bark burst into flames.

"Why would you do that!?" Shard roared, staring Inferno down with all his might. Fierce tears slid down his snout.

Inferno had the decency to look at least a little guilty. "I know it hurts, my little soldier, but I'm only doing this because of how much I love you. I want you to be the best Shard possible. Immersing yourself in the feminine will do nothing to accomplish that." And then, he simply walked away, letting Shard's art — his escape, his passion — shrivel into cinders.

Shard had continued to paint, hiding his work from everyone, but he had never forgotten the betrayal he had felt that night. He couldn't stand up to Keeper and Inferno, not without being hit or laughed at. But maybe —

The other dragons' magic vanished. Shard's eyes snapped open. "Hey! What gives?"

"What do you think?" one of the other sorcerers called back. "If you can't funnel your fair share of energy in, then don't act surprised when we cut you out of the spell!" Cries of assent echoed around the field.

Hot embarrassment coursed through Shard's cheeks. He mumbled an apology, scared to speak up. One of the backup sorcerers, a tall dragon with swamp-green and black scales named Bog, started towards Shard, his dark red eyes narrowed.

"What seems to be the problem here?" Bog asked, hovering in the air above Shard's spot. He flapped his wings loudly, the grain rippling in the gust.

Before Shard could even so much as open his mouth, someone called out, "Shard's not doing his share of the work!"

Bog tilted his head. "Oh, really? That's not like you, Shard. Well, go for a little fly and come back when you're feeling better."

"Th-thank you," Shard stammered, surprised, but grateful for the understanding. The sun hung at its zenith, shining with springtime warmth. Birds chirped in the far distance, their song calming and melodic — perfect, soothing weather.

As he ascended though, a few stray words from the other sorcerers drifted up with him. "Why are you letting him off so easy?" one demanded. "He's such a wimp; coddling him is only going to make him more insufferable!"

"I know, I know, but he's still a dragonling! He has plenty of time to toughen up," Bog whispered in hushed tones. It was clearly not meant for Shard's ears.

The heat in Shard's cheeks flared from embarrassment to anger. As he simmered and soared, he asked himself: why did he feel so bad in the first place? These dragons didn't care about him, or appreciate him. Why should he care so much about what they thought?

Even the soft earth at the riverbank and the cool, sparkling water did little to assuage his mood. Shard's mind flashed back to his own magic lessons, to those long-but-rewarding hours he'd spent with his mother. Perhaps befriending Ellen was imbecilic. Perhaps it would get him killed. But Shard knew he couldn't go on like this, being beaten by Keeper, scorned by the tribe, and pushed around by Inferno. He wanted a friend *so* badly, and moreover ...

Perhaps befriending a human could be his own little revenge.

5

S CHOOL THE NEXT MONDAY passed by in a haze. The teacher droned in front of the smartboard, his lectures flying over Ellen's head until finally, the last bell buzzed. As she stood to leave the classroom and its rows of desks behind, she folded into the throngs of students as they chatted among themselves, their voices a uniform, thrumming conglomeration of sound.

Once outside in the courtyard, the Safe Zone still bright in the early afternoon, she reached into her pocket and fired off a message to her father. *Going to the compendium after volunteering, will be home late.*

Students crowded the courtyard, chatting and playing on their phones. Ellen knew they'd be going home soon, though, for the school didn't like students waiting beyond when extra help ended. Ellen probably should have stayed for extra help herself, given how hard that morning's test had been, but she *had* to go to the compendium.

She hadn't even made it to the stone archway when her phone rang. Exhaling, Ellen looked at the screen again: it was her father.

"I just wanted to tell you, be careful on your way home!" Franklin's staticky voice reverberated through the speaker. "If it gets dark, you need to be aware of your surroundings, all right? We're getting deliveries at the food bank tonight; I don't want the trucks not to see you until it's too late. Anyway, I need to get back to work. Have fun at the compendium!"

"Thanks," Ellen said. "See ya." She hung up, then breathed her own sigh of relief. Talking to her dad could be so stressful sometimes.

You know how anxious he is! she berated herself, shame flooding through her. *If you act ungrateful, he'll leave you all that much sooner.* She bit her lip, trying to force down the rising wave of guilt. It was so much easier interacting with the kids at Shady Orchard — they were supposed to leave her one day, after all, to find homes of their own with new parents. In a way, it somehow reminded her less of ...

Well. She knew exactly who. Ellen shook her head. She had children to care for and research to do.

The reference section was located on the second floor of the compendium. Instead of a hard flooring like the first floor, there was a cushy brown carpet. A few kids younger than her crowded around a digital board with an ad for the Guild — *Keep Us Going Another Day!* — all with starstruck awe playing across their faces. It was a feeling Ellen knew too well.

As it turned out, the compendium had only a single, slim volume on dragons. Even as she sat down at a reference table, Ellen had a sinking feeling that there was not much to be gleaned from it. Less than an hour later, she learned she had been right: the book contained not a scrap of information about magic rings or talking dragons — only things she already knew, like the fact that firearms didn't work outside the Safe Zone even though nobody knew why. That was a question someone smarter than her would have to answer, though. Goddess knew, many had tried.

Well, it's not over yet. I still have one place I can get information on dragons ... Shard himself. They'd been meeting most nights for nearly half a week now, and she had yet to ask him much about what dragonkind was like.

She stood and hurried back down the stairs, her feet carrying her two steps at a time, eagerness hastening her pace. She reached the first floor, the doors a straight shot from the stairs.

"Ellen? Is that you?"

Ellen halted. Looking around, she spotted a familiar face just a short distance away, a stack of books piled high in her arms, short sleeves revealing flawless, toned light-brown skin. Breathing deep, Ellen stammered out, "O-oh ... L-Lana, right?"

"Hey, you remembered!" Lana Pai grinned, flashing the most dazzlingly pearly-white teeth Ellen had ever seen, her chocolate eyes rich as ever. Ellen wanted to lie next to Lana and stare into those eyes, their bodies soft and entwined for hours on end ... Her heart skipped half a beat as she banished lascivious images from her mind — she refused to stare like some kind of pervert.

Then Ellen noticed where exactly Lana was standing. The other girl was in front of a large, bronze plaque shielded by a glass case. There was one like it in every compendium.

Ellen's feet carried her closer as if on their own. Lana's cheer faded, replaced by something more somber. They both fixed their sights on the plaque, hanging five feet tall on the compendium's beige wall, polished to a sheen, its inscription staring right back at them.

To those who perished in the greatest tragedy mankind has ever known. We remember you. May you find peace with the Goddess Pandora.

A frown tugged at Ellen's lips. In the corner of her eyes, she saw a sober, contemplative look on Lana's face, her lips pressed just that much thinner.

It happened fifteen years ago — the Generators' one and only freak malfunction. Power had been out for barely three hours, but dragons had flown in and nearly incinerated three whole prefectures — three-eighths of the whole Safe Zone. The tragedy was called the Night of Flames, a night when wanton death and fire had lit the sky orange.

Ellen had been a mere two years old, but if she closed her eyes, she could still conjure the hazy phantoms of acrid smoke and ghostly wails.

"You too, huh?" Lana said all of a sudden, her eyes still intent on the plaque. They burned with the sorrow of loss.

Ellen frowned. What did Lana lose that night? But then, what good would it do to ask? Inviting her in, talking, sharing anything about themselves ... it would just make it all the more painful when they had to part ways — Ellen didn't have friends for a reason.

That was when she saw it. There, held within Lana's arms, at the very bottom of her stack was a slim tome. On its spine in embossed, yellow lettering was the title, *The Depths and Limits of Draconic Sorcery: A Semi-Comprehensive Guide.*

Ellen gasped. "Whoa! Where did you get that? ... Er, I mean." She coughed into her fist and resisted a groan: that had been *such* an awkward transition. "S-sorry."

Lana giggled, though whether it was genuine or out of discomfort, Ellen couldn't tell. "No, you're good. I didn't mean to pry. I'm just here to donate these to the reference section anyway. If there was one that caught your eye ..."

"W-wait," Ellen stuttered, fighting past her anxiety. Cries of *Don't talk to her! Don't get involved!* resounded in her mind. "You're just ... donating books? Like, getting rid of them?"

"Mm-hm. I wanted to recycle, but my mom insisted they had to go to the compendium. It's kinda dumb, really. I sure hope they take them."

Ellen agreed it was stupid, though for different reasons — physical books were precious rarities in a day and age where so much was online. Why would Lana's mother have them, much less want to get rid of them? All she said was, "Huh. Yeah, I guess they might just tell you to recycle them anyway ..."

"I know, right? If you want any of these, they're yours. Heads up, though: they're all pretty stuffy. There aren't even any comics or anything."

Ellen stammered as she tried to think. Her fingers rubbed together nervously, sticky sweat pooling on her palms. A boy and his mother walked by in the corner of her vision as she opened her mouth, ready to decline.

Except.

Except she had gone into the Wildlands four nights now and lived. Except she had met with a dragon, an enemy of the human race itself, and survived. Her fist clenched beside her, resolve welling up inside her chest. She could do this.

"Hey, thanks," she said, forcing a delicate smile. "I'll just take the one on the bottom there ..."

Lana proffered the stack, and Ellen slid the book out from the bottom. It felt heavy in her arms, weighty with knowledge. She ran her fingers over the rough, aged cover reverently.

Gong! Gong! Gong! A mahogany grandfather clock on the second floor chimed seven times. The PA system crackled to life; the compendium would close in fifteen minutes. Patrons started to rise from their seats, shuffling towards the stairs.

"Thanks again. I'll see you at volunteering, yeah?" Ellen said, part of her wishing for no such thing, the rest wishing for it dearly. Lana responded in kind, and started to walk to the clerk's counter, her steps soft against the carpet. Ellen herself started to make for the front door, then stopped, a heavy sigh caressing her lips.

Am I really gonna do this? ... Yes.

She groaned, her eyes dancing upwards. Nonetheless, she turned around and bounded back up to Lana.

"Ellen?"

"Hey." Ellen stalled, her words floating away before she could gather them on her tongue. Why was it so much easier to talk to Shard than another human? "Um ... I really appreciate you doing this for me. Let me know if there's anything I can do to pay you back, okay?"

Lana blinked. "Oh, you don't have to do anything, it's fine."

Ellen paused, tempted to accept Lana's refusal. Then she thrust her free hand into her pocket and pulled out her phone. "Well, if you think of anything, let me know, okay? If you want to exchange numbers, you can text me whenever."

"Oh uh. Sure! Here, let me just ..." Lana rummaged through her pockets, holding the stack in one hand. The next moment, their phones buzzed, and their contacts updated automatically via local wireless.

By the time Ellen got home half an hour later, it was still bright out, but not for much longer. She let herself into the apartment building, muffled noises from other tenants coming from closed doors. The elevator *dinged* open to the third-floor.

As she approached their apartment at the end of the hallway, she noticed two things: first, the unmistakable aroma of her father's lentil soup. Her stomach growled, the mere hint of her father's cooking dancing across her tongue. Secondly, she heard a song coming from the other side of the door, a pop number she had never heard before.

Pushing the door open, the sound of the kitchen fan roared to life in her ears and mixed with the music. Franklin stood in front of the stove, stirring a large pot. He was singing along with the music, seemingly unaware of her presence as the music blared out of a stereo. Ellen began to approach, when suddenly, the song changed.

The first notes played. Her legs locked — she couldn't move. Color drained from her cheeks. A horrible chill invaded her ears. She knew this song. She had to get out. She had to cover her ears. She had to —

The lyrics started.

You're trembling, and that's fine
I have damage, and it's mine
I hid in freezing darkness, afraid that I might fall
Locked in my last bastion, angry in its walls

Images flashed in her head. Her mother, Estelle. Hair, blonde as honey, her eyes, blue as a crystalline lagoon, twinkling lovingly ... She had sung the song — she had written it herself — her voice melodious and comforting, every night for the first eight years of Ellen's life ... And, then, there was her body, hanging lifelessly in midair ...

Before Ellen knew it, she had fallen to her knees. They crashed hard into the tile kitchen floor as she clutched herself, her arms tight around her middle. Her breathing harshened; vaguely, she knew that the song was no longer playing and her father was rushing over to her, shouting her name over and over again. He wrapped his arms around her, pulling her close, but it was too late. The last thing she registered was his look of panic and crushing guilt.

Then, he was gone. She felt as though she were plummeting even farther than the ground, losing herself in the abyss of memories flashing before her eyes. She was eight again, at the lower school; little boys and girls lined up to wait for their mommy or daddy to come take them home, but not Ellen's. The crowd thinned little by little ...

Adults, whispering when they thought Ellen wasn't paying attention, looking at her with thinly-disguised pity ... Had she done something wrong?

Stop! I don't want to think about this! her mind screamed, as if these memories didn't shape her every waking moment as it was.

Franklin finally arriving, pale with worry, walking her home as the autumn breeze blew warningly ... Ellen's mind, racing with thoughts of what might have happened to Mama ...

Everything came into hypervivid focus for a moment, playing before her eyes like a video. They rode the elevator to the third floor, the carriage rumbling as it ascended, Ellen grasping her father's hand tight, squeezing as much comfort and familiarity out of it as she could.

Then everything blurred, like it had been photographed by an unsteady hand. Feet softly hit a carpeted floor, Franklin's keys jangling as his own shaking hands turned them in the lock. Shoving the door open, his heavens-piercing cry of "Estelle!" as he rushed to the bedroom, Ellen following close behind him, only to find it empty.

Realizing the bathroom door was closed ...

Stop, stop, stop, stop ... STOP! STOP!

Her hand, grasping the doorknob, the cool metal stinging her hands like frost.

Turning the knob, her heart beating in her throat in the past and present alike, opening the door. It creaked on its hinges, ominous, discordant.

And there — she found Estelle Delacroix, her mother, hanging motionless from the ceiling, a noose around her neck.

Ellen's eyes shot open. Just like that, she was out of the dream and back in the kitchen, gasping for air, drenched in thick globules of sweat. She tried to speak, but all that came out of her mouth was something halfway between a choke and a rasping caw.

Her mother had committed suicide — her mother had *left*. She never wanted to live through that again, for if she didn't have anything to offer her own mother, what could she do to make anyone stay at all? It was that exact reasoning which had led to her life goal: she would bury her pain in the Guild, fighting to protect everyone, the most important thing she could give.

"Ellen! Ellen, talk to me!" Franklin was shouting, still holding her close. His voice trembled, and though she could not see her father's face, she knew his eyes were wide with fear. "Do I need to call a doctor!?"

"No, no, I'm fine ..." Ellen was still panting heavily as she lifted herself into a sitting position. The kitchen resolved around her. "I'm sorry I worried you."

Franklin disentangled himself from her, joining her on the hard floor. They spent a moment in silence before he said, very quietly, "It's my job to worry about you, Ellen. You haven't had an episode like this in so long ... I'm so sorry I had the song playing. I should have deleted it off my phone years ago."

Maybe he should have. But Ellen couldn't be angry. Not when that song was all he had left of his wife.

Her breathing started to even out, and Ellen insisted she was fine once more, urging him to go back to cooking. Ellen laid out her schoolwork on the kitchen table, but for the most part, she just felt sick. The apartment still seemed quasi-blurry, almost illusory. Several times, when Franklin was not looking, she gripped the table as hard as she could, savoring the smooth wood beneath her fingertips, letting it anchor her.

Within the hour, dinner was ready, and they sat at the table opposite each other. Empty thoughts raced through Ellen's mind, undefinable and vast, a sharp, spectral infinity. She stared into the red liquid specks at the bottom of her drained bowl, saying nothing.

She felt a hand on hers, and looked up to see her father, reaching from across the table. He was smiling weakly when he took in a breath. "You're going to be okay, Ellen. I promise. I think the big problem is that you're so alone all the time. You don't spend time with anyone outside of volunteering. I know other people can be confusing, but not all of them are bad."

Ellen thought about this. She thought of her father, there before her. She thought of her mother, gone forever, a betrayal she never wanted to relive. She thought of Lana, a girl she barely knew but maybe, just maybe, she wanted to get to know, and she thought of the children at Shady Orchard, whose happiness she wanted to nurture.

And to her surprise, she thought of Shard. He was putting his life on the line for her. She would have to pay him, certainly, but even so, that he had not sunk his claws into her flesh, that he had not scorched her to ashes, might just mean something impossible.

"Um, Dad," she started, her voice small.

He leaned in, trepidation written over his face. "Yes, Ellen?"

"I uh, had a question, but it's a bit of a doozy ..."

Franklin smiled again encouragingly. Anticipation radiated off him.

Her palms were clammy again. "What was the Night of Flames like?"

His smile vanished. "The Night of Flames? Well, if you really need to know ... Just ... give me a moment." His eyes glassed over, as if he were staring at some unknowable horror. For a second, Ellen was sure she had said the wrong thing, that he was going to get angry.

Instead, he breathed deeply, and spoke. "The Night of Flames ... It was hell, Ellen. Buildings burned. People burned. If the fire didn't kill you, the smoke did. The night sky was red with flames. I ... I'm not sure how I survived. People I knew and loved didn't. I ... I'll never forgive the dragons. They're all monsters, every last one of them."

He produced a tissue from his pocket and dabbed at his tearing eyes. "I'm sorry. That's a painful subject ... What brought it up?"

Ellen opened her mouth, but no words came out. How could she tell him the truth?

Franklin's eyes narrowed at the silence, a look in between suspicion and alarm written over his face. "You're not thinking about the Guild again, are you? I told you, Ellen, I'm not letting you drop out of school to join, especially not with your impair —"

"No, no!" Ellen hurried to say, putting up her hands like a barrier. Her joining the Guild was an argument they'd had time and again, one she did not want to repeat. Even without his permission, she could join on her own when she came of age in two years. Now that she had a real tutor, her dream was more within reach than ever before. "I'm not asking that, don't worry. It's just ..."

He's going to leave you, chorused the usual warning, *just like Mom did.* It almost stopped her — but only almost.

"It's just, that was only a few dragons that night, right? Not *all* dragons can be evil, can they?"

Franklin's Adam's apple bulged; his brows shot up as if bouncing off a trampoline. "Ellen, I don't know where you got that idea from, but it is *dangerous!* Dragons are feral monsters. They can't even talk! This is about the Guild again, isn't it? Ellen, you are *magically impaired.* If you join the Guild, the dragons will kill you, do you hear me?" He spoke with panicked urgency, his whole body suddenly rigid with fear.

Ellen stared back, heart thundering in her chest. His face contorted, white as bedsheets. He was moments away from yelling; she was sure of it. But his expression softened. He sighed, slumping back into his chair, his brows resting again on his eyes. "Please, Ellen. There are things you can't do, but that doesn't mean you aren't important."

"Thanks, Dad. I'm sorry I made you worry," she whispered at last. She had, she discovered, shrunk back like a turtle into its shell. "A-are you okay?"

"I'm fine," he said, but she had already leaped up, offering to make him some calming tea, ignoring his protests that he didn't need any. When those failed, he went on, "I'm sorry, I shouldn't have yelled. Ellen?" He was trying to get his daughter's attention as she rummaged through the pantry for a teabag.

"Yeah, Dad?" she said, but her focus was drifting. Something her father said had stuck out to her: *Dragons are feral monsters.*

But they couldn't be, not if they talked. Ellen thought back to the book she had gotten from Lana, laying now in her room, yet unread. How much of what was inside it was true? How much of what humans thought they knew was wrong?

Maybe ...

"Ellen, you need to make friends. I promise you, all this worrying about dragons and the Guild will fall to the back of your mind once you start to heal."

Ellen turned the faucet on. Water cascaded into a pot, a staticky white noise backdrop as disparate threads of thought coalesced into comprehension: maybe, by seeing Shard ... she was doing exactly what she needed to.

6

T HE SUN HAD LONG since set when Shard emerged from his shelter. The stars once again lit the sky, and he once again stored their energy, glowing lightly. As far as the ear could hear, there was quiet. Not even the wind blew. Shard sighed. A weight had been lifted. For the rest of the night, he wouldn't have to deal with other dragons.

Even Keeper was Agito-knew-where with Firebug. She'd shown up at the brothers' shelter a short time ago, while Shard had pretended to sleep. He'd kept one eye cracked open ever so slightly though, and the image of Firebug draped lovingly over Keeper's body as she snuggled up to him made Shard shiver in disgust.

What does she see in him? Shard thought. That dragoness was all over his brother, and for what? His personality? Perhaps she thought courting the chieftain's nephew was some way to gain power. Perhaps she wanted to become his Bonded partner so that when they mated, their dragonlings would be part of the chieftain's bloodline.

Urgh, mating. Shard shivered at the very idea. It was something he personally hoped to never subject himself to. The whole experience sounded utterly repulsive to him. He couldn't begin to fathom why so many of the other drakes seemed to actively *want* it.

"Shard!" called out a voice, the last one he'd wanted to hear just then. He looked around for its source. "Over here, my little soldier!"

Oh great, Shard thought as he looked up. The chieftain was approaching him from above, his wings making loud flapping noises, and for a moment, Shard was worried that all the dragons asleep in their shelters would wake.

Inferno touched down to the ground, skidding a little as he did so, leaving tracks in the cool dirt.

"Hello, Chieftain," Shard said, fighting back a grimace. He'd forgotten that the older dragon had wanted to meet him. "Er, I mean, Uncle Inferno." Such a loving address still felt wrong, rotten like a hunk of rancid meat.

"Ah yes, progress! How wonderful!" Inferno smiled so widely that his fangs showed, his head rearing back as he laughed heartily for a few terrifying seconds. Presently, however, his expression morphed into something more solemn. "Now, I imagine you're going to charge your magic, but you shouldn't be up too late. Always try to replenish early in the night, yes?"

Shard had to keep himself from grimacing again. "Yes, sir," he replied, marveling at his bad luck. His whole body felt tingly and twitchy, like if he stood still any longer, he'd burst. He kept sneaking peeks beyond Inferno, in the direction of the river, trying to see if there was anyone there. If Inferno noticed, he didn't react.

"Excellent, my little drake, excellent! Now, I did mention I wanted to talk to you, yes? I apologize for not following up with you sooner; being chieftain is its own special kind of ordeal, as I'm sure you can imagine!" He chortled good-naturedly. Shard dared not react with more than a weak chuckle. Inferno continued, "As I'm sure you know, your cousin Spearhead's fourth hatch day is in just a few moons."

Shard nodded — but what his uncle was getting at? Surely, he didn't need Shard to help prepare the celebration so far in advance?

Inferno looked to the left, and then the right, then the left again before leaning in conspiratorially. Shard couldn't tell how much of it was for show. "What I haven't shared with anyone is that my little drake is deathly terrified of his first Starsight vision."

It took Shard a second to process this. Spearhead was scared of having a Starsight vision? "Why?" he asked before he could stop himself.

44

When he was younger, Shard had wondered what it would be like to have Starsight — to be able to see the future. From what he knew, the visions were often vague, and being able to experience them at will was a learned ability, but even so! He had thought: *How amazing would it be to know not just what could be, but what would be?*

And he'd then learned if you didn't have a father with Starsight, you had to contract the Starblight sickness to get the power. There had been only a few cases of Starblight in his lifetime, all of them from when he was too young to remember. But tales of the illness still swirled around the tribe in hushed tones, tales of the dragons who had contracted it. Nearly all of them had died — and after those days of fevered anguish, the ones who survived were never quite the same again.

Inferno sighed. "I'm not sure, to be perfectly frank. I think Spearhead's afraid of what he'll see — or what he won't see. But, the little tyke's going to be chieftain one day, and he must develop his power to lead the tribe properly. If he's too weak to use it, then I'm not sure what will become of the tribe."

To be fair to Inferno, neither was Shard. The entire tribe planned their year around Starsight visions. When to hold holidays, when to plant what crops ... even knowing when it was going to storm was something they needed Starsight for.

A smile crept across the older dragon's muzzle. "Not to worry! I have a plan, but I need you for it."

"A plan?"

"Yes, my little soldier!" He chortled a few times, seeming very proud of himself. "All I need is for you to tell him what happened to your mother. That will help him realize just how essential Starsight is."

The world seemed to grind to a halt. A high-pitched whine trilled in Shard's ears, whispering something he couldn't quite make out. His vision wobbled as he spoke. "You ... you need me to tell him about my mom ... so he'll use Starsight ..." The pieces were all falling horribly into place. "Are you saying that ... that ..."

Inferno frowned. He'd said the wrong thing and he knew it. "Well, just as an example, you see ... What happened was unavoidable; Starsight's not an exact art, but it could be used to prevent similar unlucky setbacks ..."

No. No way. He can't be serious. Nasty rebukes ricocheted in Shard's head. He blinked back the tears threatening to cascade from his eyes, and beat down his urge to scream and shout and yell. What could he do? Yell at Inferno and be shredded into a thousand little pieces?

"I understand, Uncle," Shard said at last, his voice less than a choked murmur, because if it were any louder, it would be an ear-piercing bellow.

Inferno breathed a sigh of palpable relief. Then, he was all smiles again. "Excellent! I'll be sure to let him know you want to talk to him. Thank you sincerely, Shard."

Shard nodded. He didn't trust himself to speak. Inferno bid him adieu and took his leave, his powerful pawsteps a stamping diminuendo in the spring night. Shard barely breathed until the chieftain's gait vanished entirely.

And then the dam burst and he galloped, letting his four legs carry him through the village as fast as he could. Soon, he ended up at the river, where the rushing water raged in his ears. He wanted to sleep. He wanted to shout at the top of his lungs. He wanted to kick himself in the belly. Even the energy of the shining stars wasn't helping tonight.

"Gah!" he spat, panting as he slammed a paw into the ground, flattening the grass with a *thud*. He took a deep breath, filling his lungs with air, then plunged his head into the river. Freezing water stung his eyes, but he did not care. Shard screamed loud and rough and raw into the muffling current, expelling as much rage as he could before surfaced, gasping for air.

Inferno might have known! He could have foreseen her death, could have *done* something to save her. Shard had considered it before, but he had always decided in the end that it wasn't Inferno's fault. But the way he had just described Stardust's death, her murder: *an unlucky setback.*

Shard swung his paw again, only for his blow to pass harmlessly, unsatisfyingly across a patch of flowers. He wanted to paint something, literally anything, to take his mind off this red-hot fury.

Calm down! He still had to teach Ellen that evening, and he would not be seen acting so shamefully. His mother had taught him better than that. With a great effort like pushing over ten trees at once, he forced his eyes closed, blanketing the world in darkness. Breathing deeply, he pretended the air flowing in and out of his snout was tranquility itself. It even worked, a little. By the time he opened his eyes again, he felt, if not good, then better; like he had breathed the worst of it right out of his body.

He sat there for a bit, reveling in the night. Insects buzzed all around him as the river continued to warble pleasantly. Grass swayed in the breeze, and like a flash of lightning, inspiration struck — this would make for a great picture. He glanced from side to side hesitantly. Nobody was around. Surely a little drawing couldn't hurt, could it?

Tracing a single claw through the dirt, he began to sketch the scene around him. A wide smile broke out on his snout, his eyes sparkling with wonder as he looked up periodically from the ground to check his surroundings. True, drawing with a claw was not nearly the same as working with paints, but it carried its own special kind of artistic majesty. Soon, he had nearly forgotten his encounter with Inferno. His mood transformed slowly from sour to buoyant as he became absorbed in his art, shutting out everything else.

"Hey, what're you drawing?" Ellen asked, suddenly, from mere inches away.

He let out an alarmed yip.

7

CHIRPING CRICKETS filled Ellen's ears the second she teleported to the riverbank. Shard was hunched over what looked like a drawing, and from a cursory glance, it looked intricate. But when she greeted him, he flinched like a startled cat.

"Oh, Ellen! H-hi! Y-you're here early tonight," he stammered. Quickly, he ran his paw through the dirt, dusting away the sketch. He turned to face her, smiling anxiously. His fangs glinted, but his body seemed ... smaller, somehow, like he was curling up into himself.

"No I'm not? I was just asking —"

"Well, let's get started. You ready?"

Ellen huffed frustratedly, but sat down at the riverbank anyway. "All right. Let's get to it." When Shard said nothing, Ellen cleared her throat loudly.

"I'll tell you when you've had enough," Shard mumbled, his gaze still pointedly turned away from her.

She pushed her magic outwards, feeling it reach past her body, but this time, instead of pushing it in all directions, she decided to try pushing it in only one — down. She pushed it down into the ground, worming her way through the specks of dirt and gravel. She could feel life in the earth: bugs, worms, even some plant roots. Such an amazing feeling, she thought this was, being able to feel the energy of another life, of multiple other lives within her consciousness. Soon, though, she felt herself starting to tire.

And then her face turned green. She barely had time to lean over before her dinner came rushing up through her mouth and splattering on the riverbank.

"What the hell!" She yanked her feet out of the river so they didn't get vomit on them. "I thought you were gonna tell me if I was pushing myself too hard."

"Sorry!" Shard groveled, pressing himself against the ground in what seemed to be a bow. "Really, I am, I just, I just —"

Ellen rubbed her temples and sighed, cutting him off. "Well, that's great. Just … what's going on with you? I thought you said you were going to teach me magic." As soon as she spoke, trepidation coursed through her. What could have happened to put a *dragon* — an all-powerful force of nature — in such a tizzy?

"It's … not important."

"Shard," Ellen said, finding a surprising boldness within herself. "I nearly ruined this shirt because whatever's eating you has you distracted." The edges of fear began to cloud Shard's face. She sighed. "Listen, it's clearly bothering you, and I want to learn magic and not lose any more food than I already have. So just …" It felt like jaws were closing around her; she had to have been bothering him. A pregnant pause later, she sighed and pinched her nose. "Sorry, sorry. I shouldn't be prying into your life like this."

The fear vanished from Shard's face, but now, his eyes seemed to be staring at something far away, eyes unfocused, as if he were remembering. Ellen frowned — had she hurt his feelings, somehow?

"No, no, you're fine." Shard rose from his crouch and shook his head. "Sorry for being such a grump about this. I'm really glad you cared enough to ask."

Ellen's mouth hung open. Every time they met, she was reminded that this dragon, this great beast of fire, was so *gentle.* Nothing like she had imagined. More and more, she was convinced that her dad was wrong, that not all dragons were evil. Before her, his scales shimmering ever-so-slightly in the night, he even seemed fragile, like she could crush this apex hunter with just the right words.

50

She scratched her nose awkwardly as a cricket's chirping cut through the silence. "You uh … don't have anything to thank me for just yet. Now come on. Spill it."

"Well … I was expecting you to judge me. You know. For drawing like that."

"Wait, that's all? Dude, so you were drawing. I've seen people do it before. No biggie." Of course, humans drew digitally on their computers, not on the ground, but that didn't matter.

Shard scrunched up his face, like he couldn't quite believe what he was hearing. "It is a big deal! Art … art is something only dragonesses are supposed to do. When you showed up on me all of a sudden … I kinda freaked. Everyone always judges me for doing that, and I thought you were too." He let out a humorless puff of air. "I know, I'm stupid, I should have realized a human might be different from a dragon. I just … I …"

Ellen said nothing as Shard trailed off. This conversation was getting far too personal. But she couldn't just shut him down, and, she realized with a jolt, not only because she didn't want him to get offended and call off the lessons. Her head felt like it was swimming in fog for a second, like she was floating above herself and looking down at the conversation from on high.

"It's just that … well, I don't really get along with the other dragons," Shard admitted. "They don't think I'm tough enough, but I've seen what toughness does to you. Keeper, my brother … he's the toughest dragon in the tribe, and he's always beating me up whenever he wants, but especially if he thinks I'm painting. I guess I'm just used to it. I'm sorry."

That caught Ellen's attention. "He beats you up? Isn't there anyone you can go to about this?" The sounds rang hollow in her own ears. Dragon or not, what kind of deranged monster did that to his own brother?

Shard just shook his head. "The only adult I've told is my uncle, the chieftain, Inferno. He said that roughhousing builds character." The very mention of the chieftain's name made his expression curdle.

"But what about your parents? Can't they do something?"

Shard lamely batted a rock into the river. It landed with a *plop,* little waves rippling outwards across the dark blue surface. Finally, he replied in hushed tones, "My mom is dead."

Seconds passed silently as it all sank in. None of it felt quite real, an ethereal whisper passing through her ears almost meaninglessly. Ellen hadn't even considered ... "What about your dad?"

Shard let out a sound that was halfway between an amused snort and a hateful laugh. "My dad ... well, he's not a good dragon. He ... he ..." Shard trailed off. Ellen didn't push.

"And I'm not allowed to paint because that's something the dragonesses are supposed to do ... At least, that's what everyone else thinks, and I have to keep all my art secret because of it. Sorry, I hope I'm not sharing too much."

Ellen bit her lip, staring down at the crystal-clear water as the moonlight danced across the surface. Was this why Shard alternated between being a smart-aleck and a quivering mess? Why he flinched at the barest hint of anger?

A strange feeling bubbled inside her. No one should have to be hurt like that. Not by their family.

"I'm sorry," she whispered after a moment. Though she expected that this was transient — that whatever bond they were forging, it would end once Shard got his payment — she felt, for a moment, warm. "You shouldn't have to deal with that. And ... I want you to know that I won't hit you. No matter how angry I get."

In the starlit night, Shard stared at Ellen, who found herself staring right back. She'd thought before that people and dragons had similar body language, and she still held by that. There was once again something unmistakably human about his face — surprise and anger and grief and sadness and gratitude too, all wrapped up in that one stare. Then he looked away and peered out into the distance.

"Thank you. That means a lot."

"Yeah," Ellen said lamely. She realized she had *no* idea what to say. Should she comfort him more? Play it off as no big deal?

"You're not half-bad, Ellen. You know, for a human," Shard teased, grinning slyly.

Clean Wildlands air filled Ellen's nostrils as she snorted. "I think I'm gonna go home for the night. I wanna change into something that doesn't smell of barf. Try not to make anyone else blow chunks while I'm gone, okay?"

Shard laughed, crisp and clear. "No promises." The breeze picked up, rustling blades of grass. A toad punctuated the moment with a creaking *croak.*

Ellen reached for the ring. But a curious glint shone in Shard's eyes: "Hey, actually, could you do something? We've been building your magic strength for a few days now ..." Ellen's heart skipped a beat. "I think you might be ready to try some actual spellcasting again."

"No way." Her reply was automatic, disbelieving. Her free hand dropped from the ring to the dirt. Each individual grain of soft soil screamed against her palm as the moon moved behind a cloud. "Are you sure? I mean, like you said, it's only been a few days; shouldn't I wait a bit? I mean, you know, so I can —"

"Ellen," Shard cut in, his voice commanding yet kind all at once. "I'm not saying we're done. I'm just saying ... try it."

Ellen swallowed, heart pounding, and without saying a word, she nodded. Slowly, she climbed to her feet, and clenched her hands into fists, holding her arms in front of her like she'd seen in pictures so many times before. But what if it failed? What if she could never do it? *What if, what if, what if?*

The moon peeked out from the clouds, illuminating them in silvery light.

"Go on," Shard encouraged, smiling, and Ellen took a deep, calming breath. *Can't put it off forever, Delacroix.*

She punched the air. Shimmering air sailed across the river, *whooshing* into a tree on the opposite bank with a light *thud.* The trunk shook ever so slightly, branches swaying, leaves whispering from the impact as pollen scattered.

"Oh my Goddess." She looked at Shard, who had leaped to his feet, beaming with the kind of pride only a teacher could have. There was only one thing she could tell him, her voice breathy as she uttered two words she had thought she would never say to a dragon: "Thank you."

8

THE NEXT MORNING in the Clearing, Shard ate his portion of vegetables silently, not daring to look up from the ground. It felt like everyone's gaze was prickling across his scales, as if they all suspected his treasonous bargain. He was sure their eyes were boring into him; his stomach lurched every time someone so much as twitched.

Yet, nobody decried him as a traitor. Inferno ate perched on his podium, unaware of Shard's nighttime dealings. Keeper did not hit him. In fact, when Shard let himself into the shelter last night, Keeper had been fast asleep for the second night in a row, snoring soundly. Now, he too was focused entirely on his meal. Even with Firebug cuddled up against him, her black scales standing out against his red-and-scarlet ones as she cooed and batted her eyes at him, he didn't seem to notice Shard one bit.

Soon, breakfast ended, and the day began. Shard eventually was able to relax as he supplied energy to the crops, and he made a point of relishing it. Sitting underneath the sun, letting its warm rays wash over him, he let out a contented sigh.

Before, Shard had wondered if he was betraying his tribe by teaching a human magic. But now he'd come to a conclusion: he didn't care. For the first time in his whole life, he was making a friend, someone who laughed and smiled with him, someone who didn't hit him, someone he was proud of.

If it was so wrong to have a friend like that, then so be it.

9

T HE HUM OF AN ELEVATOR had always comforted Jess Flint. Whenever he felt that low-pitched *whirr* nestling itself deep inside his bones, it meant he was on his way somewhere important. That he was about to get something done.

This particular morning, the Commander of the Guild stood in the City Hall elevator as it rocketed to the top floor, keeping his eyes focused on the door rather than the clear plexiglass walls. Heights always made him dizzy, which was perhaps ironic, given that he had spent so long standing on poles raised high above a pool back when he played blastball.

As the elevator climbed ever-higher, he thought about what a shame it was. If he could look out the glass, he'd be able to see the entirety of Haven City, illuminated by the moon in the early morning darkness ... or at least, that would have been the case if the dome weren't there. But the silver glow of the dome blotted out the picture he'd seen so many times in his dreams, pasting a metallic hue over the city. He hated that. Invaders had taken what was rightfully theirs. Humanity deserved their world back.

Of course, he thought, nervously flexing his wrist, *even the Safe Zone might not be ours anymore.*

The elevator halted at the top floor, though the doors did not open. Jess pulled a card out of his pocket, then swiped it through a reader embedded in the elevator's control panel. The red indicator light turned green and the doors rolled open with a *ding.* They revealed a short passageway that terminated in a waiting room, tinted glass windows letting sunlight stream in. Beyond that lay the ugly burgundy waiting room. Jess would paint over it in a heartbeat if he could. There were a few chairs and a desk off to one side, a short man sitting behind it.

"Commander Flint," said the receptionist chin in a nasally, high-pitched voice. "Chancellor Robertson isn't expecting you for another few hours."

Jess's lips twinged irritably. He knew that the chancellor was a busy woman, but this was important. "I just need to see her as soon as possible."

"I'll see if she's free." He picked up the phone on his desk. "Chancellor Robertson, Commander Flint is here. May I send him in?" The speaker hissed as the person on the other end sighed loudly. Before Jess could react, the receptionist placed the phone back on the receiver with a *click.* "She'll see you right away."

"Thank you," Jess said, and made his way towards another passage, this one leading directly to the chancellor's office. However, instead of being blocked by simply a door and a keycard reader, this security system was far more complex. Here stood a tall, thick bulletproof door with a metal grate, next to which was a fingerprint reader, above which was a retina scanner, and next to those was a tube where he had to submit a sample of saliva. It made sense: she was the leader of the human race, after all. Even he had bodyguards at all times, though he wasn't always allowed to know where they were. But being delayed like this still made him nervous.

Behind Jess, the receptionist hit a button, and the whole gray apparatus lit up, a green LED arrow displaying next to the fingerprint reader, a prompt to place his finger on the reader first. Once he had that taken care of along with the saliva sample and retina scan — that was his least favorite part; the laser was bright and hurt his eyes — the metal grate lifted with a rumbling and a beep. Finally, the dense metal door creaked open, revealing Chancellor Robertson's office.

It was a spacious, circular room lit by a glass chandelier that always surprised Jess, both for its size and out-of-place elegance. It hung in the center of the ceiling, casting bright light across the gray and white tile floor, luminescence which more than made up for the lack of windows. Up against the far wall stood a row of filing cabinets, which Jess knew were filled to bursting with papers. It was hypocritical, really, trying to switch the whole Safe Zone to digital and then keeping her own documents as hardcopies. Being able to access things on computers was convenient, and they both had some of the best cybersecurity teams available in their employ; there was no need to fear making the jump. Also, Jess was a little jealous — how in the Goddess Pandora's name could she organize all those files?

Behind a large, wooden desk was the woman herself: Chancellor Ayla Robertson. She was a serious-faced woman with rippling muscles underneath her suit-and-tie attire. Leaning over in her chair, she rested her elbows on the desk, covering her mouth with her tented hands. Even sitting down, her massive size and impassive stare made Jess feel like she was looming over him.

"Commander," she said coolly, though that did not necessarily mean she was angry. Robertson's idea of professionalism, Jess had learned, was to be as unemotional as possible. Or maybe she was like this all the time.

"Good morning to you, too," Jess said cheerfully, turning on his most infectious smile. "I hope my text this morning wasn't too unexpected. I know I'm an excellent conversation partner but —"

"Flint, I'm not in the mood for your circumlocutions this morning. What did you want to talk about?"

Perhaps she was a *little* angry. Oh well. He should have known that a 5:30 AM text was a risk; not that she ever would consider putting her phone on vibrate. Jess cleared his throat. "I believe the dragons have found a way into and out of the Safe Zone."

Robertson said nothing. She did not even move.

"… Chancellor?" Had she not heard him?

Robertson's eyebrows rocketed upwards before settling. She said dryly, "Oh. You're serious. Dragons, inside the dome. Really? Not only is that an impossibility by itself, but if there actually were dragons in the Safe Zone, why has no one noticed?"

"I believe they have taken measures to hide from us. But —"

"And how exactly did you come to this conclusion?"

Jess held back a sigh. Without saying a word, he brought his fingers to his face and slowly, dramatically traced the scar on his cheek. Even despite the situation, the rough texture flung his mind back years to a night sky bathed in ash and red, to buildings crumbling around him as heat scorched his body and screams pierced his ears. Most of all, it brought him back to a giant, green and hideous dragon raking its abominable claw across his face.

Jess had fought back, punching a gust of air at the monster mid-slice. His eye had been saved, but at the cost of a bit of the dragon's talon breaking off, lodging itself in his cheekbone. It was there even now, an infinitesimal bump beneath his fingertip. On the Night of Flames, he had lost two things: his unscarred face and his wife.

Yet he had gained a few things, too. Ever since that horrible night, he had been able to *hear* dragons, understand their speech, and even more amazingly, he could *feel* their horrible magic. Robertson was the only one he had told. No one else could know that the man who led the Guild had been tainted the very thing he was supposed to protect them from.

Chancellor Robertson said nothing, her eyebrows knitted in thought, so Jess continued. "Nearly every night for the past two weeks, I've felt sorcery pulsing across the dome. *Something* is entering and leaving the Safe Zone. None of us are safe so long as that remains true."

Chancellor Robertson exhaled far too deeply for so early in the morning, and massaged her temples wearily. "Jess," she began. "Your abilities are useful, to be certain, but utterly unique. We don't know their limits or parameters at all. Furthermore, there's been no sign of a dragon, none of the chaos or carnage one would cause. And moreover, why would they just cross back and forth across the dome, doing nothing? Wouldn't they just kill us all and be done with it?"

With a start, Jess realized she was exasperated — she still didn't believe him. His lips pursed with frustration; he didn't care if she saw or not. "With all due respect, Chancellor Robertson, you've never been outside the Safe Zone. I coordinate the orichalcum runs and I fight in them. I've been face-to-face with those winged monsters more times than I care to count, and I've nearly died to them just as often. I've seen people, good people, die." He sucked in a sorrowful breath and thrust a finger right at his scar again. "They ruined my *face*. I promise you: I know sorcery when I feel it."

A guilty throb pulsed in Jess's chest — he might have laid it on a bit thick there, but it had worked. The Chancellor stared at Jess one last time, this time softly, the way someone might look at a friend.

"Jess," said Robertson at last, "I'm hesitant to believe you, not because I think you're lying, but because I think you're scared. However! It's true that you've had more experience fighting dragons than me. Goddess knows we wouldn't be here today without your efforts. Perhaps I should consider that you have interpreted your powers correctly. If you can promise me that you aren't letting your disfigurement cloud your judgment, then I will give you a chance to prove me wrong."

Jess met Robertson's inquiring gaze head-on. "I promise, Chancellor," he said immediately, sincerely, and without hesitation. This was the chance he'd been hoping for.

The barest hint of a smile tugged at Robertson's aged face, and in that smile, Jess could see warmth. Then it was gone. "Good. I'll make arrangements to put more resources at your disposal. I expect you'll bring me evidence in the next ... let's say four months."

Jess had expected a time limit of some sort. Even still, a bead of sweat rolled down his neck. "Thank you," he said.

With that, he was shooed out of the chancellor's office. He passed by the desk receptionist, rode down the elevator, and walked through the now-bustling foyer of City Hall, where thankfully, nobody approached him. It wasn't until the glass double doors slammed behind him that he allowed himself to sigh. Cool morning air blew through his brown bangs as his gaze hardened with mounting tenacity.

Four months. He had four months to find whatever monster had infiltrated their world ... and destroy it.

INTERLUDE

A CONVERSATION AT THE
CENTER OF THE WORLD

D ARKNESS SURROUNDED the woman in the black cloak. To her left and right, above her and beneath her, lay the vast expanse of the universe. Stars and comets and moons and planets shone, countless heavenly bodies sharing their light to paint a picture of the cosmos.

The woman floated in the starry rift, staring intently at a single blue planet. If she focused, she could see its oceans, its mountains and trees; its life, from the tiniest microbe to the largest dragon. She wanted to be there herself so very, very badly. Alas, she could not leave her position for long.

"It's pointless, you know," whispered the frightened one. His voice weighed heavy with sorrow and exhaustion, the voice of a warrior who had fought one too many battles — the kind that can never be won, but must still be fought.

The woman in the cloak said nothing. She did not even turn to face him.

"Please," he begged, and now she knew that he was grasping the bars of his prison cell simply because she knew *him*. "Please, give up. You're making this harder on me, and you're making this harder on yourself, too. When you lose our little game, you'll be crushed."

She bit her lip.

"You know how they are. Mortals never change, humanity and dragonkind alike. We've had so much time to understand these creatures, so much time to learn everything they're capable of. How different could these two be?"

Finally, a sigh escaped the woman in the black cloak, the first sound she'd made in days. There were many ways she could respond, but only one answer did the question justice.

She said, "I love them. They *will* stop you."

PART TWO

GROWING CLOSER

10

THREE MOONS LATER, Keeper woke an hour before dawn, sleep falling from his eyes as little specks of dust. Yawning loudly, he stretched, reaching his forepaws in front of him and extending his tail. Sometimes, he wished he had something softer to sleep on than the shelter floor, but he'd toughed it out his whole life. He wasn't about to start complaining now.

In the corner, Shard gave a slight grumble and pawed at his snout. Then he was snoring peacefully again. Keeper stared at the blue and turquoise dragon, eyes narrowing — but only for a moment. He had better things to do than focus on *him.*

Spreading his wings, Keeper flew to the roof of the shelter, opening it with the enchanted slat that made it retract. But this slat was special. He had paid for an extra enchantment for it — with a very large bear he had killed all by himself — that made it glow, but only when someone was looking for it. It had been quite the trade, but the thing almost paid for itself, just because he didn't have to ask Shard for help opening the roof when it was dark. Agito above, he hated that sniveling wuss. But it would be okay. Keeper would prove he was better, *was* proving he was better, simply by being who he had to be.

The clear, starry sky hung above him as dewdrops dripped off leaves and shrubs. Peeking out from his shelter, Keeper sneaked a glance to his right, then his left, then again in both directions. It was ridiculous that someone as tough and masculine as him — the toughest and most masculine in the whole tribe, just ask him! — had to be so sneaky. But, he could *not* allow himself to be seen doing this. He almost didn't know what would be worse: everyone's laughter, their mocking glares, or his own shame at having let himself been caught.

Satisfied that nobody was watching, he rose further into the air. With a tap of his claws against the shelter, the roof slid itself back into place, thundering like an avalanche. Keeper winced, his heart skipping two beats — had the roof always been so loud? He looked one more time in each direction. Nobody was stirring. At long last, he set out.

Once clear of the village and ensconced in the forest's greenery and its chirping insects, he set to work as quickly as he could. It was a difficult task in the dim predawn light, but Agito knew he couldn't do this during the day.

Normally, he would never even dream of such an undertaking, but this was for Firebug's sake. And Firebug? She was the most wonderful dragon in the tribe — ever, in Keeper's opinion. She was smart, beautiful, and most importantly, she was all *his.* He knew everything about her, and she knew everything about him. He knew exactly what to say to her, always knew how to make her smile and laugh, and she always knew how to lift his spirits when they were down. They were meant to be together. They had been friends for as long as Keeper could remember, and today, he was going to give her a gift. Not because it was her hatch day, not because it was any special occasion — but because she made him happy and she deserved it.

Something tugged at the back of his mind. The thought that maybe he was weak — that he didn't deserve anything — but he shook his head to clear it.

By the time the sun started to rise, brightening rays of light warming the cool forest, Keeper was plucking one last flower. He made a few dexterous adjustments, shoved the finished product into a small cloth pouch, then set off. He had asked Firebug to meet him at dawn, and he would not keep her waiting.

Keeper made a half-circle around the Clearing rather than going through it, then he moved into the surrounding forest again.

He stole through a particularly thick patch of bushes, branches and needles prickling at the undersides of his paws. The rustling felt near-deafening. More than once, he almost turned back.

Finally, he saw her; Firebug was waiting for him, her black scales glistening in the rising sunlight. She faced away from him, unaware of his presence — perhaps he hadn't been so loud as he'd imagined. Her head was lifted to the sky almost reverently. Keeper stayed silent for a time, unwilling to destroy such a beautiful image.

"Hey, babe," Keeper said at last, hoping he sounded suave and not like the choked-up, anxious mess he felt inside. Firebug gave a small gasp, but then turned to him. Her eyes shone; just for him, he was sure. "I got you a present."

Shyly, he placed the pouch on the ground and scooted it towards her. Firebug stared at it for a second, the glow in her eyes dimming. Keeper's stomach dropped — what if she didn't want it?

But then she slowly reached out to take the pouch, falling to her haunches as she grabbed it with her front paws. "Hm, what's this?" she began. Her expression brightened again as she reached inside and pulled out a garland, a loop of vibrant purple and deep blue flowers tied together by the stems. Their earthy, floral aroma was strong in Keeper's nostrils.

"Oh, Keeper," she breathed admiringly, turning it over in her paws. "This is so sweet of you ..."

"Put it on," he urged. He couldn't wait to see her wear it.

She nodded and hesitantly, gingerly slipped the garland around her neck. Excitement built and burst in Keeper's chest — it *was* perfect on her. She was perfect.

"Is this why you called me here so early? Did ... did you make this yourself?"

Keeper cocked his head upwards, smiling smugly. "What can I say? I'm just a real sentimental guy."

If Firebug was bothered by his arrogance, she did not show it. She only nodded. "Yeah," she said softly, not quite meeting his gaze.

"What?" he asked.

"Nothing."

"Oh, by the way ... Don't tell anyone you got that from me. Can't let everyone know I was messing around with flowers, am I right?"

"... Of course," Firebug said after a moment. He leaned over, pressing his snout against the side of hers. A giggle escaped Firebug's muzzle, and she swatted at him playfully. "You wanna eat together this morning?"

"You know it, babe."

They were just beginning to make for the Clearing when it happened. The sun moved out from behind a cloud, stray rays of light from the dawn catching Firebug's black scales just so. Bright flecks of white speckled her body and glittered in the sun, like a vein of astoundingly perfect diamonds. The garland accentuated the effect, the colors mixing dazzlingly. Keeper's heart felt like it stopped, right then and there, for he had not known such a cherubic dragon could exist. To him, Firebug looked like a comet streaking through the night sky — nothing short of a breathtaking sight. His tromping footsteps faded to nothing as he stopped.

"Keeper?" Firebug tilted her head, concern coloring her voice. "What's wrong?"

"Nothing, nothing." He shook his head and walked on. But, he reflected later that day, standing in a field with his flock of sheep, it was in that moment he realized in his heart of hearts what his destiny was. He wanted to be with Firebug forever, and for that to happen ...

Well, he was going to have to ask her to become Bonded to him.

11

THE RHYTHMIC, LATE JUNE drizzle rolled down Ellen's nose as she walked to Shady Orchard, her yellow coat not quite keeping her dry. Hazy mist swirled at her feet, but she was just glad school was over. She'd gotten back a mediocre grade on an essay — the unit had been on the history of mining town in Frontier Prefecture — which was by far her least favorite kind of assignment. She could never quite organize her thoughts on paper.

Oh well, she thought. *I have a lesson with Shard tonight, so that's something to look forward to.*

Her magic lessons had been going well. Mostly, they were doing the same breathing exercise over and over again, but her ability to expand her senses was improving slowly, the magic sense bubble bigger and bigger each time. She and Shard had been meeting almost nightly, and to date, they had yet to be discovered — and thank the Goddess for that. Ellen had no intention of dying any time soon.

More recently, the two of them had started swapping stories about their lives. Once Shard had calmed down around her, he'd liked hearing about human society, and for her part Ellen had to admit she liked hearing about how dragons lived, too. She'd had no idea that sorcery played such an integral role in Shard's village; it helped grow crops, healed the sick, which were powers Shard himself had, and there was a special brand of it that could even be used to predict the future. It all left an excited tension in Ellen's chest that she did not quite know what to do with.

There was the matter of the ring, too, which even now adorned her finger, glinting as it caught a porchlight in the gloom. Ellen was no closer to uncovering its origins, but its power and restrictions had become clearer. First, as she'd already known, she had to twist it thrice to use it. Second, it only worked when she and Shard were both alone. If either of them was in the presence of another, the ring would tighten on her finger if she attempted to work it, and then automatically teleport her as soon as they were by themselves. Thirdly, it always took her to Shard directly. Once or twice, she'd tried going early and ended up in his house, or shelter as he insisted it be called, instead of by the river. Luckily, Keeper hadn't been there, but Shard had still shooed her away — and with good reason. The memory still made Ellen's heart skip a beat.

Ellen stopped, standing still in the rain, eyes on her feet. If she joined the Guild, she would have to fight dragons. Kill them. Could she, knowing that dragons like Shard existed? She shook her head. This wasn't the time to think about that.

Turning onto North Yew Street, the orphanage came into view. Lights shone in the windows. As always, she rapped on the front door before entering. Presently, it clicked open, revealing a harried-looking Robert. Heavy breaths heaved his chest up and down. Slippery, sweaty beads ran down his neck.

"Oh thank the Goddess, you're here!" he exclaimed between wheezes. He doubled over, resting his hands on his knees. "There's a fly loose in the living room and the kids are freaking out!"

"... so squish it?" Ellen quirked an eyebrow as she crossed the threshold, unslinging her backpack from her shoulders.

"I'm trying, but the little bugger keeps getting away!"

Ellen sighed, pinching her nose. "Dude, there's a fly swatter in the office. You can just —" A child's high-pitched shriek pierced the air. Something, be it glass or ceramic shattered, and the wails of crying children rose in the air. "You know, I'll go get it. You go calm everyone down."

"Thanks, Ellen. You're a lifesaver."

The office was a cramped, windowless room in the back of the building. Here, the Shady Orchard staff would type out paperwork, take phone calls, and handle other administrative minutiae. As Ellen approached it, she strode through the kitchen, which today smelled of savory red sauce and tofu balls. The cooks paid her no mind as she passed across the tile floor, fans whirring and pots steaming.

Something was wrong, though. Today was Lana's day to cook, yet, Ellen noted with a pang of disappointment, Lana was nowhere to be found. Or so she thought. Finally, outside the office, a red Venetian door barring her way, Ellen heard noise coming from inside.

"Mom, please just listen to me," Lana pleaded, her voice cracking as Ellen had never before heard. "He's my dad; I want to see him!"

Is Lana on the phone? Ellen wondered. But then she shook her head — this wasn't something she should hear. She could get the fly without the swatter. But as she walked away, another voice stopped her dead in her tracks.

"I don't care. Elementals need to help us keep the dome up, not waste their time on games. No daughter of mine is going anywhere near a blastball arena to watch a bunch of suicidal idiots toss a ball around."

"But Mom, I —"

"I said no!"

Ellen hurried away, keeping her head down, her face a bright scarlet. One of the cooks looked up from his sizzling pan as she strode by, but Ellen couldn't focus on that. She knew that voice. It belonged to Ayesha Pai — the director of Shady Orchard, and if she had heard right, Lana's mother.

Ellen stayed late that afternoon, not once catching a glimpse of Lana as she read to and played with the kids. Soon, they were called to dinner. Ellen declined to join them, instead waiting on the front porch. It was raining harder now, the occasional flashes of lightning illuminating the sky.

As time dragged on, the hour growing ever later, Ellen reached into her pocket and pulled out her phone. She scrolled to the wiki page for blastball, and began to read. She knew the basic idea of the game, as anyone in the Safe Zone would, but had never bothered to really learn the nitty-gritty of it. Videos of players in spacious, jam-packed stadiums filled her backlit screen, showing them standing on pillars above a body of water, batting the ball around with their water magic as they hopped from plinth to plinth, using aeromancy to balance.

"Wow ..." she murmured, her breath fogging her screen. These players all had such command over their magic. Her aeromancy was much stronger now, but when she used it, it was an all-encompassing wind, rather than something concentrated or delicate. Would she ever achieve that kind of mastery? She clenched her fists, resolving to work even harder from now on.

Eventually, the door creaked open, and out stepped Lana. Her brows were furrowed, an unmistakable unease on her face. Ellen's heart beat hard, but she swallowed, willing herself to ignore the overpowering rhythm.

"Uh, hey, Lana," she said. Her cheeks felt hotter than hot, but still she looked Lana square in the eyes, slipping her phone back into her pocket as discreetly as she could.

"Hm? Oh! Ellen, you're here late. Were you waiting for me?" She carried a yellow umbrella at her side.

"Uh, yeah, I was," she said. Reaching into her backpack, she produced a slim volume — the very same one Lana had lent her. There hadn't been much useful in there, but the gesture still counted for a lot. "I wanted to give you your book back ... and to apologize. I overheard you talking to your mom before ... Kinda heard some personal details I don't think I was supposed to."

Lana frowned, but did not take the book. "... What exactly did you hear?" Ellen told her. The whole time, Lana said nothing, merely listening with the same disquieting look. When at last Ellen had said all there was to say, Lana still remained silent, her face brightening and dimming as the porchlight flickered.

Ellen wanted to speak, but she waited, listened, watched, made sure to catch any sign that Lana might be angry. After what felt like a rain-soaked eternity, Lana sighed, hand against her chest as her shoulders sagged.

"Oh, thank Goddess," Lana exclaimed, relief lingering on every syllable. "Finally, I have someone I can talk about this with. Here, let me put that in my bag ..." She took the book from Ellen, who blinked. She hadn't expected this.

A nervous blush crossed Lana's face. "Sorry, sorry! I should explain. Basically, my dad and I were going to go see a blastball game in Hadkirk City on Saturday. My mom — the director here — hates blastball because she thinks it steals away potential recruits from the Guild. I mean, she hates my dad too, but she'd never say so out loud. That's divorced life for ya, I guess."

The drumbeating rain slowed. For a second, Ellen expected moonlight to peek through the clouds — but then she remembered they were in the Safe Zone. With a jolt, she realized that she had to say something. "Yikes. That sounds ... complicated. I guess you were looking forward to this."

"A bit, yeah. Blastball is kind of my favorite thing," Lana admitted, scratching the back of her head. "But hey! Enough doom and gloom. It's not like I'll never see my dad again, and I'm gonna join the blastball league when I'm old enough anyway! Forget about watching the game, I'll get to play it! I'll be fine, you know?"

That could have been the end of it. Ellen could have said nothing, could have let the moment slip away to keep herself safe. She almost did. But a certain blue-and-turquoise face popped into her mind of its own accord, grinning like mad. There in the crisp Wildlands air, they laughed together, learned together, shared magic ...

Breath hitched in Ellen's throat. Could she have that with someone else?

"Hey, uh ... Is there anything I can do to help? Maybe I can say something to your mom to get her to let you go? It's stupid that you can't go see your dad."

Lana shook her head, smiling sadly. "My mom wouldn't listen to anyone on this, trust me. I mean ... Unless ..."

She stopped; her jaw quivered infinitesimally. Ellen knew that gesture — it was what someone did when they were scared, when they were considering something outrageous. Lana's eyes swept furtively from side to side, then suddenly, she leaned in, her nose inches from Ellen's. Red heat flushed her cheeks again, and this time not from shame. Lana's lips were right there, red and soft, close enough to make out every last, beautiful bump and ridge ...

"Will you do something crazy for me?" Lana's voice was barely a whisper, her breath warm as it tickled Ellen's nose. It smelled savory, but also floral. Was that lilac body wash?

She had never been this close to another girl before, and it sent shivers up and down her spine. Was Lana really oblivious to what she was doing? "Y-yeah?"

One last sweeping glance. "Will you help me lie to my mom? We can tell her I'm at your place on Saturday!"

"I ... I guess?" She spoke slowly, hesitantly. "I'm not sure that's —"

"Right, sorry." Lana pulled back and scratched the back of her neck, looking away, her lips drooping. "I guess that's kind of a pretty big thing to ask, huh?"

Bzzt, bzzt! Ellen's phone vibrated, piercing the evening rain. The screen lit up, a message from her father displayed. She pulled back from Lana as she checked it.

Ellen, said the message, *where are you? Are you all right? Do you know what time it is?*

"I gotta go," Ellen said, her face absorbed in her screen as she furiously hammered out a response. She'd completely forgotten about her dad; he must have been worried sick.

"What's wrong?"

Ellen shook her head, rubbing her temples as she imagined her father driving himself crazy as he paced the apartment. She shoved the phone back into her pocket. "I was supposed to be home like, an hour ago."

"Oh, yeah, you gotta hustle," Lana agreed. "I'll catch you later?"

Ellen stopped halfway down the front steps. Her hand gripped the wet, cold banister. The porchlight flickered on once more, outlining Lana in a halo of yellow as she gazed expectantly.

The barest hints of a smile forced itself onto her lips. This had to be a mistake, but she couldn't help herself. Lana was just too damn pretty. "I'll think about it, okay? I did ask if I could help, after all."

Lana's face shed its anxiety, sprouting a smile more subdued than sunny, but genuine all the same. "Thanks, Ellen."

12

THE NEXT DAY before work, Firebug sat in the Clearing, eating her morning meal of berries and grains from a carved, stone bowl. Keeper was nowhere to be found that morning, so she dined alone for the first time in a while. Not needing to coo at and cuddle with him was liberating.

It was a cool, cloudy morning with a breeze that promised rain. Firebug quite liked the rain. It was refreshing, and it meant that, if it did start to pour, she and the other dragonesses got to weave their baskets inside the Meeting Hall, the large shelter Inferno and his council used for important discussions instead of outside.

Of course, there was something more important than basket weaving for her to do today. She had her job too, of course, but before that she was going to finally talk to Chieftain Inferno.

Inferno, the closest thing she had to a father. The imposing red and scarlet dragon sat atop his podium, eating and laughing heartily with Gnarl, a councilmember with two shades of gray in his scales. The chieftain looked so approachable like that, Firebug thought wistfully. She wished she knew him better.

I've got this, she thought.

The thumping stampede in her stomach did not cease. What she really wanted was one more night to fine-tune her plea. The fate of the tribe was at stake. She just had to convince everyone else of that.

With a steadying breath, she took heavy steps across the Clearing, approaching Inferno. She saw Emerald and Spearhead eating together, still only partway through their portions. As she passed them, Spearhead's head jerked up — the little dragonling knew exactly what Firebug was doing. He gave her a hopeful, supportive smile. Alas, Emerald knew what Firebug planned as well. Reproving eyes warned her wordlessly: *Don't.*

Well, too bad, she thought, resisting the urge to say something snarky. This was *her* time to shine.

"Chieftain Inferno!" Firebug called out as she got closer. A sudden gust blew, perhaps as an omen. Inferno looked up from his conversation with Gnarl, the other dragon shooting Firebug a frown. She decided not to care just yet.

"Oh! Hello there," Inferno said, almost like he was surprised his own daughter was talking to him. Not that she blamed him — the sound of his voice sent a thousand little nervous thunderbolts up and down her tail. "How are you today, my dear Firebug?"

"I'm fine," she said, thankful her voice did not rasp or crack. "I did have something to ask you, though. Do you have a moment?"

"Of course," Inferno replied, and for a second, hope dared to flutter in Firebug's chest. "But perhaps we should discuss it later. I was just about to call an end to the meal. Let us talk tomorrow morning — I'm sure you'll be too tired tonight after a long day of work." With that, he announced that everyone was to proceed to their jobs, and before Firebug could protest, he flew off, low enough to the treetops that leaves rustled with each wingbeat.

"Now is good, actually!" she called, watching him shrink into the distance. Frustration fizzled in her chest. Inferno's claim that she would be too tired be damned, she *needed* to have this conversation with him.

"You shouldn't have talked to him like that, Firebug," Gnarl admonished in his deep, gravelly voice. He raised his head arrogantly.

"What do you mean?" She kept her voice as even as possible. She had an inkling, but wanted to hear it for herself.

Gnarl snorted. "Not right for a dragoness to talk to the chieftain on his podium. You should've waited until later."

Again, frustration churned Firebug's insides, anger building like venom. A third voice joined the conversation. "Oh, I'm very sorry, Gnarl," Emerald groveled, sidling up by Firebug and ever-so-minutely pushing her aside. Very obviously a command to play along. "My daughter is very sorry for her impudence, I'm sure. Aren't you, Firebug?"

Jaws tight, Firebug silently weighed her options until finally, she relented with a small sigh. "Yes, I am sorry."

Gnarl grunted. "Get to work, you two." Then he flew off, his wingbeats fading into the distance.

The Clearing was mostly empty now. Most of the drakes had gone. Dragonesses were forming a circle, getting ready to weave baskets for the day, a task Firebug would be joining soon — they had to be ready for the harvest, after all. Despite herself, Firebug stifled a groan. If she had to weave one more basket, she was going to snap.

"My dear, sweet dragonling! My dear, sweet, impossibly dimwitted dragonling. Are you really such a scatterbrain?" Emerald was, as her name implied, green. Not a brilliant green like an actual emerald, but a duller shade. Her purple eyes glared critically at Firebug, like a hawk about to swoop in for the kill. She wanted to protest, but she was sure her tongue would only get her into deeper trouble still.

Emerald took her daughter's silence as a cue to keep talking. "You know dragonesses can't talk back to a councilmember!"

Firebug found herself nodding lamely. The anger was suddenly, if not gone, then dampened. "I know ... I just — Inferno's the closest thing I have to a father, right? I figured —"

"He's your *step*-father, for Agito's sake! There is no blood connecting you; it's not the same." Emerald looked like she wanted to tear her scales out in frustration. All of a sudden, another sharp gust blew, cool like the sudden frosty dread in Firebug's stomach. She knew exactly what her mother was about to say. "If you want to be part of the chieftain's family so badly, then hurry up and get Keeper to ask you to be Bonded with him!"

Firebug stiffened. "But Mother, I've told you about ... about what I've seen." She leaned in, not wanting to attract the others' attention. "The tribe, the shelters, everyone here, burned to the ground by a giant —"

Emerald barked an ill-humored laugh. "Firebug, darling, we've been over this! Not only have you not had the Starblight sickness, not only did your blood father not have the power, but you. Are. A. Dragoness. It is impossible for us to have Starsight!"

Firebug frowned. Flashes of smoke and flaming ruin had bombarded her for weeks now, their acrid scents lingering in her nose. The visions were weak, vague, but Starsight often was at first — and if these visions weren't Starsight, she didn't know what was. "I just need him to train me," she argued for what felt like the umpteenth time. "The absolute worst-case scenario, we find out it's nothing and walk away with just a little wasted time."

Emerald sighed, shaking her head exasperatedly. "If you really think this danger is coming, that's all the more reason to hasten your relationship with Keeper. The drakes don't care about what we have to say! Come on stronger, drop all the hints you possibly can. By being with Keeper, not only will your dragonlings be part of the chieftain's family proper, but Inferno will listen to your ideas through Keeper. We've been over this! Honestly, what is wrong with you!?"

That question sank into Firebug's flesh like a knife. Why should Inferno only have to listen to Keeper? What was so bad about listening to *her?* Just because he and Keeper were related by blood, it was apparently different! Not to mention all this "dragonling" talk. What if she didn't want dragonlings?

And there was one more thing. "But Mother, I don't..." Her mouth snapped closed of its own accord; she had never told Emerald this before.

"But ...?" Emerald cocked her head expectantly.

The weaving had begun, dragonesses all lined up to create baskets and other products out of reeds they gathered by the river. Some even magicked up cloth, the grains and fibers shimmering and stitching themselves together.

Firebug glanced at them, longing burgeoning in her heart. She wished she had sorcery. She might be able to use it to save everyone. And sometimes, she thought it was perhaps the one thing dragonesses and drakes could share beyond dragonlings.

"I want to save everyone, Mother, and I can't be sure Keeper will listen to me, even if I become his mate. And ... there's something else," she whispered as she held her mother's gaze. She gulped, but Emerald said nothing. Firebug decided to get on with it. "I ... I don't think I love Keeper."

Emerald pulled back, her eyes burning fervently. An angry snort issued from her throat, a little bit of hot smoke rising from her nostrils. "Come with me. Now."

Firebug opened her mouth to protest, but her mother was already stalking away. Now she'd done it. She followed after Emerald, keenly aware of the lack of attention from the other dragonesses. Maybe they didn't care. Maybe they did. A glance their way only showed them working.

Up ahead at the Clearing's edge, where the wide-open space met the trees, Emerald was tapping one of her front paws impatiently, as if Firebug was somehow taking too long to cover the exact same distance at the exact same pace.

"Firebug," Emerald hissed when her daughter was close enough to hear. "Do you know why I am Bonded to Inferno?"

"... Because he asked you to be?"

"No." Emerald shook her head emphatically. Her face hardened. Firebug had seen that look only a few times before.

"When your blood father died — may Agito bless his dearly departed soul — when the humans rolled into our village in their strange, metal monstrosities all those years ago and stole our orichalcum and slew him, and I was surrounded by smoke and the crumbled remains of shelters and your siblings' shattered eggs, I realized I had a *duty*. A duty, *to you*, to give you the best life you could possibly have when you hatched. You think I loved Inferno when he proposed to me? Not on Agito's right wing! But I knew you needed the chieftain's protection. You need to find the best father for your dragonlings, Firebug, when you one day have them, so they can be protected, too." The powerful look faded. "What's so bad about Keeper, anyway? You've been friends since before your first hatch day; surely you must feel something for him!"

Firebug blinked, her scales feeling very tingly all of a sudden. "I just ..." The words died in her mouth.

As she stood there, trying to say anything, her anger ebbed and gave way to resignation, and she just felt tired. Keeper could be very sweet and accommodating, usually. Maybe Emerald truly was right. Perhaps there was something wrong with her. So, after a moment's silence, she answered, her voice as delicate as the gossamers spun by spiders in the fall: "I don't know."

Emerald breathed. She reached out a warm, rough wing and brushed it against the side of the younger dragoness's snout.

"It will be all right," Emerald said, smiling kindly as she looked into Firebug's eyes. "Everyone makes mistakes, but the important thing is that you learn from them. I love you, and I want what's best for you. Sometimes, we just have to accept the world the way it is, even if it isn't perfect."

"... I know, Mother. I love you, too."

"Wonderful, darling. Now, we both should get to work. I'll see you tonight." And with that, Emerald's wing dropped from Firebug's snout as she flapped both her wings and took to the sky.

Firebug stood for a moment, feeling very cold for some reason. Then, with a sigh, she walked to her spot in the weaving circle, the other dragonesses welcoming her, and picked up her basket. Yet she could only stare at it blankly. Her forelegs felt heavy, like boulders.

"I'm not feeling so well," she told the weaver next to her, an elderly dragon of nearly one-hundred-and-seventy named Brightness. "I'm going to go for a fly, try and clear my head, you know? I'll be back soon."

"Of course, Firebug," said Brightness. Despite her age, her paws moved nimbly as she threaded the strips together, holding them between her claws. "I'll save your spot for you."

"Thanks."

And with that Firebug ascended, letting her mind wander among the infinite blue.

13

THAT AFTERNOON, the orphanage had a different reader coming. Although she would much rather be headed to Shady Orchard, Ellen found herself with nowhere to go but home. As she treaded down the sidewalk, summer heat lapping at her skin, her apartment came into view. The three-story brick building had a neon-pink cat graffitied onto the side, a touch that had always tickled Ellen, if not the older residents. In front lay a nascent garden, filled with a variety of fruit- and vegetable-bearing plants. Solar panels adorned the roof, much like nearly every building on the street.

Ellen was fumbling through her school uniform's shirt pocket for her key when the front door swung open. Standing before her was her father, wearing a T-shirt and shorts. His skin, pasty from countless days spent behind a counter, seemed almost out of place in the blazing sunlight.

"Dad?" Ellen tilted her head. "You're home early."

Franklin nodded, a frown creasing his forehead. "They're installing new security cameras at the food bank. The workers say it's going to take until morning, so I have the rest of the day off! Was just about to go for a walk, actually."

A bird, hidden from sight, chirped happily as a thought struck Ellen. "Can I come with you? It's been a while since we've just hung out." Her heart caught in her chest for a split-second — wouldn't he feel like she was intruding?

Luckily, his stress-wrinkles relaxed as he beamed, eliciting an embarrassed blush from Ellen. "That'd be wonderful! I always love to spend time with my little girl."

"Dad, c'mon, I'm hardly little," she complained, but her lips curled upwards anyway. She liked knowing her father cared.

They walked through Echo Woods, opposite the direction of the upper school, chatting all the while. Tall, brown oaks were planted at every street corner, their deep-green leaves swaying in the breeze. The roads were devoid of cars, and only a few people seemed to be out and about. At least at first.

As they neared the park, Ellen spotted a repair truck parked in front of a telephone pole. A gondola was extended from the roof of the truck, and a man in a neon yellow uniform was hammering something to the pole — a camera, from the looks of it.

The repairman gave one last *thwack* with his hammer, and the gondola retracted back into the truck with a mechanical whirring. As the truck pulled away, Ellen caught a glimpse of the lotus flower logo plastered on the side — the Guild's logo. *Huh. Why would the Guild be installing cameras on telephone poles?*

Finally reaching the park, Ellen and Franklin saw a crowd had assembled around a makeshift stage set up on the grass, upon which stood a woman in the center. Three men flanked her on either side, each standing at attention with their hands behind their backs. The woman stood behind a podium, which Ellen noticed also had the Guild logo on it.

"Dad, I think this is a recruitment drive for the Guild!" Ellen nudged Franklin with her elbow, pointing excitedly across the street. This wasn't the first one she'd seen — now that she thought about it, there had been at least three in the last week alone. Still, she couldn't help but grin. When she joined the Guild one day, she would be able to protect so many people — her dad, the kids at Shady Orchard ... No one would ever have to feel the loss she had once felt.

Shard's face flitted in front of her eyes, a wry grin exposing his fangs. She blinked the image away, shaking her head. It couldn't hurt to just look, could it?

Franklin's lips twitched nervously. "Again? I could have sworn they just did one yesterday." He sighed. "We can watch, if you want."

For a second, a cold flash of anxiety struck Ellen. Had she upset her father? But then a microphone crackled to life, and her brain switched into hyper-focused mode.

"Citizens of Echo Woods!" said the woman on the stage, booming with authority. "Do you like the life you lead? Do you love your fellow humans?" She paused dramatically, surveying the crowd with a piercing look. "It could all end in the blink of an eye."

Nods rippled throughout the crowd. There were a few "mmhmms" but also, a few annoyed grumbles, to Ellen's great surprise. "They've been here every day this week," someone muttered. "And those new security cameras! It's not like anything's changed, is it?"

The recruiter went on to summarize common knowledge, that the Generators could run out of orichalcum at any time, that dragons were always on humanity's doorstep, that any night could be a new Night of Flames. Ellen frowned. The increased recruitment drives, the surveillance ... was the Guild worried about something?

"And that is why," the woman onstage continued, making eye contact with the entire front row, "we want *you* to join the Guild!"

Light applause rippled through the park, but Ellen only half-heartedly joined in. Something nagged her as she tried to reason through her concerns. Was she missing something? *Had* something changed? Based on the disgruntled expressions she saw in the crowd, she wasn't the only one put off.

The recruiter called forth anyone who wanted to join the Guild, offering contact information to all who expressed interest. As people started walking forward, Franklin placed a firm hand on Ellen's shoulder.

"I'm not going to sign off for you to join," he said firmly. "You know how dangerous it is out there."

She grunted. The beginnings of a sarcastic quip welled up, but she forced it down. She was the only family he had left, and he was the only family she had, too. Meeting his gaze with as gentle a smile she could muster, she said, "Dad, it's fine. I can wait until I'm old enough to join on my own."

That didn't seem to reassure him much, but the crowd was dispersing now, and the sun had started to set. The Safe Zone was getting dark. "I know, Ellen. I know," Franklin said and for a second, he looked remarkably tired. With a glance at the recruiter and her subordinates — they were talking with the hopeful members now; one of them stoked a flame in his palm, and the recruiter nodded approvingly — Franklin walked away, Ellen trailing after.

It wasn't until later that evening, over a steaming plate of spaghetti and meatballs that realization struck. Between the security cameras and the increased recruitment, could the Guild perhaps be scared of something *in*side the Safe Zone? Something they thought was dangerous? As her father got up from the table to answer his ringing cell phone, Ellen let her fork fall with a light *thump.*

Could it have something to do with her and Shard?

14

S HARD WAITED FOR ELLEN patiently, humming to himself and drawing patterns in the dirt with his claw. The river lapped at the shoreline a short distance away. A cloudy sky covered the stars, but even so, a small grin tugged at Shard's snout.

With a deep breath and a dreamy sigh, he gazed up into the dark, gray-blue heavens. He and Ellen had been meeting secretly for several moons now, and not only had they not been discovered, but against all odds, they actually seemed to be on the road to friendship. She was funny, a dedicated student, and even better, she didn't hit him when she got angry. She even was all right with him painting.

He wanted to keep seeing her like this forever.

As always, she appeared beside him without warning, blinking into existence where the grass met the water. Yawning, she extended her arms out wide above her head — Shard always found it so endearing to see her stretch like that, hearing her make that noise. Dragons usually stretched by extending their wings to the side and their forearms in front of them. Seeing something so different was just a tad fascinating.

"Hey, sleepyhead," he teased.

"Hey." Ellen exhaled. She sat down on the grass, but did not face him, instead looking up at the sky, then sighed again. Before he could ask why, she shook her head. "You ready to get started?" She met his gaze now, and he saw that something seemed … wrong.

Shard couldn't quite tell what. Perhaps it was the way her lips twitched ever-so-slightly, or the way she seemed to be looking far away even as she looked right at him. Something must have shown on his own face, for Ellen said, "What?"

"Well, it's just … you seem kind of off. You okay?"

"It's nothing," she said, but brusquely.

"Well, that's not worrying in the slightest," Shard replied. "Is this some weird human thing? You can talk to me, you know." The knot that always tightened in his chest gripped him. He swallowed. *This is Ellen,* he reminded himself. *She's not going to hurt you.*

"I mean I guess it's a human thing?" Ellen bit her lip as a nearby cricket chirped. "It's not that big a deal."

"C'mon, Ellen. I am an expert at finding things out. A champion, even." Shard nudged her with his wing, which brushed gently over her shoulder and exposed neck.

For some strange reason, Ellen laughed. It was short and clipped, like she didn't really want to. Clapping her hand over her mouth, her cheeks flushed. It was the sort of reaction one might get if they were to lightly trace a leaf over the underside of someone's paw.

A devilish grin tugged at Shard's mouth. "Are you ticklish?"

Ellen just swallowed, her throat bulging, which was all the answer Shard needed. "I swear to the Goddess, Shard, if you even so much as touch me —"

"You'll tickle me back? Oh no. Whatever shall I do."

"You are such a smart-ass." Ellen rolled her eyes, and Shard frowned.

"Sorry. I uh, didn't upset you, did I?"

But she was smiling as she shook her head. "Nah, you're good. I'm just … thinking. It's a few things, really."

He sighed, grateful she wasn't angry. "Do you wanna talk about it?"

At first, Ellen's gaze reached into the distance, her eyes unfocused and contemplative. "It's just … we're taking a lot of risks meeting like this, aren't we?"

"I mean, yeah?" Shard said slowly. At his paws, a little worm burrowed through the dirt, wriggling as it buried itself deeper into the rich brown soil.

Then Ellen looked him right in the eyes and her fears came tumbling out all at once in a breathless, anxious rush of a sentence. "I think my government might be onto us. I don't know how they know or how much, or what they'll do if they find us, but I — but I — I don't —"

"Whoa, whoa, slow down there," Shard said, fighting his own sinking feeling. "What happened? Why do you think that?"

"They're ... observing us more. We've got these ... tools that let us see places without being there, and the Guild is setting them up — the Guild's members are the people who fight dragons. And they're trying to get more people to join the Guild, too." Ellen heaved a sigh, massaging her temples. "Now that I'm saying it, I guess it doesn't make sense: if they were onto us, why would they start now, so long after you started training me? I'm not doing anything different that would have tipped them off."

Shard hesitated. "Do you think we need to stop?"

A hundred thoughts danced across Ellen's face before she shook her head. "No, I'm sure I'm overthinking it. Besides, I promised I'd pay you for all this; still gotta get on that."

A breeze kicked up, carrying a floral scent. Shard inhaled through his snout, getting a calming whiff of daisies. "Awesome!"

But Ellen still seemed off, her brows knitted in thought. Shard remembered she had said something else was wrong, too. "You know," he offered, "if you're not up to it, we can take it easy on the magic tonight."

She looked at Shard, her head shooting up like she was startled. "Huh," she said after a time. "Maybe it'd be okay if we just hung out."

They talked for a while after that. During a lull in the conversation, she gazed up at the cloudy night sky wistfully. "No stars tonight, huh."

"Not a one, I'm afraid," Shard said. "Guess you're gonna have to look at them at home."

Ellen shook her head. With a dreamy melancholy, she said, "Can't. The dome blocks out the sky. It's a shame, though. I love looking at the constellations when I'm out here."

"The what?"

"They're basically stars people have noticed look like they're in patterns. Or, well, noticed them before the dome went up seven hundred years ago. The only people who see them now are" — her voice caught for a second so short that Shard barely noticed it — "are Guild members."

"Patterns? So they're like paintings in the sky?"

Ellen nodded, stroking her chin thoughtfully. "I guess that's one way to look at it. You sound awfully impressed, though. What's the matter, jealous of a little human imagination?"

"A little bit, yeah," he admitted, unable to think of a witty retort. "I don't think I ever would have come up with something so creative. It must suck not being able to see them at home."

Ellen bit her lip. She was on edge again. Crickets filled Shard's hearing, soft as a lullaby. Before he could ask what was wrong, she gulped audibly.

"Thanks for checking in on me before, yeah?"

Shard shook his head, confused. "Huh? Anyone would have —"

"I mean it!" Ellen stamped a hand on the dirt and leaned towards Shard. Her eyes were lit with a fierce kindness the likes of which Shard had not seen from her. "You're teaching me magic, even though I'm a human, and you laugh and joke and talk with me every day … You're a good dragon."

Moments passed as Shard's pulse thundered in his ears. The river splashed against the bank, spilling over his claws. "You — you really think that?" he whispered. "You really think I'm good, Ellen?"

A sputtering string of syllables fell from her lips. Finally, instead of looking away, instead of running, she met his gaze head-on, and gave a single, emphatic nod.

"Ellen," Shard repeated. He rasped, gratitude choking him. "That means so much to me. Thank you."

Ellen's smile was transcendent. "Listen, I'm gonna go home." She stood but bent over, dusting her clothes off with a *pat-pat*. "I promised someone I'd do them a favor. I'll be back tomorrow, yeah?"

"Definitely." Before he could stop himself, Shard added, "And Ellen? I think you're good, too."

"… Thank you," she whispered. Then, she twisted the ring thrice and was gone, leaving the dragon with nothing but the wind and water for company. He stayed there for a time, watching the grass as it swayed in the breeze.

"She doesn't think I'm a monster ..." He was sure he would never know why, but the very fact of it heartened him. A drowsy yawn escaped him — it was getting late.

On the way back to his shelter, however, something unexpected happened. As he was passing by the Clearing — he went around it rather than through it in case anyone was there — he heard two familiar, hushed voices. The gravel crunching beneath his feet suddenly seemed loud as an explosion. He didn't dare move another inch, corking his breath lest that too give him away.

"... are you sure?" Firebug's voice came hesitantly.

"He was pretty clear." This one was Spearhead. "He's definitely going to ask you tomorrow."

Why were Spearhead and Firebug in the Clearing so late at night? They lived in a shelter together; couldn't they talk there? Did they not want to wake their mother and Inferno?

Firebug groaned. "I can't do this. He's my friend, but I don't want to spend my life with him! There's so much more I want to do than be someone's mate! Did you overhear him saying anything else; did he —" Firebug stopped midsentence, only to groan again. Shard assumed Spearhead had shaken his head, but more importantly, Shard himself was eavesdropping — and that would never do. Using a little magic to mask his steps, he made for his shelter.

It wasn't until he had slipped safely inside, his head upon the hard ground and Keeper's snores vibrating in the closed space that he realized what Firebug must have been talking about. Shard's eyelids jolted wide open. For whatever reason, Spearhead and Firebug thought that Keeper was planning to propose to Firebug.

And she didn't want to say yes.

Why, though? Keeper was always going on about how perfect their relationship was, and with their constant displays of affection, surely she felt the same? What had Spearhead heard Keeper talking about?

By the time the sun peeked out from the horizon, bathing the Clearing in vibrant midsummer dawn, Shard still hadn't found an answer. Sitting in his usual corner, he munched quietly on his grains and berries.

Dragons chattered as they ate. Spearhead sat with Emerald, but, Shard noticed, the little dragonling kept glancing over to Firebug, who was talking with Keeper. His twin brother seemed to positively glow, but also completely unaware of Firebug's worried aura. Her eyes darted left and right as if looking for an escape.

It occurred to Shard that Spearhead might have had a Starsight vision of Keeper proposing, but that was an awfully specific first vision. From what Shard understood, Starsight started vague and became more and more specific and controllable as the Starseer practiced. Had Spearhead overheard Keeper telling one of his friends about it? That seemed more likely but ...

With a frustrated growl Shard shook his head. *I'm not going to get to the bottom of this by myself.* He stared at his leftover crumbs. Inferno or one of his councilors would call an end to the morning meal soon, and the day would start. Once that happened, he could forget all of this and leave Keeper to his own business. After all, Firebug could just say no, couldn't she?

Of course, I've *never been able to say no to Keeper, not without getting hit. What if ...* Shard gulped. It was almost too horrible to think about.

But if it *was* true ...

Shard's paws started moving on their own, his throat drier than noon on a midsummer day. Even as fear jabbed into him, icy cold on all sides, Ellen's horrified reaction in his head spurred him on. Was that what Firebug needed, too?

"Um, excuse me, Keeper ..." He had lowered his head, making himself small. With a calming breath, he straightened out.

Keeper shot him a withering glare, and he shrank back again. "What's up, *little bro?*" The words were thick with menace, and there was a just-threatening-enough look on his muzzle. Shard pressed on.

"I just need to borrow Firebug for a second, is all. Just wanna ask a few questions, no biggie." He laughed, trying to sound as casual as he did with Ellen. It came out sounding very, very wrong.

"We were in the middle of something important," Keeper near-growled.

I am so getting beaten up later.

"It'll be fine, don't worry," Firebug piped up, looking visibly relieved. Shard hoped that didn't mean he was right. "What do you need, Shard?"

"It's a little private ... Nothing super bad, but if we could just talk over there before work starts? It won't take long; you'll blink and then go, 'damn, that was speedy as all get out.'"

If Keeper had looked angry before, he looked about ready to claw Shard's innards out now. Well, it was too late.

Firebug blinked. "Yeah, sure. See you tonight, Keeper!" Did she really not see the murder radiating from Keeper's wings down to his claws? Giving his cheek a light nuzzle, she parted from Keeper, and followed Shard a short distance into the forest.

Birdsong echoed around them, bright and bouncy. Light filtered in through the treetops, painting a scene in stark contrast to the lump growing in Shard's throat. He was making a fool of himself, he was sure, and she'd probably get angry at him for even suggesting —

"So, what's up?" Firebug asked curiously. Shard gulped again. His legs felt wobbly, but he could already imagine Ellen telling him to believe in himself. With a deep breath, he opened his jaw, and everything came tumbling out so fast, Firebug merely blinked. "I did not catch a word of that," she finally said.

Shard took another deep breath, cool against his sandy tongue, and, more slowly this time, he asked, "Keeper doesn't hit you, does he?"

Firebug blinked again, harder this time if it were possible, more uncomprehendingly. "... No? Why do you think that?"

Shoot. "Oh, uh, n-no reason." He wished he could play this off somehow, but he was too frenzied to come up with a lie. He tried to draw upon the confidence Ellen inspired in him. "Just a question, you know, dragon to dragon. I mean, I might have heard you talking to Spearhead last night, but, c'mon, who hasn't vented to their little brother about stuff before?" He nudged her with a wing. But when Firebug's eyes went wide, guilt stabbed Shard. "Sweet Agito, I'm sorry. I wasn't eavesdropping on purpose; I just was out for a walk. Promise." He knew how unlikely it sounded; he certainly wouldn't have believed himself.

"How much did you hear?" Firebug didn't move to hit him, didn't move at all, but her cracking voice told Shard everything.

"Just that you didn't want to be Keeper's mate."

"Oookay. Not too bad, then." She let out a breath. They shared a chuckle, Shard's more nervous than hers. "I mean, please don't tell him I said that, but ... Wait." Her eyes narrowed again. "Why would that make you think he was hitting me? Is ... Is Keeper hitting *you!?*"

Shard's stomach dropped. "You can't tell anyone!" he pleaded, his snout inches away from Firebug's. "That'll just make it worse!"

"But —"

"Listen, I'm glad he's not hurting you, but you have no idea what he's capable of." Shard pulled back, his blue and green eyes staring deep into her purple ones. He was rattling with fear as if caught outside on a winter night. She *couldn't* tell a soul. Word would get back to Keeper, and Keeper was already going to hurt him for having talked to her in the first place ... He affected as playful a grin as he could. "I know it's tempting to rescue a damsel in distress like me, but come on — there's like, a billion better-looking drakes than me."

"All right, everyone! Morning meal is over!" Inferno called out, his voice booming from the other side of the trees. The sounds of dying conversations and shuffling paws carried to them as the transition to working began.

Firebug glared at him, her features sharp as knives, and Shard knew his joke had missed the mark. "I'm going to help you. I don't know how, but it's the right thing to do. He can't get away with this." Firebug turned and made for the Clearing.

Shard found himself rooted to the ground, staring as Firebug shrank into the distance. Every inch of him from his wingtips to his claws screamed at him to run and hide. And yet, if she was serious, if she really did try and rein in Keeper ... His jaw hung open ever so slightly. Was another dragon showing him kindness? It didn't add up. But if Ellen had taught him anything, it was that the world around him wasn't always the way he imagined.

Just before the trees swallowed her, Shard called out. "Firebug? I'm sorry; I shouldn't have tried to joke about this. And thank you." She turned back and shot him a quick, determined smile. Then she was gone.

15

ELLEN LAY IN BED that evening, wide awake. The lights were on and the dull din of her father's music wafted in from the kitchen. The running faucet meant that Franklin was cleaning up.

In her hand, her phone displayed her contacts. It was a short list populated mostly by emergency numbers, but there was also her father's, Shady Orchard's ... and Lana's. Ellen's thumb hovered over the screen, resisting her desire to tap the icon. But only for a second.

Ring ... ring ... Ellen's heart beat against her ribcage, threatening to burst free.

"Hello?" Lana picked up at long last. Before she could back out, Ellen forced herself to follow through.

"Hey, it's me. I thought about what you asked. I'll do it." There. She'd said it.

"Suh-weet! Thanks a bunch! And uh, Ellen?" Lana appended, her voice softening. "You uh. You can come too, if you want."

Ellen catapulted into a sitting position, letting her feet dangle over the edge of her bed. Confusion wrinkled her forehead. "Huh? Wasn't the whole point of this so you could go see your dad?"

But Lana had a response for that. "You are doing like, so much for me with this. I literally cannot begin to tell you! And I love texting with you, but we never hang out outside of volunteering! It's two birds with one stone like this, you know?"

Lana likes texting with me. The statement took root in Ellen's mind, her thoughts latching onto it as it echoed in her ears. Could she really trust that? *Shard thinks I'm good,* she reminded herself.

There was one more thing. Lana had said the game was in Hadkirk City. Hadkirk City had a *huge* compendium, even bigger than the one in Haven City. There might even be something on the ring. If she could find some time to go there after the game ...

"Lemme talk to my dad, okay?" Ellen said, struggling to keep her voice neutral even as a hint of glee seeped in. "I gotta get his permission if I'm gonna go anywhere."

"For sure. Lemme know tomorrow!" And then, the line *clicked* shut.

Ellen locked her phone, and waited for the buzzing in her mind to die down. When it didn't, she yanked herself out of bed. It wasn't even eight-thirty yet. She had time before her magic lesson.

Standing, she ran her fingers over the rough, hardcover spines of the books on her shelf. A nostalgic sigh escaped her lips. How many times had she read these all cover-to-cover? Ten? Twenty? It was a miracle her father had been able to get out of donating them to the compendium after the Night of Flames, and, second to the ring, they were her most prized possessions. The atlases were all horribly incomplete owing to humanity's ignorance about the world beyond the dome, but still, her heart swelled as she imagined all the places she could go once she joined the Guild. Mountains, lakes, vast expanses of adventure, excitement and the chance to protect her people ... and yet ... and yet ...

Her hand stopped. Her truly favorite book had never been printed, for it had been written after the Night of Flames. Ellen reached for her phone again and brought it up on the eBook app. The cover was a picture of the book's subject, a light-skinned man in his late forties with chocolate-brown hair and deeper-brown-still eyes. He wore a stern expression, but not one without emotion. He seemed proud in this photo, like a more reserved version of Ellen's father and how he might look on the rare occasion she did well on a test.

The man's name was Jess Flint, and he was the Commander of the Guild.

Swiping through the digital pages of a memoir he'd published several years ago, Ellen scanned passage after passage, cursory readings meant more to jog her memory than anything else. The memoir, titled, "Where We've Come From and Where We're Going," was an account of how he'd come to be leader of the Guild. According to it, he was the descendant of the Guild's founder, and as a result, he'd initially resisted even joining the organization, feeling that he would be pigeonholing himself.

"But," read one of Ellen's favorite quotes, not just in this particular book, but of all time, "I realized we all have our place in this world, a place where we belong. We all have our role to play. To turn our back on what we are meant to be is to turn our back on ourselves."

And so, he had decided to join the Guild, rising through the ranks and becoming the organization's leader in less than eight years. He'd found where he belonged. And Ellen wanted to follow in his footsteps so very badly.

I think you're good, too. Shard's voice looped in Ellen's mind. A slight smile tugged her lips upwards before fading as quickly as it came. She took a deep breath. The Guild *couldn't* be onto them, yet she couldn't help but feel like *something* was wrong. Nobody else seemed to think so, though. There hadn't been any news reports on the increased recruitment drives or anything. There had been some minor complaints about the new cameras, but if anyone cared beyond that, they hadn't said anything.

Closing the reader app, Ellen thought of Franklin's words from three months back. "They can't even talk," he had said. *But they can. Shard's not a monster. And I'm going to keep seeing him.* But, she wondered, and not for the first time, if she were to hunt for orichalcum, she'd have to kill dragons. More and more, the thought made her uneasy.

Soon, it was eleven, time to go see Shard. Shoving aside the Guild with a shake of her head, she twisted her ring three times. And then she was not by the riverside, but in Shard's shelter, next to a battered, bloody, blue and turquoise dragon. His eyes stared at nothing, unfocused and glassy as his chest heaved with every breath. He couldn't have been conscious.

Ellen's stomach lurched violently as she sucked in a sharp breath.

"Shard!" she hissed, dropping to her knees. It took everything she had to keep her voice low. "Shard, wake up! Are you okay? Shard!"

An aggrieved moan escaped his snout, and then he was silent, the only sound a crackling torch on the shelter wall. Ellen reached out a hand, and gently, tenderly placed it on his scratched-up, bleeding underbelly. Shard yelped animally. Ellen recoiled reflexively with a gasp. Warm cruor dirtied her palm.

She wanted to call for help, beg anyone who would listen, but no one here would help a human. They might aid a fellow dragon perhaps, but maybe not, if Shard was right about his tribe. Could she call for help and teleport home before anyone saw her? No. She couldn't just abandon him.

"I have to do something," Ellen half-said, half-gasped. And by the looks of it, she had to do it *now.* But what? She didn't know anything about medicine, much less medicine for dragons.

Think, Ellen. Think! Digging deep into her mind, she ransacked her memories, hoping that something, even the smallest detail or offhand comment could give her a clue. He liked painting, he was good at magic, he was self-pitying ... the first time they met he hadn't attacked her ... he liked the nighttime ... he liked apples ... his brother was awful to him ...

Oh sweet Goddess, Ellen realized. *His brother must have done this.* She had no idea why, or even how, given Shard's healing power, but that was the only explanation she could think of, and — oh no, what if his brother came back and saw her here?

Tears tugged at the corners of her eyes and her vision clouded as her head spun. Shard was going. He was leaving; this was *it.* She'd never get to talk to him again, never hear him tell her she looked funny when she was mad. She'd never make fun of him again, she'd never give him his payment — bile bubbled in her throat.

"Shard!" she commanded, forcing the vomit down. Her voice was choked and her palms sweated, but she pressed on. "I swear to that Agito god you dragons believe in, you better not die!" He said nothing. Ellen heaved a great, guttural sob.

The torch flickered out. Complete darkness filled the shelter. Was this how Shard was going to die? Surrounded by nothing, not even the light of the moon he loved so much?

Wait.

What was it that she had thought before?

... he liked the nighttime ...

... Shard could heal ...

... light of the moon ...

"Holy crap."

Ellen exploded out of her crouch. Shard had told her once that their shelters' roofs opened with magic, and though she couldn't use earth magic, she was certain she could blast the roof off with wind.

Taking a deep breath to steady herself, Ellen reached out with her magic. Though she might not have been able to see with her eyes, she could use her powers to guide her. She could only faintly feel Shard's lifeforce, but it was there, all right.

But even with her improved power, Ellen only had theoretical knowledge of proper form. Her father had gotten her a doctor's note and pulled her out of the basic magic lessons most students received in lower school. *And what if he doesn't heal just from moonlight? What if he needs to be conscious to use his magic?* Ellen shook her head. There was no time to worry, only to act.

A deep breath in. A deep breath out.

Eyes shut, she let her essence expand into a magical sense-bubble. Arms tucked in at her sides, she squatted into horse stance, which probably wasn't even the right position to take for this, but it was the only position she knew.

Another deep breath in. Another deep breath out.

Ellen's fist shot up like a rocket. A maelstrom slammed into the ceiling with an audible *rush* and a deafening *thud.* No starlight broke through, but Ellen wouldn't be daunted. Her other fist pounded the air, sending it crashing into the ceiling, and this time, there was a *crack.*

One more time!

Ellen pushed up with both arms, and the ceiling blew off like a volcano. Moonlight filled the shelter, and Shard's scales began to glow. That had to be a good thing, right?

That was when Ellen realized that maybe blasting a ceiling sky high with herself and a critically injured dragon underneath it was a dumb idea. What goes up, must come down.

And the two of them were most definitely down.

Time seemed to slow to a halt as Ellen jumped from thought to wordless thought in a matter of milliseconds. There was no way she could safely blast all those rocks away, not all at the same time. Some of them would land outside, but the majority were headed straight for her and Shard. If she had earth magic, she could slow the debris, or even push it elsewhere, but all she had was her air. In fact, most elementals didn't awaken earth until their early twenties, and almost never before they awakened fire, and she was magically impaired, besides ...

No. She didn't have time to look at his glowing form, but she knew one thing: she wanted to live, and she wanted him to live. And for that, she had to protect him. She had to try. Adrenaline pumping through her veins, knowing she only had one try to get this right, she yelled, focusing her energy into her push. She didn't even think about who might hear her. Not daring to look up, she flung her arms upwards, her palms open like stop signs.

She waited a second. Then three.

It was at the five-seconds mark that the sounds of voices and pawsteps shook her back to reality.

"Did you hear that?" came a voice Ellen didn't recognize. Another dragon; a very young one by the sound of it. "It sounded like — sweet Agito, Keeper's roof is floating!" Ellen raised her head. Above her, the earthen detritus hovered in midair.

"No way," she mouthed. She couldn't believe it — impaired or no, she was using earth magic.

"Whoa, you're right!" a second voice said. This one sounded older, more feminine. "What happened?"

"Let's go check it out!"

Ellen swallowed: there was no time to celebrate.

As quickly as she dared, Ellen lowered the remnants of the roof, carefully bringing her arms down. The process became harder as the rocks got closer to the ground, gravity's pull on them strengthening, but the tromping of pawsteps hastened her. Rocks *thumped* gently in a circle around her and Shard.

Ellen sighed, relieved, but she wasn't ready to relax. Yet, there was nothing more she could do. Her fingers inched shakily towards the ring. She twisted it once, twice ... and then hesitated, looking towards Shard as he lay there. Would it be all right to leave him alone like this? Did she even have a choice?

With one last nervous glance towards his prone form, she twisted the ring a third time ... just as the barest hint of a black snout peeked over the earthen red wall. An instant later, she was back in her dark bedroom, her heart pounding in her ears.

Had she been seen? No, that was impossible. She had disappeared too quickly for whoever that had been to have seen her, and rushing back now would make things worse. She twisted the ring thrice anyway. It clamped down on her, the telltale sign that Shard was not alone. The dragon she had seen, perhaps? Hopefully, whoever had discovered him would bring help. Unless they didn't. Unless they —

A deep yawn forced her mouth open, her eyelids fluttering. Pursing her lips, she forced herself to accept there was nothing she could do right now and she needed to sleep. First thing tomorrow morning, she would visit him, but for now, she pried the ring off her finger, and forced herself to lay down, focusing on the soft mattress. The dim green light of her star stickers soothed her as they faintly illuminated the ceiling.

With another yawn, she ordered her eyes shut. She would see Shard just as soon as she could — she just hoped he was okay.

16

SHARD WAS NOT OKAY. His bones ached like they had been ground to dust. His wings burned like they were on fire. Whenever he tried to open his eyes, the light stung as if he were looking into the sun. Every time he tried to move even a little bit, even lifting a single claw, it felt like being run through with ten spears. And yet, as he lay on a bed of soft flowers and grass, in the village's healing hut with a damp, odiferous poultice on each wing, he couldn't help but think of how strange this all was.

First, when Keeper had left the night before, he'd closed the roof. When he, Shard, had been found, the roof was gone, blown apart by some unseen force. Second, the remains of the roof that had fallen inside the shelter had left him completely unharmed. Third, and strangest of all was, that by all rights, he should have been far, far worse. When Keeper had stormed in last night, Shard had known he was in for a rough time. He hadn't had time to process anything beyond his brother's rage-filled visage before Keeper raked razor-sharp claws across his snout. He had cried in agony, but a fireball came hurtling at him before he could recover, burning his chest. Keeper batted Shard's head down, sending it crashing into the hard floor.

Things got a little fuzzy after that. But he did recall, very clearly, Keeper snarling ferally about Shard stealing Firebug, the acrid scent of fire, and beneath the pain, a hope that this last beating, more intense than any previous assault, would kill him.

As the day passed and dragons came in and out of the healing hut, Shard lay with that last thought, doing his best not to dwell on it. He had recovered enough that he was no longer drifting in and out of consciousness, so instead, he tried to piece everything together. He had already figured out that after the roof collapsed, his magic had kicked in and healed him — more confirmation of how badly he'd been injured. Magic only took over like that when a sorcerer was in grim straits indeed.

The hut was deathly silent. Shard wished it weren't; noise might mean a conversation he could listen in on and distract himself with, and Agito knew he needed a distraction. As if he didn't hate himself enough, now he wanted to die? How shameful was that? He'd promised to teach Ellen magic and they were still only on the very basics. But truthfully, he wasn't entirely sure she'd miss him if he disappeared. Maybe she would. Maybe she wouldn't. But nobody in the tribe would care, right?

He groaned loudly. He just wanted to sleep and not think about this and deal with it maybe never.

"Shard?" came the healer's voice, an elderly dragon named Brightness. She hadn't yet asked how he had ended up so hurt, but curiosity shone on her face. "Are you all right?"

"I'm fine." Shard was surprised to find that moving his mouth didn't hurt.

"Excellent. Try standing," replied the healer. Shard opened his eyes and followed her command, only to wince as pain shot up his legs. "Oh dear. I think you should stay another night, at least."

"Can't I just heal with my magic?" This earned a "tut, tut" from Brightness. Shard knew why: too much magic, even healing magic, could actually be a strain on the body. Rejuvenating oneself from the edge of death to full health could actually end up hurting a dragon more in the long term. "Okay, yeah, stupid question." Not that it was the only stupid thing he had thought about that day and ...

Oh shoot. He'd missed a lesson with Ellen last night. "I'm going for a walk," he said hurriedly. And with that, he rushed out of the healing hut, and scurried to the riverside, doing his best to ignore his aching body.

The sun had long since set, but the stars did not brightly shine this night. Clouds covered the sky in patches, remnants of the morning's rain, leaving the night dimmer than usual. No breeze blew, but the air still felt cooler than it should in the summer. A few dragons passed by him as he scampered along. It even looked like one of them was about to ask how he was, but before she could, Shard had long since passed her. By the time he considered that making a big scene and rushing out might not have been a good idea, he was already at the river. The air felt better in his nostrils without the hut's overwhelming herbal pungence, so he closed his eyes and took in a few deep breaths. In the darkness behind his eyelids, he tried to ignore his foreboding dread.

17

FIRST PERIOD HISTORY was a bust. Ellen's fingers barely moved, her keyboard making only the slightest sounds as her teacher scribbled diagrams on the whiteboard in erasable marker, and the same held true in Earth science and literature. Even in the moments where she could think, all she could think about were the questions burning in her mind. Was Shard okay? Was he even alive? Had his brother come back and finished the job? The ring had refused to take her to him that morning, tightening instead when she'd twisted it.

And that was before she remembered that she might have been seen.

By lunchtime, Ellen was about ready to pull her own hair out. Sitting at one of the wooden picnic tables in front of the school, she stared down at the unappetizing gray blob the cafeteria insisted was meatloaf, knowing that it was only going to get cold in the unseasonably cool breeze. Across the street, there was another recruiter, barking on and on about the need to join the Guild, but right now, Ellen didn't have the mental bandwidth to fret over them and Shard.

Shoving the meatloaf aside, she groaned loudly and slumped. Some students at the next table raised their eyebrows at her, but Ellen simply stayed with her shoulders drooped, staring up at the cloudless sky, tinged silver by the dome.

She was this close to sneaking off and checking in on Shard right then. He might not be out by the river tonight, and his brother had to be out hunting or herding or something, so maybe now was her best chance. But no; if the ring wouldn't take her, he had to be with someone, maybe a healer, and she had volunteering today, anyway. Letting down all the children at Shady Orchard was not an option.

Maybe this was how her dad felt all the time. Agitated. Fidgety. Fretful. It must have been exhausting.

The sound of a single pair of footsteps captured Ellen's attention. Glancing around, she spotted Lana approaching, a tray of half-eaten food held in her hands.

"Hiya!" Lana chirped. "You seem kind of out of it. Need some company?"

"I'm fine, really. But uh, sure, you can sit here. I'm all alone, anyway." Truthfully, she welcomed the distraction. As Lana took her seat on the bench, Ellen noticed a table on the other end of the courtyard, filled with faces staring Lana's way. "What brings you here, changing seats in the middle of lunch? Won't your friends miss you?"

Lana shook her head. "They're trying to hook me up with some guy from the debate team. I can never get a word in edgewise when they're like that."

Was that a note of resentment Ellen detected? Was Lana even attracted to guys? Straining against the burgeoning heat in her face, she tore her attention away from the table with Lana's regular lunch buddies. "Ugh, that sounds rough."

"Eh, it's not so bad. Not like I can control them, you know?" She lifted a mug from her tray to her lips and nearly gagged. "Urgh, gross! This tea's freezing cold."

Ellen cleared her throat questioningly. "You got tea in June?"

Lana shrugged. "Tea calms the mind, and I've got a test next period. I don't wanna get a bad grade, you know?" Then, she flicked a small ball of fire from her fingers into the cup; a steamy sizzle wafted up from the tea.

Ellen gazed on, wordlessly admiring the feat. She'd known Lana was an elemental when she said she wanted to play blastball, but not that she had already awakened pyromancy so young. She almost didn't care that it was illegal to use fire magic so carelessly, for whenever the two met, it seemed as though she learned something new about Lana. Fear thrummed in her heart each time, but more and more, she didn't mind it.

"So. This blastball game tomorrow," she said when she realized she'd been staring. "Who's playing?"

"I didn't tell you? The Agreste Prefecture Fireballs and the Haven Prefecture Slayers."

For just a moment, Ellen's mind went blank. "You're kidding. The Slayers? That's Jess Flint's old team!"

Lana's lips creased thinly for just a moment. "Yeah. I guess you're a fan of his?"

"Yeah! He's —" Ellen had almost said "the author of the most important book in my life," but stopped herself. "I read his memoir," she settled on, trying to play it cool. Her enthusiasm burst out anyway. "And I *loved* it. He's so witty, and insightful too! It almost felt like he was talking to me through the page."

If Lana noticed Ellen's stammer, she didn't comment. "It's a good book, yeah ..." Here, she trailed off, as if unsure herself what to say. Ellen raised an eyebrow, when finally, Lana finished, "I have *no* idea how he found time to write a memoir and run the Guild!"

"I guess geniuses like him are on some kind of other level ..." When Lana looked away, Ellen frowned. "You okay?"

"Oh yeah, I'm fine. Did you talk to your dad yet?" A blue truck with the words "Echo Woods Food Bank" on it whizzed by on the street, while Ellen fiddled meekly with her earlobe. How was she going to explain that she'd been too busy worrying about her dragon friend to talk to him?

"Not yet," she admitted. Lana's face fell and Ellen rushed to add, "Don't worry, let me text him right now! ... And, done. I'll let you know as soon as he — oh, he's responded already."

True to her word, her phone had buzzed within seconds. Franklin's message read, *Ellen, of course you can go! I'm so excited that you have a friend you can spend time with, but be careful! Hadkirk City is all the way in Agreste Prefecture. It'll take time for me to come and get you if anything goes wrong!*

Ellen smirked. That was her dad, all right. "Guess who's got permission to hang out with you?"

Lana grinned just as the bell rang. The girls rose from their seats, lunch trays grasped in their hands. "I'll tell my mom I'm at your place. See you tomorrow?"

Ellen meant to give a simple "yes," but instead blurted, "I'm really glad you wanted me to go to Hadkirk City with you. I promise I won't ruin your time with your dad." The words were out before she could stop herself. She blushed nervously — surely she'd said the wrong thing.

Yet, Lana's eyes twinkled kindly. "You won't, I promise."

By the time Ellen sat down for her next period, the classroom's lemon-scented air freshener strong in her nostrils, she felt more relaxed. She could now think clearly: her best bet to check on Shard was to go tonight, when they had a lesson planned. If his magic had healed him, he would be there. If not, she would do what she could to help him, and then, she would go to Hadkirk City with Lana and have a great time.

Even with worry for her scaly friend biting at her chest, she was able to take a deep breath, and exhale. The warm air soothed her.

18

THE RUSHING RIVER joined a chorus of cicadas in a cool, summer moment that dragged on and on. It felt like centipedes were crawling all over Shard. Where was Ellen? Had he missed her?

Just as he was about to return to the healing hut, she appeared. The second she saw him, her nose scrunched up, her eyes shone wetly. She bounded towards him, and for a second, he tensed — she was going to attack him! But her arms wrapped around his neck, practically tackling him as she stood on her tippy toes to do so.

"Oof!"

"You're okay!" Ellen choked through her tears. "Oh my Goddess, you're okay!"

Something strange but welcome rose in Shard's chest. He hadn't been hugged like this by anyone except his mother. Lifting his paw gingerly, he patted her on the back.

"Happy to see you too, Ellen," Shard managed as she squeezed his airway tightly. "Could you ... loosen up a bit? I'm a little sore ..."

Ellen pulled away, wiping a tear from her eye. Her face sparkled with an elation Shard had never seen before. Was she really so happy he was alive?

"How did you know I was hurt?" he asked.

"When it was time for our lesson, I saw you laying there, half-dead! I ..." she trailed off, a difficult expression on her face. Whatever she wanted to say, it seemed hard for her. "Sorry about your roof, by the way. I know I did a pretty slapdash job getting you moonlight."

"Wait. That was you? But that means you'd ... you'd have had to ..." Everything clicked into place, and Shard couldn't have been happier — or more confused. "You used earth magic!"

"Damn straight I did!" Ellen puffed out her chest.

"But since when can you ... ?"

"I don't know!" She grinned giddily. "I must have awakened it right then and there. All your training really paid off!"

"Well, I'm not normally one to brag, but I guess I am a pretty great teacher."

"Don't get too full of yourself," Ellen ribbed. But her smile faded, and she scratched her nape nervously. "There *is* something you should know, though ... I uh. Think I might have been seen, actually? When I was saving you, I mean."

Shard's jaw clenched. He gripped the dirt beneath his paws as he simply stared.

"Goddess to Shard!" Ellen said, waving her outstretched palm in front of him. "Hey, you in there? We need to think of a game plan!"

A frog croaked, bringing him back to reality. "I ... I don't think we do," he admitted with a sigh, realizing the truth as he spoke it. "If someone had seen you, I wouldn't be here right now. We definitely haven't been caught."

"You sure? I'm sure I saw someone peeking in right before I left."

"Trust me. You might have seen someone peeking in, but they definitely didn't see you."

A second later, it was her turn to heave a sigh. "You're probably right. It couldn't hurt to be a little quieter from now on, though. Way you laugh, I'm surprised you haven't woken up your whole village, am I right?" Her teasing lilt returned, starlight illuminating her face.

Shard, however, suddenly felt like he was caked in mud. Unclean. Dirty. He looked away, his earlier misgivings worming their way back to the forefront.

"You okay? It was just a joke."

A million and one thoughts raced through Shard's mind. A million and one ways to ask what he wanted to. He bowed his head, unable to look at her any longer. Tears pooled in the corners of his eyes. They silently cascaded down to the ground and as they did, Ellen's mouth hung open, and that just felt like one extra blow to his chest, because his tears weren't just of relief for being alive.

What if he died and she didn't miss him? What if nobody did? What if Keeper tried again tomorrow, and the day after that, and nobody did anything? What if nobody cared? A raw sob escaped him.

"Hey ..." Ellen timidly reached out a hand, but didn't touch him. It just hung in the air before she withdrew it, frowning.

Shard desperately fought the urge to bawl loudly and hysterically. His whole body trembled as he choked down another sob. "Why do you like hanging out with me?" The words tumbled out on their own.

"... What?"

"Why do you like hanging out with me?" he repeated with force. "I act all confident and snarky, but that's just to hide how much I hate myself! Everyone wants me to be strong and a drake and a vicious warrior, and the very idea of being that repulses me, so why?"

Ellen didn't reply; her face was unreadable. Did she really not care after all? Finally, she said, "Well, I mean, you are teaching me magic ..." But it was nervous, like she didn't really mean it.

"So that's it?" Shard pressed.

Ellen pursed her lips together, placing her hands up like a wall. "Dude, I'm gonna pay you for the lessons, I promise."

"And then what? Are ... are we just gonna go our separate ways? Once I've taken you as far as I can, are you just gonna leave me?" Shard looked at Ellen, and she stared back. Her posture loosened, her eyes wide, yet glazed over. She said nothing, and Shard's heart sank. "I should go. I'll see you for our lesson tomorrow."

"No more lessons," Ellen declared. "And no payment either."

Shard's heart ached. He had really thought ... but then, perhaps it didn't matter what he thought. He unfurled his still-sore wings and turned.

And then she made a plea as forceful as he had ever heard: "Don't go!"

19

A MILLION AND ONE thoughts swirled in Ellen's mind. A million and one things that could go wrong. A million and one reasons to back out.

None of them were good enough. Deep down, she knew that she could either say what she had to ... or lose Shard forever.

"When I was little, my mom ..." Ellen began, her mouth dry as a desert. "My mom took her own life. I felt lost. I felt betrayed. I felt ... abandoned. Every day, I live with that. Every day, I can't help but think that someone new is going to leave me. I can't make someone else feel like that. I can't do that, not to you."

The change on Shard's face was the difference between a brick wall and an open door magnified a thousand times, and this emboldened Ellen. Her voice did not rise, but as she spoke and heard her own words, she knew that no one could take her truth for lies.

"So screw the lessons! I know my limits now; I can practice on my own. I meant it when I said you're good, Shard. You're not just a teacher — you're my friend."

The next thing she knew, Shard's wings were cocooned around her. His face was bright, lit up like she'd never seen it before, like the whole of Haven City on a dark, winter night. "You're my friend, too, Ellen! I … I'm so sorry you lost your mom." His leathery wings felt sturdy, strong, but familiar. Like safety and home. They felt like family.

"I'm sorry you lost yours." She hugged back, and they stayed like that for a time, her arms around his scaly chest, his heart beating in her ears. Faint whispers tantalized her ears, tendrils of sound in the register of Shard's voice … Slowly, they resolved into words, but it quickly dawned on Ellen that she was not hearing with her ears …

I have a friend! I finally have a friend, and she's the best friend I could have asked for!

Images flashed in Ellen's head. Her and Shard, by a lake on a gray day, the grass around them wet with rain. Pure white light, engulfing them each. A giant egg, cracks rippling across it. And then the two of them, sitting in a meadow at dusk, eyes closed, smiles of utter contentment on both their faces …

They broke away from each other at the same time, gasping, and the voices in their minds cut off. Yet, that was not the strangest part: in front of her, Shard shone a dim golden color. Ellen could feel her jaw slowly dropping as her eyes widened; Shard's face mirrored her own.

"Ellen, you're glowing!" he exclaimed. And he was right. When she looked, there was indeed a silvery shine to her skin. Ellen mouthed words of astonishment as she flipped her hands from side to side, examining them.

They stared at themselves, then each other, then themselves again, their amazement only growing as the glow faded, leaving only chirping crickets behind.

Ellen dared to speak first. "… What was that?"

"Well … I think we just glowed and heard each other's thoughts … I don't know what that other stuff was though."

"Wow."

"Yeah," Shard agreed, eyes wide. "Wow."

"Whatever this is …" Ellen spoke slowly, choosing her words one at a time. "… has to be because of this ring, somehow. I don't know where it came from, but it brought me to you. It has to be at the center of all this."

Shard nodded. "I think that maybe, whoever gave it to you … I think they might have wanted to bring us together."

Now there was an idea. Who would want to bring a human and dragon together? Who could?

Shard cleared his throat. "To uh, backtrack a bit ... I'm sure no one saw you, Ellen. If they knew what we're doing, trust me, I wouldn't be here right now, and neither would you. But I'll keep an eye on things, see if anyone is acting differently."

"Thanks, man," she said with a relieved sigh. A gentle breeze played with her bangs and the grass beneath her. "And be careful! Goddess knows I don't want you getting hurt."

"I think you mean, Agito knows." He winked wryly.

"Same thing, ya big dork."

Shard pouted at her, and for a second, she thought she'd messed up. But, at the same time, something rose in her chest, light and bubbly. Before she knew it, she was tempering belly laughter into soft chuckles. Shard was not far behind, caught in his own giggling fit. Eventually, their mirth died down and Shard sighed.

"I should probably go. I kind of took off in a hurry. Our healer is probably wondering where I am."

"Sweet. I'll see you, then. Promise." Ellen reached for her ring, but did not twist it. A thought had just occurred to her. "Say ... There's no way anyone could let Keeper get away with this, not even your crappy uncle. This might be your chance."

"My chance? What do you —" He stopped, blinking as confusion changed into astonishment. "Sweet freaking Agito ... You don't mean ..."

"You know I do. It's time to finally give Keeper what's coming to him."

20

FIREBUG SAT on her haunches in the Clearing, staring at the sky long after everyone else was asleep. The cloudy sky had cleared, leaving the stars in full view as a cool wind caressed the treetops and her scales alike.

Keeper *beat* Shard. *Hit* him. That much was clear, whether Shard wanted her to tell anyone or not. She herself had come upon his mangled body just last night, woken when she heard a loud crash. It was a sight she would not soon forget.

Could it be, she feared, that Keeper had nearly killed his own brother? Firebug didn't like Shard, per se — until today, he had always been so mild and inoffensive that it felt like he was trying to wrap up conversations as quickly as possible so he could be rid of you — but he was still another dragon.

She shuddered. It was like she didn't know her oldest friend anymore. Not to mention what she thought she'd seen: a human in Shard's shelter — a human, of all things! It had been for the briefest of moments, but ...

She closed her eyes. Maybe if she could induce a Starsight vision, she could learn something. But all she saw were the backs of her own lids. A hot, flame-filled snort escaped her nostrils — what good were these visions if she could never master them?

"Uh, Firebug?" came a familiar voice. When she opened her eyes, there was her brother, standing in front of her. Instantly, a weight lifted.

Spearhead, being younger than Firebug — nearly four to Firebug's nearly six — was short, even for a drake so young. Not that it mattered. Spearhead was the one drake who always listened to her. He even believed her about the coming disaster.

"Hi, Spearhead," Firebug said. Now that she thought about it, the young dragonling seemed ... off somehow. He kept fidgeting and shifting his weight from side to side. "Are you okay?"

"Yeah, I — are you thinking about Keeper?"

"... Maybe. Okay, yes," she amended when his eyes narrowed. "How could I not, after Shard was found half-dead? I'm on track to be the lifelong mate of a dragon who beat his own brother." She knew she should be more worried for Shard than herself, but if Keeper had it in him to beat his own brother, then what would he do to his Bonded mate? She hadn't seen any warning signs, though admittedly, she hadn't looked for them ...

But she couldn't even say no if he proposed, for not only would her mother never forgive her, but then all the *other* drakes her age would move in on her like she was some sort of trophy. It wasn't like she hadn't seen all their barely-concealed lustful leers.

"Keeper always makes you feel sad, so he's a jerk," Spearhead declared emphatically. He plopped down beside her, kicking up a small cloud of dust. "I'm sure Daddy will make everything okay, though! He always knows what to do!"

Firebug exhaled, looking up at the starlit sky. She wasn't sure she wanted to talk about this anymore. "There's one other thing ..." she began, but a lump caught in her throat. Was it worth panicking him? She wasn't even sure she'd seen it anymore.

"Yeah?" Spearhead tilted his head coaxingly as cicadas trilled around them.

Firebug knew she had to tell him. If anyone would believe her about this, it was her brother. "I think I saw a human in Shard's shelter."

Spearhead made a sound halfway between a snort and a gasp. "You don't think the human was the one who hurt Shard, did you?"

It would have been so easy to say her best friend was innocent, that the human was responsible. But as much as she wanted it to be true, it didn't add up. "No, I don't. The way the rocks moved — slowly, like they were deliberately being let down ... I think it was human magic. And if it was a human, why wouldn't it pummel Shard with them? The only thing I can think of is that it wanted to get Shard some moonlight, that it wanted Shard to heal, but ..."

Spearhead's eyes were glassy as he tried to puzzle through this. "But that doesn't make any sense ..." he murmured — Firebug's thoughts exactly.

"I might not have seen it anyway, to be honest. It was probably just a trick of the light." She laughed evasively. They weren't going to get any answers about this tonight.

And then the Clearing was gone.

Flames crackled before her eyes, gnawing at the woods, hot cinders rising in the sky. Screams echoed in her ears, desperate and feral. A giant towered above her, standing in the center of the village on two legs, hunched over. It glowed a bright, ominous white. Each step it took sent horrible quakes through the ground. Dragons Firebug had spent her whole life with swarmed around it in the air, spewing their own flames at the giant. It swatted them away like flies with its two enormous arms. Some swerved out of the way, but others were sent hurtling to the ground.

The giant turned; its gaze fixed on Firebug. Her breath came in jittering huffs as she stared back, willing her terror to be defiance. It opened its eyes, and Firebug saw two bloodred sclera.

"Firebug!"

Spearhead's voice cut through the vision, dragging her back to the present. He stared at her, worry wrinkling his face. Without having to ask, Firebug knew that he understood.

"Sorry, sorry," she forced out, still panting. A chill had settled in her wingtips. "That's the first one in a while; caught me off-guard."

Spearhead nodded gravely. "I feel something too, Firebug. I feel like something is coming. Something we can't take back."

Dread bubbled in Firebug's stomach. Whatever it was, whatever her half-brother felt, it was linked to her own visions. She was sure of it, and though he did not say it, Spearhead was, too.

But they didn't have time to worry for long. The next morning everything began to change.

INTERLUDE

STARDUST FALLS

S HARD'S MOTHER, a dragoness named Stardust, had had her throat slit by her Bonded mate Blizzard. It had happened in the dead of the night smack-dab in the middle of winter two years ago. Shard had slept right through it. The next morning, he and Keeper were awoken by two dragons hauling her body out of the shelter.

"What's happening?" Shard had asked, his voice small. Why was his mother laying so still? Where was his father? The world seemed hazy.

But the older dragon, with his black and red scales, had just looked at Shard and shaken his head sadly before his partner opened the roof. They flew off into the bright, snowy morning. Shard watched them disappear, his gaze transfixed on his mother's corpse.

Mere hours later, the council had held Blizzard's trial. Everyone gathered in the Clearing, the ground covered in snow. The whole time, Shard and Keeper had stood side by side, neither of them looking at each other, Keeper's barely-restrained seething heavy in Shard's ears.

What Shard remembered even more clearly about that day was the look of confusion on his father's face ... almost as if Blizzard didn't understand what had happened, or what he had done wrong. He insisted that he would never hurt Stardust, that he loved her more than life itself, that he had always wanted to be by her side, that he had always been *on* her side. Even through his dumbfounded stupor, he recounted the tale of how she had come to the tribe, a traveler looking to settle down, and he had begged and pleaded for Inferno to allow her to stay. Yet, anyone could tell Blizzard's heart wasn't in it, his voice weak, his words garbled by stammering.

Inferno's judgment had been swift and merciless — guilty. Blizzard was to be banished. Yet even as the blue dragon took to the skies, never to be seen again, he insisted that he was innocent.

Once upon a time, Shard wanted to believe his father. Now, his blood roiled at the thought of him. Blizzard had been found with blood on his claws, and there had been no one else in the shelter save the four of them, and he had the sheer gall to pretend he was anything but a murderer. What did he expect everyone to believe? How could he commit a crime so vile and think to play dumb?

They cremated her later that evening. As Chieftain Inferno and Smasher, another dragon in the tribe, laid Stardust's corpse on a bed of orichalcum, Shard wanted to say something, anything to eulogize his beloved mother, but no words would come.

Inferno jerked his head at Shard, a wordless command: light the pyre. That was when the tears began, loud, vicious howls of grief the likes of which Shard would never produce again. Inferno turned his attention, and silently made of Keeper the same request. Keeper walked over to the silver beads of orichalcum on which his mother lay, and set them alight with a puff of flame.

As the fire caught, the adults began to sing their dirge. It was a solemn, mournful song, nothing like the happier melodies Stardust had sung in life. The fire began to melt the snow, the orichalcum slowly charring. An overpoweringly floral smell filled Shard's nostrils as the fire spread to what remained of his mother. In the air, the snow mixed with little specks of silver light, shimmering points borne of the orichalcum beads, swaying back and forth as the fire burned. Shard knew what was coming next. He wanted to look away, but he knew he would regret that for the rest of his life.

The silver dots began to swirl as the outline of a dragon came into view. Slowly, the dirge came to an end, reaching its climax — one long, miserable note — and when it finally finished, the image of a giant, living Stardust floated above her smoldering corpse, an effect of the burning metal.

Shard stared at the translucent ephemerality. This phenomenon, a window into the afterlife, only lasted seconds. He wanted to savor it. His mother's ghost said nothing, as ghosts never did, instead searching the tribe with her eyes. Quickly, her gaze fell upon Shard, and Shard only. He tried to choke out something, to let her know that he loved her, but all that came out was something like a croak.

Now, as he lay in his shelter in the present day, the torchlight dying down to embers, he thought back to that time. Would Keeper be brought to justice if Shard told his side of the story, or would he feign innocence like their father had? And, if he did, would Inferno believe him? He hadn't believed Blizzard, but ...

"I have to do this," Shard reminded himself, his voice a determined whisper. "I have to tell them what Keeper did."

PART THREE

A DAY IN HADKIRK CITY AND A TRIAL IN THE TRIBE

21

T HE FIRST TRAIN to Hadkirk City left at 8:30 AM from the Echo Woods train station, but even before then, the sun was out. The weather app had promised a scorcher of a day with hardly any wind.

Ellen looked up at the sky above through the lens of the ever-present silver dome as she stood on the platform, a backpack slung over her shoulder with one of her books and a map of Hadkirk City lest she get lost. Of course, there was a map on her phone, but what if it ran out of batteries?

I sound an awful lot like my dad, she thought, amusing herself for a second.

The Echo Woods train station had three elevated platforms and an asphalt road running below them. Ellen waited for Lana on Platform C, from where westbound trains departed. Across from it was Platform B, upon which there was yet another Guild recruiter giving a speech. Largely, he was saying the same things as the lady in the park, but he was saying them louder and more ferociously, barking them, almost like a dog. Some of the people opposite him were nodding their heads in approval, others stared, dewy-eyed and enraptured by his zeal.

Ellen nervously cracked her knuckles. Thoughts of *the Guild is onto us* and *they know, they know,* ricocheted around her head.

It's fine, she told herself, taking a deep breath. *The Guild is not after you. Right now, you're going to the Hadkirk City Compendium and finding out what's up with this ring. And besides, you have a fun day with Lana ahead, too. And her dad, I guess. I hope he likes me.*

... I hope they both like me.

"Hey, Ellen!"

Suddenly, Lana was bounding up behind her, waving an arm excitedly, dressed in her most beautiful outfit yet, a spirited golden sundress with a light blue floral pattern that cut off just above her knees. On her head sat a beige sun hat, secured with a neck strap, and pinned to her ears were cobalt studs. Two white sneakers adorned her feet.

A magnificent blush crimsoned Ellen's cheeks. She had never seen the other girl look so radiant. Perhaps she should have worn something cute too, so that maybe Lana would like the way *she* looked. Her black polo and blue jeans would have to do.

"Er, hi. I — I like the hat," she forced out, stiffly raising her palm in greeting. Her phone was still in her hand. She quickly shoved it back inside her pocket, cheeks flushing that much hotter.

Lana giggled. "Thanks! My dad got it for me."

The loudspeakers crackled. "Attention please, attention please. The 8:30 train to Hadkirk City will be arriving soon. Please stand clear of the tracks and behind the yellow line."

Lana scratched the back of her neck with a nervous chuckle. "Looks like I got here just in time! Sorry that I cut it so close, though. I slept right through my alarm. Kinda had trouble sleeping last night."

"Ouch. Better rest up on the train." Ellen turned her head to hide her ladybug-red blush.

Lana tilted her head. "You okay? You seem ... off, today."

Ellen's heart beat so hard, she thought it was trying to break free of her chest. "I'm good. Don't worry," was all she said.

The jet-black train roared into the station, drowning out any more conversation. Commuters lined up to get into the train as it screeched to a halt. The doors mutedly slid open, passengers pouring out.

Inside, Ellen glanced around for a place to sit. The brown leather seats were six on each side of the train, every two rows facing each other and sharing a window. Several seats had already filled up.

"I call window seat!" Lana rushed to claim a space near the back of the car, squeezing past a gaggle of businessmen in navy blue suits. They shot her dirty looks, but she didn't notice.

Quirking an eyebrow, Ellen sat across from her. "You know there are, like ... ten window seats in here, right?"

"Okay, yes, but this one is gonna have the best view, trust me. When we're passing through the farmlands, the train is gonna be traveling with this side at the front — we'll get to see everything first! You'll love it, pinky promise."

"Er, well. I mean ... I see food in the gardens at home all the time, but I guess I can keep an open mind." *That sounded far more suave in my head.* She placed her bag on the seat next to her; anything to avoid sitting still with her sun-hot blush.

"It's not just crops. There are also windmills! And yeah, okay, that's a weird thing to get excited about, but I think they're super cool and really calming to look at. They just go round and round and there are so many of them, all spinning in sync —"

Ellen couldn't help but crack a grin. Lana's excitement was as infectious as ever.

"Attention please, attention please," the PA system cut in. "The 8:30 train to Hadkirk City is now departing, making stops in Cresting, Westville, Bell Vale, and Hadkirk City. Please stand clear of the doors."

Then, the doors closed and the train steadily started to move, gaining speed as the passengers slowly left the scenery of Echo Woods behind. The slight hum of electronics filed Ellen's ears. Lana started nodding off, her head bobbing every few seconds before she would shake it and return to staring out the window.

"You can sleep if you want. I won't be upset." Ellen left out that it might help calm the stampede in her chest.

Lana opened her mouth to protest, but came a yawn. "Ugh, maybe. But I invited you! It'd be rude for me not to talk. And I do wanna hang out!"

"Do you read a lot? You said you liked comics, right?" Ellen blurted out all of a sudden, and she had to fight not to cringe. *So awkward!*

Lana blushed. Twirling a strand of her hair, she replied, "Honestly, not really. The dataweb comics I follow are about it on reading. I'm more of a video game kind of girl, anyway. I play them with my friends Ayako and Priyanka all the time."

"Really?" Ellen hadn't pegged Lana for a gamer. "Do you and your dad game together, too?"

And there it was again — that very same disquiet whispering across Lana's face before morphing right back into a cheery smile. "Nah, he really isn't into games. When we hang out, we mostly just — " Whatever Lana had been about to say vanished beneath a second yawn, louder and wider than before. "Buh, excuse me. Okay, yeah, you know, maybe I should close my eyes for a bit."

"Hey, I've got my phone and a charger; I'll keep myself busy."

Lana nodded and rested her head against the seat. "Be sure to tell me what you think when you see the countryside, okay?" Then, she was out like a light.

Ellen exhaled, relieved. Her phone read 8:50. The blastball game was at noon, and the train would arrive in Hadkirk City half an hour before then. The butterflies in her stomach sputtered back to life, sharp and jittery. Before she had met Shard, Hadkirk City had been farther than she could ever have pictured herself going. People in the Safe Zone did travel, but mostly just for work or to visit family. Her life had always been in Echo Woods, and she had always thought it would stay there until she made it into the Guild.

Shaking her head, she reminded herself that almost every evening for the last three months, she had been taking a journey that could have been any number of miles into the Wildlands. By comparison, Hadkirk City was practically the same as walking to the food bank.

As for the blastball game, it was at Switch Arena, which was named for Switch Corp, the telecommunications giant. Of course, that name had been given long before Ellen was born — phones and communications were now handled by the government. What would it be like, she mused, living in a world where money determined everything rather than a monthly resource allotment? At the very least, the arena was right near the train station, and only a forty-minute walk away from the Hadkirk City compendium, where she hopefully, possibly, maybe might find some answers about the ring. Ellen held up her finger and peered pensively at the silver band of metal that had changed everything. Light from beyond the window reflected off it.

Outside, the Safe Zone raced past her. Green grass and purple, yellow, even orange crops endlessly blurred together in field after field.

The windmills had yet to appear, but Ellen got a clear view of the silver dome shimmering in the distance. The very dome that protected humanity from all dragonkind. It had been her dream to fight for this barrier, for the excitement, for glory, and to protect humanity.

Her mother's face flashed through her mind, an empty image of what Ellen never wanted to lose again. Thinking about it was like sinking, like leaving her body in the train far behind.

Lana stirred halfway through a snore, snorting in an inelegant nasal rumble. Her eyes fluttered open, yawning through wide-stretching mouth. "Hoo-boy! I feel much better now! ... You okay, Ellen?"

"What? Oh! Yeah. I'm okay. Just ... thinking."

"You need to talk about it?"

Ellen's hands wrapped loosely around her hard plastic phone case as she pressed it to her chest, wondering if she should say her piece. It would accomplish nothing, she was sure. But she wanted to be wrong.

"I guess I was just wondering ... you ever think how great it would be if we could be friends with the dragons?" Ellen's chest tensed, ready for Lana to snap indignantly. She had to sound crazy, suggesting something like that.

Yet, Lana simply stroked her chin, humming thoughtfully. It dawned on Ellen that she was by some benevolent act of the Goddess considering it.

"I think it might be nice, yeah," Lana said deliberately. "I don't ... I think we shouldn't have to live under a dome. And my parents would ..." She stopped, shaking her head. "What brought that up?"

Ellen blinked. Lana's parents would what, exactly? Did it have something to do with the plaque at the compendium? "Oh, nothing. Just being a mushy idealist, I guess."

"I feel that, girl. I think we need more people like you."

Ellen's heart leaped, and a great, but terrible thought reared its head: *I really do have a crush on her, don't I?*

And the next thought, terrible, but great: *I think I might be okay with that.*

Presently, the train screeched to a halt at Hadkirk City Station. As soon as Ellen stepped off the train, a wave of heat rained down on her from above and radiated off the pavement beneath their feet, even worse than it had been at the station this morning, sweat pooling on her nape. Beside her, Lana practically hopped from foot to foot. Ellen lagged just a bit behind, her throat dry. She wished she had brought water.

On the other hand, Hadkirk City was magnificent. Buildings jutted up from the ground, reaching for the top of the dome. People swarmed in cacophonous droves, all headed in the direction of the blastball arena, a building so large it was visible for miles around. It towered over everything, and in front of it, two silver statues of the Goddess Pandora greeted visitors. As Ellen approached, she decided the statues had a certain majesty about them, though whether that was from their calm, yet stern expressions or simply their grand size, she was not sure. She snapped a photo with her phone. Perhaps Shard would appreciate the art.

There was a Guild recruiter here too, shouting through the same speech as the ones in Echo Woods did. Thankfully, the throngs of arena-goers all chattered as loudly as a roaring pride of lions, nearly drowning out the recruiter. In the massive crowd, Ellen could spot little boys and girls with their parents, university-aged kids of all body types and skin colors, fans dressed in red and gold, the colors of the Haven Prefecture Slayers, but many more dressed in the Fireballs' green and orange and more.

Was the inside of the arena like this too? Ellen half-imagined herself in her seat in the blastball arena, enjoying the air conditioning, but the other half was a prickling suspicion that the noise would be even worse.

"Come on!" Lana called out, turning around as she skipped backwards down the sidewalk with a smile. "We're gonna be late!"

Hastening her gait, Ellen asked, "When are we meeting your dad?"

"He's gonna meet us inside." That some of Lana's brilliance died was not lost on Ellen. There was obviously tension between Lana and her dad, but it couldn't have been that bad, could it? He had asked them to spend the day together.

Should I ask about it? But wouldn't that kill the mood? Aren't we supposed to be hanging out and having fun? Ellen went in circles as they neared the front of the queue. By the time she finally screwed up the courage to ask, the bouncer called out, "Next!" Ellen nearly swore.

She and Lana both reached into their pockets; their tickets were QR codes on their phones. A man in a green booth scanned them, a flash of red from the scanning gun accompanying a computerized *beep.*

The man's eyes widened. "Just a moment, Ms. Pai," he said, nervous all of a sudden. He quickly called over a burly-looking lady. "You will be escorted to your seat by my associate here. Enjoy the game!"

Ellen frowned. Why were they getting such preferential treatment? Their new escort beckoned for them to follow her, lips thin with impatience.

Directly inside was a large, brightly-lit foyer before the actual playing field, floored with white tiles. Milling, booming crowds made their way to the proper entrances for their seats. The woman muscled through, cutting a path for her two young charges. Ellen kept hoping Lana would explain, but her friend suddenly seemed nervous, chewing her lips like some kind of tic and keeping her head down. Ellen tapped Lana on the wrist. "You okay?"

Lana gave a guilty, unhappy chuckle. "I'm sorry. I shouldn't be like this. I should have told you." She shook her head, looking like she would prefer to be anywhere else.

"Like what? Told me what?" Ellen asked, gentle but prodding. She had never seen Lana this anxious before. "What's wrong?"

They were climbing a staircase, their footsteps swallowed by the roaring patrons, and Ellen only now realized that they seemed to be heading to the third floor. With an electric jolt, Ellen remembered that the third floor was the VIP box. What kind of connections did Lana's father have to get a seat there?

"Here we are," said the tall lady, turning around to face them all of a sudden. "Enjoy the game."

Instead of the cramped bleachers that made up the rest of the arena, there were only three seats here, all equally spaced with plenty of legroom. In the center one sat a man. He faced outwards, towards the playing field. Against each wall of the box were men in black suits, each wearing sunglasses and both of them had an earpiece. Bodyguards?

Ellen gave a brief, breathless glance at Lana; her dad had to be in some incredibly important government office to get this kind of protection. Was it really all right for Ellen to be joining them? Lana looked away.

"Sir," said the tall lady. She gave a slight bow then planted herself by the entrance to the VIP box and went still, staring straight ahead.

The man gave a slight start. "Oh, you're here!"

Ellen's heart stopped. She knew that deep, masculine voice. Even over the din of the crowd, it boomed in her ears with all the force of a radio turned up to ten. She had heard that voice on the news; she had heard it on the dataweb; she had heard it in her sleep.

The man rose. As he turned to face his daughter, he revealed his dark-brown hair and chocolate-colored eyes and skin suntanned by years spent in the Wildlands.

No way.

But the scar on his left cheek clinched it.

"Jess Flint," Ellen squeaked. As if in slow motion, her lips curled up in a giant grin. She was here, *with Jess Flint,* in the same room, not even ten feet away!

For a moment, Flint stared at Ellen, silently, his expression stony and stoic. Except it wasn't. In that brief moment of silence, Ellen saw something on her idol, something dark and foreboding. She saw surprise, yes, but also fear.

Then, Flint's lips quirked upwards, an aura of amusement about him. "In the flesh. I hope I'm not too disappointing."

"Oh, all, not at no! I mean, not at all. I um, I liked your book! The autobiography, I mean. It uh, it changed my life. Not that your work at the Guild isn't good, too! I just, I wanted to uh, thank you. I want to say thank you. Yes. Thank you. Is what I wanted to say." Heat rushed into Ellen's cheeks, a hundred times worse than when she had been nervous with Lana that morning. Even with the glare he'd shot her, taking to Jess Flint made her feel stupid and giddy all at once.

Lana, meanwhile, looked at him with the same conflicted expression from before. *It's almost like she doesn't want to be here,* Ellen noticed. *But that's ridiculous; this was her idea. She's asking me to lie for her to be here! Does this have something to do with the look he gave me?*

"Wait a minute ..." Flint said, a playful glint in his eyes. "I know you!"

"You do?"

"No, not you! You!" He looked past Ellen. "Pumpkin! You came!"

A nervous chuckle escaped Lana's lips. Ellen cocked her head, then looked from Lana to Flint to Lana again and back to Flint. The gears in her mind sputtered and churned.

"This is so great," Flint gushed as he pushed past Ellen to wrap Lana in a hug. "I'm so glad you're here, pumpkin! Looking forward to today's game?"

"You bet I am!" Lana said. She swallowed, like it was hard to say that. Completely at odds with her cheery voice and wide, vibrant smile. "The Haven Slayers are my favorite team, Daddy!"

Ellen finally found her voice. "Wait, wait, wait. Lana, your dad is *Jess Flint!?*" No wonder Lana had had all those books about dragons — of course the Commander of the Guild would have that kind of literature.

"That's right. I guess my little pumpkin here didn't want to ruin the surprise?" Jess said with a bouncy grin. Lana chuckled nervously and ran her fingers through her hair, pushing stray strands off her glasses. "But enough about me! Sit down, you two! The game starts in twenty minutes, that's plenty of time to talk!"

Talk. With Jess Flint.

Ellen suddenly felt even dizzier, but she forced herself to take the rightmost seat, ignoring the suited man hovering imposingly just a few feet away from her. At least the chair was comfy.

"How have you been?" Jess was saying as he and Lana took their own seats. Jess took the leftmost seat; Lana, the center. "How are your grades? Did you decide if you're going to the University?"

How does he not know all this stuff about his own daughter? Ellen marveled. But her focus shifted when for a fraction of a second, Lana pursed her lips.

"I've been so great, Daddy!" Lana said, happy again. "I can't wait to tell you all about it! My grades are great, but I don't know if I'm going to the University yet. Honestly, I still wanna go into blastball, but Mom's taking some time to come around to it."

Jess Flint laughed appreciatively. "Ah well. We can't force her, but something tells me she'll see it our way one of these days. You'd be amazing at this game, let me tell you. And hey," he said, suddenly leaning over to Ellen, "it seems you have some friends! Tell me, Ellen, how did you and Lana meet?"

"We actually volunteer together," Ellen said. The words came hesitantly, like if she misspoke even slightly, her idol would never forgive her. "At Shady Orchard."

But rather than anger or rejection, Flint's brows knitted in confusion. "Shady Orchard? In Echo Woods?"

Ellen blinked. "Yeah?" Next to her, Lana sunk into her chair, her face furiously red.

"Um, Daddy," she said. "I told you, Mom moved us to Echo Woods to be closer to her work. I haven't lived in Bell Vale since December."

Flint blinked. "Oh, right! I'm sorry, it's just been so long, and with everything at work —"

"It's okay." Lana pressed her lips into a thin line.

"Really, I am sorry, pumpkin, it's just, with the Guild —"

Flint continued to talk, but Lana had gone quiet. A lump rose in Ellen's throat; she had never before seen Lana without something to say.

She needs an out.

"So, the Guild, huh?" Ellen interjected as loudly and cheerfully as she could. Flint dropped off midsentence, like he wasn't used to being interrupted. "That must be one hell of a career, huh? Risking your life, finding orichalcum ... Those dragons probably run for their lives when they hear the leader of the Guild is coming for them! I bet they have stories they tell their little dragonlings, like, 'don't overeat, or the big bad Jess Flint will get you!'"

On one hand, Lana didn't seem angry anymore. On the other, she now stared at Ellen, eyebrows raised, her head tilted. Flint, meanwhile, smiled anxiously, his eyes darting from side to side as he looked for a response.

"Well, I am pretty handy in a fight," he finally said, "but I doubt dragons tell their kids stories about me or much of anything. Dragons, telling stories ... makes for an interesting picture, doesn't it?"

Oh, right, Ellen remembered. *I'm the only one who knows dragons are intelligent.*

"Speaking of!" she said, trying to spin this positively. "I bet with all those new cameras you've got, you get all sorts of cool pictures!"

Flint frowned. Ellen wanted to smack her forehead.

Before she could have a fraction of another thought, the lights dimmed, a spotlight shone down on the arena, and a buzzer sounded. The crowd's cheers erupted, a concentrated burst of noise. Ellen gulped.

Below them, the playing field, which was many feet lower than the bottom stands, began to fill with water. A number of off-white pillars stood there, each one large enough to stand upon and aligned in a grid. At the farthest ends of the grid were two plinths taller than the rest — the goalposts.

Each team had already taken their marks. Three players from the Slayers balanced on their own pillars, dressed in the team's traditional red and gold. At the opposing end of the grid were three players from the Fireballs; they too balanced on top of the pillars, wearing orange and green. They hunched, ready to pounce as the crowd cheered wildly for their home team.

On four massive screens hanging from the arena ceiling red numbers worked backwards towards zero with each passing second. Ten ... nine ... eight ... seven ... With each new digit came a beep. In the corner of her eye, Ellen saw Lana's gaze intensify tenfold. For the first time since they entered the arena, she was smiling, and that lent a grin to Ellen's lips, too.

Three ... two ... one ...

Bing!

A ball dropped from up high towards the center row of pillars. Two players from each team rushed towards it, hopping from pillar to pillar. Ellen knew that they were using air magic to help themselves move as gracefully as they did, much less stay on the narrow pillars' tops.

Loudspeakers hummed to life and a male voice reverberated through the arena. "Ladies and gentleman, welcome to Switch Arena this fine Saturday. We've got what promises to be a heated game going today ..."

The first player reached the ball, a young man from the Fireballs, no more than a few years Ellen's senior. He sprung into the air, aided again by his air magic, and punched at the ball as he met it. A carefully controlled blast of wind assaulted it, sending it flying diagonally down at the Slayers' goal.

One of the Slayers had stayed back towards the goalposts, the goalie. The ball hurtled at her, but she was ready for it. With a lightning-fast twitch of her arms, she raised a tendril of water up from the pool surrounding the match, and neatly flicked the ball away.

Ellen's mouth gaped. Seeing these elementals play on her phone had been one thing, but seeing them in person was on a completely new level. A part of her resented her father for denying her the chance to train, to achieve that level of mastery, but the rest of her was too busy resolving to practice even harder with Shard.

The whole arena thundered, but especially Lana. She rounded on Ellen, shaking her by the shoulder and gesturing frantically at the playing field. "ELLEN! OH MY GODDESS, ELLEN! DID YOU *SEE THAT!?*"

"Yes, yes!" Ellen pulled away, a little startled. "I'm right here!"

"Right, sorry. My bad." Lana was still grinning as she turned back to the match.

Despite the sensory overload, Ellen found herself with a smile of her own. She had never really gotten out of her head long enough to notice how good it felt to see someone else happy until recently.

The match continued, high-flying displays of air and water magic knocking the ball back and forth. Points were scored, a buzzer ringing each time only to be nearly drowned out by the roaring fans. The commentator narrated the game, offering no lack of bias towards the Fireballs — being the home team had its advantages, Ellen mused, but she found the whole thing a little much. It was just so loud, and though the game had started off easy enough to follow, soon there was so much water and air and jumping that she quickly lost track of what was going on, instead losing herself in Lana's whoops and cheers.

In fact, the only real problem was that the few times she looked away from the match, she could have sworn she caught Flint glaring at her with the same malicious, fearful aura she had sensed before.

The troubles magnified at halftime. Just as the lights came back on, one of the suited men in the box with them approached Flint. He tapped on his shoulder and whispered in his ear. Even without seeing her face, Ellen could see the joy drain from Lana's being.

Finally, Flint turned to them, frowning. "I'm very sorry, girls, but there's an emergency. There's a truck that's broken down outside the dome. I've got to organize a rescue." He stood and ran towards the door before looking over his shoulder. "You two can watch the rest of the game, and Lana? I'll make this up to you."

Before either of them could say anything, Jess Flint and his bodyguards hurried out of the VIP box and vanished from sight. Ellen turned to see Lana hugging herself and staring at the ground with glossy eyes. She was starting to understand why Lana had wanted her here so much. "You okay? You seem ... upset."

Lana sighed as she let her arms fall to her side. "Eeeeeeh, I wouldn't go that far," she replied, teetering her hand like a seesaw. "I just ... I thought this was going to be different. It's been months."

Ellen swallowed. She knew how awful it must feel to have a parent but not be able to see him, but she had no idea what to say. Should she be comforting? Say nothing? Lana stood before Ellen could decide.

"Goddess Pandora, Ellen, I'm sorry. I need to get some air. You can finish watching the game if you want."

A small smile crept across Ellen's lips. "Thanks, I appreciate that, but honestly, it's way too loud in here."

Lana snorted. "Thanks for putting up with it, then."

The loudspeakers crackled back to life as the action down on the field came to a stop. "Ladies and gentlemen," announced the PA system, "we'd like to take this intermission to honor the fine Guild members who make our society possible! Without them, we would have all fallen on the Night of Flames fifteen years ago! Let's have a moment of silence to offer both them and all those who have lost their lives to dragons, and remember: the Guild is always recruiting!"

The noise stopped. All around them, people in the bleachers clasped their hands together in prayer; if someone had dropped so much as a needle, Ellen swore she would have heard it.

Slipping out of the VIP box, they walked back the way they came. Lana tromped down the stairwell, her steps echoing with each angry stomp, her head hung low. As they reached the lobby, the noise inside the arena exploded again, and a thought occurred to Ellen. "Hey, Lana?"

"Hm?"

"If you don't mind ... there's actually somewhere I'd like to go."

22

T HE FIRST TIME Firebug had played with Keeper was the same day she had first thought she might be someone important. She was a little less than a year old.

It happened during Rest, a holiday where the whole village would gather together out in the cold during the day, and at night they would all go to their shelters and simply spend time together. During the daytime, there was a hunting contest for the young, eligible male dragons, who would then share all their catches with everyone else, and at night, the single, young dragonesses would paint. In the morning, a judge, usually the oldest female in the tribe, would declare a single painting as being worthy of being hung in the council's meeting shelter.

The winner of each contest would share a traditional flight dance, a ritual performed in the sky with swoops and dives and turns, while everyone else watched and oohed and ah-ed. The story went that if the two dancers were courting, or if they ended up Bonded even years down the line, then both of them winning their contests was a sign that they were destined to be together forever and ever.

In fact, that was how Firebug's parents Emerald and Ace ended up being Bonded. As Emerald was very fond of telling Firebug, Ace had harbored feelings for her for quite some time, but had never worked up the nerve to tell her. When they were both selected for the dance, Ace was emboldened, and finally told Emerald how he felt. The two were an item from then up until Ace's death at the hands of humans. Every Rest for as long as Firebug had been alive, Emerald would stay inside for the flight dance, a sad, faraway look in her eyes — the only time Firebug ever saw her mourn her first love. The rest of the year, she was Inferno's mate first, and everything else second. Sometimes, when Firebug was alone, she wondered what Ace had been like.

On the day Firebug first heard the story of the Chosen, she had been in the corner of the Clearing, watching the festivities with rapt attention, too shy to join in. Dragons laughed merrily and chattered, the light and warmth of the torches all around the Clearing illuminating the winter evening. Some of the older dragons even drank a special juice made with a green berry that ripened only in the fall and, when consumed, slurred your speech and made you act funny. Firebug did not yet understand why that happened, but she knew that many of the grownups enjoyed the way it made them feel, and that the juice was only had during Rest. Spearhead's egg had yet to be laid, so this was the only Rest in her memory where she was not with her half-brother.

"Firebug!" came a voice. Firebug turned to see a dragon with red and darker-red still scales staring at her curiously. He was only a little taller than her. "Why are you alone?" Vaguely, she knew that this dragon was Keeper, and that Inferno liked him very much.

Her stomach turned underneath the young drake's penetrating gaze. "Why do you wanna know?"

Keeper sidled up next to her, unbothered by her rudeness. Firebug remembered that he seemed far less imposing up close. "My mommy and daddy say Rest is for fun! You can't have fun if you're alone."

Firebug tilted her head, confused. "But I'm not alone! I'm with everyone in the tribe. You're a dummy."

Now, the drake did seem to get angry, narrowing his eyes. "Am not! And you're not with anyone, you were just alone." He went quiet for a moment, pouting. When he spoke again, there was palpable hurt in his voice. "I just wanted to be nice ..."

Firebug looked away, but kept one eye trained on Keeper. Mommy and Inferno had said that being mean was bad, and she realized now that she had been mean to him. Besides, he smelled like blueberries. "I'm sorry ..." she said, and he smiled.

The two of them stood there the rest of the evening, quietly watching the other dragons in the tribe. It was the most soothing silence Firebug had ever known.

Sometime later, Inferno flew onto his podium. He cleared his throat before sending a stream of blue-hot flame blooming brightly into the air. Now, she was right in front of the podium and could feel the blast of heat, and, along with everyone else, immediately quieted. Keeper was next to her, his eyes fixed on his uncle with a kind of reverent, sparkling awe.

"Friends and family," Inferno said, his deep voice booming, "tonight, we celebrate! Not just Rest, and not just the flight dance, though we celebrate those both with hearty vigor. But we also celebrate something else. Something many of us have waited our whole lives for." Whispers bubbled around the Clearing. Firebug remembered thinking that the grown-up dragons sounded like they knew what he meant, but did not quite believe it.

Inferno unfurled a single wing authoritatively, and everyone went silent again, their eyes focused on him with rapt attention, even Firebug. She had no idea what they were talking about, but it sounded very exciting, so she too looked on, her heart beating in anticipation.

"We celebrate ... for my most recent Starsight, which has revealed to me that Agito's Chosen, he who shall conquer the humans, and restore dragons as the rightful masters of this Earth, walks among us!"

Cheers had erupted among the crowd. Afterwards, she and Keeper had squabbled over which of them might be the Chosen, which had devolved quickly into a contest of, "Uh-huh! Nuh-uh!"

For the longest time after that, Firebug had held onto to the hopes that maybe she really could be the Chosen. She fantasized about how great it would be to have a God-given role and how everyone would have to listen to her and revere her and think she was important. The fact that she would kill the humans that stole their orichalcum and her blood father was just a bonus.

And yet, Agito's Chosen had never come. How could everyone have forgotten Inferno's grand declaration? Were they really so ready to blindly follow him? Was there something she did not know that they did?

As Firebug approached the fields many years later, she found herself again wishing she was Agito's Chosen. Other dragons moved about behind and before her, chattering as they carried grains and gathered fruits in reed-woven baskets. Firebug could not make herself pay attention to their exact words, but they sounded shocked.

How could they not? Just that morning, Keeper, the nephew of the chieftain and her once-upon-a-time best friend, had been approached at the morning meal, publicly arrested, and locked in the council's shelter, facing trial. His charge? Attempted murder.

Firebug let out a shaky breath and looked down at her paws. Her eyelids sagged like they were weighed down by a bag of sand. She could just hear her mother already, too, harping to the tune of something like, "Oh, this is just dreadful, Firebug! Keeper's going to be disgraced, and you'll lose your opportunity to be his Bonded mate! How could you let this chance slip by you?" The very thought made her blood roil.

She sighed again. She could see Shard in the distance, his eyes closed. His scales glowed with a bright white aura, as did the other sorcerers'. Above her, the sky was a clear, cloudless blue. Beneath her, ants marched in a single file line, carrying a leaf.

Firebug steeled herself. She had to talk to Shard.

And then she saw a shadow looming from behind her, blotting out the ants.

"Firebug, my dear," came Chieftain Inferno's voice, breaking Firebug from her reverie.

"Y-yes, Chieftain?" she said, doing her best to hide her surprise. Her adoptive father had always intimidated her by virtue of his height. Even now, she had to resist the urge to shrink back.

"Firebug." The chieftain spoke again. He sounded soft, even concerned. "I know you and Keeper were very close. Someone of your ... disposition may be unable to handle what happens to Keeper tomorrow, should events take a course neither of us want. Please know that whatever happens, all will be as it should be, and that is something to take solace in."

"I'll be fine," she said without meeting his gaze, although she wasn't quite sure she meant it. And then inspiration struck. "Actually, I —"

"That's wonderful, my dear," Inferno interrupted. "Now, you need to get back to work, no dilly-dallying around here. I suppose I'll go check on Spearhead, make sure he's holding up well." He shook his head regretfully. "All this, such a short time before his fourth hatch day ... oh, what a pity."

"Oh, there's actually something I wanted to say ..." Firebug began, but Inferno had already taken flight. She called out for him to wait, yet his figure shrank into the distance, not for a moment stopping to look back. She grunted angrily, a puff of smoke leaving her nostrils.

She glanced over to see Shard, still channeling his magic into the crops. She supposed she could wait for him here, focus on asking him about the human she thought she'd seen. It would certainly feel less like pulling out her fangs.

Spearhead's words from the previous night echoed in her mind. *"Something is coming. Something we can't take back."*

Firebug launched into the air, beating her wings fast and hard as she chased after her stepfather. If nothing else, the sky felt cool against her scales even as she simmered. She had always loved that about flying, and the freedom of the endless, rolling blue.

"Wait!" she called out. The effect was immediate, bringing Inferno to a stop as if someone had lassoed his neck. He turned midair, his head tilted.

"Firebug?" he said. "What's the matter? You really should be working on baskets now."

Firebug bit back a retort. She had to stay calm. "Yes, and I will be really soon, but I have to talk to you!"

Inferno sighed dramatically. "All right, but keep it quick. We both have things to attend to after all." Though she would not put it into words until much later, Firebug knew, deep down, that this was a turning point.

Concisely and with conviction, she told him of her visions of the giant and its carnage. She left out the part about the human — best to stick to the bits she was absolutely sure about. Inferno remained quiet the whole time through, listening attentively, even nodding a few times. Hope began to blossom in Firebug's chest, that maybe he would take her seriously.

"And that's why I think you should train me in Starsight!" she finished.

Inferno blinked. They both hovered in the air, sunlight catching Firebug as a cloud moved out of the way. Inferno opened his mouth, and out came a deep, hearty rumbling — he was laughing, Firebug realized. Her jaw dropped.

"Oh, my dear Firebug!" he guffawed. "Don't be silly! There's no giant coming, for something so terrible would surely have shown in my Starsight — and you certainly haven't such a power. You're a dragoness! No, my dear. I'm sure you're just stressed from everything that's happened."

"Wh-what? No, I —" Firebug began to protest, but Inferno cut her off, the mirth fading from his expression.

"I think you need to rest today. I'll tell the other dragonesses that you're excused from basket weaving, so please, don't worry about Keeper. You need only focus on doing what you must."

And then he was gone, for real this time. Firebug stared after him, watching his figure shrink into the distance once more. She lowered herself to the ground and slapped at it with a front paw, kicking up a little cloud of dirt.

She was in the village now, the reddish-clay shelters surrounding her, the Clearing visible in the distance. No one was around to pay her heed when she let out a frustrated growl.

Would no one ever believe her? Her mother wanted her to focus on romancing Keeper. Spearhead remained convinced their father would fix it. And their father thought she was hysterical over Keeper!

And Keeper himself! He had changed so much. What she wanted more than anything else right then was her best friend back.

"Sweet Agito. Screw this," she grumbled, and turned around, heading for her own shelter. Her steps, once poised, determined, full of purpose, were now unsure and ginger, weighed down with exhaustion. She tried so hard to be heard — but no one wanted to hear what a dragoness had to say.

What if they were right?

23

ABOUT FORTY MINUTES after leaving the game, Lana and Ellen stood in front of a four-story brick building with a grand stone staircase leading up to it. On either side of the staircase was a ten-foot-high, chrome-silver statue of the Goddess Pandora, wearing her famous silver and gold dress, the Goddess Raiment. The statues each held a sword, crossing each other above the staircase and forming an archway.

The street here was, unlike the ones near the station, filled with foot traffic. People rushed by on the sidewalk, and the street too had people milling about, even in the heat. Some gave Lana and Ellen the stink eye as they pushed their way through. Each time, Ellen bit back the urge to say something rude.

"This place seems so ... imposing," Lana said. She kept glancing at her phone, which had the maps application running. "Are we sure this is the place?"

Ellen shrugged as she slipped her own phone back into her pack. "That's what the maps say, at least. Besides, look." She pointed to a metal sign on the wall at the landing at the top of the stairs. "It says 'silence your phones; quiet inside' over there."

Lana squinted, holding her glasses by the frame as she struggled to make out the writing. "Huh. I guess it does. You know I'm kinda surprised they have two giant Goddess statues and not a sign for the compendium itself."

"Maybe they just think she's pretty and wanna stare at her."

Lana swatted lightly at Ellen's shoulder and admonished, "Oh, you stop that." But she was smiling, her eyes lit up, and her tone was playful.

Ellen smiled back, and they ascended the staircase.

The doors to the Hadkirk City Compendium were tall and grandiose double doors, nearly twice Ellen's height. Ornate golden patterns covered the wood, much like the ones on the famous Goddess Raiment. It was almost like a house of worship, Ellen thought as she pushed the door inward.

Then she saw the inside, and her mouth dropped. If the outside was grandiose, then the inside was positively *lavish.* The lighting was low, and the whole place smelled of paper, quieter than a winter night as everyone stared intently at their books. One could hear the turn of a page from the other side of the building in here.

Next to Ellen and Lana, there an elderly lady sat behind a desk, typing notes on a computer, her fingers moving nimbly across a touchpad keyboard. Just ahead, a large central area filled was filled with reading tables and public-use computers, people hunched over both, absorbed in books or the dataweb. Beyond that, on all sides, rows upon rows of shelves filled the building, each one stacked to the brim with books.

And that was just the first floor. When Ellen looked up, she could see three more levels built around the central reading area with glass partitions to make sure nobody fell down. Even more shelves covered these upper floors. And, finally, there was a stained-glass skylight, lending the building a yellow tint.

Ellen gulped. Not even the Haven City Compendium was this grand.

"You sure they have comics here?" Lana whispered in her ear. Ellen could feel the other girl's breath on her skin, enticingly warm.

"Um, yeah, probably. Let's uh, let's ask the clerk ..." Ellen shook her head to clear it. She turned to the elderly lady behind the desk, then asked in the barest hint of a whisper, "Miss? We're from out of town, but I'd like to do some research; could we have some help?"

"I'm just here for the graphic novels," Lana chimed in.

The librarian looked up from her ledger, her wrinkled face calm and kind. "You've come to the right place for research. We have a diverse selection of both reference material and pre-Night of Flames comic books."

And so it was that Ellen and Lana, each armed with a text message filled with recommendations, went to separate sections, agreeing to meet back near the entrance later. As Ellen rode the elevator up, her stomach tightened. The librarian had warned them that they would not be allowed to take anything home with them. If she wanted to find something about the ring here, it had to be today.

The elevator *dinged* open. Ellen took a step forward onto the third floor. It turned out to be much larger than it had appeared from below. Shelves rested upon much of the gray-and-black carpet, but there were also some tables to sit down and read at by the partitions at the edge of the floor. Seated at several of these tables were a variety of people, but the one thing they all had in common was the stacks upon stacks of books.

Ellen quirked a smile. In another life, perhaps she would have taken up writing. Goddess knew she enjoyed a good novel, and her history books and atlases, too. *Maybe there's still time for that,* she discovered herself thinking. *Maybe I can write about dragons and help people find more dragons like Shard.*

Actually, perhaps there was merit to that idea: maybe bringing humans and dragons together was exactly her calling.

One step at a time, Delacroix. Put that on the backburner, Ellen thought, but she couldn't help but feel like there was a bounce to her gait now.

By the time she had gone through the list of reference numbers, she had pulled four books off the shelves, two of which were wafer-thin. Hugging her haul to her chest, she headed back to the elevator. Books had been spread out across three different aisles, with one of the reference categories carrying over to the next aisle, a fact she had not noticed, and had caused her to spend about fifteen extra minutes looking for the last book. She was half-expecting her phone to buzz with a text message from Lana, asking what was taking so long.

Ellen and shook her head. She could not think about that now, would not. Lana had looked so sad before; Ellen needed to focus on making her happy again as soon as she had done her research. But on the other hand —

Bam!

Ellen's forehead smacked into something hard as she rounded a corner. Yipping as she lost her balance, her books flew every which way. With a pained groan, she rubbed her throbbing forehead, the room around her spinning.

"Hey, watch where you're going!" came an angry hiss. "These are all priceless!"

"S-sorry," Ellen stuttered as her surroundings came into focus. Kneeling on the ground in front of her was a woman, probably about a few inches shorter than Ellen, frantically snatching up books that now lay strewn on the carpet with gloved hands. They looked different from the ones Ellen had dropped, their covers ornate, their spines ivory-colored, and even as she scurried, the woman seemed to be managing the books as delicately as she could, placing them gently back into a box.

As Ellen got to her knees, she reached towards one of the books. "Here, let me —"

"No, no, it's fine," the woman said, a panicked lilt to her words. "These books are all very old; they shouldn't be touched with unclean hands. Oh, I'm going to be in so much trouble for this ..."

"I'm really sorry. I'll just get my stuff picked up ..." By the time Ellen gathered up her last book, the librarian was already rushing away. Letting out another sigh, Ellen began to get to her feet, hoping that the woman was not in as much trouble as she seemed to believe.

That was when Ellen saw it, clear as day. There, beneath one of the shelves, laying on the carpet, was a book with a decorative cover, just like the ones that she had just been told were priceless.

"Oh, crap." She got back on her knees to fish the book out. As her fingers neared the book, she paused. Her hands weren't sterile — they could damage the book. But then again, it was probably better for it to be touched briefly than left lying on the floor until someone found it again.

Ellen grasped the slim volume, and edged it towards herself, doing her best to ignore how gross the dust and cobwebs felt on her skin. Then, when she had the book, she sat back up, and took her first good look at it.

Her mouth dropped.

On the cover was a stylized picture of a strange, many-winged creature, painted in such a way that looked almost like stained glass. Rays of sunshine filtered down onto it, backgrounded by a blue sky and fluffy clouds; a dragon reached up towards the sun, as if trying to grasp it in his paws.

Ellen's tongue felt dry. What she had in her hands was priceless, a book about dragons that could contain information on the ring ... and one that likely was not available to the general public, either.

Ellen had a choice to make. She could either return the book to the front desk and explain what happened, or she could read it and risk damaging it.

You might never get this opportunity again. If you want to know what caused the most miraculous thing to ever happen in your life ... this could be the answer. She exhaled, trying to let out all her fear and misgivings, but to no avail. *Just read the first few pages. If you don't think you'll find anything, you can put it down.*

She cracked open the slim volume, and instantly knew she had made the right choice. In script as clear and legible as the newsfeed on her phone, even on the yellowed page, there was written a title:

"The Sad Story of the Gods Agito and Pandora."

The story of Pandora, the Goddess who had gifted the Generators to humanity from on high, was known to even the smallest child, but Agito was a name Ellen had never heard until just a few months ago. The compendium worker had said this book was old. Could it be that knowledge of the dragon god was commonplace among humans once upon a time?

Ellen looked up then down the corridor. No one was around. With one last glance in both directions, she slipped the book into the pile of books she was allowed to have, stood, and hurried past the elevator, carrying the stack close to her chest.

She hurried back downstairs, two steps at a time, where she found Lana reading near the entrance. The dark-haired girl sat at one of the tables she'd seen when going towards the entrance, her nose buried in a comic. Taking a seat for herself, Ellen whispered, "Hey." She plopped her stack of books onto the beige-colored wooden table.

"Hey, that was quick." Lana replied. Her sight fell on Ellen's books. "Damn, that's a lot of books. You think you'll be able to read them all?"

"It's not that many, if I can read fast enough." Another blush crossed Ellen's face. Did Lana just want to get out of here? "I think. I mean, we have a lot of time, right? If you wanna go, I'll be quick. I —"

A cascading giggle cut her off. Mischief shone in Lana's eyes as her lips arched upwards. "Relax, Ellen, it's fine. You know, you act aloof, but you're really pretty shy, aren't you?"

"I, uh …" Ellen paled.

"Don't worry. Your secret is safe with me." Lana winked, once with each eye before returning to her comic.

"Oh, um … thanks?" Had Lana been *flirting?* Or was she just reading too much into it? The *click-click-clicks* of the public computers filled her ears like the ticking of a clock.

Ellen threw herself into reading. She only had so much time before they needed to leave, so she skimmed only the chapters she thought most likely to be useful. It was far from a perfect method, but it was the best she had.

But, by the time she had finished the second book, it was already 4:15. If she wanted to make the 5:30 train home, she would have to finish up soon.

Across the table, Lana snored gently, her head resting upon a thick graphic novel. *Jeez,* Ellen thought. *She really didn't get much sleep last night, did she?* She wondered if anything had happened to keep Lana up so late, and for a second, she reached her hand out, intent on waking her friend and asking.

But then again, Ellen still had yet to find anything about the ring. By now, she believed Shard when he said he hadn't made it, but the fact that she still didn't know who had was maddening. If she wanted to read the Agito book, now was the time.

Ellen snuck a glimpse at it without moving her head. "The Sad Story of the Gods Agito and Pandora" lay hidden under another book, just barely peeking out.

Ellen scanned her surroundings, her heart pounding hard and fast. A woman a few tables over hunched over her phone. The crisp crinkling of a page turning drifted into Ellen's ears; when she turned around, she saw that it was from the elderly gentleman sitting right behind her, though he did not seem to notice her. Some kids were sitting at the public-use computers, tapping away at games.

Everyone seemed caught up in their own world. If Ellen could pretend that she was doing nothing wrong, she could read this old, priceless book, and return it before anyone noticed it was gone. She grasped it in her hands. For a moment, she simply stared at it, her heart beating in her ears.

Ellen pursed her lips. She had to do this.

24

*L*ONG AGO, *when the Earth was still young, there were two beings of awesome power: Agito and his sister Pandora, who hailed from beyond the stars. Yet, after an epoch of wandering our planet in solitude, they grew lonely.*

From tears shed by the goddess Pandora were formed the first humans, their infant bodies sprouting out of the ground like flowers. From blood pricked of Agito's own veins was formed the first clutch of dragon eggs, all hatched under the sweltering sun.

From that day on, the gods lived in a luxurious palace, worshipped and loved by humanity and dragonkind alike. The mortals, meanwhile, lived side by side, if not in unity, then in uneasy peace. But no matter how their gods begged, or pleaded, or commanded, they would not open their hearts to one another. Pandora appeared to accept this, but Agito could not.

Then, everything changed when humanity and dragonkind clashed in a war as violent and brutal as no other. Dragons fell to the humans' weaponry, their bullets and missiles steadily driving them to the brink of extinction. Humans were slain again and again not only by claws and fire, but by arcane might as well, darkness threatening to engulf the world.

Agito's sorrow hardened into a gelid frost. "I will brook no more! You have shown to me you cannot honor your gods' wishes, and so you shall face retribution." He descended from the clouds, lightning crackling in his palm, ready to deliver judgment upon the tremoring mortals.

But judgment never came, for at that moment, Pandora channeled her immense power into one devastating strike upon her brother, banishing him to the center of the universe for all time. Then, she created seven pillars, each one black as night, and arranged them in a circle. "This shall be the realm of the humans. No dragon may enter it until such time as I deem you are all of you ready. Until that day comes, I shall protect you."

She shed one last tear, and then she was gone. Where she went, no one knows. If she still protects us, none can say. And so, we await her return ...

25

E LLEN READ THE WHOLE TALE front to back. When it was done, she closed the book, and found herself staring at nothing. Something pulled at her chest, something else filled it.

She thumbed through one last time, looking for a sign, a hint, a clue. There was nothing. The compendium was dimmer now, the light of the sun outside fading with the afternoon, draping Lana in the disappearing daylight.

Ellen was about to reach over and tap her on the shoulder, but, inspired by the sheer control the blastball players had over their powers, tried a different tactic. Flicking her fingers, she sent a light burst of air wafting over to Lana, no more powerful than the ones she used to make.

Lana roused and yawned loudly, earning glares from several patrons. "What time is it?" she asked, ignoring them. Inside, Ellen wanted to pump her fist — it had worked.

"Almost time for us to go. It's nearly —" here she checked her phone — "Yikes, it's nearly 5:30. We missed our train. Guess we gotta take a later one."

"Man, I slept a while, huh?" Lana stood up, but paused, her eyebrows knitted in concern. "Are you okay? Your breathing is really heavy."

Ellen leaned into the table with a sigh, resting her chin in her palms. "I dunno ... I guess I thought ..."

"You're mad at me, aren't you? You have every right to be. I'm sorry I dragged you into this, Ellen."

"It's uh. It's fine? I'm not really sure what you're talking about." Ellen tilted her head.

Yellow light from above glimmered over Lana's soft, pained face. "You know how I asked you to come? Well, I wanted to get back at my dad for never spending time with me, for always being busy with work. I guess I wanted him to be a little hurt that I'd bring someone when we hadn't seen each other in so long. But I shouldn't have lied to you, especially not when you're going out of your way to cover for me."

Ellen frowned. On one hand, she hated being deceived, but on the other ...

"I guess not," she finally admitted. "But I saw what stuff was like with you and your dad. And I ... I know what it's like to be angry at your parents when they should be there. It's kind of the worst. Just ... be honest next time you want something from me, okay?"

"Okay. I promise. I *do* like you, you know. I wasn't lying about that part." Lana proffered her pinky, a smile on her face. They shook on it. Today had been worth it.

The girls stepped out into the late afternoon. This time of year, it was still bright out, but as Lana hurried down the stairs, Ellen lagged behind. Happy though she was to see Lana happy, she was no closer to finding the truth about the silver ring. And beyond that, she wondered what was happening with Shard. Had he told Inferno what Keeper had tried to do? Would Inferno believe him? These dragons, these faceless names held her best friend's future in their decisions.

Lana stopped and turned as she passed under the statues' sword-arch at the bottom of the steps. "You coming?"

"Yeah, just a moment!" She exhaled and shook her head, adding in a mutter, "I'll check in with him tonight." Then, she hurried after Lana.

For years to come, Ellen couldn't pinpoint exactly when they lost their way. Perhaps it was when the clouds rolled in, and she and Lana started fretting over whether or not it would rain, causing them to miss a turn. Or maybe it was when Lana's phone ran out of batteries and she suggested they try and go the rest of the way without a map for the thrill of it — they were so close, she had said, what could the harm be? Perhaps if Ellen had realized she had left her backpack and phone at the compendium sooner, they could have doubled back, retrieved it, and avoided the whole mess.

Regardless, by the time a distant bell tower rang seven times — seven *gongs* that echoed across their surroundings: rows and rows of increasingly derelict buildings and apartments with their paint peeling off, windows boarded over, and cracked, weed-infested sidewalks — the knot in Ellen's stomach was fit to burst. They'd asked for directions three times already, and each time, they had gotten more and more lost. At first, she had been irritated. Now she just wanted to go home.

The streets were empty, but the sound of a crying baby echoed through the neighborhood. A dog barking in the other direction punctuated the infant's cries. The acrid scents of marijuana and, if Ellen had to guess, stronger drugs mixed in the air. She'd never done drugs herself, but she knew classmates who did. They were all horribly, horribly illicit — especially if you were an adult. She did not want to know what kind of adults would turn to drugs, how desperate for relief they would have to be.

"I guess we could ask for help again," she suggested as they passed what looked like a bodega. There was a sign atop the door that she presumed was supposed to say "Johnny's," but half the letters had peeled away. Peeking inside the tinted window, she saw burly, unshaven men chugging booze by the checkout counter. Their cheeks were flushed red. One of the men locked eyes with Ellen through the window, his glare empty and menacing all at once. She shivered; looking away immediately as a chill ran down her spine. It wasn't even eight o'clock yet. "Not here, though."

"This place is giving me the creeps so bad," Lana moaned. She was hugging herself now, hunched over.

"Hey, listen. Let's focus on getting out of this place." Ellen placed a comforting hand on Lana's shoulder. Heat flushed her cheeks for a split second; Lana felt so delicate beneath her palm. Ellen coughed and pulled away. Lana didn't react.

They had walked less than another block when Ellen noticed a tall, darkly dressed man with a bandanna covering the lower half of his face. He slinked down the otherwise-empty sidewalk, hunched over, slow but steady. Ellen chose to wait and see what would happen, trying to ignore the lump in her throat.

Two blocks later, the man was still steadily creeping along behind them. Lana had yet to notice, but if Ellen's chest had been pounding that morning on the train, now it was hammering. "Lana," she whispered, her words choked, "I think we're being followed."

"What?"

"That man. He's tailing us."

Lana peeked over her shoulder, her eyes going wide as she gulped loudly. "Let's turn a few times, see if he's still there."

Ellen nodded. They made a right at the next intersection. The man was still there, walking unhurriedly. Did he know that they had caught on? Ellen couldn't be sure. Then they turned left at the next intersection, and right, then left, then right again, and each time they turned, she glanced over her shoulder, and each time, he was still there.

By now, the sun was starting to set, the cool shade of night rolling in. Even worse, Ellen still had no idea where they were or how they were going to lose this stalker. For once, her dad's constant panic didn't seem so insane.

"I have an idea," Lana muttered, leaning in.

"Yeah?" Ellen asked under her breath, trying very hard not to think about how much she liked having Lana brushing up against her like this.

"There's an alleyway up ahead, see? We cut through there and lose him on the other side. On three, we'll make a run for it."

"... Okay. One ..."

"Two ..."

"Three!"

They ran. Their feet slammed into the sidewalk with each stride they took, the alley nearing ever-faster. Ellen did not once look over her shoulder. All that existed now was the sprint, the wind whipping through her hair, and the promise of safety. After an agonizing eternity, they finally veered a hard right into the alleyway.

The alley didn't go through to the next street over. It ended midway, a dark brick wall bisecting the narrow passage. The path swung right just before the wall, but could they risk going further in?

"Crap." Ellen looked back again. The man loomed, tall, imposing, menacing.

She snapped her head back in front of her, her mind already made up. "Keep moving!" she shouted, and grabbed Lana by the hand, pulling her along as the dark-eyed girl yelped.

The footsteps of their would-be assailant quickened, hard and without rhythm as he raced forwards. She could smell him all the way from here. He smelled of body odor and nicotine, though as he ran, he made no grunts or pants. Ellen did not dare look back to see if he was gaining. She just kept looking ahead, hoping, praying to the Goddess that on the other side was a chance for escape.

There wasn't. Instead of another street, Ellen and Lana were greeted with the boarded-up back door of a building. A window was next to it, but it too was covered in wooden boards.

Ellen's stomach soured like milk. She was sure she heard the sloshing of blood in her veins, trying vainly to keep her breathing steady.

Think, think, think! There had to be something, anything they could do. Could they fight? Ellen had air and earth magic, but could she use them in an actual fight? "Lana, you're an elemental. How much magic do you have?"

Lana's face lit up, and she nodded, still panting. "I have air and fire; I can try to burn through that wooden barricade."

"No, don't. You'll just end up setting the whole building on fire before we can get through it."

Lana threw her hands in the air with a frustrated huff. "Well, what do you sugg—"

"Both of you shut up! And put your hands in the air if you want to live!"

Ellen froze. Her mind felt like it was an empty desert plain and a crowded city street all at once. Vaguely, she heard Lana squeak.

"I said, PUT YOUR HANDS IN THE AIR!" The voice barked with a trembling rage. Cutting off the way back out into the streets, was a tall man with sickly-white skin, like he was dying of some rare disease. His face was gaunt, and through his loose-fitting clothing, the outlines of his ribs were visible.

Ellen complied, raising her hands above her head. As cold sweat slipped down her nape, her heart pounding in her ears for what seemed like the umpteenth time that day, she looked at one thing only: the dull silver handgun clutched in the mugger's hands.

"Wh-what do you want?" Ellen asked, trying to sound calm in the face of the firearm. She knew she was failing miserably, but she had never seen a gun in person before. It was illegal for civilians to own one.

The thief took one hand off his weapon, and with a flourish, a ball of flame ignited atop his palm. "Your valuables!" he barked. "Give me your valuables!"

Ellen's stomach dropped. What did she have that this man would consider valuable? Her phone was sitting miles away in a backpack in the now-closed compendium. Even if she wanted to give him something, all she had was ... she blanched.

"I said do it!" the attacker snarled, brandishing his gun. He waved his casting hand. With a crackling *swoosh*, an arc of acrid-smelling flames rushed through the air, dissipating before it reached the girls.

For a moment, Ellen fiercely wished they were in the Wildlands where he could pull the trigger all he liked and the gun still wouldn't shoot.

"Okay, okay! We'll cooperate, just don't hurt us!" Ellen pleaded. Her voice cracked and strained.

"Good. Reach into your pockets. Turn them inside out so I can see what you have. You first, glasses. Hand over your earrings."

"A-all right ... T-They're yours."

She was behind Ellen, and so, Ellen only heard Lana's hyperventilating until there were two light *thumps* and a tinkling *clink* one after another.

The mugger extinguished the flame in his hand and pulled on the air with his fingers. The cobalt earrings swept across the ground and leaped into his hand. Lana sobbed sharply as he pocketed them.

An image of blasting the man with her air magic so hard his skin flew right off his bones popped into Ellen's mind. She wanted to smack herself for it. What was important was getting both herself and Lana out of here alive, and any idiot knew that elemental powers or not, he had a gun. Those were a threat to even the most powerful elemental.

"You next, blondie."

"But I don't have anything ..." Ellen swallowed hard, then slowly, deliberately reached for her pocket. She assumed — hoped — that once he saw she didn't have it, he would let them go. She only had one other valuable item after all, but it was so plain, he couldn't possible think much of it ...

"The ring," the mugger growled, his voice slimy with hunger. "I want the ring."

Ellen's blood ran cold. "What?" she croaked. Immediately, she knew that was the absolute wrong thing to have done, for the man's lips curled into a manic smile. His boney face seemed somehow even more malicious.

"Oh no, this ring? It's just plastic, nothing special. You could find one of these things anywhere." Ellen hurried to backtrack, but even as she spoke, she knew her screechy, cracking voice betrayed her.

The flames flared in the mugger's palm again as he took one menacing step forward — a warning, unspoken but potent.

Ellen nearly gagged as panic squeezed her chest. She couldn't give him the ring. She *couldn't.* She'd never finish learning magic. She would never get into the Guild. She would never go back into the Wildlands.

She would never, ever see Shard again.

"I said, give me the ring!" With an ominous *click,* the thug cocked his gun, aiming directly at Ellen's chest.

"Ellen ... what are you doing ..." Lana spoke under her breath, a panicked singsong to her words.

"You have ten freaking seconds! Ten ..."

Her father's voice echoed in her mind again, this time clearer than ever before. *"It's too dangerous. It's too dangerous. It's too dangerous."* The words reverberated over and over again, bitter irony bubbling on Ellen's tongue. The Wildlands were the place she had felt safest her entire life, while now, here in the supposedly Safe Zone, her life was in danger as it had never been before. She would not back down. She would fight: for herself, for Shard ... Or else she would die trying.

"Six ... five ..."

Ellen exhaled and reached out with her magic. She pushed it as far as it would go, farther than it had ever gone before. And she felt it. She felt the thug's lifeforce at the edge of her consciousness. She could feel his every movement, every shake and tremor and breath.

"Three ... two ..."

He gripped the trigger. Lana shrieked, but even that could not break Ellen's laser-focus. She knew exactly what to do.

"One —"

Ellen *swung.* Her arm moved upwards lightning fast, a typhoon-like gale rushing the criminal mid-word. Little specks of dirt and street-grime pelted him, caught in the wind. The man's aim faltered beneath the incredible force, and with a deafening *bang* his bullet strayed from its intended course, rocketing into the building behind Lana and Ellen. It dented the brick.

The man's face contorted in pure shock, but Ellen dared not stop. She flailed with her other arm, sending a stalagmite bursting up from the ground and knocking the gun out of his hand, followed by another blast of air that sent the gun flying up and onto a fire escape. The man watched as the gun sailed through the air.

"Lana, run!" Ellen grabbed her friend by the wrist and pulled her forward. They barreled back down the alleyway, charging past the still-flabbergasted criminal, and charged back into the street.

They ran, not checking to see if the man was following them, though Ellen was sure he was. All she knew was that after a block of running, the wail of a police siren filled her ears, and her stomach sank even further. Were they going to be arrested on top of everything else?

But, for some reason, Lana yanked free of her grip, and actually started running back in the direction they had come. Ellen whipped around, ready to knock her upside the head for being a fool, when she saw the car, blue with yellow lettering that read, "POLICE" on it in all capitals.

Lana started banging on the window of the passenger side door until two officers, an elderly, dark-skinned man and a younger, brunette woman got out. Before they could say anything, Lana burst into tears.

"Help us!" she begged. "There was a maniac with a gun and my friend and I just barely got away! Please!"

The officers exchanged a look. The lady jerked her head towards Ellen. "That your friend over there?"

"Yeah, that's her, now please, help us get out of here!"

Suddenly, what Lana was doing made total sense. Of course she would ask the cops for help — Ellen wanted to smack herself.

"Please, yes, I just want to go home," Ellen added. The thought of her dad freaking out when he heard what had happened flashed through her head, but she was too tired to worry about it.

"All right. Get in." The lady reached for a radio on her hip; static reverberated as she called for backup. "My partner will take you to the station." And just like that, the brunette cop plunged into the alleyway, her gun at the ready.

As Ellen and Lana sat themselves in the cushy back seat of the cop car, though, Ellen found she wasn't relieved, only suspicious. "Why," she asked as the car drove away, its engine humming, "were you here with your sirens blaring? If you were chasing someone, why stop for us?"

The man's eyebrows twitched for a second. Ellen saw it in the rearview mirror. She thought she saw surprise on his face, mixed with a bit of pity. They turned a corner as the cop spoke. "We heard someone screaming, followed by a gunshot."

"You mean ... you got a report of that?"

"Nope. We heard it ourselves."

Ellen opened her mouth to ask more, but shut it as the car started to slow. Outside the window, she saw a sign. "Gallop Creek Police Station."

The breath rushed out of her like a deflating balloon; she felt like an idiot. Not only had they managed to leave Hadkirk City, they'd been mere blocks away from help this entire time.

Next to her, she saw Lana staring at her lap, tears streaking silently down her face. Ellen opened her mouth to say something comforting, but Lana jerked her ahead away with a harrumph. A moment later, Ellen realized she was very pointedly not making eye contact.

Huh!? Really? She had saved Lana's life, and now she was angry? It didn't add up!

The police car pulled up to the station. "All right, girls," said the officer. He had a serious expression on his face. "Let's go."

They were led into the station, a small, blue building. As they walked, Ellen's eyes darted from side to side, in case the mugger had followed them. Thankfully, it didn't seem so.

The inside of the precinct was probably the nicest place she had seen since they had left the compendium hours ago. Though it reeked of lemon air freshener, it had pristine walls and a black linoleum floor. Behind a desk sat a heavyset man, hunched over as he scribbled on paperwork. The older officer led them right past the younger man.

He said, "I'm going to have to ask you a few questions. Then, we'll call your parents."

"Questions?" Ellen repeated, her eyes narrowing.

"You're not in trouble, don't worry. We just need to know what happened."

"Let's just go with it." There was a bite to Lana's voice now, one Ellen had never heard before. It was enough to shock her into following along.

They were ushered into a brightly lit room in the back of the building, where they explained what happened. The officer took notes on a digital notepad, and after he made them tell their story twice each, he nodded, seemingly satisfied. He told them that the man they described matched descriptions of a mugger in the neighborhood. After radioing several officers and telling them to be on the lookout for an emaciated white man with a gun, he brought Lana and Ellen to a phone. He told them each to call their parents.

"Ellen?" her father said when she called the landline. "Is that you? Are you all right? You said you would text when you got on the train!"

"I'm fine," Ellen started, before realizing that that wasn't entirely the truth. "I mean, I wasn't fine before. I ..." She trailed off. How was she going to explain any of this?

"Ellen? Ellen, are you there?"

She swallowed. It was best to bite the bullet. "I'm here, Dad. I ... I got lost, left my phone behind, and a, uh, a thug tried to rob Lana and me at gunpoint."

For a long second, her father did not say anything. Ellen pictured his mouth hanging open in shock and she braced herself.

"GUNPOINT!?"

"Dad, please don't worry! The police came and saved us and the only one who got hurt was the thug. I'm at the police station in Gallop Creek now, and everything really is okay ... I'm sorry I worried you."

Even as his hyperventilating slowed, Ellen had to wince again. She hadn't meant to put him through that. "You're not going to lose me, Dad. Not today."

"I'm glad to hear it, Ellen," he said softly. "Can I speak to an officer?"

Franklin and the tall cop talked for a few minutes, during which time the officer introduced himself — "Officer Jeffery Crews," he said — and there were a few "Mmhms" and "uh-huhs" and the officer assured him that the girls really were fine. He promised to get Ellen on the next train home, and Franklin promised to be waiting for her at the station.

"Your turn," Crews said as he handed her the phone. Lana reached for the phone, shooting Ellen a glare deadly enough to wilt flowers.

Why is she so upset!? No matter how hard she tried to think of something, nothing came.

Jess Flint's voice crackled through the speaker. The conversation was mostly the same as the one Ellen had had with her dad, and ended with Jess Flint saying he would come get Lana himself and that he would be there in less than half an hour. The phone clicked as Lana placed it on the receiver.

"I'd like to charge my phone, Officer. Is that all right?" Lana said curtly, her lips pressed into a thin line. She was very pointedly looking right past Ellen.

Crews nodded, flashing them a comforting smile, and led them to what looked like a doctor's waiting room. Its walls were painted beige and lined with wooden chairs. In the center was a walnut-colored table, bare save for some half-eaten sandwiches. The lemon air freshener from before tickled Ellen's nostrils.

"This is our break room," Officer Crews explained. "Bathroom's down the hall. Ellen, I'll be taking you to the train station in about half an hour. In the meantime, make yourselves comfy."

"Thanks," Lana said, then mumbled something Ellen didn't catch as she took a seat, pulled out a white charger, and plugged her phone in. Her face visibly relaxed as the phone pinged and lit up, but not by much, which just made Ellen's breaths even shorter as she wracked her mind for whatever had Lana so ticked.

She took a seat across the room, the table dividing the space between them. Reaching for her backpack, she was met with a harsh reminder when her fingers found nothing. Sighing, she remembered that she had no charger, no phone, and no way to pass the time.

Wait. Ellen froze, eyes going wide. She had promised to meet Shard this evening, and there was absolutely no excuse for not going to see him tonight of all nights. She glanced around the room, searching for a clock, but there was none. She bit her lip, holding a frustrated growl back.

Lana's phone had charged enough that she was playing a game, jabbing the screen with her finger again and again. Chiptune music and sound effects issued from the tiny speakers.

Ellen sighed. "Hey, Lana," she said, trying to sound casual, "do you know what time it is?"

"It's 9:30. Why?" Lana did not look up from her game.

"Oh, um ..." Ellen stammered, knowing it unwise to divulge her true reason. "Just curious." At the very least, she was not supposed to see Shard for another hour and a half, so she had time. "Well, even with everything, I guess having a dad so important he can own a car must be kinda nice ..."

Lana looked up from her phone and glared. Her eyes were narrow with disbelief and her lips were pursed tight with anger. Ellen's inhaled sharply — she had said the wrong thing, and she knew it.

"I don't know if you've noticed, but I am freaking *pissed* at you right now. What the hell is so important about that stupid ring that you tried to use magic against a freaking *gun?* Actually," she interrupted herself with a bob of her head, "I don't care what's so great about it. Those earrings were important to me, but clearly you think your stuff is more important than mine *and* our lives. So you can just stop talking and leave me alone."

Ellen's eyes bulged, her mouth agape. "Dude, I *saved* our lives. I beat the guy, didn't I? I'm sorry I couldn't save your earrings, really, I am, but what's to say he wouldn't have shot us after he got our stuff?"

"If he wanted us dead, he would have fired from the start! Oh, and, like I said, you didn't save our lives, you risked them. Do you know how *lucky* you got with that windblast? There was no way you could have predicted the exact moment he was about to shoot."

Scrunching up her face in amazement, Ellen let out a scoff. She hadn't been taking lessons the past three months for nothing. "I'm not a complete newbie at magic. I know how to reach out with it to expand my senses."

"Yeah, uh-huh," Lana said with a scowl. "Tell me all about how you used magic to do something that magic *can't do.* What do you think I am, stupid?"

Ellen rolled her eyes. "You clearly have no idea what you're talking about." Either that or Lana had no training, but she *had* to know how to expand her magic — it was the first, most basic thing she, Ellen, had learned.

Lana snorted. "I really shouldn't have asked you to come today." Without another word, she turned to her phone and hammered the volume button all the way up.

Ellen clutched the sides of her seat. The hardness of the chair and her aching fingers distracted her. Before she knew what was happening, something wet stung the corners of her eyes. She blinked once, and then twice, and then bolted out of her seat.

The ladies' room door slammed shut behind her, and then a stall door, too. Ellen's fist collided with the wall. Red-hot pain sparked in her knuckles. She didn't care. Today was supposed to have been fun! So how had things turned out like *this*?

A deep, hot breath welled up and flowed out of her throat. Her whole body loosened, not with relaxation, but resignation.

"I won't cry." Ellen wiped away her tears, her voice barely a whisper. Today had been a disaster, but even if things with Lana ... deteriorated — she sobbed tearlessly — she still had someone else who cared about her. That had to mean something, right?

26

S HARD LAY IN HIS SHELTER, resting his head on his paws. He was alone, save for the starlight pouring in his broken roof. He'd have to hire someone to fix that, but he wasn't sure he had anything he could trade for such a service. If he were a dragoness, he'd offer his paintings, but as it was, those had to remain a secret.

It's not so bad. I get to charge my magic, Shard thought. Not that his powers would do him any good tomorrow. He would have only himself to rely on during the trial.

"Trial." He mouthed the word as if it were holy and unutterable. There was finally a chance, the slimmest, most infinitesimal possibility that Keeper would be punished.

He hadn't thought going to Inferno would accomplish anything. But Ellen believed it would, and he believed in his friend, so he approached the chieftain's shelter that morning. Every step sent twinges of pain shooting through his legs. Several times, he had himself nearly convinced it was useless.

And yet.

When Shard told the chieftain what had happened, the older dragon's eyes had widened in alarm. The two had conversed outside Inferno's shelter just before dawn; the world around them was tinted blue in the ending night.

"Shard ... these are very serious accusations. However, given that you are my nephew and your current ... indisposition" — he gestured a foreleg at one of Shard's cloth bandages — "I have no choice but to investigate."

Inferno sighed, and dipped his head, bringing one of his wings to rest against his horn as if he needed a steadying touch. Though the red and scarlet dragon was still much bigger than him, Shard thought he looked small, perhaps for the first time in his life. An ember of hope smoldered in the younger dragon's heart.

"Rest assured," Inferno vowed as a cool breeze picked up, carrying the scent of dirt and flowers. "I will never let anyone hurt *my* dragons." And with that, he had spread his wings and took to the sky.

As he stared up at the night sky, the memories of the day replaying in his mind over and over again, Shard half-expected to wake from this wonderful dream and find Keeper ready to scorch him alive. But that never happened, and best of all, it kept on not happening.

Ellen appeared in front of Shard, who instantly perked up, his ears twitching as he rose to his paws. "You're here!" he said, so excited he nearly forgot to whisper. But her face was beset with a terrible melancholy. "Are you okay? You seem wiped."

Ellen laughed weakly. "I've ... I've had kind of a rough day."

Shard frowned. He didn't think Ellen had ever been so forthright so quickly with him when she was upset. "Oh no, what happened? Actually, wait," he said, pointing up to the sky. "We're totally exposed here. If someone flies overhead, we're screwed."

"Oh. Right. I'll meet you at the river in five minutes." She reached for the ring, her shoulders slumped, and eyes half-lidded, like all the energy had been sucked out of her. For a heartbeat, he forgot how nervous and incredulous he was, and wished there was something he could do for her.

"Ellen?" Shard blurted out. "You've never ridden on a dragon's back before, have you?"

She stopped and looked at him like he had just suggested that monkeys lived on the moon. "You're suggesting you parade me around for everyone to see for miles around. Really?"

"I mean ... just down to the river. Everyone's sleeping, so if we go fast enough, nobody's gonna notice." Even saying that, he heard how foolish it was. Yet, for the first time in as long as he could remember, the chorus of voices in Shard's ears, the ones that went *stupid, stupid, stupid,* were easier to ignore.

"Maybe tomorrow, Shard," Ellen said, still sounding weary. "I just wanted to know how things went with your uncle."

"There's going to be a tribunal tomorrow. Keeper and I are going to each go before the council and explain our sides of the story, then they decide who they think is right."

Ellen tilted her head. "They just ... decide, just like that? Don't you guys have to present evidence?"

"No? They just go with whoever's version of events matches what was seen. Why would we present evidence when everything is already right there?"

"Never mind." A pause. "Just be sure to think of something for how the roof broke. You can't exactly tell them it was me."

Shard nodded. He hadn't thought of that. "I'm feeling pretty good about my odds, though. There's no way they can side with Keeper after the time I had to spend in the healing hut."

One last sad smile graced Ellen's lips, filled with regret that Shard could only half-identify. "Okay. Hey, I gotta go. I'll talk to you tomorrow." She reached for the ring, then paused, her eyes fixed on Shard. He felt something emanating from her, something fierce and unshakeable — her whole-hearted trust. "Good luck, yeah? You deserve to be safe." And with that, she twisted her ring and vanished.

Shard stayed there, unmoving. On some level, he had always known Ellen's words to be true. But, hearing them spoken aloud by someone else, someone he cared for more than anyone else ...

Though he might not like Inferno, he knew that when the chieftain said he was going to do something, he did it. Firebug too had been concerned, even appalled when she had found out.

With a calming breath, he let the stellar magic of the night sky flow into him, warm and familiar. He lay down again, rolling onto his back and exposing his underbelly to the sky. His scales glowed as he stored power. His eyes drifted shut.

And then the heavy flapping of wingbeats echoed in Shard's ears. His eyes shot open. As the world around him came into view, illuminated by the million specks in the sky, so too did Firebug landing before him. Her eyes were wide, her mouth hanging open. She seemed jittery, shifting her weight from side to side as she breathed heavily.

"F-Firebug?" Shard bolted upright. Somehow, he knew exactly what had happened.

"What was that," Firebug said, and not as a question. Her words carried an air of disbelief, spoken quietly as if she herself did not know what she was saying. "What *was that?*"

Oh crap. Shard stood. He kneaded the gravelly dirt beneath him nervously, but he wasn't about to give up without a fight. "W-what was what?"

"The human!" Firebug hissed, and now there was a crazed look in her eyes. A hundred little lightning bolts thundered in Shard's ears — he'd been found out.

Firebug paced back and forth now, ranting in hushed but wild tones. "I mean, I thought I'd seen one with you the other night, but I wasn't, you know, sure or anything! So I figured I'd talk to you about it, but then I realized maybe now of all times wasn't the best time to talk to you about it, but as I was flying back home, I saw it again! *What even!?*"

"I-I can explain!" he yelped. And yet, to his great surprise, Firebug placed a claw against his snout, shushing him.

"Quiet!" she whispered urgently. "Do you want the whole tribe to hear?"

Shard shook his head, too bewildered to speak — wouldn't she want everyone to know he'd been consorting with the enemy?

Firebug removed her paw. An exhausted sigh escaped her mouth, and she cradled her head in her wings. "That human ... it *talked.*" When her wings fell away, they revealed her face, and now, he could see that she wasn't angry, wasn't bloodthirsty, but confused. "How can a human talk? Did you ... magic it? I mean, it vanished into thin air, so ... you did something, right?"

Despite everything, this was an opportunity. Maybe, just maybe, he could convince her to keep his secret. She had understood Ellen, after all — maybe she could understand the full truth. Being honest was risky, but at this point, what wasn't? It was now or never.

"I ... I didn't do anything to her. I've been able to talk to her ever since we met."

Firebug blinked. Shard knew he had her attention. As calmly as he could, he explained everything. It was almost bittersweet, giving away his most precious secret, but it had to be done.

176

The whole time, Firebug listened, not asking any questions, patiently waiting for Shard to finish. When he was done, she stayed exactly where she was, not moving a muscle. Starlight passed over her scales as the clouds moved, her little white specks twinkling like stars themselves.

"Please," Shard begged. "Don't tell anyone. Ellen is my best friend in the world. She would never hurt any of us." As he said it, though, a little voice piped up in his mind. *Then why does she want to learn magic?*

"I don't ..." Firebug began, only to trail off. Her gaze hardened. Now, it was her turn to share something. "There's something you need to know: I have Starsight, and I think I've been having visions of your friend. I think she's going to destroy us all."

Shard blinked. That was a lot to take in. He wasn't even sure he'd heard right.

"You don't believe me, either, do you?" A deep frown creased Firebug's face. She looked away, bitterness narrowing her eyes.

Shaking his head, Shard fought the urge to say he didn't. He couldn't let this go wrong. "It's not that! This is just so ... I dunno? I didn't think dragonesses could have Starsight!"

Firebug heaved a sigh. "Neither did I, until a few moons ago. My powers are weak but I've been having visions. In each and every one of them, I see a giant, bipedal ... *thing* destroying the entire tribe."

"And you think it's Ellen? Why would she do that?"

"Because!" Firebug exploded, a dam built from moons of frustration finally bursting. Her paws gripped the dirt, leaving clawmark trails. "This is a —" She caught herself and leaned in, quietly hissing again. "Because she's a human! Humans kill us and steal our orichalcum. What else could it be?"

Shard winced. Every inch of his body told him to run, that she was going to hit him. But then, her eyes widened. When she looked at Shard, he saw something not angry, but vulnerable ... and hopeful. "Wait. You *do* believe me? You believe that I'm having visions?"

Shard's mouth hung open as he stammered for a response. Then, one came to him, and he knew it was the only possible answer. "I ... I do. I don't think the visions mean what you think they do, but Agito knows everyone's been wrong about what drakes can and can't be. Why can't they be wrong about dragonesses, too?"

Wind whistled above them. The moon vanished behind a cloud as crickets chirped, a natural nighttime symphony. On Firebug's face, conflict warred — should she believe him or not?

"Listen," he implored. "I swear, my best friend is not going to turn giant and destroy us. I'll help you find out what your visions mean, but please! Don't tell anyone about her."

And that was exactly what Firebug needed to hear. "All right. But you better not go back on your word, got it?"

Relief rushed through Shard's veins. Things really *were* looking up. "Wouldn't dream of it."

Their promise now made, Firebug wished Shard luck in his trial tomorrow. If she wanted to talk about Keeper, she did not show it.

When he slept that night, Shard heard a soothing lullaby his mother had sang to him in his dreams. He hadn't thought of it in nearly two years, but the lyrics were every bit as vivid in his mind as they were then.

I hid in freezing darkness, afraid that I might fall
Locked in my last bastion, angry in its walls
And then one day, by chance I found your light

27

THE PITCH-BLACK LIMOUSINE'S engine hummed as it sped down the roadway, dirt and gravel crunching beneath the wheels. The inside smelled of Jess's favorite fragrances, rosemary and lilac. A man in a dark suit gripped the wheel, tapping his fingers periodically. One of the benefits of being the Guild's Commander, Jess supposed — not only did he get a car, he got someone else to drive it for him.

He had always loved driving at night. The world seemed to fall away as he was chauffeured wherever he needed, save for the glowing lamps that dotted the road's edges every so many feet and the occasional emergency vehicle rushing by. But for now, he could appreciate his chauffeur and focus on what, or rather who, was in the velvety back seat with him.

Lana pressed her head into Jess's side, burying her face in his arm. Her breathing was heavy, yet wavering, as if she were trying not to cry. What happened to her today must have been awful. Jess was just glad she was okay.

When his phone buzzed, he had been at one of the Generators, just a few dozen miles from Hadkirk City. The impossibly tall, stygian tower loomed over him, a stark contrast against the pale silver dome, beyond which lay trees and shrubs and empty grassland farther than the eye could see. Jess hated looking out there. He'd left the safety of the dome enough times to know the Wildlands were an ugly, vile place.

At the base of the tower were two technicians, monitoring the machine with various beeping gadgets and gizmos that Jess only mostly remembered how to work. Three other men hefted a bag fit to burst with orichalcum over the brown dirt, dumping it into an opening at the Generator's base. When they were done, two more field operatives brought an equally-large bag, and with a hearty "heave-ho!" they poured the silver beads in, then slammed the cavity shut.

Jess nodded with lips set thin. That much orichalcum was good. It might last them a while. Then his phone had rumbled against his leg, and he dashed off to make sure Lana was safe.

In the morning, he would have to go into the Guild. He would have to ascend to the highest floor of Headquarters, and sit once more behind his desk. He would have to deal with planning orichalcum expeditions and assigning different teams to different deposits. He would have to monitor the extra security footage from the cameras he'd had installed all over the Safe Zone, combing through it for even the slightest hint of the source of dragon magic. But now, for the first time in months, he could spend time alone with his sweet, smart, wonderful, beloved daughter.

As if on cue, Lana yawned. "You must be tired," he commented. If his evening had been trying, hers had to have been outright terrifying.

"I'm gonna be okay, Daddy." Her voice had a noticeable quiver.

"I know, pumpkin. Are you sure you don't need me to do anything?"

"Nah, it's fine."

She gripped tighter on his arm.

Jess patted his daughter's head. He had already contacted Ayesha to let her know what had happened. Ever since the Night of Flames, their relationship had taken a turn for the vitriolic, and now, he had scant love left for the woman. Still, divorced or no, if they shared anything, it was their love of Lana. She deserved to know.

He had sent word by text, rather than calling, and had yet to hear back. Jess sighed and breathed in deeply. She couldn't set aside her petty and immature hatred of him to talk about her own daughter? It was pathetic — and it was all the dragons' fault. If he could raise Lana himself, he would, but with all the time he had to devote to work, Ayesha was the only one who could do it.

"Hey, I know! Why don't you tell me about how you've been lately? Oh Goddess" — realization struck — "I think it's been two months since we've talked, just you and me, in person."

Lana's eyebrows drew together, though just for a second; but, in that second, Jess saw a flash like deep hurt. Then it was gone. "Yeah, that'd be nice."

And so, they talked for what felt like hours. Lana told Jess all about school and how her classes were going, her friends Ayako and Priyanka, and Priyanka's new boyfriend, and her magic lessons between volunteering at the orphanage. Finally, the topic turned to the day's events.

With a small, tired voice, Lana asked, "Do you think they'll catch him, Daddy?"

Jess wanted to answer yes, but Lana was old enough to hear the truth, ugly as it might have been. "I don't know, pumpkin. Gallop Creek ... it's a rough area. The cops there already have their hands full. What were you doing all the way out there, anyway?"

Lana looked away, twirling a strand of hair. She had long since taken off her sun hat, which now lay on her lap. "My phone ran out of batteries ... and I thought, 'why not just go the rest of the way by memory?' It could have been fun, you know?" Jess had the suspicion that that wasn't the whole truth — perhaps, that had something to do with the distinctly-absent earrings Lana had worn at the game — but he ignored his gut feeling. "I wish you could do something about that guy. Being the Commander of the Guild has got to give you some connections, right?"

Jess laughed like a glass bell, beautifully and fragilely. If he had the kind of power Lana envisioned, then the Safe Zone would be a very different place indeed — it had taken such a long time for him to get the clearance for the cameras alone. He couldn't imagine ever being allowed to do actual police work. "Not enough, I'm afraid. But your friend Ellen must have given the guy quite the surprise. If we're lucky, she scared him straight."

"Urgh, Ellen is the last person I want to even think about right now. She could have gotten her and me killed all over some stupid ring, and then she made up some lie about 'expanding her senses' with her magic to justify it. How ridiculous is that!? I could have died today!" She scoffed, eyebrows slanted, and Jess knew he had to say something.

But his body had gone numb. He forced himself to breathe and focus on the present, though the sudden disorientation did not leave him.

"You're alive, pumpkin," he said, aware of how hollow and unconvincing he sounded. "I know it's scary, but you're going to be okay. Besides, I'm sure Ellen had her reasons." He reached out a hand and placed it on his daughter's shoulder, trying to work through the horror she had just instilled in him.

Lana, for her part, seemed completely unaware. "Thanks, Daddy. I think ... I think I wanna just sleep now, though."

Jess nodded. "All right. Sleep well."

Lana opened her mouth, about to say something important — or so Jess thought, but instead, she said goodnight and closed her eyes. Resting his head against the soft seatback, Jess made a point of not falling asleep, even as Lana's chest began to rise and fall, the air from her nose tickling his arm.

The whole time, his heart pounded wildly in his throat, a twisted, triumphant smile pulling at his lips. He'd been right all along — there *was* dragon magic inside the Safe Zone. Weeks of searching had all but snuffed out any hope he'd had of finding the source, but at long last, he knew it had to be none other than Ellen Delacroix. From the moment he'd set eyes on that girl, he'd felt something deeply, unsettlingly wrong from her and he now knew exactly what. Countless battles with dragons flashed through his head, their barked orders and animalistic roars accompanying each memory. He knew that dragon sorcery could expand senses — but human magic could only ever control the elements. How, then, had Ellen done exactly that? How had she even known that the technique existed?

There was only one explanation: Ellen Delacroix was a dragon merely disguised as a human. It was something that should be unthinkable ... yet everything about this was truly out of the ordinary.

Jess's smile fell as the car passed under a streetlamp, his face reflected in the window for a split second along with Lana's sleeping eyelids. His word wouldn't be enough for Robertson, not yet. He'd need to actually see Ellen casting magic — the claw in his cheek would tell him if it was elemental magic ... or dragon sorcery. Only then would the Chancellor believe him.

I've still got a month left, he thought. *I'll make this work.* He glanced down at his daughter, snoring soundly against his arm — music to his ears. He had to protect her and indeed all of the Safe Zone. It wouldn't be easy, but he would prove Ellen was a dragon ... at any cost.

But first, he'd have to falsify some documents.

28

K EEPER AWOKE to a claw poking his side. "Get up," came a voice. Stirring, he placed it as Thorn, one of the oldest dragons in the tribe. "I said, get up!" Thorn poked him again, harder, more painfully. They were in the earthen meeting shelter where Keeper had been imprisoned yesterday. The roof was open, early morning light streaming in from a cloudless sky.

"All right, all right," Keeper grumbled, getting to his paws. He yawned, pangs of hunger gnawing at his belly. He ignored them. He was a drake, after all; he could handle being a little hungry. Instead, he focused on Thorn with as much defiance as he could muster. That was hard, given the elder dragon's missing right eye. It made him feel like he was kicking a little dragonling.

"The trial's starting. You will present your version of events. Shard will present his. The council will then decide which we believe."

"Yeah, I know," Keeper retorted. "I'm not freaking stupid."

Thorn snorted, a smokey cloud puffing out his nostrils. Then, he gestured for Keeper to follow him out the open roof.

The thought of just making a break for it seemed awfully appealing. Not that he would actually do that. Inferno wasn't actually going to punish him — he, Keeper, had just been living the life Inferno had taught him. He'd been defending what was his. *You're tough, you're awesome, you're strong,* he chanted mentally, a mantra of courage and survival. Today, he would prove to everyone that they should have been paying attention to him all along, that he was *better* than Shard, no matter what their stupid, weak mother had thought, no matter what anyone thought.

I'm strong, I'm strong, I'm strong. When I win this stupid thing, I'm gonna make Shard regret trying to steal Firebug.

When he touched down in the Clearing, he saw his uncle on the podium, and three councilors the ground. The entire village had gathered. Keeper gulped.

Thorn took his place in front of the podium beside the other councilors: Gnarl, Noir, and Scar, and Inferno cleared his throat with a loud rumble. "Will Shard please come forth?"

Behind him, Keeper heard an unfamiliar pawstep rhythm. At first, he thought someone was looking for a better view of the action. Then he realized the someone was nearing him.

No way. It can't be …

Approaching the center of the Clearing was none other than Shard. But that was impossible. Shard was weak and groveling and pathetic. Even when he tried to stand up for himself, the little runt just needed some roughing up and he would run with his head hung low. But the dragon Keeper saw stood firmly, almost even proudly, as he approached the podium. This was someone who had faith in himself.

Suddenly, Keeper was a mere year old dragonling again. In his mind's eye, he saw his brother and mother leaving the shelter, going off for yet another magic lesson in the middle of the night, leaving *him* behind.

Can't I come, too?

I'm sorry, Keeper, but this is Mommy-and-Shard time.

But you always —

Don't bother your mother, Keeper. She'll play with you when she can.

But Daddy, she never plays with me! It's not fair!

Fire churned in Keeper's belly. He didn't know where Shard's poise had come from, but he would stamp it out forever. Firebug would love him, and only him.

"Shard, Keeper," Inferno said with a nod to each of them. "Let's begin."

29

S HARD FELT WOBBLY in the legs. He was so lightheaded, he thought he might pass out. His mind screamed at him to turn tail and run. But he couldn't. He wouldn't. Ellen believed in him. Even Firebug was rooting for him. He had to stand tall.

His joints taut, his wings folded, long, scaly tail curled around his side, and his head held high, he looked the councilors straight in the eyes. They all stared back impassively. Even Inferno seemed to have shed the sad gleam in his eyes. That made sense, Shard supposed. They all had a job to do.

"And so, in the name of our tribe's peace and the God Agito," the chieftain was saying, "I, Inferno, shall pass judgment today on these dragons in whatever form I deem necessary.

"Shard. You may tell your story first."

The world blurred into a hyperreal facsimile of itself. The gentle breeze whispering through the treetops and passing over his body, the yellow sun vanishing behind a cloud, taking its light with it, the stares of the tribe around him boring into his scales. He could feel his chest constricting, and when he opened his dry, arid mouth, his breath scraped against it formlessly.

The whispering crowd's reactions passed through Shard's ears. Little bits of chatter, muffled yet clear all at once. "What's he doing?" "Why isn't he talking?" "Is this some kind of game to him?"

"Shard." Inferno coughed meaningfully and spoke again, more firmly this time. "I said you may begin."

For a heartbeat, Shard swore he felt the brush of someone's clawtips against his. He stiffened, gasping slightly, but did not look away from the chieftain. *You can do this, Shard,* came a voice he had not heard in over two years, and now, he did look around, searching the Clearing in a daze. That was his mother's voice.

"Perhaps," said Gnarl, his voice thick with impatience, "we should let Keeper speak first."

"Wait!" Shard cried out. "I'm ready to talk now. Sorry, I just had to gather my thoughts." He did not know what he had heard. But he did not need to.

When nobody said anything, Shard told them. He told them how Keeper had charged in that evening and beat him. How he had nearly died, saved only by the light of the moon and his healing powers. Here, he left out the parts about Ellen, and wove a tale of how in his half-conscious state, he must have broken the roof with his magic; a believable enough fib, he hoped.

As he regaled them, the councilors continued to stare emotionlessly. One would nod every now and again, or they would grunt, but that was it. Shard forged onwards, until finally he had said everything he needed to.

"The next thing I knew, I was coming to in the healing hut," he finished. Relief washed over him. It was like the tide going out, carrying his tension along with it. The sun peeked out from behind the cloud, as if congratulating him for having done what he could.

Inferno stared at Shard with a piercing gaze, as if he were sizing the younger dragon up. Shard forced himself to stand firm. Finally, Inferno nodded, as unreadable as Shard had ever seen him, and turned his gaze to the left. "Very well. Keeper. You may go next."

Keeper snorted derisively. "Ugh, finally." The councilors exchanged glances, but he plowed on, speaking in an odd mix of disinterest and haughtiness. "Hey, whatever, it's cool. You gotta give everyone a fair chance, even if they —"

"Keeper. Tell us what you think happened." It was Noir who spoke. He stared down at the young red dragon, unimpressed. "And please, keep your opinions to yourself."

"I can't say what I think, but here's what I *know* happened: Shard tried to steal my girl. I mean, I couldn't just let that slide, right? Like Inferno always tells me, a drake's gotta be strong."

For the first time since the trial had begun, Shard saw genuine emotion in the councilors' eyes: shock, in some, understanding in others ... but in Inferno's slit-thin glare, Shard saw something the chieftain had not expressed in front of Shard, not ever: rage. The rest of his posture remained unchanged. But still, Shard saw fiery anger; he was sure of it.

Keeper paused, taking in the dragons' disapproving glowers around him. He cleared his throat. "I mean ... Yes, I attacked Shard. He tried to take Firebug from me."

Gasps resounded in the crowd. Shard wanted to see if he could catch Firebug's reaction, but he had lost track of her. He shook his head, forcing himself to refocus.

Keeper swept his gaze in a semi-circle, glancing at all the villagers before zeroing in on Inferno. He spoke accusatorily, even angrily. "But that doesn't mean I meant to kill him! I was just doing what you taught me to do — being strong, and protecting what was mine! If you didn't want me to do that, why the *hell* did you drill it into me?"

Nobody said a word. Were the other dragons appalled? Were they nodding in agreement? Shard dared not look around, and neither did the councilors, who merely kept their gazes trained on Keeper. A low ringing buzzed in Shard's ears, as his paws kneaded at the ground beneath him. If Inferno sided with Keeper now ...

"Normally, I prefer to consult with my advisors before making a ruling," Inferno said, his voice level but icy. "Today, I will do no such thing."

Keeper looked particularly pleased with himself.

"I believe you tried to murder your brother, Keeper. You will come with me to the council's shelter so I can mete out appropriate punishment."

"... What did you say?" His grin evaporated.

Shard could scarcely believe it. Inferno had sided against Keeper? He stared on dumbly, unbelieving. Within his chest swelled hope, almost even triumph. *Stay focused. It's not over yet.* But the ringing in his ears had stopped.

"I said," Inferno repeated through bared fangs, "that you will come with me. Now."

"What?" Keeper flared his wings, stomping forward. "Are you joking? Are you JOKING!? I did exactly what you taught me to do!" Inferno opened his mouth to say something, but Keeper shouted over him. "I've spent my whole LIFE doing exactly what you said! I'm strong, and a drake, and tough, just like you wanted, and — and now you're going to side with HIM?" Keeper bellowed, raw and hurt, his breathing heavy. Thorn, Gnarl, Scar and Noir bristled, but Inferno remained all but frozen in place.

"You love HIM more than me, don't you? All of you do! Can't you see how weak he is!? Am I not good enough for you? That's what this is about, isn't it! I'm not good enough for you!"

"Keeper —" Inferno began, getting in only that one word before Keeper roared like a feral beast.

A single, actual tear streamed from Keeper's eye. Shard's jaw hung open. He had never seen his brother cry; the thought that maybe, just maybe, Keeper might have feelings beyond rage and smugness flashed through his mind.

"I trusted you!" And then, Keeper did the absolute worst thing he could have done. He charged forward, his claws bared as he leaped into the air, fire crackling in his mouth.

Before the councilors could act, Inferno's eyes flashed. He opened his mouth, but instead of fire, a wave of golden magic surged out his jaws. It hit Keeper square in the face, and he crumpled, hitting the ground with a *thud.*

No one said a word.

Inferno flew off the podium, his flapping wingbeats breaking the silence as he landed near Keeper's all-but-unmoving form. "Everyone," he announced, businesslike. "I apologize that you had to see my nephew act so dishonorably. I will be taking him to the council shelter for discipline on top of his punishment. You are all to go about your day."

Then, with a flash of golden light and a *crack* like thunder, they vanished.

Gasps and murmurs spread through the crowd; hushed, anxious tones. "What was that?" "Did Keeper just attack the chieftain?" "Did *Chieftain Inferno* just attack his *nephew?*" "What is happening here?"

"You heard him!" Gnarl shouted. "Everyone, stop sitting around like little sissy dragonlings and go do your damn jobs!"

As everyone slowly started heading out to their workstations, mumbling among themselves, Shard wanted to shout for joy. He spread his wings and made for the fields, lighter than a feather. As he settled into his spot in the pentagram, golden grains surrounding him beneath a sunny blue sky, he channeled his magic into the growing spell. Even while he focused on the magic, he felt relaxed, limber even. After Keeper had all but self-destructed like that, there was no way things would be the same ever again.

Tonight, he could introduce Ellen to Firebug, and the three of them could together work on deciphering Firebug's visions. Everything was finally looking up. For the first time in so very long, he might finally be safe.

30

A FTER A NIGHT SPENT on the railway, Ellen awoke in her own room. She lay in her soft bed, staring up at the star stickers, which glowed in the blueish early morning.

Her dad had been waiting for her when she stepped onto the platform, eyes underlined with dark worry, but his voice kind and comforting. Officer Crews had even been kind enough to pick up her phone and backpack from the compendium.

Everything worked out in the end.

Except Lana hates me.

Ellen hoisted herself out of bed. Her father snored resonantly the next room over, a rarity at this hour. Normally, he was getting ready for work, bustling about the kitchen and taking large swigs of steaming coffee. She gulped — she must really have worried him.

The trial's probably started by now.

She stared at the ring on her finger, moon-silver, catching the morning light. Would she ever know where it came from? Perhaps that did not matter. She squeezed her eyes shut. Placing her palm on the ring, she breathed a calming breath, and hoped as hard as she could that things had worked out for her scaly friend.

31

K EEPER'S EYES DRIFTED OPEN, but he saw nothing. Total darkness engulfed him ... where was he? Soft dirt and pebbles pressed against his underbelly and paws, but for some reason, his wings and tail and all four of his legs were numb with pins and needles.

He tried to move. He couldn't.

What's going on? Where in the hell am I? The thoughts raced through his mind as his breathing quickened. It was as if chains had been affixed to him, locking him in place. He tried to open his snout to call out, to demand to be let free, maybe even to scream for help, but his muzzle refused to open. *When I get ahold of whoever did this ...*

"Ah, good. You're awake." A friendly, even jolly voice greeted him, one Keeper had heard too many times not to recognize. There was a *whoosh,* and a solitary torch burst to life. In the dim light, he could see one dragon, tall and menacing, his eyes glowing like burning coal.

Inferno.

Everything came rushing back. The trial, the verdict, his utter, embarrassing failure ... A powerful urge to hurt his uncle seized Keeper, but he still could not move, no matter how he struggled against his unseen bonds.

"Now ... how am I going to teach you your lesson, my dear boy?"

MY *lesson!?* But he hadn't done anything wrong!

"Oh, don't you give me that look," Inferno said with a stillness that belied fury. He began to stalk back and forth like a slithering snake. "You tried to hurt one of *my* dragons. You admitted to it yourself, in front of the whole tribe. The roughhousing between you and him, that I can stand, but I cannot allow attempted murder to go unpunished, my dear Keeper."

Inferno slinked out of sight, but Keeper could still feel his uncle's presence, still hear his soft-yet-deafening steps. Keeper wanted to roar. Didn't his uncle know that the so-called "roughhousing" had actually been him showing Shard who was in charge?

"I suppose I could hit you," Inferno pondered aloud, "but I'm not sure that would hurt enough. You might come up with some rationale about how I cheated, given your current incapacitation, and besides, I might lose control and cripple you permanently, mightn't I? I don't want to hurt you too badly, just the right amount."

Unwelcome warmth pressed against the side of Keeper's snout, a tickling against his ear as Inferno breathed gently against it. Keeper found his anger ebbing. Something all too familiar seeped in to replace it.

"Now, now, don't be scared. This is for your own good. I want you to be the best you can be, and the first step towards that is to recognize who's in charge — me."

Scared? Me, scared? No, I don't get scared. I scare others. I am dominant and strong.

Inferno lifted his paw, and for a second, Keeper thought he was about to strike. Instead, Keeper was suddenly shivering — he could move again.

"I didn't try to freaking kill him! Agito's claws, I just wanted to teach him a lesson!" Keeper shouted, hoping that if he were loud enough, he could drown out whatever this horrible sensation inside him was.

Inferno chuckled darkly. "My dear Keeper, it's far too late to change your fate now — now, now, don't bare your fangs at me. I will defend myself if you make it necessary. I just want to hear what *you* think would be an appropriate punishment, hm?"

"Wh-what?" Keeper stammered. *Don't be a coward!* he mentally shouted at himself, but before he could say anything more, Inferno spoke again.

"Oh come now, it's not that hard. How do you think I should punish you? I suppose something long-lasting would be best, something that constantly reminds you to stay in line. I could cast a spell that saps you of your strength ... Hm, yes ..." Inferno's eyes became glassy, like he was deep in thought. "I need you to be able to perform your chores, so perhaps you should always be only the second strongest dragon in any given group." Inferno's face brightened with smug self-satisfaction.

"Don't you dare!" Keeper shrieked as he leaped to his paws. His muscles shouted in protest, like he hadn't moved in days. "I *need* to be the strongest!"

"And why is that?" Inferno asked pleasantly. Keeper's mouth dropped. How could Inferno not know? The answer was obvious! But he kept staring expectantly — he was actually asking.

"What are you talking about!? You were the one who taught me that I had to be strong to take what I want! Was it all a damn LIE!?" A voice in the back of his head whispered that maybe yelling wasn't a good idea, but he ignored it. Fire boiled inside him, bursting to come out.

The pleasant look vanished. "Of course not," he spat. "But this isn't about me. This is about you, and the fact that you tried to hurt one of *my* dragons!"

"What do you mean, 'yours?'" Keeper's jaw clenched as he stared his uncle right in the eyes. Inferno inched forward, one paw in front of the other, his steps slow and deliberate.

"Everyone in this tribe is mine. Shard is mine. Spearhead is mine. Emerald is mine. Firebug, Smasher, Bog, even you, Keeper — you are all *mine*. Only I can make you into who you are all meant to be, and I will not allow anyone to interfere with that — not even you." He stopped, his snout just a blade of grass's length away from Keeper.

Keeper's whole body felt hot, but he refused to budge. He would not kowtow to his uncle, he told himself, even as he felt his breath catch in his throat. He wanted to strike Inferno again, to spray the fire inside himself out all over Inferno and watch him burn, but it was all he could do not to recoil.

"Oh dear. I didn't mean to say all that. But now that I have, I suppose there really is only one punishment I can mete out."

Keeper's heart pounded wildly. *What's he talking about? What's he going to do to me?* Finally, he found his voice. "I am not your plaything."

"I do not *play* with my dragons, dear boy. I *guide* them. And as I was saying, it seems there's only one way to keep you on the right path." He pulled away and smiled, tenderly and gently. In that moment, Keeper thought, he could have believed that Inferno genuinely cared about him, even as he spoke the most horrifying, horrible words possible:

"You will agree to a binding curse."

And so, by the time he flew out of the council shelter, a bevy of dragons waited outside, staring eagerly, like they couldn't wait to see Keeper reduced. In the back of the crowd, he saw Firebug, and standing next to her was *him.* Shard. So, it was true then. Firebug and Shard *had* been going behind his back. Why else would a drake and dragoness be close to each other?

"Move!" he yelled, making a point of showing his fangs. He could still do that, at least. He muscled his way through the crowd, the others giving him a wide berth as he approached Firebug.

But when he reached her, he couldn't bring himself to even try and be aggressive. Not with her. He stared at her for a second, as something wet stung his eyes. He shook his head violently. Weakness was something he would never — could never show again. He flashed Shard as hateful a glare as he could muster, and tromped into the woods.

What else could Keeper do? His life would never be the same.

32

ELLEN AND SHARD sat side by side on the riverbank that night. The sky above them had clouded over since the morning, but the humid air of the summer night still weighed on Ellen's shoulders. It was almost like swimming in a pool. She wanted to tell Shard all about what had happened in Hadkirk City with Lana and Jess Flint, but that could wait.

"So ..." She had a feeling she already knew what had happened at the trial.

"I can't believe this." Shard stared at the other side of the river with such intensity that Ellen almost thought he could see something she could not. "Nothing's changed."

"You're sure, right? You're sure that he wasn't punished?"

Shard shook his head, still not looking at Ellen. "Of course he wasn't. He just ... came out of the shelter and went back to herding, like nothing had happened. He was surly and seemed kinda pissed, but what else is new? He's probably at the shelter right now, just ... just waiting to sink his fangs into me."

The corners of Ellen's lips sagged downwards as her stomach started to twist. "This is really bad, huh?"

He fixed his gaze on a dragonfly buzzing across the river, jerking hither-thither as it swarmed. "You were right, you know," he said, his voice empty. "We *had* been seen."

Ellen gasped, alarm bells going off in her head. She looked around, half-expecting a barrage of dragons to appear from the trees and scorch her.

"No, no, it's fine," Shard hurried to say. "She heard you talking, too — Firebug, Keeper's girlfriend. She knows you're good. I was going to introduce you to her, you know. I thought we could all be friends."

"Man, replacing me already? I feel so expendable." Ellen smiled half-heartedly. Maybe getting their usual banter going would make things better. Maybe if nothing else, she could help him forget for a while.

Shard looked at Ellen for the first time since they had sat down. Two empty eyes met hers, and as he spoke, his whole body seemed to quiver. "Oh, sweet Agito, Ellen, I'm doomed! All that, *all that,* and everyone takes Keeper's side *again*! What if they just think I'm a liar? I mean, why wouldn't they? Inferno ruled in favor of me, and Keeper just walked out of the council shelter a free dragon. And of course they did! They all think I'm just a waste of space!"

Ellen reached out a hand and placed it on Shard's side. Strangely enough, his scaly body felt warm. Dragons were supposed to be cold-blooded reptiles, so why would his body be warm? There was so much she didn't know. "You know, Shard ... it kinda seems like you're the one who thinks you're a waste of space."

Shard stared at Ellen wordlessly. An owl cooed in the distance. "Yeah. That too," he admitted at last, before they drifted back into silence. After a time, he sighed. "This is it, huh? End of the line."

"I mean, Firebug believes you, right?"

Without joy, Shard smiled. "Firebug believing me is good, but ... I'm not sure I can live in a tribe where almost everyone is okay with me being beaten like this. And if I did leave, where would I go? I need to eat, and I can only live off the land until winter. I mean, I guess I could hunt if I really had to, but I hate eating meat! I always think of the animal dying when I try."

"You're a vegetarian?" Her mouth hung open a little. A vegetarian dragon. Now that was a thought.

"Wait, there's a name for it?"

"Uh, yeah. Lots of humans choose to eat only fruits and veggies."

"Huh ... Well, there you have it. I'm a — what did you call it? A vegetarian. And I hate to say it, but I need to live here to eat through winter. I guess I could go live with another tribe, but then who knows if they'd accept me? My tribe accepted my mom when she came here, but I think that's just because she was really good at magic. I mean, I'm okay at it," he added at Ellen's cocked eyebrow, "but I'm nowhere near on my mom's level. And I've heard horror stories of dragons trying to go to a different tribe only for them to find that they're closer to the orichalcum deposits and then the human kills them and that's why the tribe accepted them in the first place, because they didn't wanna die out, and there's nothing I can do anymore and I can't take this!" Shard scrunched his eyes shut and covered his head with his paws as if they could block out the world.

At last, Ellen understood. The knot inside her felt tighter than ever before. She was scared for Shard, too. "This was your best chance for safety, wasn't it?"

Shard opened his eyes and nodded. He growled and struck the river, water splashing. "I'm so sick of being his clawing toy!"

Ellen laughed without humor. "I wish I could bring you back to the Safe Zone," she found herself saying.

"Heh, yeah right. A dragon in the human world. That'd go over well." Shard let out a mirthless chuckle of his own.

"Okay, but what if we disguised you, somehow?" It was impossible, but the thought was too tantalizing to let go. "Like, you magicked yourself to take human form and that somehow got you past the dome."

"You know ... That'd be nice, actually." He lifted himself off the ground, sitting on his haunches like a cat. An excited grin was slowly playing across his snout. "I could learn to do that writing thing, and maybe paint!"

"Hey, yeah! We have art lessons! You could study painting and go to school with me, at least until I graduate ..."

"And I could eat all sorts of vegetables without being pressured to eat meat ..."

"And you could go to art shows and learn more about painting ..."

"And I could make friends with other humans!"

"And you could have a nice, warm bed to sleep in at night with blankets!"

"I don't even know what that is, but I want it!"

Inspiration struck Ellen. "And you could live with me and my dad. We probably couldn't tell him you used to be a dragon, but maybe he could adopt you!" She gasped and looked Shard right in his excited eyes, feeling her own enthusiasm bubble up. "We could be brother and sister!"

"Yeah!" Something harmonious, even melodic emanated from Shard, a sound of sheer contentment and peace — he was laughing. It rose up in the air and surrounded the two of them like a warm embrace, and although Ellen did not join in, the horrible sensation in her stomach was melting away.

At least, until Shard stopped laughing and gave a heavy sigh. "It'll never happen, though. Even if I could transform myself, there's no way I could fool the dome into thinking I'm human. I'd still be a monster on the inside."

"Hey, you're not a monster, man." Frustration twinged beneath those gentle words. How could she make her friend see himself the way she did?

"Yes, I am. I'm a dragon." He said it with such finality that Ellen wanted to fight him on it all the more.

"That doesn't —"

"I'm literally teaching you magic that you're going to use to kill dragons. If you don't think we're monsters, then how in the name of Agito do you justify that to yourself?"

Ellen didn't quite have a response for that. Everything she might have said jumbled together, one big, tangled mess of reasons and nothings. Jess Flint and Lana flashed in her mind's eye, but she blinked them away. "Maybe I used to think dragons were all monsters, but you're not. I don't want to be part of the Guild anymore," she at last admitted, her voice low. "Not if it means hurting dragons like you. I want to do something important with my life, but … I'm starting to understand more and more that that's not the way! You're a good dragon. Maybe there are other good dragons, too. Maybe someone in the tribe can help you if you reach out! I mean, what, was your *mom* a monster? You loved her, didn't you?"

Shard's gaze hardened, but it was too late to take it back — too late to worry that he would wash himself of her. The sheer rush of her determination to get through to him kept her from backing down.

"She was different!" Shard retorted. "I mean, she wasn't violent, for one thing! She was always kind, and tried to find the best in dragons and she sang me lullabies and never hurt anyone and always looked for the solution that made everyone happy! And guess who killed her? My dad! Her mate!" Ellen gaped; had she ever heard that part before? But Shard wasn't done yet. "He came home one night and slit her throat with his claw while we all slept and then had the gall to play dumb the next day!

"She was the most amazing dragon in the world, and she taught me magic and she taught me how important it is to be good to others, and I just wish I could see her again, but I never will, because nothing ever goes right for me! I tried standing up for myself, and nothing changed! Nothing ever *will* change! I still have my stupid uncle to deal with and a beating waiting for me at home and I'm going to spend every day for the rest of my life knowing nothing means anything when everyone hates me and I just wish ... I just wish ..."

The world felt muted somehow as Shard stood there, on the verge of sobs, his body hunched over and trembling. Ellen wanted to say something, but she had no clue what. So instead, she waited for him to speak. And then, finally, he did:

"Sometimes, I wish I could just *die,* you know?"

He said it so casually. So nonchalantly. The way Lana might complain about getting a bad grade on a test.

"So that's it, then? You're just gonna off yourself, just like that? It's that easy for you?"

In a small, but dark voice, Shard said, "I don't really have a plan, so ... I dunno. Maybe."

"You don't mean that." It was a warning. She hoped that maybe, just maybe, he had not understood what he'd said.

For a transient instant, hurt twisted his face. "I didn't ask to hatch. If I could have had the choice, I would have never decided to be alive in the first place."

Ellen's mouth hung open, her hand balled up in a shaking fist. "I can't believe you. Don't you have any idea how much I'd miss you if you died!?"

Now, it was not hurt on Shard's face, but venomous loathing, primed to sting both Ellen and himself. "You'd forget all about me if I were gone! And I wouldn't blame you! *I'm not worth remembering!*"

Just like that, Ellen exploded. Rage and despair and loneliness billowed out her mouth like lava. "Really? Really!? I *just* told you two nights ago how my mother killed herself! Do you have any idea how hard it was for me to tell you all that? And now, you're telling me that *you* want to kill yourself, too?" Icy-hot pinpricks seared her face — it took her a moment, but she registered she was crying.

Shard flared his wings, his own tears streaming freely. "I don't know what else to do! I don't know how to deal with feeling so horribly so intensely all the damn time! I just want everything to stop! There's nothing here for me anymore"

Ellen stabbed the air with her finger. A guttural grunt scraped her throat. "What the hell, Shard?! I thought you were my friend!"

Silence. The space between them now seemed insurmountable, as wide, teary eyes stared into wide, teary eyes. Ellen had never seen him look so destroyed. She thought, for a moment, that maybe, just maybe there was something else for her to do.

"Ellen, I ..." Shard began, but he cut off midsentence. He looked defiantly away.

She sighed, shaking her head. "I should go, Shard. Good luck with whatever you do."

Gripping the ring that had started this all, it occurred to her she might never know where it came from. Perhaps it would never matter. She turned the ring thrice, and the Wildlands were gone. In their place was her room, dark and still and lifeless, devoid of wind or chirping crickets.

Something hard squeezed her throat. She wanted to punch the wall, or throw her books across the room, or pull out her hair — anything to get the anger out as her chest heaved up and down with furious breaths. The ring sat on her finger, mocking her, taunting her with what it had promised her.

May you bring peace and love to this world that needs it so. That sheaf of paper was still tucked away between books on her shelf. It had seemed cryptic at the time, but now, she wanted to laugh at its naivete. The world needed peace? The world needed love? What a load of crock. What the world needed was to stop dangling shiny things in front of her before yanking them away, and what she needed was to stop chasing after those gilded lies.

Ellen tore the ring off her finger and chucked it across the room. It hit the wall with a *clack*, and fell limply to the floor. A section had broken off, leaving the ring forever fractured. Numbly, it dawned on her she would never see Shard again.

She had left him behind.

INTERLUDE

THE BEGINNING OF THE END

I N THE CENTER OF THE UNIVERSE, a certain someone shook their head sadly. "I told you, sister. Even with all the power in the world inside them, they never change."

The woman in the black cloak said nothing, simply staring ahead impassively.

He didn't like that. "You're going to have to let me out eventually. You've spent these years playing your game, but I too, have a champion, and you and I both know he is stronger. Please, save yourself the heartache and just give in."

She turned around, and only now did she speak. Her lips were set in a thin line, her eyes hard like stone, her whole face steeled with determination. "It's not over."

"Of course it is! You made your play, and it failed! We just saw their bond shatter over something perfectly solvable. There's no coming back from this!" The prisoner glowered at his sister. He knew he couldn't intimidate her into freeing him, but she surely knew what folly this all was.

And yet, the woman in the black cloak shook her head sadly, as if *he* was the one who misunderstood. "Don't underestimate them. Love will triumph in the end."

His eyes widened, he sucked in a sharp breath and for the first time in eons, the god Agito screamed.

PART FOUR

SMASH THE WORLD'S SHELL

33

"ELLEN?" SHARD WHISPERED. He kept hoping that she would come back, longing for her to tell him, "changed my mind, sorry," or "Hah! Fooled you!" and for everything to go back to normal.

Only the moonlight answered him, shining indifferently above.

Shard collapsed to the ground with a *thump.* His belly collided with the dirt as a splitting headache seared his temples. The river wet his snout, approaching and receding unchangingly.

I hurt her really badly, didn't I? Now, there really was a single option left to him, one thing that would make the roaring emptiness inside him vanish. All he had to do was stick his head under, and wait for his air to run out. Simple as that.

Oh sweet Agito, but what if it hurt? What if his chest burned from holding his breath for so long and he came up gasping for air? What if he tried to kill himself and he failed and everyone found out and they mocked him for that, too? And what if Ellen really did come back, only to find him dead?

He tried to force himself to his paws, but a wave of vomit surged up from his stomach and into his mouth, chunky and rancid and vile. With great effort, he was able to lift himself enough to deposit his sick into the river. It washed away on the current.

"Shard?"

His heart skipped a beat — but no, that wasn't what Ellen sounded like. He twisted his head in the direction of the voice and found himself looking blankly at Firebug.

Firebug seemed to be waiting for him to say something. When her only answer was the trilling cicadas, she took the initiative. "I heard some yelling. Who were you fighting with? Was it ... you know?" She glanced from side to side, making sure the coast was clear. "Was it your human friend?"

"... I don't think we're friends anymore." It came out as a hoarse, nauseous croak.

"Oh ... okay? What do you — I mean, we're safe, right? She's not gonna come back with an army of other humans?" Anxiety burned on her face.

Shard thought about this. At last, he shook his head. "No, I don't think she is." Ellen had said she didn't want to hurt anyone with her magic — he believed her.

"Okay ..." Firebug sighed, clearly unsure if she should push. "Listen, I'm gonna talk to Keeper, okay? I don't know what the hell Inferno is thinking, but Keeper can't get away with — A-are you crying?"

He wiped his eyes with a foreleg. "S-sorry ..." Firebug wouldn't be able to do anything, but he appreciated the effort all the same. "You don't have to talk to him, though." *Not when I don't intend to stick around.*

"Yes, I do! You're not the only one who's hurt by this, okay?" Firebug snapped. A fierceness alien to Shard sparked about her. It took him a second through the sticky haze clouding his brain to realize she didn't mean Ellen's departure.

"... you don't actually love Keeper, do you?"

When Firebug finally responded, it was a single, heated grunt — years of frustration releasing all at once. "He used to be so *good.*"

"I'm sorry." Steady breaths kept Shard anchored, but barely. He couldn't find it in him to ask how Keeper could ever have been good.

"You look like crap," Firebug remarked, not without concern. "I guess you and her really did have a fi—"

"I think I'd just like to be alone," Shard cut in, his voice still soft. "Thanks for sticking up for me like this." He wanted to say more. Right then, he couldn't.

"... Oh. Okay," Firebug said after staring a long while. "We can go over my visions another time, I guess." She sounded jilted, but if she had more questions, she kept them to herself. Soon, she slipped away through the trees, rustling the curtain of greenery as she vanished.

Shard remained by the riverbank the rest of the night, barely sleeping as the swell of chirping insects filled his ears. When he did sleep, he dreamed of death. Slow deaths, drowning deaths, deaths by incinerating himself with his own fire, flying up into the sky and letting himself plummet to the ground ... And yet, no matter how hard he thought, he couldn't think of a way to end himself without pain.

34

WHEN HER ALARM went off at 6:00 AM, Ellen reached over and silenced her phone, and spent the next half-hour staring at the ceiling. Cars rumbled by on the street below, echoing in the dark, curtained room.

Despite herself, the ring caught her gaze, or what was left of the ring, anyway. It lay exactly where it had slammed into the hardwood floor, its pieces taunting her.

I'm never going to see him again, she reminded herself. Last night, that had been a relief. Now, it felt like gouging her tongue out.

By 6:30 AM, she had given up on falling back asleep. At 6:45, Franklin knocked on her door. "Ellen, are you awake? You're going to be late for school."

Ellen said nothing but threw off her covers. She could feel sorry for herself later. Without bothering to get dressed, she ambled towards the kitchen, wearing only her pajamas, her eyes half-lidded.

Her father stared at her as she approached, the edges of his mouth twitching like a rabbit. Ellen could tell he was struggling not to ask why she wasn't ready for school. Steam wafted off a cup of coffee. Hopefully he wasn't chugging the stuff to keep calm. It always just made him more anxious in the end; Ellen hated seeing him like that.

She plopped down in front of the table, frowning.

"I set aside a bowl for you," her father said, gesturing with his coffee hand a pot full of oatmeal on the stove. On a hook on the wall next to the oven rested her dad's pink apron, which smelled strongly of sweetener. *The pink apron. His favorite. He must be feeling extra shaken.*

As Ellen sat back down with her meal in front of her, Franklin asked, "Are you feeling well this morning?"

Ellen froze. Then, gently, deliberately, feeling her throat bulge as she set her spoon down. It *clinked* when against her plate.

There were many ways she could answer that question. Answers like, "I'm feeling fine." "Never been better." Or, "Everything is horrible." "People do nothing but hurt me." "I'm all alone."

"Sweetie?" Franklin asked, his voice cracking. Ellen braced herself for the deluge of well-meaning but inane questions, tension building in her chest as she prepared to go off at her father.

"I messed up." The sentence was out of her mouth before she knew what she was saying. A door had been irrevocably opened, and even as she tried to shove everything behind it again, it was too late. If she didn't let some of the hurt out now, she'd burst.

"Sweetie, what's —"

Ellen spoke again, choking on her words as a sob caught in her throat. "I messed up, Dad. I made Lana hate me." *I made Shard hate me, too,* supplied the susurrant void in her head.

"Honey, I'm sure that's not —"

"I thought, maybe I didn't need to join the Guild. I was thinking, maybe if I make friends, it won't hurt so badly, but I got into a fight with Lana and now she's gone, and it feels just like when Mom killed herself!" Her fist crashed into the table. The plates and silverware all gave a *clang* on impact.

"Oh, Ellen," Franklin said, his voice drowning in sympathy so syrupy-thick it made her want to choke. She hated feeling so *broken.* "I don't know what happened with Lana, but I am proud of you. I know how difficult other people are for you, and you *tried!* There will be other friends in your life."

Once, the prospect of more friends would have scared her, but now she didn't think she cared. That was the worst part, really. So much had happened yesterday, and she wasn't even sure she felt anything about it anymore beyond perhaps *defeated*. She certainly didn't feel hungry.

With a few giant gulps, she downed her glass of water and stood. "Thanks Dad. I'm going to get dressed and walk to school. See you tonight."

He saw her off with an uneasy smile.

The day was going to be sweltering, but for now a lukewarm morning air hung around Ellen as she walked to school. Before she knew it, she was standing in front of the school gates, as if she had simply appeared there instantaneously. Inside the courtyard, students milled about.

She blew a blonde strand of hair out of her eyes and strode through the gates, keeping her gaze fixed on the front doors. Nobody paid any attention to her as she walked forwards, all of them staring at their phones or chatting with their friends.

I'm just fine with that, she thought, right before the school doors opened and Lana came out. Her eyes were baggy as she hunched over, clutching her schoolbooks to her chest like a security blanket.

Everything seemed to stop as the world faded into silence. It was as if the space between her and Lana were a narrow passage and everything else just did not exist anymore. Lana's brown eyes caught Ellen's. Something played across them. Anger? Regret? Sorrow?

All three, Ellen decided as something like life flickered inside her chest. Maybe things with Lana could still be salvaged? Then Lana turned her nose up and walked away, and the hope fizzled out, leaving nothing behind.

35

F IREBUG SAT ALONE. Rain threatened to pour from the dark clouds up above as a harsh wind whistled through the trees. The other dragons seemed to be hurrying through their morning meals, wolfing down their grains and fruits before the storm broke. Even the chieftain seemed agitated, constantly shooting glares at Keeper, who sat in a corner of the Clearing, prodding his food with his claws but not eating it.

Firebug couldn't bring herself to eat either.

Everyone had seen Keeper attack the chieftain yesterday, but a few dirty looks aside, no one seemed to mind that the younger red dragon had gone unpunished. He'd been taken to the council shelter, and then he had just walked away, consequence-free. Firebug couldn't bear to think of what he'd do the next time she was alone with him. Would he reprimand her for not taking his side? Would he demand she never talk to another drake again?

And Shard himself claimed to believe her about her visions, but he was perhaps the most dangerous dragon in the tribe. He had been friends with a human after all. Perhaps he still was, and this yelling match they'd had was some sort of fabrication? But why go to the trouble of all that?

She wished she could talk to this Ellen character herself. What a thought — talking to a human! But clearly it was possible.

Firebug noticed she was tensing her foreleg, as if preparing to strike someone. Her gaze floated from Keeper's sulking form, then to Chieftain Inferno, who was talking with Noir, before finally landing on her own, black paws.

A vision flashed before her eyes. Flames, heat, smoldering corpses. A giant biped, two leathery wings, an impossible, bright golden light ... and the screams of all the dragons of her tribe.

The Clearing returned to Firebug's vision as ragged, hot breaths heaved her chest. She stood there a moment, letting her breathing even. Again, she had seen the future, and again, she was powerless to change it. If she were Noir, or Thorn, or even just male, Inferno would take her seriously. He would listen to her about the disaster, which she could feel nearing by the day.

Was she truly the only dragoness who cared about the way she was treated? Weren't there any other dragonesses in the tribe who were sick of being less than the drakes? Surely *someone* was sick of being belittled and relegated to raising dragonlings and making pots and baskets and being banned from hunting and herding and farming. Her mother seemed to practically flourish under these restrictions. Even Brightness, the oldest dragoness in the tribe, never talked back to a male dragon, even when he was being rude. Wasn't there anyone she could talk to about this besides Spearhead?

Just then, the first raindrops trickled from the sky, hitting the ground with a *plop, plop, plop,*

"All right, everyone," Inferno yelled. "If you're working in the fields today, now is the time to start. If you've been assigned another task, be sure to work on it in your shelter!"

Firebug sighed. Today, she was on healing hut duty with Brightness, responsible for preparing salves and poultices. She spread her wings, meaning to take to the air and fly to the healing before the storm got too intense.

But then her eyes landed on Keeper, who had stayed put. She swallowed deeply, for she knew what must be done.

Approaching him, she saw his eyes light up. It was like seeing the silly, stubborn, kind drake she had once cared for. Still, she knew he wasn't that dragonling anymore.

"Hey babe," Keeper said. He stood, and suddenly his muzzle was pressed against her neck as he affectionately nuzzled her. "I've missed you so much these past few days."

Her cheeks went cold. "Keeper, wait," she said as firmly as she could manage.

He pulled back and frowned, tilting his head. "What's up?"

In her mind, her mother was already berating her for letting her chance slip by her. *Make him want you, Firebug; it's the only way. Think of your dragonlings!* But Firebug didn't want to think of her dragonlings. She didn't *have* any dragonlings.

Summoning more strength than she had thought she could, she looked Keeper dead in the eyes and told him the truth. "You're not the sweet little drake I grew up with; you're violent and angry and entitled. You attack other dragons. I don't know what happened to you, but I want none of it. I don't exist to make you feel good about yourself."

Other dragons, male and female alike, looked on with interest, whispering among themselves. Emerald gaped speechlessly, mortified. *I'm sorry, Mother,* Firebug thought. *But it would never have worked.*

Then she brought her focus back to Keeper. Instead of hitting her, instead of looking even the smallest bit angry, there was an undeniable look of hurt on his face. "I get it," he said. Even his voice was breaking. "I know how it is."

Firebug could not tear her eyes off him as he flew away, holding in her breath, like he might come back at any moment. When she was finally sure he wasn't, she let it all out in one big rush: she had said no. She had said no to the dragon who she had spent the last six moons wrapped around as though she were a vine. Perhaps she should have felt bad that their friendship was well and truly over ...

But she just felt relieved.

36

S HARD LAY LISTLESSLY in his shelter, sprawled out along the ground. A new roof covered him in darkness, bought with meat he wouldn't have touched anyway. He hadn't the energy nor the inclination to light the torches; he barely even cared to work in the fields, much less focus on the pentagram spell. The crops would be behind schedule. The others would surely be angry, but even that couldn't lift this fog of lethargy. He knew he was supposed to go see Firebug, but he'd already put off their meeting for four days. He wasn't sure he could face her now.

Sleep came to him in fits and spurts lately. When the riot in his head became too much to bear, he'd open up his stash of paints and paintings and stare blankly at a canvas. Occasionally, his paws would move of their own accord, splattering crushed red berries onto a painting, and Shard would pretend it was his blood.

Sometimes, it really was his blood.

Harvesting it was easy enough. Cathartic, even. All he had to do was slice a claw along the back of one of his ankles, right where there weren't any scales, and blood would come seeping out, all the bile and anger along with it, a little reminder that he was finite. No one seemed to have noticed yet.

The roof opened all of a sudden, sending a pulse of fear shooting through him. Was Keeper back? He scrunched his eyes shut, hoping to pass for asleep.

Rhythmic flapping filled his ears as Keeper drifted down. "Damn, it's so freaking dark in here." There was the *whoosh* of flame breath and suddenly, brightness from beyond Shard's closed eyelids illuminated the shelter.

Scritch, scritch, scritch. Keeper lightly kneaded the dirt.

Well, I guess I'm not painting tonight. Somehow, the thought was amusing — as if that was his biggest problem — and Shard let out a snort.

His eyes flew open as his heart beat wildly, years of etched-in fear shooting through him. He'd just given himself away, what was Keeper going to do, would he hit him, or — or — or —

Keeper snorted derisively. "You're a real lucky bastard, you know that?" He sat there, yawning sleepily and curled up in a ball.

Shard stood. Each step renewed his aches and pains, but he cautiously backed away from his brother nonetheless. Just because Keeper wasn't attacking right away didn't mean he wouldn't.

"I'm not gonna hit you, you wuss."

Before Shard knew what he was doing, he barked a cold and humorless laugh. "Well, that's a first!"

"Oh, what the hell ever!" Smoke puffed out of Keeper's nostrils, but the next instant, his anger vanished. He looked tired — not like he hadn't slept, but like he had pushed himself too far. "*I* should have gotten the damn magic. Everything would have been perfect."

Shard blinked. That was a new one.

"If I had magic, I'd be unstoppable. Not even our mo — I mean, not even our unc —"

Keeper's jaw snapped shut, his throat bulging as he gagged. In the space between moments, the stink of jealousy and rot and somehow the color gold assaulted Shard's nostrils. Just for a moment, though. As quickly as it had come, the impossible scent was gone, and Keeper was shouting again. "Nobody would be able to hurt me, okay! That's what I'm trying to say!"

"What's that supposed to mean," Shard began to ask, but Keeper cut him off.

"Shut up! I don't need sympathy from you."

On any number of nights since past, Shard would have prostrated himself and begged for forgiveness. But now, he was through with that for good.

"Sweet freaking Agito, you're an ass! I hate you so much it makes me *sick*." Shard hocked a wad of saliva at the ground. Seething pants came and left him, heavy, hot, horrid. For the first time in days, he finally felt something more than nothing.

A dangerous look crossed Keeper's face as his own rage swelled, but Shard didn't care. Whatever Keeper threw at him, it didn't matter. He *wanted* to be hurt. He *wanted* to feel pain. He wanted Keeper to bite and claw and kill him, because he certainly hated Shard enough and then Shard would not have to deal with anything and just be *done.*

Yet, Keeper merely huffed one last time, and once more rested his head on his paws. Soon, he started to snore, as if he hadn't a care in the world. Shard scoffed, half in disgust, half in disappointment.

Keeper's words echoed in his mind, unbidden.

Nobody would be able to hurt me.

The torches were slowly starting to die, darkness once more encroaching upon the shelter, but Shard didn't want to sleep anymore. He opened the shelter roof, emerging into the night. Stars shone brightly alongside the waning moon. Shard let a bit of their magic flow into him, though they did not make him feel filled like they once might have.

Nobody would be able to hurt me.

Down below, everyone else rested in their shelters, leaving Shard alone with the seed of an inkling of a start of an idea. He didn't have the words for it yet, but he could feel its terribleness embrace him like a suffocating cocoon. Under the light of the moon, as the wind brushed over his scales and stung the slowly-healing cuts on his ankle, he knew somehow that he had learned something indescribably important about his brother.

Nobody would be able to hurt me.

And — this was truly the scary part — maybe about himself, too.

37

F IVE DAYS AFTER she destroyed the ring, Ellen walked in the door from school, and stopped. Her jaw fell open as she stared at the scene before her, seeing but not comprehending. Somehow, for some reason, sitting at her kitchen table was Jess Flint, calmly smirking as her father fumed red.

As the door clicked shut behind her the conversation braked to a halt. Franklin and Flint both turned to face her. Cinnamon air freshener, sweet-smelling but dissonantly dreamlike punctuated the scene.

Her father, clad in his favorite pink apron, let out a small squeak. Flint's grin grew infinitesimally — it didn't register until later, but he looked like a man who had won. In the back of her mind, Ellen wondered why there didn't seem to be any bodyguards nearby, unless the building was being watched from afar.

Ellen opened her mouth, but the hammering in her chest made everything come out wrong. "J-Jess Flick, I mean, Jint Fless, I, uh, uh, um, Jess —" Her face turned a brilliant shade of scarlet, her cheeks burning.

"How's Lana doing?" she blurted out, and immediately felt even stupider.

Franklin raised an eyebrow, and for a heartbeat, Flint frowned. That quickly flipped one-hundred-and-eighty degrees in the blink of an eye.

"Oh, she's fine," he said, an amused note in his voice. If Ellen wondered whether or not he knew about their fight, she forgot to be curious a moment later. "But let's not focus on her. I'm here about you."

"Me?" She pointed at herself, feeling out of place in her own home.

With a bright, inviting smile, Flint responded, "Why don't you sit down and join us, Ellen? I have some documents I think you should see." His eyes snapped towards a plain manila folder that had been sitting on the table, the seal unbroken.

"Now wait just a minute here," Franklin growled. "You can't just waltz in here and act like you own the place!"

But then, he and Ellen shared a look, and in that moment, something passed between them, though she wasn't sure what. Sinking back into his chair, he massaged his temples. "I'm sorry. I suppose you have a right to hear this, Ellen."

"Hear what?" She was about to pop from all the suspense. Not bothering to take off her shoes, she took a seat next to Flint, and oh Goddess Pandora, she was *inches* from Jess Flint himself.

"Ellen," Flint said without not even a trace of irony, "how would you like to join the Guild?"

Whatever reaction Flint had been expecting, Ellen was sure she couldn't give it. This had to be a prank. A joke. It didn't make any sense.

"I can't," she said, shaking her head. "I'm underage; my dad hasn't given me his permission." Did Flint's face darken for that split second? Ellen couldn't tell.

"No, he hasn't. But when we caught the man who assaulted you, we learned some ... rather interesting information about your magic ..." He trailed off, a knowing look in his eyes.

Oh no. Had they found out about Shard?

"He'd had a bodycam on him, did you know? Utterly disgusting, he was. Liked to watch videos of himself robbing young women. Yet, when we watched the video of you, we saw your magic — and what magic it is! You are what we call a High Arcane Potential Individual."

"A what? I've never —"

"Heard of it?" Flint chuckled. "You wouldn't have. It's a recent discovery, and highly classified at that." He reached for the manila folder again, passing it to Ellen. She ran her fingertips over it nigh-reverently, soaking it in with touch.

"You'll find information in there you can't find anywhere else. I trust you won't share it with anyone. But given your innate ability, it should suffice to say I want you to join the Guild. I'll have to evaluate your magic myself, of course, but if I like what I see, I'll want you as my personal student."

Ellen gawked. A few months ago, she would have leaped at the chance then and there. Her, a personal student of one of the greatest elementals alive? Beloved and revered by all in equal turns? Even now, the prospect tantalized.

"I have just one question." Franklin frowned guiltily. "You say Ellen has particularly strong magic, but she can't — she's been magically impaired since she was a kid."

Ellen wasn't even angry; that was a fair point. She'd improved her magic greatly, but only thanks to her training — without Shard, she'd still be the same girl who could barely magic up a paltry draft. She eyed Flint, trying very hard not to pay any mind to the suspicion growing inside her.

And yet, for the first time since he had arrived, Jess Flint actually looked annoyed. His lips pressed into a thin frown, his nose just barely wrinkling. After a single, brisk sigh, he responded. "Actually, it's believed that a misdiagnosis of magical impairment at a young age is quite common for HAPI individuals. Based on the limited data we have, it seems that the impairment symptoms clear up on their own as the person in question gets older."

He stood. Smiling wanly — perhaps threateningly, Ellen wasn't sure — at her father, he said, "Well, I really do need to go now. Orichalcum runs to organize, recruits to train, all that jazz. Oh, and for the record, Mr. Delacroix, as Commander, I have full authority to accept minors into the Guild, even without their parents' permission — especially HAPIs. I hope you'll keep that in mind."

He switched his gaze to Ellen; it was devoid of the contempt he'd shown her father. She gazed back, trying to measure what was a performance and what was not. "Guild work is difficult and dangerous, but highly rewarding. If you're willing to work for it, I know that we can do great things together. I'll be dropping by tomorrow for your answer."

And just like that, he waltzed out the door with a skip in his step, shutting it behind him with a muted *clack*. Ellen and Franklin sat there for what seemed like hours, dazed. The kitchen clock ticked on, heedless of the once-in-a-lifetime chance she'd been given.

Three months ago, this offer would have had her jumping up and down like a toddler. But three months ago, she hadn't known dragons were every bit as intelligent she was. She hadn't known that they felt and thought and laughed and loved.

Finally looking at her father next to her, his face ghostly pale, she knew she couldn't do this to him. He was so scared of everything, the last thing he needed was a daughter in a career of life-or-death danger.

But then, how could she ever be useful to others if not in the Guild? How could she protect people? Goddess knew she was horrible at making friends. Goddess knew she was worse at keeping them. She felt tired and alone and miserable, and a career in the Guild could easily be her ticket to something better.

I have a choice to make.

"I'll be in my room, Dad." Before Franklin could say a word, she sighed, stood, and shut herself in her room. Outside her open window, the setting sun slowly plunged the world under the dome into darkness. A truck rattled along the street, two men were having a loud lovers' quarrel, and a dog barked in the distance — a fitting soundtrack to this lonely suburbia.

Was it bad that she actually *missed* Shard? She wanted to hear him laugh and joke and to nudge him when his wry comments missed the mark. Ellen sighed, feeling something heavy and intangible. It was too late for regrets, for without the ring, she had no way to get to the Wildlands and back safely. Even if she joined the Guild, her trips out into the world would be as a soldier, not a student or friend. If she met Shard ever again, she'd have to kill him.

Assuming he hasn't killed himself already.

She couldn't ignore the way her stomach lurched.

38

F IREBUG PACED back and forth in the mist-covered Clearing
early the next morning. No one else was around, which was
fine — Inferno got there before anyone else, and she needed to
talk to him alone. Shard had proven to be utterly useless— he was
too busy moping in his shelter to help her.

The skin beneath her scales burned hot and itchy as visions
of chaos tried to pull her under. Whatever was coming was coming
soon. She ran through possibility after possibility, explanation
after explanation. Not a single one seemed good enough.

"I just have to talk to him," Firebug assured herself in too-shaky
tones. "I just have to try." Whatever happened from there was up to him.

Tromp, tromp, tromp. Pawsteps heralded Inferno's arrival, his
silhouette taking shape in the fog. Firebug's heart caught in her throat.

Moment of truth, she thought.

"Firebug?" Inferno called out. "Is that you? What are you doing
out here so early?"

C'mon, don't be nervous. "I was a little restless," she admitted.
Immediately, she regretted it. Anxiety belied weakness, and Inferno
hated nothing if not that.

Now that he was closer, though Firebug could see his head drooping and his half-lidded eyes. "Perhaps you should go back to sleep, then."

Something about him was off, but what? Had his visions showed him something? Inferno simply waited with an intense and inscrutable gaze.

"Remember what I told you about the other day?" she asked, paws tensing.

Inferno frowned and rolled his eyes. "Oh, Firebug, not this again. There is no monster coming. Hurry back to the shelter. There's still some time before you need to be up for the morning meal."

"But Inferno —"

His eyes blazed, anger finally breaking his dreary demeanor. "You know full well I would have seen such a thing in a vision. There is no giant of light coming. You are merely stressed from what's happening with Keeper."

"No, I'm not, actually," she retorted hotly, flaring her wings. Maybe a little aggression would finally do the trick. "I've been seeing this vision for moons now! Are you sure that maybe your Starsight isn't all that great?"

Immediately, Firebug knew she had poked a hornets' nest. Inferno flared his own wings out, growling deep and throaty: a warning if there ever was one. "Ridiculous! Are you honestly trying to tell me that not only do you somehow have Starsight, but it's stronger than mine? You are a dragoness. Instead of coming up with these ridiculous stories, you need to focus on your role here."

It was the same song and dance as always — *you're a dragoness. You have your part to play. Play it.* Firebug was sick of being told she was less.

"I do have Starsight! It's not strong, but I have it. And if your power is so great, why couldn't you prevent the humans from killing my father?"

Inferno roared, snapping his jaws animally. Firebug winced without meaning to. "Do not question me like that *ever* again," he snarled. "Now go find some way to make yourself useful, you ungrateful dragonling. I suggest you weave some baskets."

And then he spread his wings and took off, leaving Firebug on the ground, breathing hard and heavy as she collected herself. Finally, a sort of cool resolution settled inside her. He wanted her to

be useful, but he had such a limited idea of usefulness — and that was his problem. She'd save everyone her own way. She just had to —
Wait.

Firebug's jaw dropped as an idea hit her like a sack of rocks. Why hadn't she thought of it sooner? Even if Shard had completely flaked out on his promise to help her, he had still *believed* her about the giant, hadn't he? Maybe it wasn't because he was some open-minded gentleman: what if ... he was in on the plan to destroy them?

She paced back and forth, muttering to herself as she thought it through again and again. She didn't know why — perhaps he wanted revenge on his brother — but the more she thought about it, the more it seemed like a possibility, a surety. She really had been going about this all wrong, after all — she didn't need to get Inferno to tell everyone what to do. She didn't need a drake at all.

She just would have to tell them all herself. From there, their destiny was up to them to seize.

39

HALF AN HOUR before her alarm rang, Ellen was up and wearing her summer uniform, a white button-up shirt and a black skirt. She strode towards the kitchen, only to find her father sitting at the table with his laptop, the blue glow of the screen illuminating his face. She frowned. She'd gotten up this early specifically to avoid him.

"Can we talk, Ellen?" he asked as he looked up from the dataweb. His features were soft. Imploring. Scared. His usual self, then.

Franklin seemed to take her silence as a "yes," for he closed his laptop with a *click*. And yet, as she looked closer, for some reason, it was like she saw something in him that he had never shown before. Defeat? Understanding, maybe?

Ellen shook her head, pre-empting him. "I'm not —"

Franklin put up an open palm and took a quavering breath in, and then out. He was being vulnerable, she realized. He was scared, yes, but he wanted to talk about it with her — that was enough to make her stay.

"I've been so terrified to think of you out there, Ellen, risking your life, fighting monsters with sorcery and fire and boulders and torrents flying everywhere. I've said this before, but I ... I saw what happened on the Night of Flames. I've seen those *beasts* up close. If you got hurt, I'd ..." He took in one more deep breath just as a crease of worry started to streak across his forehead. "But I've also known for years that you're hurting. You're angry and lonely, and I kept urging you to reach out to other people, to forget your dreams of joining the Guild, without actually listening to you. If you think going out into the Wildlands will help you live your best life ... I think you should go for it."

Slowly, almost in spite of herself, Ellen sat down at the table across from her dad, as if pulled by a magnetic force.

"... Okay, wasn't expecting that. But I'm not ..." she trailed off, rubbing her fingers together anxiously. Images of herself in the Wildlands flashed through her mind, hauling sacks of orichalcum to a truck, fighting dragons with her magic. She thought of being useful, she thought of being needed, valuable.

"I'm not going to join the Guild."

Franklin frowned, scrunching up his nose in confusion. "What? Why?"

She scratched her cheek hesitantly. "It's just ... what's joining the Guild going to solve, Dad? Yeah, I'll be bringing home orichalcum, and that would be good, don't get me wrong. But would that really make me useful? Would it make me valuable? It's not like there aren't a thousand other elementals in the Safe Zone."

And to Ellen's surprise, the confusion vanished from Franklin's face. There was something knowing in his eyes, something warm. "Ellen, you bring so much joy to my world. You don't have to feel like you're protecting someone to belong in their life."

A chill slipped down her spine. The *tick, tick, tick* of the kitchen clock echoed deafeningly. Franklin reached out a hand and placed it on her. "Your mother's death wasn't your fault. I hope you know that."

Ellen shook her head, disbelieving. How could that be true?

"Take the day off from school," he said sagaciously. "Think about what you want. If you want to join the Guild, I'll support it. If you want to finish your diploma, I'll support it. No matter what happens, I will always love you."

A few long seconds later, she nodded.

Even with her reprieve from school, she went for a walk. Under the gray sky, Echo Woods was more or less empty. As she strolled around the neighborhood, images of Shard and Lana flashed across her eyes of their own accord, like stills from a movie. Try as she might, she could not force them away.

Passing by a community garden, its crops in summery multihued bloom, it struck her — this was the way to Shady Orchard. "What am I doing?" she asked herself. There was no possible way they'd want her there, not after she'd helped Lana lie to her mother — to the owner.

Unless ... Unless, perhaps, they did. Perhaps her years of service to the kids would count for something. She thought of the children's faces, their laughter pushing her onwards. Presently, she came upon the Shady Orchard building, and without hesitating, rapped on the door.

"Ellen?" Robert said when he opened it, frowning. "Don't you have school?"

"I uh. Free period," she hastily lied — not that she wanted to, but Robert didn't need to know everything. "I just wanted to talk to Ayesha, really quick."

"Uh, okay?" He looked like he wanted to argue, but led her back to the office anyway. They passed by the living room where she had spent so much time reading to the children here. It was empty now, for most of the children were in school, but still, Ellen thought of all the service she had given Shady Orchard. Surely it had to be worth something! She crossed her fingers ...

Finally, she knocked on the closed office door, two sharp notes piercing her ears.

"Come in!" Ayesha Pai's muffled voice came, the sound of a clacking keyboard audible beneath. Ellen inhaled, one last big breath before she faced the music.

The door creaked on its hinges, revealing Ayesha at her desk, absorbed in her laptop. It struck Ellen, in that calm before the storm, just how much she looked like Lana ... The cherubic face, the slender body, the sparkling, chocolate eyes ... As soon as she saw Ellen, her expression curdled.

"What are you doing here?" Ayesha's two narrowed eyes were piercing in their intensity.

"I came to help," Ellen said, truthfully. "I'm not going to school today."

"Not only did you *help* Lana lie to me, but she could have died because of you. I think you've done enough."

237

"What? I saved Lana! I'm sorry I lied to you, but Lana is alive because I helped her!"

"Really now. You helped my daughter?" Her tone became frostier by the syllable. She shut the laptop with a definitive *click,* and leaned forward, as if relishing the moment. Ellen gulped. "Ellen, I know you eavesdropped. You *knew* that I didn't want her seeing that horrible man or playing that reprehensible game. But you, in all your teenage wisdom, having known my daughter for less than half a year, thought you knew what was best for her, thought you could override me, her mother!"

"I just ..."

"You just wanted to make friends, I know." Ayesha let out a long, exhausted sigh. She seemed to, if not calm down, then cool off, rubbing her temples. "You need to leave. I appreciate everything you've done, but you're not welcome at Shady Orchard anymore."

"But the kids —"

"You should be in school. Go." Ayesha opened her laptop again, as if opening the book on a new chapter. Ellen waited, silently, desperately wracking her mind for something to say.

At last, she nodded meekly, and walked back out the way she came.

Half an hour later, she sat at the kitchen table, alone. Outside, rain fell in a torrential downpour, percussing down on the apartment building's roof. Thunder boomed and lightning flashed, illuminating the apartment for a split second at a time. Wind howled from the other side of the window.

Before her were the pieces of the ring, laying one next to the other on the table. With a deep breath, she grasped one piece in each hand and fitted them where they had split. They meshed perfectly. Would they bring her back to Shard? Ellen didn't know. She wasn't even sure Shard would want to see her again, or if she wanted to see him again, either.

You don't have to feel like you're protecting someone to belong in their life.

Your mother's death wasn't your fault.

The remnants of the ring dropped to the table as lightning clapped outside again. She massaged the bridge of her nose. Jess Flint wasn't coming until the afternoon. She needn't rush this.

Someone rapped on the door, two short, sharp bumps. Ellen gasped, suddenly alert. Could it be Jess Flint, here already? The knob turned, back and forth, jiggling loudly as the door remained unopened. Was someone trying to pick the lock? Taking in a deep breath, Ellen felt her chest tighten. She stood, inching slowly forward to look through the peephole.

And then a pale white hand passed through the closed door.

A scream rose in Ellen's throat but jammed. Time seemed to slow down as the hand continued to protrude from the wood, followed shortly by an arm, then a torso and legs and a head, all gliding through the door as if it weren't there at all.

Impossible. People couldn't slip through solid matter. And yet, somehow, a black-robed figure now stood in the entryway. Her face — the parts of Ellen's mind that could still work thought they were a she — was obscured by a hood.

She raised her hand, bringing it up towards her face.

Adrenaline pounded through Ellen's veins. Without thinking, she punched the air, sending a shimmering windblast rippling towards the cloaked lady. She held her hand up like a stop sign, unbothered. The blast dispersed with a whispering *whoosh.*

Ellen's jaw dropped. How the hell had she done that?

"Ellen, please," the woman said, her hand falling to her side. There was something familiar about that voice, something like a glass of warm milk in the dead of winter. "I'm sorry I had to scare you like that, but there's not much time."

Dizziness assailed her as the room began to wobble around her. She *did* know that voice — but it couldn't be. It *couldn't.* "You know my name?"

The woman sighed. "Perhaps this will hasten things." Ellen could only stare as the hood came down, not believing what her mind told her she saw: two eyes, each one bluer than the deepest lake, porcelain white skin, shoulder-length honey blonde hair that curled near the ears and a smile as soft as snow.

"No way ..."

A pained smile crossed Estelle Delacroix's lips. "I'm so happy to see you again, Ellen. But time runs short. Shard's life is in danger, and if you do not save him, all will be lost."

40

E ARLIER, SHARD'S EYES opened after a restless night. He had drifted in and out of wakefulness, never sleeping for more than an hour at a time. His side ached and his wing felt sore; he had definitely slept on it funny. A dusty cough scraped the roof of his mouth.

Across the shelter, Keeper was just stirring, groaning as he stretched out his paws in front of him and stuck his tail in the air. Standing, he stared at Shard with half-lidded eyes. Shard just looked away.

Keeper was only too happy to respond in kind. He opened the shelter roof with an enchanted panel in the wall of the shelter, and took to the cloudy sky. Once the staccato of his wingbeats dimmed, Shard shifted onto his stomach and moaned, head sagging to the ground. It was going to rain today; he could feel it in the heavy air. Working in the fields, pumping energy into crops that were going to get water anyway while he got drenched for hours and hours sounded unbearable.

As he lay, not even bothering to close the roof, the usual thoughts started to well up inside his head, flying around like a hundred buzzing flies. *What are you doing,* the thoughts taunted him. *They're going to beat you for this, and you'll deserve it. You're proving everything they've ever said about you by being a lazy wimp. You can't even face the day!*

He could even hear the scolding he'd get from Inferno. *Shard, you must do your part to help the tribe! You mustn't laze around like this!*

"Screw it," he muttered. Going out and facing everyone was just too overwhelming, consequences be damned. Closing the roof with his magic, he resigned himself to being a little late.

Almost on its own, his claw slid towards his wrist, slicing through the exposed skin, right where his scales stopped. There was a flash of pain. Blood seeped out the cut, red and sticky, but relief was instantaneous. He still wanted to die, but now he could go on for just a little longer.

He exhaled, shut his eyes and channeled a bit of magic into the gash he'd made, sewing it shut. It already was a bit sore from having used healing magic like this so many times, but better sore than bleeding.

How would his mother have reacted if she saw him hurting someone, even himself? He didn't want to know.

Thunder crashed above him. He had been right about the rain.

He wasn't sure how much time had passed before the roof opened again. Perhaps it had been just a few minutes, or perhaps it had been a few hours. Sleep had finally decided to grace him, but he felt no better rested. All he knew was that all of a sudden, heavy drops of rain were soaking him as Chieftain Inferno flew down into the shelter, his wings beating loud and clear. Scowling deeply, he glared at Shard with ice in his eyes.

For the space of a second, Shard's heart pounded. But then, his face fell, and his worry ebbed, replaced by exhaustion. What did it matter if Inferno had found him shirking work? If the trial proved anything, his uncle didn't actually punish dragons, and even if he did, what was the worst he could do? Hit him? Keeper did that all the time. Say he wasn't masculine enough? That would be nothing new.

"This is a problem," Inferno said curtly. "We're already behind schedule because of your lackluster spellcasting, and now you're two hours late? I expected better from you." He paused, waiting for Shard to say something, then closed his eyes, a deep breath as his posture sagged. "I had assumed you'd be happier now that your brother knows not to take his roughhousing too far."

Wait.

Shard perked up. "... What do you mean by that?" Something pulled at the back of his head, a feeling that something, somehow, was wrong about this, but he couldn't place what.

Inferno started to sigh again, but he froze mid-breath. Alarm spread across his features, his eyes widening by a magnitude. He paced through the shelter, sniffing as he went.

"What are you ..." Shard began, only to go silent when he saw that his uncle wasn't just pacing — he was following a scent trail. Inferno stopped. At his feet lay the patch of ground where Shard hid his paintings.

"Why is there a spell on this bit of earth? What's underneath the ground here?"

Shard's blood ran cold. He gasped, realizing that that was exactly the wrong reaction just a moment too late. A jet of green flame blew from Inferno's mouth. The second it hit the ground, rather than fizzle out from the rain, it spread, but not as fires normally do. This fire spread in a line, then turned, then turned twice more until it was a square outlining the entirety of Shard's hidey-hole.

I can't lose this, too.

Inferno tapped the dirt with his claws. It ruptured open, creaking like an earthquake as the rocks crumbled to dust.

Resting on his haunches, he reached two paws down into the pit and grasped a painting in each. The emerald flames did nothing as they touched his scales. He sat there, trembling, and Shard could tell he was shifting his gaze from one painting to the other. Then he chucked them at the wall. Both hit, one after another, colliding with a horrifying *crack.*

"Hey!"

Inferno ignored him, taking out two more canvases.

"Stop that!" Shard lunged, meaning to dive in and save his art, only for Inferno to shove his nephew aside. He skidded, scraping his side across the ground, though by now it was changing into squishy mud. He grunted painfully.

Inferno turned his head slowly, like he was fighting against a flow of molasses, until two golden slits glared at Shard. The whole shelter seemed to quake as he stomped a paw. "I gave you an order! First Keeper, then Firebug, now you? I swear on Agito, everyone thinks they can just do what they want today! Do you and your brother have ANY concept of what I try to do for you?"

"Uh, what?" Shard staggered to his paws and scoffed. If he focused, he could ignore his throbbing ribs.

"If it weren't for me, you very well would be dead! Your brother wanted to kill you after the trial; I could see it all over his face!"

"And you just let him *walk away!?*"

Inferno flinched, the anger on his face dissipating ever so briefly before returning in full force. "I'll have you know I gave him a stern talking —"

"Oh, yeah, sure, right. A stern talking-to, just like you did the first time I came to you about his 'roughhousing!' Face it, the only reason I'm not dead is Keeper's waiting for the right moment to kill me! And you're just standing around, acting like everything's sunshine and rainbows!" Shard spat for emphasis. Mist had started to swirl into the shelter.

Frustration seemed to tangibly seep from Inferno's very body as he growled. "I promise you that your life is not in danger, not anymore!"

"Because you talked to him, I know. I mean, maybe I should just go find him right now, ask him to finish the job! He'd be *glad* to do it. And you know what? The worst part is that I think he's right to want me dead!" At long last, everything inside him spilled out. His eyes shut tight, his head angled towards the ground, he shouted over the beating downpour for all the world to hear: "I'm worthless! Completely, utterly worthless! I'll never be strong enough for anything or anyone! No matter what I do, it's never good enough!"

A new wetness stained Shard's cheek. It wasn't the rain. Between belabored breaths, he opened his eyes and glared defiantly at his uncle.

Yet, the chieftain said nothing, simply glaring back at Shard as heavy breaths came and left his snout, his back arching and falling as he seethed. Lightning flashed, illuminating Inferno's furious features. Behind Inferno, the rain soaked Shard's paintings, the colors bleeding across the canvas, hours upon hours of hard work pooling at the bottom of the hole in a colorful slush.

All of a sudden, it was as if someone had shone a light on Inferno's face. "Hmm … yes …" His lips curled upwards ever so slowly. It was as if the pieces of a puzzle had clicked into place. "Perhaps … perhaps you're onto something, Shard! But first, let's get out of the rain, shall we? It's awfully wet in here."

Shard nodded, suddenly very tired again. He wasn't sure if he was angry that Inferno had agreed so openly that Shard would never be good enough, or relieved to hear it said outright. Waving his paw — the good one, not the one he'd been cutting — he closed the shelter roof.

"Good, good." Inferno nodded approvingly. "Now, as for my idea ..." For some reason, he was talking much faster, almost as if he were rushing to say his piece. "What if you didn't have to try to be good? What if you had someone to just *tell* you, hm? Think about it! You'd never have to worry about doing something wrong! You would be as Agito intended for you to be!"

"How would that even work?" Shard sighed wearily. "I can't just —"

"Oh, but you can! All you have to do is agree to let me do just a *little* bit of magic on you."

"What, like a binding curse?" He scoffed. There was no way, no way at all that anyone would ever suggest that, not even someone like Inferno.

His jaw dropped when he saw what the chieftain did next — he grimaced. He gestured tentatively. "Well, 'curse' is such a strong word ... I prefer to think of it as more of a binding *enhancement*, don't you?"

The weight of that sentence hit Shard like a boulder. What Inferno was suggesting ... it was unthinkable. Evil, even. A binding curse was a horrible, taboo bit of magic that once cast would bind its subject to the whims of the caster. Anything the caster commanded, the target would have to do, with absolutely no ability to refuse; their body would simply move on its own. The only upside to this curse was that the target always had to agree to the curse beforehand; it could not be inflicted without consent.

"No, no I don't!" For the first time that day, Shard's exhaustion was replaced with something else: horror. "It's not an enhancement at all, cursing someone like that! You could take away their free will, you can strip them of everything that makes them who they are!"

"Well, yes, but ... wouldn't that be good for you?" His face lit up again. Inspiration had struck once more. "It's no great mystery that you hate yourself to pieces, my dear Shard. Why wouldn't you want to be someone you might like?"

A tinny whine rang in Shard's ears. As much as he hated to admit it, that actually struck him as a pleasant prospect. Liking himself ... what would that be like?

Inferno ventured a step forward, encouraged by Shard's hesitation. "Yes, I can see you like that idea, don't you? And just think: the others might like you too, once I've changed you! Once you no longer are servile and bland, they'll flock to you! You'll have friends for the first time in your whole life, my dear nephew!" He grinned, his ever-sharp fangs on full display.

Shard, though, was thinking just about having friends. He didn't like most of the dragons in his tribe, but had he ever really taken the time to get to know them? And even if they were still terrible, he could become someone who would like them. This could be his chance to finally do everything right!

He shook his head. "No. No ... I can't," Shard repeated, but with less disgust than before. "You can't just ... *choose* who someone else is."

Inferno took another step forward, then another and another. Now, he was mere inches away, and they stared into each other's eyes. It suddenly felt claustrophobic in the shelter, as if Shard had nowhere to run.

"Maybe ... you'll even be able to win the heart of a dragoness! That would be wonderful, no?"

He wanted to protest, but his mouth felt like it was sealed shut. His wings felt heavy as a bag full of grains at harvest.

"Think, Shard," Inferno whispered, his voice brushing seductively against Shard's ears. "You'd never have to be lonely again. You'd never have to be hurt again!"

I want to say yes, Shard realized. If he did, he'd never have to worry again. He'd never have to hate himself again. He'd never feel lonely again. And deep down, wasn't that what he had always wanted — to be accepted? His heart thumping like a rabbit's foot, Shard took in a deep breath.

"I can't."

Inferno pulled away, tilting his head. "But why ever not?" he asked, sounding more confused than anything else.

"Because ..." Shard waited for an explanation to come. Why ever not, indeed? He couldn't think of an answer for the life of him. And then, the words started to form in his mind and on his tongue.

"Because ..." he began slowly. "Because I've had a friend before. It ... it wasn't for very long ... And it wasn't — it wasn't everything I wanted it to be. It hurt sometimes. But it was ... good. It was what I needed." As he fumbled to pull the half-formed ideas from his head out into the world, everything started to become clearer to him. He stood taller, spoke louder. "I loved her — I still do. I wouldn't trade my time with her for the world. And I don't know why, but she liked me too, just the way I am. Even if she's not with me anymore, I think she'd be really sad if I were gone."

Shard breathed in one last time, plowing through the fast-darkening look on Inferno's muzzle. He had to say this, for even if he was only just coming to understand this now, every word contained a kernel of truth he could learn to believe.

"So, I won't. I'll be myself, and no one else. I can't let you or anyone else take that away from me."

Contempt burned in Inferno's eyes. Hateful. Angry. "Of course," he spat. "Stardust. Your *mother*. How could I forget that toxic stain on my life?"

"Excuse me!?" Shard wasn't sure if he was angry or confused — he hadn't been talking about his mother at all.

"I knew she was trouble from the day she showed up completely out of nowhere, but my idiot brother was smitten from the word 'go!' I allowed Stardust to stay in the village for Blizzard's sake, but she insisted on subverting me every opportunity she got!" Something was changing in Inferno, something dark and primal bubbling to his surface. He began to pace again "Always trying to make suggestions to me, always trying to tell me how to do my job! Imagine that — a dragoness, an outsider at that, trying to tell me how to take care of *my* dragons!"

Finally, he came to a halt, glaring at Shard. "Stardust *died for a reason!* If you think her loving you is proof that you're the best version of yourself, you're an imbecile!"

"No! My mom was —"

"An imbecile, as well!" Inferno cut in, bellowing five times louder. He spat again — *ptooey!* A great gob of saliva landed on the still-muddy floor. "You're not strong! You're a weakling, and a coward! *I* can make you good! *Only* I can make you good! But if you want to ignore my sage counsel — if you want to just go on hating yourself, then it makes no difference to me! Just know that it was *me* — my magic, my strength and my love for you — that's kept you safe!" He turned back to face Shard's paintings. "As for these wretched things ..." He opened his jaw, and summoned a giant stream of flame. The paintings burst alight, *popping* as they burned.

Shard knew he had no time to waste. He rushed forward, only for Inferno to crash into his side, knocking him against the wall. Pain burst in his wings and behind his eyes. He struggled to get to his paws, but found he couldn't, collapsing again with a *thud.*

Inferno waved his paw and the roof started to creak open. Rain poured in again, drenching Shard. "I expect to see you in the fields tomorrow. Reconsider my offer, too, and this time … come to the decision that will make you happiest." He spread his wings.

Something tugged at Shard's mind. Something Inferno had just said, but what? Shard hurried through every possibility, for he knew he had to piece this together then and there — or he would never do it at all.

"What …" he choked out with a cough. 'What' indeed? Inferno hadn't said anything out of the ordinary, had he? Why did Shard think something was wrong here? Everything just hurt so much, inside and out; it was all so painful. And then it hit him, right as the roof finished opening.

"What did you do to Keeper?"

Inferno froze. But only for a moment. An instant later, his shock was replaced by a neutral expression. "I don't know what you mean." And yet he stayed — almost like he wanted to hear what Shard was going to say next.

Shard struggled to his paws, successfully this time, even as he almost slipped on the mud. Everything had clicked into place, but it was not only anger that this realization brought forth, but revulsion. He met his uncle's glare, his own eyes narrowed accusingly as the rain percussed in his ears like a drum. "You got Keeper to agree to a binding curse of his own, didn't you? As punishment for trying to kill me. That's why you're so sure I'm safe — he is literally unable to lay a claw on me."

Inferno didn't reply, but the way he glared told the whole story.

"How many other dragons have you cursed?" Shard asked, the question just now occurring to him. He raised his voice to be heard over the storm. "How many?"

Even if he hated everyone in this rotten village … Even if they detested and scorned him right back … Even though he wanted to just be done with the world and sleep forever … He knew what it was like to feel trapped. If he could help the others break free of their prisons, then he would do just that before he killed himself.

It was what his mother would have wanted, and moreover, it was the right thing to do.

Lightning flashed. Thunder cracked like a whip.

"Oh, Shard," Inferno said sinisterly. "I haven't cursed anyone here, save your fool brother. But you don't believe me, do you? I can see it in your eyes. I certainly can't have you telling everyone about my little secret." He lifted a glowing paw, claws bared, golden, arcane lightning crackling across it, and his horns glowed brightly. "This is your last chance: agree to the binding curse, or I'll wring consent from your bloodied flesh."

Shard swallowed, but he had already chosen his path. Ellen liked him the way he was. His mother had liked him the way he was. Even if he'd never see either of them again — even if he wanted to die just to be rid of himself — he would fight to honor what they had wanted for him. True, his mother had taught him magic was never to be used to hurt. So, he wouldn't kill Inferno — not that he was even sure he could — but he would defend himself just long enough to free everyone from their curses.

A deranged chuckle reverberated in Shard's ears as Inferno focused his manic-tinted eyes. "Get ready to hurt," he said, and breathed white-hot fire all over Shard.

41

ELLEN GAWKED, her mouth hanging open. "You're *alive!?*"

"In a manner of speaking," she answered with a cryptic nod.

Knees wobbling beneath her, the air seemed to rush from Ellen's chest. "H-how!?" she demanded, compelling herself to stay standing as the room spun. "I saw your corpse!"

"Ellen, please, there's not much time!" Estelle reached out a hand towards her daughter, but Ellen swatted it away. "You must —"

"I'm going insane," Ellen decided, grasping her temples with a panicked groan. She started to pace, back and forth, eyes fixated on her feet. "That's what this is; I've gone off the deep end."

Estelle's shoulders sagged. "No, you're not insane. If you need the truth, then I shall give it to you. Just remember, it really is the truth, no matter how fantastical or farfetched it may seem." She paused, sighing one more time. Ellen quirked an eyebrow, but came to a halt, saying nothing. How much more fantastical could things get than her dead mother coming back to life?

"I am the Goddess Pandora, the creator of humanity. I gave you the ring that brought you to Shard. I wanted to prove to my brother, Agito, the creator of dragonkind, that humans and dragons could be friends, so as to deter his wrath — you'll have read about that in the book from the Hadkirk compendium. We made a bet, him and I — we each would choose champions. I would choose both a human and a dragon, he would choose a dragon, and we would pit them against each other. Whomever picked the winning champion, would win the bet.

"The body you saw hanging all those years ago was a mortal shell, a mere vessel for my soul. When I learned your magic was not as strong as I had hoped, I knew I had to start again, but I didn't want you or Franklin to wonder where I'd gone. So, I destroyed the shell, my divine spirit completely unharmed. That is how I survived death."

Ellen stared for what felt like a very long time. Her mother stared back, her expression brazenly hopeful.

Then, she took in a deep breath. "Okay, yeah, no," Ellen said, crossing her arms. "That *is* too ridiculous for me to believe. Like, for one thing, that doesn't explain how you know about Shard. For another, if you're the Goddess, can't you just kill Agito yourself? Oh, and third, this would all make me a demigod! That's not even possible. I'm just a girl like any other."

Pandora hummed in affirmation. "Yes, you are human through and through, for so was my body when I bore you. However, you have a spark of extra power in you that lets you go beyond what a normal person can do — the ability to use draconic sense-expansion, for example. And even though I'm the Goddess, I'm not powerful enough to defeat my brother. We are equal in our abilities. As for Shard ..." She hesitated. "That is something you will discover for yourself. For now, let it be enough that I enchanted the ring to bring you to him and to give you the power to understand dragons. Without it, their words would be as animal growls to you."

Estelle waited. "That is not everything though, is it? You have another reason for not wanting to believe me. I can see it on your face. I know what it is, and I am truly, deeply sorry. I did what I had to do, wrong though it might have been. I'm sorry it caused you such pain."

Ellen's heart leaped into her throat. Indeed, a fourth reason remained unsaid, teasing her lips as fear that it might be true held her back. Cradling her forehead in her palm, she meant to sigh, but instead there came a sniffle.

"I don't believe you that you're Pandora," she said truthfully. "But you're clearly alive. I don't know how ... but you are." She looked her mother dead in the eyes, her gaze narrowed and accusatory. "Which means then that you didn't kill yourself. You chose to leave me because you couldn't be bothered to stay when I didn't have the magic you wanted me to." *Because,* Ellen finished in her mind, *I really, truly wasn't a good enough daughter.*

Estelle averted her eyes. Shame danced across her features. Outside, lightning flashed. Rain continued to fall in torrents, pounding on the roof rhythmically. "That's true."

The words struck Ellen like a bullet to the chest. And yet, she couldn't even make herself cry, not even as tears tugged at her eyes. "So I'm really not good enough for you. Me and Dad ... we weren't good enough for you to stay! Did we ever mean anything to you?" Ellen was on the verge of shouting now. "Were we just pieces on the board in your game?"

The becloaked woman shook her head. "I was wrong, Ellen. I should have waited to move on. I — I should have stayed until you were older." She choked the words out, and Ellen got the impression she had practiced them many times. "You and your father both mean so very much to me. You are family to me, no matter what it may seem. I understand the human heart well, but not completely. I did not realize how my abandonment would wound you both."

"I really wish you had," Ellen said, and now, she did start crying, tears silently dripping down her cheeks. She leaned against the wall, unsure what else to say.

Estelle strode over, placing a comforting hand on her daughter's shoulder. Ellen continued to sniffle, cherishing the sight of her mother who should be dead. It all seemed so unreal, and yet, it was anything but. Estelle — her mother — was alive and well and had lied.

"I am sorry, Ellen," Estelle said again, her voice small. "But Shard is going to die without you. And it won't be from suicide. His uncle is going to kill him."

Ellen's breath caught. She knew all too well how likely that was.

Removing her hand, Estelle flipped her open palm over to reveal a small silver ring, identical to the old one. "Use this. It won't matter if there's someone with him."

After a moment's hesitation, Ellen slid the ring from her mother's grasp. Fingering it delicately, it glinted, as if it were a holy object. But then, she supposed it was.

"I'll save him," she said. "Just this once."

253

Hands grabbed Ellen on each cheek as two green eyes locked with two blue ones. The ring clattered to the floor, rolling across the boards. For the first time in a long time, Ellen knew she had something in common with her mother as the woman's eyes went blurry with tears.

"What do you mean 'just this once!?'" Estelle pleaded. "I know you're in pain! I know you want to shut yourself away and smother everything in you that wants to reach out to other people! But what you share with Shard is a bond that you both need! I can't force you to embrace others, but Inferno's power is like nothing you have ever faced! Unless you are willing to let Shard in fully and without reservation, you both will die!"

Ellen stared at her mother uncomprehendingly. What did her bond with Shard have to do with power? In truth, she had an inkling. She thought back to the note, the one that had come with the ring. It had said to bring love to the world — somehow, this was about her and Shard's ability to love.

Estelle walked over and plucked the ring from the floor. She held it out one more time, her pleading gaze saying more than any words could.

And so, Ellen knew she had a decision to make there and then, one that could not be unmade. Her heartbeat pounded in her ears. Her throat bulged.

Shard's life was in danger.

She was scared.

Her friend could die.

What do I want from my life? Ellen asked herself. Once upon a time, it had been to join the Guild. Now …

Her lips quivered for the most infinitesimal of moments. Then, she narrowed her eyes, set her lips in a thin line, and took control of her destiny.

42

SHARD BURNED. White fire scorched his body as pain exploded beneath his scales. He was going to die; he was sure of it. An unending, guttural shriek was coming from somewhere. It sounded like his, but he couldn't tell.

The flames stopped.

"Are you ready to submit, Shard?" Inferno's voice was silky smooth, oily. Confident that he would get his way.

And that confidence burned Shard even more than the flames. Even as he heaved and wheezed, he teetered to his paws, healing himself with his reserve magic as quickly as he could manage. "I'm not done yet ..."

Inferno clucked disapprovingly, as if Shard were a naughty dragonling that had stepped just a little out of line. He opened his mouth. Sparks popped as he prepared to unleash another barrage.

He isn't even using his sorcery yet, Shard realized, just as more flames rushed at him. He rolled to the side, doing his best to ignore the wave of pain that shot up his leg. Inferno shrugged, unperturbed. His horns glowed gold as he readied a spell. A high-pitched whine sounded in Shard's ears, growing louder quickly.

He braced himself, hoping he could dodge whatever Inferno threw at him. He knew, somehow, that he couldn't, but he would try. *I have to get out of here,* he thought. He swiped the air with his paw, sending a magical signal to the roof. It rumbled open slowly — too slowly.

He wasn't going to make it out in time.

A giant pillar of stone jutted from the ground and slammed Inferno square in the jaw. He staggered, wobbling to the side.

Shard stared, bug-eyed, trying to process what had just happened. And then he saw her. Shoulder-length blonde hair. Two bright green eyes, reddened around the edges. Her unmistakable fruity scent.

"Get away from my friend!" Ellen shouted. Before Inferno could regain his bearings, she punched the air. With a whistling rush and then a deafening *crack* Inferno crashed through the shelter, carving out a hole in the wall.

Shard couldn't believe his eyes. "Ellen!" he cried out, bounding up to her. He wasn't sure if he wanted to yell at her or cry for joy. "I thought you were never coming back!"

"That was the original idea, yeah," she said, dropping her fighting stance. "I'm sorry I was such a jerk."

Shard, almost despite himself, laughed joyfully, tears pooling in his eyes. "I'm just glad you aren't gone forever."

"Hey, what's going on!?" someone called out in the distance. The sound of approaching pawsteps and loudening wingbeats sent a jolt of panic through Shard. If they found his friend, they would kill her.

"You have to get out of here, Ellen!" he barked, cringing at how angry he sounded. But he could deal with that later: her safety was most important right now.

"I can't. I have to make sure you're safe." With a focusing breath, she turned back around and brought her fists to her face, readying for battle.

Panic continued to race through Shard, his body starting to tremble. He would not let them hurt Ellen, not for his sake. She was too important to him — she was air itself, filling his lungs with breath. Excuses, insults, things he could say to drive her away, anything at all, flashed through his mind.

Inferno groaned, staggering to his paws. When his gaze found Ellen, more malice, more contempt, and more hate than Shard had ever seen from the chieftain clouded his face. For a split second, he glanced at Shard, as if to say he would deal with his nephew later. Then, he turned his full attention to Ellen. "I don't know how you're here, human, but you will die today! Your kind doesn't deserve to live!" He opened his muzzle wide, more white-hot flame spewing forth from it.

Shard sprang into action before he had time to think. It was as if his muscles had made the decision before his head had time to. He dived into Inferno's breath, blocking the flames from ever reaching Ellen as they engulfed him.

"RUN!" was all he had time to yell before he couldn't think anymore. Pain seared him once more, like a thousand bolts of lightning striking him all at the same time. His shriek spilled out of him, unbridled and without restraint. The moment seemed to drag on into eternity.

And then it stopped as a sickening *crunch* resounded. Shard blinked, bleary-eyed and woozy. Forcing himself to stand, he glimpsed Inferno reeling from a chunk of earth to the jaw. He hollered, flaring his wings as electricity sparked around his horns.

Ellen ducked out from behind Shard, and hurled more earth at Inferno with one punch after another. "I'm not leaving without you!" she declared, only for her missiles to bounce off harmlessly, landing on the ground and crumbling. A translucent shell now surrounded Inferno. Shard guessed that it was a shield. For her part, Ellen swore viciously.

Inferno's eyes narrowed into ominous slits. A throaty growl rumbled in him, escalating into a furious roar. "What manner of trickery is this? How is this human *speaking?*"

Shard's chest felt like it was about to cave in. But there was no point in denying it, and even if there had been, he thought, it wouldn't save her, only him. "I don't know how she can speak. But she's my best friend."

Inferno shook his head disbelievingly — as if he could not understand. By now, other dragons were arriving, visible through the destroyed wall and the open roof. Shard saw Emerald, Bog, Gnarl, Brightness, Noir, the twin dragonlings Biter and Cleave, and many others. They all stared on in confusion and fear, even as rain poured in, sharing bewildered looks, as if they too couldn't quite believe what they were hearing.

"Revolting," Inferno snarled, finally seeming to comprehend. "They steal your orichalcum, slay your kin — and you befriend one of them? I don't care how it can speak — you will both die here!"

Shaking his head, Shard forced more stored moonlight to heal him. Now, he could see his brother among the crowd. Would he fight alongside Inferno? Keeper's expression was inscrutable.

But no. Looking closer, Shard could see just a smidgen of hope on his older twin's face. He opened his mouth to rebut his uncle, but found he couldn't quite find the words.

Inferno took this as license to speak. He regarded all the dragons gathered, and his voice boomed over the thunder. "Shard has betrayed us! He has given into weakness and aligned himself with evil!"

Murmurs rippled through the crowd. Even though there was a human right in front of them, it seemed they were all too shocked to attack her. But that wouldn't last for long. Shard had to say something now, or he would have no choice but to fight.

Gathering whatever strength he could find, he cleared his throat loudly. "Wait please!" But no one listened. He tried again, begging them to stop, but Inferno boomed louder.

"We must expunge both Shard and the human! For Agito!"

This seemed to be the cue everyone was waiting for. Hatred ignited in their voices as they whipped themselves into a cacophonous frenzy. There were no words now, only a buzzing, angry dissonance. Shard reflexively took a step backwards. He spread his wing out, trying to tuck Ellen behind it, as if doing so could shield her from nearly half a tribe of vicious dragons.

Teeth grit against teeth as something akin to fire lit in Shard's chest. He opened his mouth, and shouted loud enough to pierce the heavens. "I said WAIT!"

Some of the dragons grinded to a halt looking very confused. Shard, yelling? That couldn't be right! Or so their faces seemed to say.

The rest of the mob, however, was far less placated. Their faces were still contorted with malevolence and their fangs were all bared. Were they under Inferno's curse, too?

Someone swiped at him, her claws shining wet in the rain. Her name was Petal, a dragoness Shard had seen many times at meals. His stomach capsizing, Shard dodged to the side, Petal's claws slicing through air and raindrops, though only just. A blast of wind rippled out from Ellen's fist, knocking the pink dragoness away. Despite the situation, pride swelled in Shard for having helped her develop her magic so much. But that only lasted for a moment. Even the dragons who had seemed cowed were starting to look bloodthirsty again.

"Everyone, please —" Shard began, determined to resolve this peacefully.

"Don't listen to him, my brethren!" Inferno's horns sparked once more as he prepared to strike. "He is tainted by human scum! He is no longer one of us!"

Something snapped in Shard just then. It had no tangible form, but he heard the loud *crack* all the same. *No longer one of us.* What a joke! He hadn't ever fit in. And moreover ... maybe he didn't have to.

He wanted to paint. He wanted to embrace his feelings and be weak every now and again. He wanted to not fight and not eat meat and not be an object of derision. That was who he was, and he had been denied his very self for far too long. In that moment, his mother's words rang in his mind. Not the ideals he had lived his life by, but rather exactly what she had told him:

Use your magic to protect, not to destroy.

Like the sun rising on a new day, something changed in Shard. What he wanted might just be worth protecting. He still would rather die than fight for himself, but if he did that, Ellen would be killed too. Agito knew she was too precious to let die.

Without thinking, he unleashed his magic. A giant wave of blue light burst out of him, carrying with it a single word magically amplified to earthshaking volume. Raindrops scattered every which way; such was the force of Shard's first and final command to his tribe:

"STOP!"

Everyone stared. Even Ellen was looking at him, pride tugging her lips upwards. Even Inferno was flabbergasted, mouth agape.

Breath came to Shard in ragged pants. Partially because he had winded himself, but mostly, he hadn't thought this would work. "I am not your enemy! *Ellen* isn't your enemy!" He jabbed the air, gesturing at her with a wing for emphasis. "Humans are the same as us — we don't have to hurt each other like this!"

"Yeah, right!" called out a voice brimming with scorn. "Humans killed my —"

"It's true!" There was a note of surprise in Ellen's voice, for she was only just beginning to understand what she was saying. "I don't want to fight — or kill — anyone. Not humans, not dragons!"

At that, the other dragons stared, twittering amongst themselves. "Did that human just talk?" "What's going on?" "This is a trick!"

"It's not a trick!" Shard shouted. "Ellen is intelligent, the same as you or me. When we met four moons ago, I was lost. I'm *still* lost. I still think about dying nearly all the time. I had no parents, a brother who beat me, and an uncle who thought that was how it was meant to be — is it any freaking wonder that I became friends with a human? She's good to me! When we're together, I feel like she actually cares about me as much as I do about her! I don't have that from anyone else here!" Hot tears streamed down his face as a soft, fleshy hand brushed against his scaly side — Ellen's.

"Shard is a good person. And ... he's helped me realize that maybe I'm a good person, too." Resolution lifted Ellen's voice into the air with a sureness Shard had never heard from her before.

Gasps ricocheted through the crowd once more. Many faces still stared suspiciously, but many more were slack-jawed, staring without understanding. *Could this be real?* they seemed to be thinking. *Is this truly happening?*

"Please," Shard implored, galvanized. There was yet more to tell them — Inferno's curse, for one — but for now, he just had to build this bridge. "We can talk with Ellen. So let's just do that — let's get to know each other."

Nobody spoke. Even the pitter-pattering rain seemed to fall away, leaving only the moment behind. Shard dared to hope this would go right.

"Stop!"

Thunder rumbled again, but this time, it was not from the storm. Only one dragon had spoken, but her roar cut into Shard and Ellen's impassioned plea. She hovered above the nearly destroyed shelter, her wings beating rhythmically. Two steely purple eyes fixated on the human and Shard alike — eyes belonging to a certain beautiful black dragon.

"I have Starsight! I have Starsight, and I've seen the future!" Firebug declared. Despite her hardened gaze, her voice had a pained, croaking quality. Shard's ears thrummed with dread. They'd been so close. "That human and Shard are a danger to us all — they turn into a glowing giant and kill every last one of us!"

Silence swept over the crowd. Ellen and Shard exchanged glances, their mouths hanging open. For a moment, it was as if they could read each other's minds, so clear was the thought written their faces:

Oh no.

43

E VERY PORE on Firebug's body felt clogged, every wisp of breath jammed in her windpipe. She was condemning Shard to death like this. But what choice did she have? If she was right, he had conspired with this human for moons now. If she was wrong ... Well, she'd seen what would happen. She *had* to be right.

"A dragoness, having Starsight visions?" Bog mocked. "Now this is just getting ridiculous!"

"Let's just kill the thieving ape and put Shard on trial!" Noir shouted. A chorus of bloodthirsty yells assented.

Inferno looked at Firebug. For a second, he couldn't tell what he was thinking. Was he angry? She gulped. But then Inferno smiled a triumphant, malicious smile and Firebug's heart sank despite herself — whatever she had done, it had worked.

"If we work together," Inferno yelled, regal and commanding, "we can overpower them!"

Shard and the human shared a fleeting glance. Then, they tensed, ready for battle, just as the first volley of flame burst forth from the dragons nearest them.

Firebug hung back, waiting to join the battle when she could — combat was not her forte, but she couldn't just run away, even as the first scream of the fight split her ears. A stab of guilt pierced her chest — someone had been hurt.

But she had started this, so she would see it through.

44

TENSION EXPLODED INTO MELEE in a matter of seconds. Before Ellen knew what was happening, Shard's tribe was upon them like hungry mosquitos, determined to wring every last drop of blood from their prey.

Ellen launched a blast of air at the first dragon to lunge forward. The bright yellow dragoness was sent hurtling up through the air, landing seconds later outside the shelter with a prodigiously loud *crash.*

As another dragon breathed a stream of fire at them, the sound of her heart pounding wildly filled her ears. Erecting a wall of earth to protect them as quickly as she could, the heatwave still felt as hot as noon on the summer solstice.

Shard's own fire sizzled in his open maw. He spewed a concentrated jet at the crowd in front of them; most of the dragons nimbly dodged out of the way. One dragon was singed. An ear-piercing scream boomed in Ellen's ears. In the corner of her eye, Shard's eyes widened in horror.

"Please, I don't want —" He began to plead once more, his voice cracking.

"Shut up!" A red figure divebombed Shard from the air; he leaped out of the way mere moments before it was too late.

Recognition fluttered in Shard's eyes. "Keeper, stop!" he said. A bolt of lightning *cracked* at him from behind — from Inferno — but a magical barrier blinked around Shard, absorbing the electricity.

For the first time, Ellen had a face to put to Keeper's name. Burly and gruff-looking, there also glistened sorrow in his tearless eyes.

Why would he be sad? The question jerked through Ellen's thoughts before claws clashed against claws. Keeper and Shard pushed against each other, their back legs digging into the dirt in a contest of brute strength. Worry lurched in Ellen's throat — she had to act. She raised her arms, but no sooner had a bulbous lump peaked out of the ground than did someone slam into her. A pained yelp broke through her lips.

Stars exploding behind her forehead, Ellen blinked over and over, willing herself to fight through the pain. A great pressure clamped her arms. She tried to move them, but couldn't — she was pinned down.

"Miserable human dreck ..." came an enraged hiss, heat splattering all over her in a sensation between being steamed and spat on. As her vision cleared, she saw a hulking red dragon. Golden eyes dark with wrath bored into her. His lips curled in twisted glee.

Inferno.

Ellen's heart jackhammered wildly, *thump, thump, thump.* Breath came to her in ragged wheezes; she was hyperventilating, and she knew it. "Why?" she gasped. "Why are you doing this?"

Inferno's temple bulged, and for a moment, icy fear shot through Ellen's veins. Was he going to kill her right there and then?

But he purred, smooth as velvet, "My, my, my ..." Without any further answer, he spread his wings and yanked her into the air. Her legs dangled as they ascended. Kicking wildly, she sent gusts of wind every which way she could. She even managed to knock out a few dragons with them, but Inferno remained unharmed.

"Keeper," he projected. "Take care of Shard. I'm going to deal with this thieving ape myself."

He hates me. On a deep, personal level. But before she could process her revelation, they were flying away. The trees shrank beneath them, the ground receding further and further away.

"ELLEN!" Shard shrieked, raw and fearful. "ELLEN!" Inhaling sharply, she dared to hope he'd gotten away from his brother and his seeming-hivemind of a tribe. But seconds passed, and he didn't follow. He was still fighting them. *Please be okay, Shard!*

Her arms started to ache as they sped through the air. With a half-ironic snort, she thought maybe they'd fall off. Neither human nor dragon said a thing, until finally, they came upon a lake, the source of the river Ellen and Shard had spent so many nights beside. The still waters reflected the gray, cloudy sky.

Inferno descended, still gripping Ellen tightly. At first she thought he was going to simply drop her and let the impact snuff her out, but he didn't let her go until they were just above the muddy earth. Ellen landed with a *squish,* muck spattering over her school uniform. With a horrified gasp, she saw that the ring had gone flying from her finger — it lay some ten-odd feet away, glinting even in the gloom.

Inferno touched down, blocking her path to the ring. For a tense second, they locked eyes, the hatred in his clashing with the conviction in hers as she lay sprawled on her side. She hoisted herself to her feet, and took a moment to appreciate just how large Inferno was. He towered over her at what had to be at least twelve feet tall, and that was on all fours. *Stay calm,* she commanded herself. *Get to the ring and back to Shard as fast as you can.*

Inferno broke the silence. "What a surprise this is! It's not often we get human visitors out here, much less talking ones." He spoke casually, even cordially. Yet, the foreboding, icy smirk on his face told Ellen she had to stay vigilant. She was itching to bring her fists up, but even as he continued, she could feel the power radiating off him like heat.

"All humans can talk, Inferno! I'm under a spell that translates for us, but I promise it's true!" Maybe, just maybe she could avoid battle — but she doubted it.

Hearty belly laughter echoed from the trees to the lake. Ellen almost wanted to laugh right back — Inferno had to be toying with her.

"Oh, that's funny. You're quite the jokester, aren't you?" He wiped away a tear with his paw. He seemed almost like a good-natured grandfather. Then his face hardened, his voice sharp like steel. "But I know the truth: even if you can talk, there is nothing worth hearing from your vile little mouths. You are all thieves."

Ellen gave a pig-like snort. Surprise overrode her fear just long enough for her to retort: "I'm sorry, what? You mean the orichalcum?

You do know we only need it because *some dragons* would fly in and torch us to death without the dome, right?"

The towering dragon's nostrils flared. "Pathetic! Trying to play the innocent, like the conniving demon you are … Orichalcum belongs to *us!* It provides us with a last glimpse of our loved ones, and you would dare claim you need it! You repulse me!"

A part of Ellen yearned to tear into him for everything he had let happen to Shard. But his power was so far beyond anything she could fight — she had to keep him talking and hope that she could think of a plan. "You've got magic, sorcery beyond what any human elemental can do! If anyone can find a way to talk to us, it's you!"

"Find a way to …" Inferno repeated himself several times, as if trying the words on for size. "Never! Never in a million years! Your putrid kind killed my sister!"

Ellen said nothing, but hope exploded in her chest like fireworks despite his hateful declaration. His bigotry had a root. Was this a sign Inferno could be reasoned with?

"I suppose *you* wouldn't know about it, though, would you? Too busy living under that ridiculous dome of yours. And really," he continued, his lips curling back into that malicious grin, "all things have a purpose. Before I kill you, let me tell you how I learned mine."

45

"ELLEN!" TEARS STUNG Shard's eyes, blurring his vision of the ruined shelter. "ELLEN!" All thoughts of the angry mob around him vanished as he shouted. His wings shot out with a *whoosh* sound; preparing to launch him into the air and follow Inferno.

Wham! A hulking red mass slammed into him. Before he had time to process the pain bursting in his skull, sharp talons closed tightly around his throat. Shard clawed at his brother's paws, but Keeper was too strong. He opened his mouth, but all that came out was a garbled croak. Fire burned in his chest, and not the kind he could blast at his brother. His head felt like it was about to burst open. Black splotches clouded his vision, swarming around in his eyes like silent bees.

I could die here. The thought vanished as fast it had appeared, comforting and alarming in equal turns. He could pass on, be done with everything … All he had to do was nothing.

"I'll kill you," Keeper whispered, ephemeral and soft, not a lick of anger imbued in those three simple words. Light refracted off his eyes — but no, Shard realized with a jolt, even as his own consciousness began to waver. His eyes weren't just shiny, they were moist. Keeper was crying. Despairing.

That's not my problem. What do I care?
Of course it's my problem. Ellen needs my help.

The pressure from his chest spread to his head, banging on his skull, *whack, whack, whack.* Blood sloshed through his veins, a torrential river. Someone called out to Keeper, egging him on to draw blood as if this were some kind of game. But it didn't matter, for Keeper simply kept his paws around Shard's throat, doing his damnedest to squeeze the life out of him.

Shard closed his eyes and the world dropped into darkness. Reaching deep inside himself, he conjured his magic, trying to channel as much as possible into his own claws. He planned to shred Keeper's face to ribbons, but ... could he hurt his brother? Even with all the hate, even after all the abuse, could he bring himself to maim or even kill?

There was one other thing he could try, but if it failed ...

Light glowed in Shard's front paws, prompting Keeper to squeeze even harder. But Shard did not attack. Instead, he did something he never thought he'd find the heart for: he reached up his paws, tenderly cupping Keeper's cheeks.

Keeper gasped. Wet droplets *plinked* from his face, landing on Shard's. Their eyes met, and in Keeper's, Shard saw surprise, and fear, and an all-consuming wildfire of anger and hurt and confusion and surprise.

And that was exactly what Shard was waiting for.

Reaching out his magic, he intertwined his aura with Keeper's. There was no known spell for this; improvisation was the name of the game. The binding curse, exposed by Keeper's heightened emotions, was like a tiny golden ball embedded in his soul. Shard's instinct was to exhale to guide his magic here, but that wasn't an option now. So, his consciousness threatening to slip even further away, Shard *pushed* on the yellow orb from every side.

Cracks spiderwebbed across it. In the physical world, Keeper wheezed and lurched, jerking his head skyward like a wolf on the full moon. A confused buzz spread through the crowd. Little wisps of air leaked into Shard's throat as Keeper's grasp weakened.

In Shard's spell-view, tendrils of gold seeped out from the fractures in the orb. Their overpoweringly acrid scent grated against his nostrils. It made him want to gag.

Along with the gold, however, came sparkling red. They were the emotions he had brought to the forefront of Keeper's mind, but

Shard didn't have time for them. Refocusing himself, he squeezed even harder on the golden ball. The cracks worsened, *crunching,* the red and gold curls spewing out faster and harder. Faint sobs fanned over from the red.

Keeper met Shard's determination with a dumbfounded look, comprehension somehow dawning. He did not — could not — release his grip entirely, but it was weakening.

C'mon, c'mon, Shard thought, as the pains in his chest howled like a storm. The world around him spun. *Almost there ...*

In his spell-vision, Shard gave one last great shove. With a sound like cleaving stone, the ball splintered, each sliver glittering as they winked out of existence. All at once, a great many things happened. Keeper bellowed like an animal in its death throes and released Shard's throat. Air rushed back into his lungs as his head wobbled and spun. The magical gold color dissipated, as if blown away by some unseen wind; the red rushed Shard, clouding his sight.

The sobbing reached a crescendo, and suddenly, Shard was assaulted with a vision. Gone were the remains of his shelter and the mob. In their place, a much-younger Keeper, small, hunched over and almost-fragile-looking wept near the riverbank. His tears mixed with flurries of snow from a gray sky, invisible to Shard from his vantage point on the bank opposite, though Keeper's shivering heaves and sniffles could not be mistaken for an effect of the bitter cold.

"Keeper? Is that you?" Shard tried to say, but the words came out funny, strained — and not just because he had just been choked.

"She's gone ..." was all Keeper said hollowly, as if to himself. Shard doubted Keeper had heard him at all. "She's gone ... and she never loved me ..."

Keeper jerked his head back and forth, spewing fire into the air above him with a roar. "AND IT'S ALL HIS FAULT! ALL SHE CARED ABOUT WAS HIM AND HIS MAGIC! NEVER *ME!*" He screamed, ragged and guttural.

Shard stared through wide eyes. Pangs of something unfamiliar gnawed at him. Had he ever thought Keeper had a vulnerable side? Had he ever known his brother to feel sorrow?

"Keep it together, my dear Keeper!" Inferno's voice came. For a second, Shard tensed — but no, this was not the real Inferno. A memory. Frost crunched beneath his paws. "You're a drake, aren't you? I know it's hard, but you must be strong!"

271

Keeper blinked, his sobs ceasing. The wind howled bleakly, sweeping him and the winter scene away, like dandelion seeds scattering across a field. Shard, though, remained still, waiting for the village — the present — to return.

Was this really what Keeper thought? Anger briefly welled up within Shard. How dare Keeper think their mother hadn't loved him! And yet ... had she? Shard wondered almost involuntarily. She had spent so much time with Shard, day after day, but never with Keeper. The thought arose without warning as the darkness became absolute. He knew he was hurtling to the bottom of the abyss, but there was no feeling of air rushing against his body.

Their argument just a few nights ago flashed in Shard's mind. I *should have gotten the damn magic*, Keeper had said.

"Oh boy," Shard mouthed as finally, he understood. This memory was from when their mother died. This despair, this anger was what had driven Keeper for so long. They both were in pain, and had been for a very long time, Shard realized with a jolt. They had dealt with it in ways that were very different, but also very similar.

An instant later, Shard slammed to a halt. He was in his shelter again on his back, staring up at the gray sky. Burning aches throbbed in his wings and his back, like he actually had just crashed into the ground.

Nobody was saying anything, their quiet complete and eerie. Had the mob taken him for dead? However, there was still sound — a staccato of sniffles and whimpers. He had heard it only seconds before — Keeper was crying here, just as he had in the vision of their past. Had he, perhaps, seen the same vision Shard had — had he relived the same memory?

46

BACK BY THE LAKE, Inferno beat his wings, and a gale knocked Ellen off-balance. She flew across the ground, bouncing like a stone skips across a pond before she came to a skidding halt. Pain screamed in her ribs. She tried to pull herself to her feet, but her hand slipped, and she found herself right back in the mud.

"It all started fifteen years ago, when I was a plucky young lad of four," he began. "I was a happy dragonling like any other; I had a father but no mother and two siblings. There was Blizzard — Shard's father. Then, there was my sister, Rain." His eyes softened and his mind seemed to travel to some far-off place. A wistful sigh floated down to Ellen. "She was the oldest dragonling from our clutch ... and what a dragonling she was! Intelligent, kind, caring ... the most perfect sister I could ever have asked for ... I would have given anything to help her, as would have Blizzard and our father. It wasn't always easy, mind you, wasn't always good ... but we were happy, the four of us."

"Then, Rain and I contracted Starblight. We spent the first few days of our illness together in our shelter. When we weren't sleeping off our fever, we were talking, laughing about the future ... We were going to do so much, help everyone ... Me with my Starsight, her with her own wits and ingenuity … It was supposed to be a blessing, a sign that the two of us were marked by Agito himself! I was *happy*, can you imagine? Happy for *her!* The other dragonesses in the village I already knew were good for only one thing, but I thought my sister was different. I thought she wasn't like the others …

"Then humans raided the village." His expression soured like a rotten grape. "They set fire to the trees, to our crops … They slaughtered indiscriminately, without hesitation as they sought to steal what was rightfully ours. Those who could fought valiantly, but there was only so much they could do …"

Inferno stepped forward, but slowly, threateningly, as if to draw out his story. Crouched low to the ground, like a wildcat waiting to strike. Ellen grimaced despite herself; she had the distinct impression she knew how this story ended.

"I would have fought, but I was scared. Scared to die, scared to even move as the fever burned within me. The screams of everyone I had ever known filled my ears … And you know what? I was *right* not to go anywhere! I was, if not safe, then hidden in my shelter! I'm a sorcerer, but a barely-trained dragonling can only do so much! And my sister — my beloved, *stupid* sister — thought she could drive back the humans herself, and at the very peak of her Starblight! I begged with her, pleaded for her not to go, but she threw herself into the fray nonetheless. If she had just listened to me, she would still be alive!" Inferno spat a great big wad of saliva into the mud.

"But I suppose that was just in her nature, wasn't it? I spent so long missing her, wishing she had just *done what I'd told her!* The older dragons laughed at me for believing in a dragoness, did you know? It was the one time in my entire life I have ever deserved ridicule. But you're female, aren't you? Human or not, you wouldn't understand what true power feels like. You wouldn't understand what it means to be able to control your destiny! All you're good for is supporting the real heroes as they shape *history*.

"I am Agito's Chosen … do you know what that means? I'm the champion of God himself, selected for greatness! One day, I'm going to figure out how to bring down that pathetic dome of yours, and I'm going to torch every last one of you to death. But for now … you'll do."

Fire gathered in his opening jaw. Ellen leaped to her feet, nearly slipping on the mud. She couldn't delay him any longer. Fighting this dragon, this monster, alone with no one to help her was idiotic at best.

She raised her arms in front of her, her lips set firm in grim determination.

47

"KEEPER?" SHARD SAID, more gingerly than he thought he could to Keeper. He twisted onto his belly and raised himself up to his paws. Every minute movement sent pain shooting up his legs and then some.

Keeper only cried. "I ... I ..." he finally spluttered before going quiet. He stared at the ground, unmoving.

Cries of, "What have you done to him!?" and variations thereon echoed throughout the crowd, bouncing back and forth as they swelled into a cacophonous frenzy. It almost sounded like swarming, angry bees.

"Get Shard!" someone yelled, and the whole crowd roared, flaring their wings and baring their fangs. Shard gulped, backing away, ready to spread his wings and take flight. He knew he couldn't take all of them on, though, not without magic, and he wanted to save as much of that as he could if he had to fight his uncle. But how could he even outfly them all without his magic?

He clenched his jaw and shook his head back and forth. He had to try. Sore as they were, he flapped his wings once, twice, three times, readying for takeoff.

Please ... Don't die, Ellen. Surviving this whole situation was going to take nothing short of a miracle. But if that was what they needed, then he would stop at nothing to make one happen.

His paws floated just a few short spaces off the dirt floor now. "Stop!"

Keeper's command rang out, clear and authoritative, shocking the mob into inaction. Their angry buzzing tampered off into confused stares. Even Shard halted, hovering midair, his mouth ever-so-slightly ajar.

"I'll handle him myself," Keeper announced through gritted teeth.

"Oh yeah?" Shard fired back. "Well, catch me if you can!" And just like, that he rocketed into the air, thinking, hoping, praying, *Please, please, please, let him be trying to distract them!*

The shelter shrank beneath him, transforming into a pinprick-sized reddish dot. Cold wind brushed against his scales as he flew, his eyes desperately scanning the ground for any sign of Ellen or Inferno.

All he could see below him was the village and beyond that, the green tops of trees and blue rivers and lakes. But he forced himself onward, even as terrible dread gripped his chest. What if he couldn't find her? What if it was already too late?

"ELLEN!" he desperately called. Yelling scratched his throat, leaving it raw and sore, but he didn't care. "ELLEN! ANSWER ME!"

His cry echoed through the forest like a twisted, mocking chorus. "Ellen, Ellen, Ellen ..." If only he was strong enough to search for her with his magic — but he could only extend his senses so far. And they could be anywhere by now! Fighting back stinging tears, he shook his head. Giving up was not an option. *"ELLEN!"*

But then, in the corner of his eye — a speck of glistening red — in the distance, by the lake — large and imposing —

Inferno! And just a small distance away from him stood ...

"Ellen!" Joy sparked in Shard's chest. He'd found her! Angling himself downwards, he dived, hurtling towards the ground. Inferno and Ellen hadn't seemed to notice him yet, though they grew ever-closer, the ground fast-approaching.

Wham!

Something heavy and fast crashed into Shard's side, pain splitting his ribs as he spun through the air. He beat his wings furiously, desperately working to steady himself. By the time he managed to regain control, he'd been knocked halfway across the village.

And there, in front of Shard, hung Keeper, nostrils flared, claws primed to slice.

Shard's stomach fell. His faith in his brother, however temporary, had been foolish. "Don't do this. I have to help her."

"Why?" Keeper demanded, glaring. Yet, he did not move, gave no indication he was about to attack.

"This is NOT the time! My friend is in danger!"

Keeper shot forward, until their muzzles were only inches apart. Hot breath from his flared nostrils tickled Shard, and for a second, it seemed as though Keeper would lash out.

"Not her!" Keeper growled. "Why did you save *me?*"

"I don't —" Shard tried to push past, only for a set of claws to clamp down on his wrist, the one he'd been slitting. Shard squealed — even with his healing magic, the cuts were still tender. But, instead of squeezing down harder, instead of wringing out as much pain as possible, Keeper let go.

"You were trying to kill me," he said, quietly but firmly. "It was either break your curse or leave Ellen to Inferno."

Keeper threw his paws up, shouting in frustration. "You could have killed *me*! You hate me enough!"

"Because I'm not like you! I don't pretend that hurting others is gonna make me feel better! ... The only thing that works is hurting myself."

Two narrowed slits fixated on him. "You make me damn sick; you know that? All goody-goody."

"I —" With a stab of annoyance, Shard realized didn't have the answers his brother sought. In the distance, he could see Inferno and Ellen. There weren't any signs of a fight. Were they talking, perhaps? Was Inferno toying with her, taunting his prey before sinking his fangs into her flesh?

"I have to go!"

All of a sudden, everything about Keeper relaxed, deflated, as a resigned, bitter sigh rushed out his mouth. "I really am a damn ass. Freakin' wasted all this time blaming you for crap. Following around our uncle like a loser. I got played real good, didn't I?" A hollow, longing sound that was a mix of a laugh and a sniffle echoed as Keeper looked away. "But I'm a drake, and that means squaring up when I gotta. Go save your stupid human girlfriend. I'll make a story up or something to keep the others busy as long as I can."

Shard hesitated, reaching out a paw despite himself. Keeper made no motion to take it, only frowning. A gust of wind kicked up, chiller and harsher up here than on the ground, a sharp reminder that he couldn't dally in the air for long. "I ... just tell them the truth, okay? About the binding curse."

Through trembling, clenched jaws came Keeper's quivering voice, tears gliding down his cheeks. "I hate you," he said with none of the usual machismo he prided himself on. Now he just looked tired.

Shard nodded, anger and sorrow and pity all vying for dominance within himself. He breathed in deep, the cold air stinging his insides, and looked at his brother, seeing more of him than he perhaps ever had.

"I hate you, too." He said it tenderly, for although he knew that he would hate his brother forever, he also was beginning to understand that for all his violence, Keeper was just as much of a scared, lonely dragonling as Shard was. That had to have been worth *something.*

Shard waited for just a heartbeat longer than he already had, hoping desperately that Keeper might say something.

He didn't, and so, Shard hurried to the lake. Powering through the sky, he set his face in grim determination. The moment of truth had come.

48

ELLEN STRUCK FIRST. She punched the air, sending a gust shimmering towards Inferno. It collided square with his chest. He wheezed, anger flaring on his face as the flames in his mouth smoked. As he coughed and choked on his own fumes, Ellen whipped her arm out again.

This time, Inferno was ready. He swayed to the left, the gale just barely grazing him as it instead slammed into a tall oak tree with a terrible *snap*. The top half crashed into the ground seconds later, but by that time, Inferno was already on the counterattack. Magic leaped along his scales, lightning shooting out. Ellen waved her arms again, thinking to manipulate the mud into a barrier between her and the lightning. The mud, however, had other ideas. It twitched for a split second before remaining steadfastly put. Ellen had a breath's time to realize she'd failed before the sensation of seven thousand needles jamming themselves into her body overtook her.

She fell to her knees. Her eyes felt like they were about to pop out of her skull. Somehow, she knew Inferno was inching ever-closer, the electricity intensifying with each step he took.

"Die!" Something hard and scaly bashed into Ellen — a paw or wing, or tail; it came so fast, she didn't get a good look — and she soared through the air. Cold wind rushed against her body as the lightning stopped. She hit the ground with a *thud*.

She pulled herself to her feet as fast as she could, breathing raggedly. Jets of flame rushed at her, impossibly hot and bright. Ellen blew hard at the ground, knocking herself backwards. She vaulted through the air once more, the fire chasing her. Her momentum ran out, and she fell into the lake with a wet *plop*. Clear blue water wrapped her in a chill embrace, but as the conflagration passed by above, it heated up.

Crap. The heat stung her body, and Ellen realized her mistake — now all Inferno had to do was breathe enough fire into the lake and she would boil to death.

Flailing madly, she dragged herself to the top. The water cooled quickly, but it was only a matter of another blast of heat before she burned again. Her head erupted from the lake. She panted heavily, urgently trying to fill her chest with air.

"Crafty little ape, aren't you?" Inferno mocked. Ellen scanned her surroundings. There! He was perched on a large rock just along the shore, his claws curling around it as he leaned forward.

His wings opened. A shockwave rippled through the air. Ellen was blown even further out into the lake, the water rising in waves from the force. Spinning as the current dragged her long, her stomach lurched.

Stay calm! Ellen commanded herself. She knew exactly how she could use this to her advantage. She punched a windblast at Inferno. He dodged easily, retaliating with yet another blast of fire.

But he hadn't been her target. Instead, the gust sent her sliding through the water. With a second effort, she had made it to the opposite shore.

Ellen turned to face her enemy, arms raised, digging her feet into the muddy bank. "You want me? Then come and get me!" Her yell echoed all around the lake, like a trumpeting stampede of rhinos. It sounded much braver than she felt.

Inferno roared, great fumes of smoke funneling out his nostrils. He launched himself off the boulder and into the air. He flew closer, closer, and closer still, beating his wings, summoning great big pillars of water from the lake.

There was a horrible moaning and the very earth beneath Ellen shook. Her feet gave way beneath her. She lost her balance, tumbling through the air. The pillars of water rushed at her loudly, moving across the lake as if pulled by invisible strings. Before she knew what was happening, the columns were crashing into her, one after another, *bam, bam, bam!* Her skin smarted; if she survived, there were sure to be welts. Something hard crashed into her — the ground, she realized in between flashes of pain.

Suddenly, in front of her, hovered Inferno just inches off the lake, his wings spread. His face was somewhere between a sneer and a snarl. "You will die, here AND NOW!"

Ellen gulped. Seeing this monster towering over her, she thought she might truly understand why her father was so afraid of dragons. "Then make me," she said, defiant to the last.

Inferno's eyes bulged. "Insolent —"

Something large and blue crashed into Inferno's side at a million miles an hour. He went hurtling across the lake, screaming like a child on a rollercoaster. There was a giant *thump,* followed by scattering birds. Then, silence.

"Are you okay?" Shard asked as he landed gracefully on the muddy bank.

"I'll be fine once you are." Ellen pulled herself upright with a grunt. "C'mon, let's get you out of here."

"I can't go," he protested, shaking his head. "I think he's got everyone here under a spell. I can break it but ..." A sniffle punctuated his sentence. "There's no reason for you to get hurt fighting him, too."

Ellen blinked. "Okay, wasn't expecting that but I can make it work. Let's kick his ass." She pounded her fist into her open palm, flashing Shard a grin — she was ready to take on the world.

But Shard shook his head. "Ellen, it's not safe here. You'll die."

Ellen shook her head, too. She knew that normally, she would run away — keep herself safe, even though it might hurt someone else. But it was time for a new normal. She reached out and placed her palm on Shard's snout.

He stiffened immediately. "Uh, what are you —"

"Shhhh." Her eyes closed and everything vanished, save for the soft ground beneath her feet and the dragon — no, the boy beneath her hand, and that was scarier than even Inferno had been minutes

283

before. Chest tight, she said what she had to, even as her voice cracked and choked.

"I'm sorry I left you Shard. I was selfish. I ... I *am* selfish. I'm rude and moody and I don't know why you seem to like me so damn much. But I'm really glad you do."

Somewhere, be it miles or inches away, she heard Inferno roaring insults and promises of death. Wind blew, unnaturally strong, her skirt and hair whipping around in the gale. They didn't have much time, but, Ellen hoped, it was all the time they would need.

"I know it's not safe here. It never has been, but I still want my best friend back, so, please — let me help."

Suddenly, two shaking wings wrapped around her, pulling her into the warmest embrace she had ever known. A tearful, trembling voice joined them. "Then I guess we're fighting my uncle together. I'll never forgive you if you die here, you know that?"

Ellen smirked despite herself, opening her eyes. "Don't hate me 'cause you ain't me."

And then, with all seriousness, Shard said the magic words, words she had longed to hear for all her life. "Hate you? I love you because you're you."

A high-pitched whine filled their ears, followed closely by heavy wingbeats. Wind rolled over them, but from behind, as if they were being sucked up into a giant vacuum, globules of mud and water rising into the air. Heat prickled at their skin.

"FOUND YOU!" Inferno yelled. "You should have obeyed me when you had the chance!"

Light enveloped Ellen's hand. It glowed, dimly at first, but grew in intensity as it shot up her arm. As golden light engulfed Shard too, she knew that this came from within each of them. Shard's rushed outwards as her own silver light rushed in turn to greet it; two metallic hues intertwining. Warmth accompanied the light, the kind she had known moments before when Shard hugged her.

Sounds echoed in her mind, an unknown cacophony of thoughts and ideas. Words stuck out from the jumble of sounds, small ones at first — paint, mother, friend, worthless, stupid — that grew in intensity as feelings joined them; anger, hot as the sun, hatred, cold as a tundra, love, as floral as a field of daisies ... These were Shard's thoughts, she realized, and he heard hers, too. But they weren't just *her* thoughts anymore ...

Her own heart flowed outward, mixing with Shard's. Her own pain, her own anger and selfishness, her fear of being left alone, her obsession with the Guild and protecting and her gnawing emptiness ...

I'm so weak, she thought, marveling at her own insufficiencies when laid before her friend's virtues.

49

THERE'S MORE, said a voice that was neither just Shard's nor just hers.

50

A ND INDEED, there was. Shard could see, hear, *feel* Ellen's essence merging with his own — her love of magic, and how when she thought she might never be able to master her own, she had instead nurtured her desire to protect and volunteered at the orphanage, day in and day out. He could taste the bittersweet longing she harbored for her friend Lana, the burning, peppery sensation this unfamiliar girl evoked in her, and the sour aftertaste of what could have been something special.

He saw his friend's beauty and worth, and the beauty and worth she saw in him reflected back. It shone as bright as a thousand sun and glowed with the mellowing comfort of the night sky.

But I'm weak, he thought, bewildered that she saw anything good in him when he was so unfathomably inadequate.

51

A SINGLE THOUGHT floated into Ellen's mind, savory like her father's cooking and melodic as her mother's voice.

52

A SINGLE THOUGHT caressed Shard's mind, nostalgic like his mother's magic lessons and soothing like a finished painting.

53

Y OU MAKE ME STRONGER.
And that was the beginning of everything.

54

THE LIGHT SURROUNDING Shard and the human dreck solidified into an orb, speckled gold and silver. Inferno relented, observing the object in front of him, his snout wrinkled in confusion. What was this? Were they hoping he would simply leave them be? Or were they gathering their strength, and merely biding their time?

It matters not, Inferno decided. They were vulnerable now. If he felt any hesitation, it was misplaced. If that fool dragonling rejected Inferno's wisdom and love, then he could reap the consequences. Shard had made his choice.

Wet, grimy earth squelched beneath him. Heaving a deep sigh, he summoned magical energy to his claws.

In one quick flourish, he swiped at the ovoid structure, his enhanced claws primed to rip it to shreds. Soon, he would be rid of both human and nephew, and his dragons would be better off for it.

Yet, his paw glanced off with nothing but a metallic clang. Inferno cocked his head. Had he not channeled enough energy into the strike? He lashed out once more, only for the same result. Again and again, he pounded on the shell, his grunts turning more and more feral with each failure, orange sparks erupting with each contact.

"What is this?" he snarled at last, panting as he caught his breath. It was the only sound in the forest, which had gone as silent as the night sky. For miles around, it seemed, everything was deathly quiet, as if all sound had drained out of the world itself. A strange sense of foreboding filled him.

Fractures rippled along the oval. A pure white shape, neither paw nor hand, but with the claws of the former and the fingers of the latter ruptured forth with a *crunch*. Bits and pieces of the oval fell to the ground before blowing away in the spring breeze; before Inferno had the chance to quite process this, another form of pure white broke free — a wing. It was large, larger than any Inferno had yet laid eyes on, but it was unmistakably a dragon's.

He sucked in a breath, apprehension popping in his ears like a snapping branch. This wasn't a stopgap for them to bide their time. Before him stood a giant egg, and whatever was inside it was hatching.

55

THEY WERE ONE. Neither Ellen nor Shard, human nor dragon, girl nor boy. They smashed through the final remnants of their shell, jagged slivers of it spraying outwards. Wind whipped around them as they rose into the air, their wings unmoving. Long, flowing locks of pure white, hair-like light flapped in the gale. Two eyes opened, one green, one blue, just like Shard's, each ready to soak in the world through new sight.

Opposite them was Inferno, himself ascending. With a malevolent roar, three burning spheres erupted from his fangs. Yet, even though the icy grip of fear clutched their heart, they thought that perhaps it needed not rule them.

A song started to chorus in the depths of both their memories. It was a beautiful melody, its singer's voice angelic and painfully familiar all at once.

You're trembling, and that's fine
I have damage, and it's mine
I hid in freezing darkness, afraid that I might fall
Locked in my last bastion, angry in its walls
And then one day, by chance you brought me light

They outstretched a hand, moving on instinct. Power burbled beneath their spread-wide fingertips; with a calm exhalation, they called upon this new and terrible strength that they did not understand. A fireball collided with their palm and fizzled into smoke. Two more flew past them, landing in the lake below with an explosive thud. Water erupted from the impact.

"You will not hurt us anymore." Their declaration reverberated, two distinct voices layered over each other and amplified many times. Inferno's forehead creased. Changing tacks, he lifted his front paws, each glowing with magic. Two beams of light burst forth with a terrible *gong* like a distorted grandfather clock.

They dived, but Inferno did not relent. They swooped and turned in the air, graceful like a bird, dodging lasers almost effortlessly. Below them, the stray beams collided with the trees, mowing them down with abandon. A single laser grazed their wing. Hot pain burst as they spiraled downwards.

Focus, focus! They flapped their wings, desperately trying to break out of the fall. But Inferno was already charging. With less than a second to spare, the being of light pulled themselves upright and pivoted to the side. The dragon-turned-missile narrowly missed. This close up, his magic prickled their skin like static.

Yet, they caught a glimpse of something terrible — his eyes now shone completely golden; no iris, no sclera, only two blocks of solid color. Time seemed to slow. Inferno whipped out his wing; a giant blast pulsated from its tip, hitting them square in the chest. Hurt boiled from their wound; they gasped, clutching their chest.

You don't know yourself
You don't see who you can be
I don't like myself
But with you, at last I can start to breathe

They forced themselves to peek through their hands at where they had been hit. But there was nothing there. No blood. Not even a scratch. Not even pain after a moment. Their mouth hung slightly ajar.

Triumph plastered Inferno's face; his lips curved upwards in a toothy smirk. "Victory is mine. Now *die*."

"We ..." they rasped. With a deep breath in, their face firmed, and they spread their arms wide, proudly revealing their uninjured body. "We will never lose to you."

Inferno's gaze lingered on their chest for a second before he snarled brutishly, then lobbed two more blasts. Yet even as they pounded the being of light, these and the three following blasts did nothing. With each successive blow, it was more and more like being tickled.

"You cannot withstand this!" Inferno raged. His smugness had decayed into fervor. "I was blessed by the god Agito! Mine is the most powerful magic in existence! Not a single living being, human or dragon can survive me! You're just a failure of a dragon and a thieving cowardly human! Neither of you are above the natural order! You! Are Not! Above! *Me!*" Each shout was accompanied by a blast.

"No," they agreed. "We're not."

We loved others, and were burned
Hands reached out; they were always spurned
I don't know how we manage; I know we both have scars
Red and numb and burning; they shine darker than the stars
But now, with you, the world can seem so bright

In a blink, they closed the gap and buried their fist in his snout, cartilage *crunching.* Blood seeped out his nostrils. They threw another punch, followed by another, and another. Each blow landed harder than the last.

But then a punch didn't connect. Inferno swayed to the side just in time. He shoved the being of light hard, sending them hurtling. Inferno charged again, but this time, they were ready.

Mustering their magic, they launched themselves right back at him. An arc of silver and gold magic formed ahead of them. Burning balls of flame greeted them, a relentless barrage as thick as hail. They weaved up — down — jerked to a midair halt — dove under a fireball, riposting with their own.

Inferno strafed. Another of the distorted *gongs* resounded — his own counterattack. He divebombed them, a golden magic arc cocooning him, too.

Clang!

The combatants clashed, two airborne titans jockeying against each other; an earsplitting steel-mill grind screeched as their magical arcs scraped together.

"You cannot have this kind of magic!" Inferno cried. Shiny tears welled in the corners of his golden eyes. "This is a trick! A ruse!"

"It doesn't matter what you think!" They strained their way forward, jaws tight, teeth gritted. "We've hurt each other, and we're still friends — that makes us *strong!*"

"*NO!*" Inferno bellowed. For the first time in his life, he was facing something he couldn't overpower. With one last grunting heave, he began to slide back through the air, pushed by the being of light.

"No, no, no!"

They arced through the sky, their positions reversing, pushing Inferno down. He struggled the whole way, relentlessly pushing back against them, not for a moment thinking to break away. But it was useless. Soil and mud erupted upwards and outwards on impact. Inferno gasped — he'd taken the worst of it.

As the veil of dirt cleared, the tribe's fields resolved into view. Golden grain flourished around them, save for the large swath they had flattened on impact. Teams of dragons, arranged in pentagrams, all opened their eyes.

"What's happening?"

"Who is that?"

"Is that the chieftain!?"

"What is that *thing* on top of him!?"

Horrified whispers filled the area, but not a soul moved to intervene, a stark contrast to before. Were these dragons all talk and no action? But maybe that was for the best. The being of light had something more immediate to deal with, anyway.

Inferno lay sprawled out at the being of light's feet, his belly facing the sky. One of his back legs had a raw, bleeding gash etched into it, and both his wings were bent at unnatural angles. "Go on, then! You're going to kill me, aren't you? That's what you want? So do it!"

Silence fell. The gathered dragons stared. An icy chill ran down the being of light's back. They *could* kill him if they wanted to. Justice — vengeance — hung there, tantalizingly easy. A single slicing claw across Inferno's throat, and ...

No! We can't! We're not murderers! argued a part of them. Ellen? Shard? They didn't know.

He has to pay! insisted the other hotly. *It's his fault we were miserable for years! He's a monster!*

Isn't that why we hated all the other dragons in the tribe, because we thought they were monsters? Isn't that why we hated ourselves, because we thought we were monstrous, too?

Killing him isn't going to make us feel better!

Inferno continued to shiver and whimper. They looked into his eyes, which had reverted from their solid gold state back to normal: gold irises but otherwise, ordinary. Reflected in those ordinary eyes, though, they saw themselves reflected. They saw a being of white light, part human, part dragon, with all the best and worst of both. They saw rage. They saw hurt, and power.

And they saw what they were going to do next. The end of the song whispered in their head, its final notes fading like the last lights of day.

So let's heal ourselves
Let's both of us break free
This world's shell
Won't decide anything for me
So let's heal ourselves
Side-by-side, we're free

You know, thought Shard. *I really am glad you came back, Ellen.*

A ring of magic burst out from them, washing over everyone as it spread. If anyone had been under a binding curse, it freed them. Two new outlines took shape at its center, and a moment later, Shard and Ellen were separate again, standing over Inferno.

They were met with a disbelieving stare. "Is that all?" Inferno said, mouth agape. He guffawed, as the telltale luminescence of healing magic engulfed his leg and wings. "This is your idea of strength — surrendering right when you have me where you want me? How pitiful!"

"This isn't a surrender," Shard said with a resigned sigh. His eyes had a faraway look, Ellen observed, like he just wanted to sleep.

Exhaustion ached in her, too, muscles burning. But rest would have to wait for now. Shaking her head to clear it, she added, "And we're not gonna kill you either, okay? But we do have some rules."

"Rules? Rules!?" Inferno parroted. He swiveled off his back and onto his belly, his legs twitching like he was readying to spring. Neither Ellen nor Shard made to stop him. "Why would I —"

Shard cleared his throat loudly. "First, you're going to promise never to cast a binding curse on anyone ever again. Second, don't order anyone around because you don't think they're strong or weak or whatever. It's stupid. And third, you're not going to follow us when we leave." He looked to Ellen. "I think that about covers it. You got any ideas?"

Ellen stroked her chin. "Hm ... Nah, that seems good."

"And if I were to just kill you both now?" Inferno took a menacing, deliberate step forward.

"I mean, you can try," Ellen said breezily. "We did just beat the crap out of you, though."

"We'll do it again, too," Shard added, "and this time, it'll be in front of everyone. Do you really want them to see you lose a fight, tough guy?"

Inferno froze. His eyes flicked back and forth, surveying the dragons gathered around him. Fear painted its dark strokes on each and every dragon present. Some of them simply stared, while others seemed like they wanted to say something, to encourage their leader.

"N-no!" Inferno spluttered, forcing Ellen to refocus. "I — I — I would never submit to the likes of you! Run if you wish, but we will hunt you down! I am the chieftain of this tribe; *I* decide how it is run! I am —"

"Wait!"

A voice cried out to them, cutting Inferno off midsentence. Ellen turned to see the black dragoness from before pushing through the crowd, dragons grunting as she strongarmed a path. Ellen tensed her fists, ready to fight again if she had to.

"I was ..." the black dragoness began, but stopped in the middle of her sentence. She swallowed, like she was struggling with her words.

"I was wrong," she enunciated slowly, lowering her gaze out of shame. "They *did* turn into a giant, but only to defend themselves from us. This is not the day my visions have shown me. If they want to go, we should let them." She looked up, fixing her magenta eyes on Ellen and Shard. "I am so sorry for what I did. I was scared, and jumped to conclusions. I put both of your lives in danger — there's no excuse for that."

"Now wait just a second —" Inferno began, but she shot him a glare so withering that even he recoiled a bit.

"They trounced you, Inferno. Have some honor. Accept defeat."

Renewed murmurs ping-ponged around the fields. In the corner of Ellen's vision, Shard stared at the events unfolding before him, his mouth hanging slightly ajar. Ellen wished they could fly away there and then, but she knew Shard needed to see this for himself.

"... Thank you, Firebug." His words were soft and filled with, if not catharsis, then understanding.

The black dragon bowed graciously.

Inferno stared at Firebug, fuming. After what felt like hours slipped by, he trained his vision on Shard. Ellen could practically see his heart hammering in his ears, saying nothing of the tension in her own chest. She tensed, prepared to leap back into battle if need be.

"Leave."

Neither of them moved. Had they heard right?

"I said, leave!" Inferno barked. "I won't follow you, but you are no longer welcome in my tribe."

The murmurs exploded into incredulous chatter.

"He's letting them go?"

"Just like that?"

"I never would have thought!"

"I —" Shard began, but shook his head. He sighed, relief seeming to flood his body. "C'mon, Ellen."

"Huh?"

Shard bent down. "Climb on," he said. "We're going flying." His mouth curved upwards ever so slightly; he was still tired, but Ellen knew that at least for now, he was happy.

And at least for now, so was she. Without saying another word, she mustered the biggest smile she could, and clambered onto his back, laying on her stomach. Then, they were rising into the air, the dragons beneath them shrinking. Shard rocketed forward and wind rushed over Ellen's skin. The sky was cold, but it reminded her of a warm, soaking bath. She had flown when she and Shard were one, but this ... this was completely different.

The fields turned into a forest, green and lush. The mountains loomed in the distance, growing closer and bigger with every mile they traveled. Ellen whooped with euphoria, waving her arms up in the air. The clouds parted at last, revealing the setting sun.

"I'm free!" Shard cheered, joining Ellen's joyous cries. He swooped through the air and Ellen nearly fell off, hanging onto his back for dear life.

"Shard!" she admonished as he leveled out, but a second later, she was laughing, and him too.

"Sorry, sorry! No more acrobatics, I promise!"

"Good!" Ellen shouted over the wind rushing past her face. "Now ... where to?"

Her gut twinged, reminding her that they had much to discuss. Perhaps, one day, Shard would leave her. She hadn't made her peace with the idea. Not fully. But for just this single moment in a lifetime full of moments that would never come back, they were riding off into the distance, the purple-orange sunset peeking out from the clouds, and they had earned a near-impossible victory.

She sighed wistfully and closed her eyes, leaning into Shard's back. She might not have known what the future would bring, but despite her fear, she could, just for now, simply be present. And that was all she needed.

EPILOGUE

IN THE DARKNESS at the center of the universe, the god Agito stared impassively. Before him was the cage he had called home for countless years, and beyond that, the woman in the black cloak — his sister, Pandora. She faced the Earth, her back to him. Neither of them said anything.

At last, though, Agito would wait no more.

"You never said anything about helping them yourself." He made a point of keeping his tone even, though he couldn't help but cross his arms. She had shut him in this cage for millennia. The least she could do was keep her word. "You cheated."

Pandora looked over her shoulder at him, smiling sadly. "Yes. I suppose I did."

Agito, too, smiled without a shred of joy.

"But don't you see?" she implored, her eyes sparkling. "They were able to let each other into their hearts. They did what you said a human and a dragon could never do, and they are both of them stronger for it. Don't you think that it's worth giving humans and dragonkind alike the chance to live together?"

Agito hissed. What sort of fool did his sister take him for? "'Stronger,' you say — as if any ordinary human or dragon could attain *that* kind of power? They only triumphed because they're your —"

"No," Pandora cut in. Her passion from seconds before was gone, replaced by hard steel. "Humanity and dragonkind are not as different as you think."

Anger spasmed in Agito's temple. He wanted to reach out and shake her; he needed to make his sister *understand* just how ridiculous her theory was, how she was only going to be disappointed, but the damnable prison kept him as trapped as ever.

Unless ... perhaps he didn't need to do anything just yet. His champion had failed, but he could see Earth just as well as his sister could — and there, in the metropolis the humans called Haven City, he saw Jess Flint, hunched over a desk. Dark rings of exhaustion underlined his eyes. The poor man hammered madly at a keyboard, revising his plans to capture Ellen Delacroix, muttering to himself like a lunatic.

At last, Agito sighed. "Very well, Pandora. Believe that if you must. But know this: humanity and dragonkind both *will* be erased, and their successors *will* be perfect. This is far from over." He leaned back nonchalantly, unbothered.

She chuckled, melodic and wan all at once. The sound grated. "I suppose it isn't."

Neither said another word for some time after that.

•   •   •

When the sun began to dip below the horizon and the daylight began to fade, Shard descended. They had put enough space between them and the tribe that finally they could rest. The air around him warmed as they neared the ground and they found themselves in a glade. It was smaller than the Clearing, but grass covered it instead of dirt and pebbles. The ground felt cool beneath his paws, which he thought was rather strange given that it had been much colder up in the air.

"All right," he said. "I gotta take a breather."

"Oh thank goodness. I feel like my arms are about to fall off, holding on to you like that." A second later, Ellen rolled off his back and landed with a *thump.*

She walked into his field of view, and for the first time since their battle, he caught a glimpse of her. With a jolt of worry, he saw her as disheveled as she had ever been. Her clothes were tattered and caked in mud. Splotches of dirt covered her skin from head to toe, and hair was frizzy and stood on end. Just to be sure, he asked, "You okay?"

"I'm ..." She trailed off. Shard was about to offer — no, demand that she let him heal her before her lips broke out into a great, big smile. "I'm really good, actually. I'm so glad you're alive, you know?" She plopped down onto the grass, resting her back against Shard's side. He had to twist a little to see her, but it was nothing too painful.

"And you got to fight a dragon for the first time, too!" he said.

"Urgh, that's the one thing I'm not doing great on. I'm not sure I ever want to fight anyone again, dragon or not." She looked away. "I guess my dad might have been onto something ..."

"Oh? I guess I spent all that time teaching you magic for nothing ..." He sniffled theatrically. "Poor me ..."

"Oh, quit it, you." Ellen playfully swatted him and he rolled his eyes. It was almost like they hadn't a care in the world.

"Are we gonna talk about it?" Ellen asked after a silence. The sky had turned a brilliant assortment of oranges and reds and yellows without a single cloud to cover it.

"Which 'it?'" Shard replied. It wasn't even avoidance — there was a *lot* to talk about.

Ellen's throat bulged. "Well ... for starters, I guess, you saw it too, right? In my head when we did ... whatever kind of magic we did?"

"Yeah, I did." When they had ... when they had *transformed* together, they had seen each other's memories. They had heard the exact same song, and they had heard it not just in their memories, but each other's. To think, the song his mother had sung him as a lullaby wasn't written for him, but instead for ...

"It was ... I mean ..." He fumbled for the right words before trailing off, hoping Ellen would say it for him. When she didn't, he took in a deep breath. "That was your mom. She uh ... she had a pretty singing voice."

Ellen raised an eyebrow. "'My' mom. Don't you mean ... well ..." Now she trailed off, hugging her knees to her chest. "All these years, I thought she was dead. But she ... she'd been watching over me the whole time, and never once thought to come back ..." She shook her head. "But it's not just about me."

Shard nodded. "How is this even possible? Your mom ... my mom ..." Deep down, he hoped that if they both pretended they hadn't seen what they had seen, then it wasn't real. But the rest of his sentence was already forming on his tongue. "... were one and the same."

Now that they had said it, the surreal impossibility of it hit them like a bolt of lightning. When faced with something so utterly ridiculous, so utterly *stupid* that it couldn't be anything but real, there was only one thing either of them could do.

They laughed. They laughed, deep belly laughter, like a chorus of dragonlings who had just discovered gross-out humor. They laughed so hard they cried, and they cried so hard they wished they could go back to laughing as the pain bled out through their tears.

"And she was the Goddess on top of everything!" Ellen guffawed. "You saw that in my head, too, right?"

"Did I see it?" Shard howled uproariously. "How could I not? Our own mother, the Goddess! You can't make this kind of stuff up!" They broke into another round of loving, pained laughter. "You know what this means, right?"

"What?"

"We're siblings! You and me! You're my big sister!"

Ellen sobered. The thought that he had gone too far, that he should have waited, struck him. His laughter came to a halt. "Yeah," Ellen said mutedly, yet with awe. "Shard ... you're my brother."

And then she splayed her arms against his side, embracing him in the best hug he didn't know he'd needed. He wrapped her under his wing as the full weight of the truth hit him.

Ellen was his sister. His sister was a *human*. His head swam; he still had no idea how any of this was possible, goddess or no, but he loved everything about it.

Then she pulled away to look Shard straight in the eyes. Only the way she nibbled on her lip belied her anxiety. "Hey ... Shard. Do you still wanna kill yourself?"

And there it was — the one thing he had wanted to avoid above all else. Shard breathed deeply. There were plenty of ways he could answer that, but which way was the truth? Reaching deep inside himself, he thought of everything he loved — Ellen, his mother, painting — and compared it against every painful thing that constrained him, every painful thing he hated and wanted to be rid of ...

310

Perhaps she took his silence as an answer by itself, but she stayed still and silent, waiting, blinking away tears.

"I … I don't know. I mean, we escaped Inferno, but now I don't have a home! I don't have a roof over my head … I can go anywhere I want, but what will I eat? I'm free, but …" He faltered. There was still one last thing he had to know before he could make a decision. "Would you miss me if I were gone?"

Two hands balled into shaking fists, as her breath visibly caught in her chest. "Absolutely! If you died, nothing would ever be the same! I'm so, so sorry I didn't act like it before."

And with that, Shard had his answer.

"I don't know," he said, softly, breathlessly. Ellen did not reply save for the way she furrowed her brows sadly, like someone had extinguished a light within her. But that just meant Shard still had more to say.

"But I'm not going kill myself. Not right now. I can't do that to you. I don't … I think I need to find a reason to live. I think, maybe, I even *can.* I just … gotta hang in there until I do, right?"

Ellen blinked before heaving a deep sigh, her chest deflating as her posture relaxed. "I guess that's good enough for now," she admitted. "And I can come visit you any time."

The sun finally vanished behind the mountains, leaving only the light of the stars. They were as comforting as always, Shard thought, but not nearly so much as his sister beside him. "That'd be great. See you tomorrow?" He his wing around her one more time, one last chance to hug his sister before this life-changing day was over.

"Hey, I'm not going anywhere just yet. I still gotta figure out what I'm gonna tell my dad. I'm not sure I can keep this from him anymore." She shivered again. "Let's just … stay here for a bit, okay?" She said it so softly, like a question, but they both knew that neither of them were going to say a single word more after that.

Instead, they drifted off into silence, and then sleep, the night air blanketing them both. They would have to face tomorrow sooner rather than later: Shard would have to decide where he was going; Ellen, what she would do now that she knew she could not join the Guild. Their lives had both irreversibly changed today, for better or for worse.

But for now, they would just stay in the moment. In the moment, they had the beautiful, starry sky, the calm, cool, air, a night filled with sweet, restful dreams … and in the moment, they had each other, too.

ABOUT THE AUTHOR

Passionate about stories from a young age, Daniel Fliederbaum spent the entirety of their first-grade year too embarrassed of their bad handwriting to pick up a pencil and actually write. When they finally learned about the wonders of digital word processing, they began a life-long love affair with storytelling, spending their elementary, middle, and high school years working on a novel which will hopefully never see the light of day.

Now that they have a degree in Creative Writing from the University of Idaho, and are earning their Master of Fine Arts, handwriting is far less of an issue. When they aren't writing, Daniel likes to spend time with friends, with their cat, and gorging themself on a steady diet of young adult fantasy, Japanese anime and *Pokémon* games.

YOU MIGHT ALSO ENJOY

SKY CHASE

BOOK ONE OF "THE FLIGHT OF SHIPS"

by Lauren Massuda

Travel to a vast world of airborne ships and floating islands.

THE SMUGGLERS

FROM THE "TRUCK STOP AT THE CENTER OF THE GALAXY"

by Vanessa MacLaren-Wray

Attachment is everything.

Mother says, "Don't name the merchandise," and "Don't let the humans see you."

A WRECK OF DRAGONS

by Elaine Isaak

Teens and their giant robots search for a new home for mankind, but the planet they discover belongs to the dragons.

Available from Water Dragon Publishing in
hardcover, trade paperback, and digital editions
waterdragonpublishing.com

Made in the USA
Middletown, DE
17 September 2023

38515040R00191